DUST CLOUDS OF WAR

DUST CLOUDS OF WAR

by

John Wilcox

Magna Large Print Books
Long Preston, North Yorkshire,
BD23 4ND, England.

British Library Cataloguing in Publication Data.

A catalogue record of this book is
available from the British Library

ISBN   978-0-7505-4364-4

First published in Great Britain by Allison & Busby in 2015

Cover illustration © Galopin by arrangement with
Alamy Stock Photo

The moral right of the author is hereby asserted in accordance with
the Copyright, Designs and Patents Act, 1988

Published in Large Print 2017 by arrangement with
Allison & Busby Limited

Magna Large Print is an imprint of Library Magna Books Ltd.

Printed and bound in Great Britain by
T.J. (International) Ltd., Cornwall, PL28 8RW

For Betty – for the last time

CHAPTER ONE

*The border between Northern Rhodesia
and German East Africa,
September 1914*

The three men stood motionless on top of the hill, looking down onto the sleepy little border town of Abercorn beneath them. To the north, the rays of the rising sun caught the southern tip of Lake Tanganyika some forty kilometres away, causing little silver reflections to bounce back and speed the retreating darkness on its way.

It was to there that the middle of the three now pointed. 'When they come, they will come from there,' he said.

He spoke in the soft, ululating tones of the black African but he and his companions were dressed alike, in the casual, loose garments of white men farming on these high, fertile plains: cotton shirts, open at the throat, well-worn riding breeches, high boots and wide-brimmed slouch hats. But they each leant on a British Army rifle and were markedly different in stature.

The black man was slim and by far the tallest. As he took off his hat to wipe his forehead – for they were only eight degrees south of the equator and although it was only a little after dawn, the sun was already hot – he revealed a tightly curled head of snow-white hair. His face was completely black but his features were not negroic. His nose was long, with flared nostrils and his lips were thin. There was an air of nobility about him and he pointed again.

'Yes, definitely from that way.'

'Are you sure they will come, Mzingeli?' The man on his right spoke as he adjusted his field glasses to focus better into the mid distance towards the lake.

'Oh yes, *Nkosi*. They already on their way. They come from Bismarkburg on the great lake.'

'Blimey!' The man on the left who completed the trio sniffed. 'The bleedin' war 'as only just started, look you.'

His voice carried the unmistakable cadence of the Welsh valleys and his sentences ended in an upwards inflexion, as though he was in a perpetual state of indignation. Which was roughly true of 352 Jenkins, holder of the Distinguished Conduct Medal and Bar and late of the 24th Regiment of Foot, the Queen's Royal Corps of Guides and the bosom companion of the other two. 'It doesn't seem right to come chargin' in straight away, now, does it? There should be a bit of a chat, an' all that, first see.'

'No time for that.' Simon Fonthill spoke almost absent-mindedly as he slowly turned the focussing wheel on the field glasses. 'The Germans have already attacked and taken the port of Taveta, a dozen miles inside British East Africa. They're bound to attack this border. It's comparatively small and lightly defended.'

He put down the glasses and turned to Mzingeli. 'But you say they are already on their way?'

12

'Oh yes. My boys tell me this. News here travel fast in the bush. They are coming down this way,' he pointed again, 'along German shore of big lake. Should be here soon.'

'How many of them? Do you know?'

'They say about three hundred and fifty.'

Jenkins gave a mirthless chuckle. 'Not exactly what I'd call an invadin' army, look you. Nothin' really.'

Mzingeli allowed himself a rare smile. 'Ah, but these are the Germans' black askaris. Very fierce men. They say some are cannibals. Germans have trained them well. They good soldiers. Mostly come from north-west of German Africa land.'

'Hmm.' Fonthill raised his binoculars again and trained them now on the little town that straggled along the plain below them. 'Do you have any idea if we have any troops down there, in Abercorn?'

'Don't think any. Maybe a few farmers, that's all.'

Jenkins sniffed. 'Well that's a bit different. Three hundred and fifty sounds a bloody great army now.' He turned to Fonthill. 'What are we goin' to do, bach sir? Go down, the three of us, an' throw pebbles at the Boche?'

'Something like that.' Then he threw back his head in consternation. 'Aaargh! I've just remembered. Northern Rhodesia is administered by the British South African Company, as opposed to the Colonial Office. As such it is not allowed to maintain a standing defence force. There might be a few policemen down there, but that's all. Come on. Let's get back to the horses and go

13

down and see. Obviously, if Mzingeli's boys are right, we haven't much time.'

They turned and, lengthening their stride, made towards where they had left their horses tethered to a thorn bush, mounted and urged their mounts along the well-worn path down the hill towards the little town.

Jenkins, at about 5ft 4ins tall, but as broad and muscular in stature as a prize fighter, fitted into his saddle with the greatest ease, for it was clear that he had ridden since childhood. There were startlingly white shoots of hair now amongst the jet-black thatch that stood up straight from his skull, like a broom bottom. A still-black moustache stretched away under his nostrils, as though some small rodent had crawled there and died. At 63, he was the oldest of the trio and his face was now so lined that, after years of campaigning under the hottest of suns, it looked like cracked leather. But the eyes, black as buttons, shone with good humour and danced now with the thought of the fight ahead.

Simon Fonthill glanced at him with affection. Aged 59, Fonthill eased himself in the saddle awkwardly, for, unlike Jenkins, he was not an instinctive rider and arthritis was just beginning to attack his joints. At 5ft 9ins his height placed him exactly between that of his two companions. A thick sweep of grey hair was pushed back above each ear but he sat erectly enough and, although his shoulders were broad, his body was slim. It was clear that age and a touch of infirmity had only slightly reduced an athleticism honed, like Jenkins, by years of campaigning in the far corners of the British Empire, broken occasionally by work on his farms in Northern Rhodesia and Norfolk, England.

His eyes were a soft brown and he would have been remarkably handsome if it were not for the nose, broken by a Pathan musket high in the Hindu Kush many years before, which had left it slightly hooked, giving Fonthill a predatory air that belied the gentleness of his expression, which in turn was unusual in a member of the British upper class foraging and hunting on the far borders of Empire.

Jenkins he had first met when the Welshman had acted as his batman in that regiment. He was always known to his intimates as 352, the last three digits of his regimental number to distinguish him from the other Jenkinses in the 24th of Foot, that most Welsh of Regiments. Since then they had served together throughout the series of 'Queen Victoria's Little Wars' that had studded the closing quarter of the nineteenth century, Jenkins earning his two DCMs and Fonthill a Companionship of the Bath and membership of the Distinguished Service Order – the second time for his services on Colonel Younghusband's invasion of Tibet, ten years before.

Their service, however, had rarely been conventional. The two had formally left the British army after the second Afghan war, preferring instead to work as scouts, often behind enemy lines or riding far ahead of advancing troops. The exception had been during the Anglo–Boer War, fourteen years before, when Kitchener had persuaded Fonthill to take command of a British

15

cavalry unit. Their comradeship – forged with each saving the other's life in constant combat – was unusual in Victorian and Edwardian times in that it crossed the class divide. Although rank and education separated them, respect and even a platonic love had long since united them.

Mzingeli had originally been employed as a tracker and guide when, with Jenkins and Alice, his wife, Fonthill had entered Matabeleland on a hunting trip in 1889. They had all become embroiled with Cecil Rhodes, however, when the latter had sent in his men to take the land by force and create Rhodesia. At the end of that conflict, Simon had bought land in the north of the new territory and installed Mzingeli as farm manager, where he had stayed ever since, only leaving to join the other two in the war against the Boers.

After the marriage of his two step-daughters in South Africa, Jenkins had joined Simon and Alice on the Rhodesian farm for a brief holiday when they all realised that the invasion of Belgium by the Kaiser, and the subsequent outbreak of the war in Europe, had suddenly thrust them into the front line here on the Northern Rhodesia–German East Africa border. Alice, semi-retired as a veteran war correspondent with the *London Morning Post*, had immediately offered her services to her editor in London and had left for Mombasa to join up with British forces rumoured to be planning an invasion of the German colony.

Simon himself had cabled his old commander, Lord Kitchener, now installed in Whitehall as Minister for War, to offer to travel back to Europe to fight, but K's response had been typically to the point. It read: 'AGE AGAINST YOU STOP KEEP POWDER DRY AND REMAIN AFRICA STOP COULD BE USEFUL IF WE FIGHT IN GEA STOP WON'T FORGET YOU STOP K.'

As they approached now the wooden houses that marked the outskirts of Abercorn, Fonthill frowned. He might be involved in fighting the Germans before most of the British army had even crossed the English Channel! His farm was some forty miles away from the border and they had ridden through the night to reach Abercorn, a town he had never visited, in the hope of discovering the state of the defences of the border. It looked very much now as though there were none.

They passed a white man ambling along what appeared to be the main street and Fonthill hailed him.

'Is there a police station here?'

'Aye. Just up ahead on the right. Although you might find nobody there. It's a bit early.'

Simon nodded and resisted the temptation to warn him against the impending attack. Better not spread panic at this point. And whatever policemen were in Abercorn, perhaps they were already preparing defences, although, looking around him, he could not see at this point how the town could be defended, sprawling, as it did, in a series of little side streets ending in the open bush.

If the streets seemed semi-deserted, however, the police station was buzzing with excitement,

17

with bare-footed black policemen, neatly dressed in the dark-blue jerseys and khaki shorts uniform of the Northern Rhodesian police force, running in and out of the door leading onto the building's stoep or verandah.

'Who is in charge here?' called Fonthill.

One of the men stopped and pointed inside. 'Lieutenant McCarthy, baas.'

The three men tied their horses to a hitching rail and walked inside. The police station seemed gloomy after the brightness of the early morning outside, but Simon could make out a tall black sergeant and a white man in officer's uniform bent over a map pinned to a desk.

'Mr McCarthy?' he called.

The officer looked up. He was clearly young, probably in his early twenties, with fair hair and a rather flushed face, and he looked harassed.

'Yes. What is it?'

'My name is Simon Fonthill and I farm about forty miles due south of here. These are my associates, Jenkins and Mzingeli.'

Jenkins gave the lieutenant the benefit of one of his great, wraparound smiles and Mzingeli nodded briefly. The young man's eyebrows rose at the black man being introduced as 'an associate', then he frowned.

'Good morning to you all. Can you tell me your business quickly? We are rather busy here.'

'You certainly are, bach,' said Jenkins affably. 'Place is buzzin' like a bee 'ive and the sun's 'ardly up, like.'

Simon intervened. 'You have obviously heard the news that the Germans are on their way to

18

attack Abercorn?'

'Yes, but I don't know exactly the way they will come or how many there are of them. My sergeant and I were just trying to see which way they would attack.'

Gesturing towards Mzingeli, Fonthill said, 'My farm manager here knows more or less everything that is happening for miles around this border. His black boys tell him that there is a force of German Askari coming along the German side of Lake Tanganyika heading directly this way. There are about three hundred and fifty of them. We believe them to be travelling due south, which means they will attack this town as the main border crossing.'

The young man's frown deepened. 'Did you say three hundred and fifty?'

'Yes. How many men do you have here and what training have they had?'

At first McCarthy's features took on an air of truculence. Then that disappeared as his face brightened.

'Did you say Fonthill?'

'Yes, Simon Fonthill.'

'Ah, forgive me, sir. Of course I know you now. You got through the Mahdi's lines to reach Gordon, I remember. And gave the Boers a bloody nose down south, fifteen years or so ago.'

Fonthill gave a half-smile. 'All a long time ago, Mr McCarthy. But now to the present. How many men do you have?'

'Ah, about forty in all, sir. And I have sent riders to bring them all in from the nearby villages along the border.'

'Forty!' Jenkins voice carried a note of derision. 'Blimey, sonny, we are goin' to 'ave our work cut out, look you. Old Jelly 'ere,' he gestured towards the silent figure of Mzingeli, 'says that the lot that are comin' down from the lake are a pretty savage bunch.'

McCarthy drew himself to his full height. 'Yes, well. I suspected that we would be outnumbered, but my chaps have had military training and are good shots. We can defend this place.'

'I am sure you can.' Fonthill drew up a chair and leant forward to look at the map. 'Have you made any plans for defence yet?'

'No, sir. To start with, we didn't know which way the Hun would be coming. But I have sent three scouts out to the north, as that seemed the obvious way. How we are going to defend the town, though...' His voice tailed away.

'Scouts are a good first move. Now, let's look at the map.' He suddenly looked up at the young man. 'I hope you don't mind me making the odd suggestion, if I can?'

'Good lord no, sir. I have only been out here for some eighteen months and have had nothing like your experience. Most of our time here is spent cracking down on thieving farmhands and the like. Please do take charge.'

'Very well. Now, Mzingeli, you know the area. Come and look at this map. Is there anywhere we could intercept the Germans and ambush them before they reach the town?'

'Don't need to look at the map, *Nkosi*. I know the ground. Road to north is straight and ground is flat. Not much cover. Only bushes and short trees.'

'I'm afraid he's right.' McCarthy rubbed his jaw ruefully. 'I was just looking to see what options we had.'

'Have you sent for help?'

'Yes. Sent a man galloping just before dawn south to Kasama. I understand that there is a small force there.'

'Good. What weapons do you have?'

'Well, we have a rather aged Maxim machine gun and the men are armed with .303 Martini–Enfield with triangular bayonets. They are good with the bare steel, as you'd expect.'

Jenkins sniffed. 'The Metfords are only single shots, though, aren't they?'

'Afraid so. I see you've got the magazine Lee Enfields. Wish we'd got them.'

Fonthill nodded. 'We brought them back with us after the Tibet show. Shouldn't have kept them but I had a feeling they might come in handy up here so I brought them with us. Mind you, they are a bit ancient, too, but at least they are not single shot.' He stood. 'Now, we haven't much time. Have you alerted the local people and called all available men up?'

'Sorry, no. Just haven't had time.'

'Right. Send someone – any magistrates here?'

'Yes, a good man. I have already sent a boy to alert him.'

'Then I suggest you send him knocking on doors, telling women and children to stay inside and keep their heads down, and the men to come here quickly bringing whatever arms they have. Your sergeant should stay here to tell him that.

21

Now, perhaps you can show us the lie of the land.'

The lieutenant barked a series of orders to his sergeant, then he joined the others as they stood outside looking up the long, straight, dusty road that led to the north. They began to walk along it. Fonthill focussed his field glasses but could see no sign of life ... except, yes, there were three tiny figures in the distance, seemingly approaching the town. The German advance patrol or McCarthy's men coming back? They would soon know.

He handed the glasses to the lieutenant. 'Yes,' McCarthy held them steadily to his eyes. 'They're my boys coming back. It looks as though they're trotting. They can cover miles like that.' He handed the glasses back. 'I couldn't see any sign of anyone behind them.'

'Good.' Fonthill pointed to a large, red-bricked, windowless building at the end of the town. 'What's that?'

'Our prison. Quite new. Our pride and joy.' He gestured. 'Those horizontal glass slits in the walls along the top are the nearest we get to windows.'

'Do they face all round?'

'Yes, except back towards the town.'

'Can you get men up there to fire through them?'

'Yes, we can put ladders and tables into the cells.'

'Right. We will make it our fortress. Put in ten men to man it, but – and this is important – I don't want them to poke rifles through those windows until they are told. Understand?'

22

'Yes, I get your drift.'

Fonthill looked around him. 'The problem is going to be to defend the town on all sides with so few men. There is no time to erect barricades, even if we could find the material. Let's hope the Germans haven't bought field guns. I suspect that, if we lie very low, the Huns will try a direct frontal attack at first, probably coming fast down the north road and into the main street here.

'If they do,' he pointed up ahead, 'we will need two small, concealed trenches, sufficient to hold, say, three men each and back from the road on either side by about two hundred yards each. If they keep their heads down, we might be able to direct enfilading fire and knock a few of them over before your chaps can hare back here.'

McCarthy nodded. 'I see. Then what?'

'Depends how many men we can summon up. The town is open on most sides, with the streets just emptying onto the bush. Is that right?'

'Not quite. On that side,' McCarthy pointed, 'the bush peters out into our little lake, Lake Chila. The ground is very swampy there. If they try to attack on that side, they could get literally bogged down, so I doubt if they will try it.'

'Well, that's one small blessing. Now, let's see. If we put six men out into the trenches there and ten in the prison, that leaves us with twenty-four police, plus us three and whoever we can pick up from the town's inhabitants. Let's say...'

Simon pushed back his hat and wiped his brow. 'Let's say something like thirty-five or so defenders left to cover the sides and back of the town.' He blew out his cheeks. 'And we shall need

23

a small mobile reserve to reinforce any area that is under the greatest attack.'

A silence fell on the little group. Somewhere in the tiny gardens attached to a few of the houses a group of cicadas began their scratchy chirping.

'With respect, bach sir, for your generalship an' all that,' said Jenkins, 'I don't see 'ow we can do it, I really don't.'

'But the alternative is to let the Boche walk straight into the town, ransack it and rampage through into the heart of Northern Rhodesia.' McCarthy was standing ramrod straight now and his voice was resolute. 'And I am not having that.'

Fonthill smiled. 'You are quite right, McCarthy, and neither am I. But I do have a plan – of sorts. Get all your chaps into the police station as soon as possible, plus the able bodies you can get from the houses. I will brief them there. Do that now, at the double, for we have little time.'

'Very good, sir.' McCarthy was about to salute, then thought better of it and doubled away, calling to his men as he went.

Jenkins wiped his moustache with a very grimy handkerchief. 'I 'ope it's a bloody good plan, bach sir, otherwise I'd say we don't 'ave much of a chance.' But he spoke with a grin and Fonthill grinned back.

He raised his binoculars once again and focussed them along the road. 'Well, it's not much of a plan, but I reckon–' He broke off and concentrated.

'There's a small cloud of dust beyond Mc-Carthy's returning chaps,' he murmured. 'Must be the Germans. Here, Mzingeli, look and tell me how long we've got.'

The black man took the glasses. 'They still a good way away. Perhaps we have an hour and a bit. Not much more.'

'Blimey!' Jenkins shouldered his rifle. 'Better get going.' He made to walk back to the station but Simon stopped him. 'I've got a rotten job for you two,' he said. 'But it's important.'

'Ah yes. Do we get extra pay and automatic VCs, then?'

'Guaranteed. Now, listen. We three are the only men with fast-shooting magazine rifles. I shall need mine in leading the mobile reserve. But I want you to grab a couple of shovels and go out into the bush, about two hundred and fifty yards that way,' he pointed, 'just in front of those foothills. Dig yourselves a small trench, disguise it with scrub, take as much ammunition as you can find, and settle in there out of sight and wait.'

'What we wait for?' asked Mzingeli.

'Wait until the Germans have passed you to attack the town from your side. Then, when they have settled, open fire as fast and as accurately as you can, so that they think there is a platoon dug in behind them. When it gets too hot for you, escape into the foothills and make your way back into town under cover of darkness. Is that clear?'

'Oh, it's clear all right.' Jenkins sucked in his moustache. 'But won't you need us in the town? At least you know we can shoot, and you don't really know that about these black coppers. Personally, I never knew a copper of any sort who was any good at anythin'.'

'Come, 352,' grunted Mzingeli. 'We don't have

time and we need cartridges and shovels from station.'

'Don't much fancy diggin' in this 'eat.' Jenkins pulled up his belt. 'But if the pay rise an' the VCs is guaranteed, we'd better get goin'. Now you be careful, bach sir. If somethin' 'appens to you, it'll be me that gets it in the neck from Miss Alice, not you.'

'Oh, get on with it.'

The two hurried away, and Fonthill took another glance through his field glasses then followed them towards the police station. He passed six policemen trotting towards the northern end of the town.

'Where are you going?' he demanded.

His air of command brooked no argument and a lance corporal replied. 'We goin' to dig two trenches either side of road, baas,' he said.

'Good. I am a British army officer. Lieutenant McCarthy has put me in charge here. Dig your trenches well back from the road, so the Germans don't overrun you. Disguise your mounds of earth and put stalks of brush in front of you so that the Germans can't see you there. And, for goodness' sake, take off those fezes when the Germans are near. Do not, I repeat, do not fire until either we open fire from the prison there, or unless you are discovered and are fired upon. Understood?'

'Ah yes, baas.'

'Double back to the town when you hear the bugle.'

'Yes, baas.'

The station was crowded when Fonthill regained it, with a handful of weatherbeaten men

26

of the town, bearing hunting rifles, drifting in to mingle with the policemen.

'Right, Mac, are all your chaps here, with the exception of your scouts and the six digging the trenches?'

'Yes. Including those away and with twelve of the townspeople, we have forty-three armed men.'

'Splendid. If I may, I would like to explain the plan, such as it is.'

'Of course, sir, go ahead, but let me introduce you first.'

The buzz of conversation in the crowded room fell silent as McCarthy, his cheeks glowing, held up his hand.

'As most of you know by now,' he said, 'we have about three hundred and fifty Germans and black askaris coming to attack the town from the north. If we let them take our homes without a fight, then we let them march through to ransack Northern Rhodesia, and our names will be mud throughout the Empire.'

No one spoke.

'So we *will* fight – and we are lucky to have with us a most distinguished soldier who has great military experience and will lead our defence. This is ex-Brigadier Simon Fonthill, CB and DSO, formerly of the British army, who will explain his plan to us now.'

The buzz returned as Fonthill stepped forward.

'We have very little time,' he said, 'because I believe that we will probably be under fire within the hour. I have already made some dispositions out in the bush to halt the Huns' stride, at least, but we have much to defend with few men to do it. I shall ask Mr McCarthy to take ten of his policemen and man the prison at the northern end of the town. That will be our fortress.

'Then I shall ask him to deploy five of his men to be under my command in the centre of the town, ready to double to whichever part of the town is under the greatest attack to reinforce that position.' Simon drew in his breath and a pin could be heard to drop within the station, so intently listening were the members of his audience.

'Now, I want those of you who are not police-men to listen carefully. I want you to go back to your homes and go to the ends of your streets that open out onto the bush and dig a small trench, deep enough to offer you protection, throwing up the soil to act as firing positions for your rifles. Dig these in a v-shape, with the point of the v pointing out onto the bush. This will enable you to direct enfilading fire onto the enemy on either side of you. I would like each of you to take up a position in a trench – as near as possible to your dwelling – and I shall reinforce you with policemen, as best I can.'

He looked around carefully at the wide eyes staring back at him. 'I am confident that we can throw the Germans back across their border.' He smiled. 'Let me tell you why. We have the greatest military advantage that any force can have: that of surprise. You will not show yourselves – any of you – until you hear the first shot fired by us, probably from the jail, so the Boche will think that the population has fled the town. We will

28

show them that we have not.

'Now go to your positions, always obey my or Lieutenant McCarthy's orders when they are given, tell the wives and children to lie low on the floors of the houses – and good luck to you all.'

He nodded and the white townsmen nodded back and began turning away to leave. But one man, burly, bearded and with a strong South African accent, stepped forward.

'I reckon, Brigadier, or whoever you are, you are leading us into a death trap.' He glowered and Fonthill recognised a strong vein of Boer truculence in his voice. 'Ach, these police here,' he gestured, 'are not soldiers and neither are we. These Germans will kill us all if we try and resist. Best to negotiate with them and let them march on south without giving resistance, if they agree to by-pass the town.'

McCarthy shook his head. 'We can't do that, Mr de Wet. There is a substantial British force coming up from Kasama; we only need to hold off the Germans for, say, thirty-six hours, and we shall be reinforced. And you're wrong about my policemen. They have all been trained by the army. We must hold off the Germans until help arrives and stop them spreading out in Northern Rhodesia.'

'Umph!' The Boer spat on the wooden floor. 'Your fellers are black and black men don't make good fighters. And they've only got single-shot Metfords, which were no match for our Mausers fourteen years ago. We should think of our women and children.'

Jenkins snorted. 'Listen, bach,' he said. 'The

brigadier and me was at Isandlwana and, although I went down, the brigadier went on and fought at Rorke's Drift. What we both saw there showed us that black fellers can fight, all right. I got a knobkerrie, or whatever you call it, on me 'ead, which put me out. Oh yes, them Zulus could fight all right, and they're black fellers.'

'Mr de Wet,' Fonthill spoke softly but everyone could hear him, for silence had descended on the room and those who were about to leave had paused to hear the outcome. 'I have great respect for the fighting qualities of South Africans – of whatever colour – but we will not force you to fight. If you wish to leave then do so, at once, and take your family with you. Those who are left will do our best to defend your home.' He looked at the others. 'Anyone else who wishes to leave may do so, but go very quickly now. The Germans will be here soon.'

Everyone's gaze now was on the Boer. Eventually, he stiffened his back. 'No, English. We Boers don't run away. I will stay.'

'Good man. Now, townsmen, back to your homes quickly and start digging. Policemen, stay here. Jenkins and Mzingeli go to your positions.'

Within moments, McCarthy had allocated his men, when a cry came from outside. 'Scouts back, baas.'

The three dust-coated scouts came trotting down the main street without changing their loping stride, then came to a halt and saluted McCarthy.

'Report quickly,' said the lieutenant.

'Germans coming all right, baas,' the tallest of

the three spoke, with no sign of the exertion caused by his marathon trot. 'More than three hundred, I think. And they have big cannon.'

'Oh blast!' Fonthill stepped forward. 'Just one big gun? And did they see you?'

'Just one big gun, baas. We keep hidden and then creep away into bush and then run. They don't see us or fire at us at all.'

'Good man.' Simon lowered his voice and addressed McCarthy. 'I had hoped they would have no artillery. If they stand off and just shell us, we could have a difficult time.'

'Hmm.' The young man now spoke softly, too. 'Would it be best, do you think, to parley with them – white flag and all that? Explain that the town is defended but say that women and children are sheltering in the houses and that they should not shell us.'

Fonthill wrinkled his nose. 'Wouldn't stand a chance, I would say. The rules of war, as I remember them, are that the town should lay down its arms and completely surrender if they wish to avoid being fired upon. If there is a Hun in charge, then he will probably be a Prussian and he will know that. We either surrender completely, or we stand and fight. Which do you want, Mac?'

The young man's high colour seemed to darken in the sunlight. 'Right,' he said. 'We stand and fight, sir.'

'Good. The artillery piece is obviously slowing them down and giving us more time.' He raised his glasses. 'Yes, they seem to be moving quite slowly. Send everyone to their positions, Mac, and give me the chaps you promised. You take

31

the Maxim. I told your chaps out in the trenches there that you would recall them with a bugle call after they had fired. We mustn't leave them to be overrun.'

'Of course not.' McCarthy barked more orders and the policemen split into groups, the largest standing by Fonthill. He looked out towards the foothills and saw mounds of earth being carefully deposited out where Mzingeli and Jenkins were digging.

'When do we start firing?' asked McCarthy.

'That is your decision, Mac. Your chaps out in those trenches either side of the road have orders not to fire until you do from the jail. So the first shot will be yours. You will be the nearest. Stay hidden until the Germans are as near as you can let them come without them splitting up to surround the town. Then surprise them – and the rest of us will follow suit. Got it?'

'Got it, sir.'

'Good. Good luck.'

'And to you.'

The young man doubled away with his ten men and the remainder grouped around Simon. He numbered off five of them. 'You will stay with me at all times,' he ordered. 'We will act as a running reserve to support whichever part of our defences are under most pressure. The rest of you come with me and I will allocate you to your positions. Do you all have full bandoliers?'

'Yes, baas,' the chorus was supportive, as were the great smiles that now split the black faces surrounding him.

'Good. Let's go.'

32

The trench digging was well under way – with some small boys helping – as Fonthill toured the town. He left one policeman with each trench, so giving him seven to defend the rear of the town, in addition to his own 'flying squad' of five. The seven he placed at strategic points – on roofs, behind walls, in hastily dug foxholes – until he was satisfied that his tiny force had been distributed as strategically as possible. Then, with his five men, he returned to the jail at the northern end of the town, taking care to avoid being seen by German field glasses.

Inside the jailhouse, the few prisoners had been herded into one cell and McCarthy's ten men had been posted high up at the now open windows, with the Maxim securely balanced to fire due north, covering the entrance to the town. Fonthill swept the bush with his own binoculars and was relieved to see that that the six men on either side of the road were well hidden, as were Jenkins and Mzingeli.

'Now all we can do is wait,' he muttered to himself.

He focussed the glasses again on the advancing Germans. They came into view clearly now. Leading the column on horseback rode three men wearing European pith helmets, followed by a string of black Askari troops wearing khaki uniforms topped by fez-like hats. It could have been a unit of the King's African Rifles. And yes, there, in the centre, was a field gun, being hauled by a team of black porters. The dust-shrouded column came on, slowly but menacingly.

Fonthill bit his lip. Could his little force of

policemen and shopkeepers hold off this advancing corps of professionals? They must try.

He called, 'Good luck, Mac. Hold your fire as long as possible. I will be in the centre of the town by the station.'

'Very good, sir.'

Simon slipped away, dodging with his men from doorway to doorway to avoid detection, until he reached the police station. There the little group waited in the dark room, leaving the door open.

'Don't fire yet, Mac,' muttered Fonthill to himself. 'Don't fire yet.'

He stole a glance round the corner of the doorpost and caught a glimpse of what seemed like a solid phalanx of soldiery stretching across the road and edge of the bush about a hundred yards from the entrance of the town. The officers had dismounted and, cautiously, revolvers in hand, were leading the advance.

Simon turned and was about to cry jubilantly to his men, 'They've taken the bait!' when the Maxim suddenly chattered into life and rifle shots could be heard from the bush up ahead. He couldn't resist shouting, 'Don't fire yet, 352,' when the jail up ahead seemed to blaze with flame and gun smoke and he saw the leading ranks of the advancing Germans fold and fall. At the same time, a bugle call rose above the firing from the jailhouse.

His men behind him in the police station began to push towards the open door, but Fonthill held them back.

'Wait until we see if the enemy manage to avoid the jailhouse and rush down the main street,' he said. 'Then, on my command, spill out and fire at will. But wait now.'

Simon eased the bolt on his Lee Enfield and slipped a cartridge into the breech. He looked out between a gap in the houses opposite and could see the little line of shrub that Jenkins and Mzingeli had erected to conceal their trench but could see no rifles protruding through. Good. That meant that the Germans had not diverted yet to circle the town.

He took another look up the main street. Yes, a group of askaris were running, heads down, past the jailhouse but close to its walls so that the defenders could not fire down on them.

'Out now!' he cried, leading the way. 'At the enemy in front, FIRE!'

The volley rang out and five askaris immediately fell, one of them clutching at his thigh. Somewhere, from one of the houses, a woman screamed. 'Fix bayonets,' screamed Simon. 'Charge!'

It was not exactly a full-scale, regimental charge: just six men, one of them bayonetless (because Simon did not possess this vital accessory), but it was enough for the remaining askaris, who turned and fled to the end of the road, melting away into the bush.

At the jail, Simon shouted up, 'Mac.'

The lieutenant's face appeared at the window alongside the barrel of his rifle. 'Yes?'

'Get your men to fire at the cannon's crew,' he shouted. 'Don't let them unlimber it to fire. Kill any man who goes near it.'

'Very good, sir.'

From out towards the foothills, Fonthill now could distinctly hear the sound of quick-firing Lee Enfields. That meant that the Germans had broken up to try and attack the town from the sides and that his two comrades had now been brought into the conflict. A sudden thought struck him. Jenkins was now 63. He could still shoot like a Bisley champion, ride like a jockey and fight like a Dervish when he had to. But could he – would he – run quickly enough when the Germans spread out to surround them? He swallowed hard at the thought of losing his old comrade. But there were other pressing matters now. Firing was coming from one of the streets running off the main road – from the side where the marshland was supposed to stop any attack from that direction.

He waved to his men. 'We'll leave the fort to hold the northern entrance. Back this way, now.'

One of the side trenches had been dug facing the lake, 'just in case'. Now, the policeman and two of the townspeople were firing as fast as they could reload, towards where a group of German askaris were advancing on them, picking their way gingerly through the unfirm ground.

Fonthill touched two of his five on the shoulders. 'Go down there and help those three in the trench,' he shouted. His reserve of six was now reduced to four. He looked across to the other side of the road. Firing was coming from 'the Jenkins side' of the town, but, as far as he could see, the men in the trenches were holding their own.

'Back towards the southern end of town,' he

cried. As he ran, puffing beside his three men, who easily fell into their miles-consuming jog, he wondered if his gamble of leaving the bottom of the road comparatively badly defended had failed. Had the enemy been able to avoid the enfilading fire from Jenkins, Mzingeli and the men in the side trenches to circle the town and attack it from the south?

The answer became clear as the rattle of single-shot musketry sounded from where he had positioned the last of his men, scattered among the houses at the southern end of town. He was about to hail one of them, on a rooftop, when the man jerked, groaned and slid towards the guttering, falling over the edge into the street. At that moment, six black askaris appeared from round the end of the last house in a group across the main street. They immediately presented their bayonets to Fonthill and his men and, uttering a shrieking war cry, ran towards them.

Simon quickly glanced to either side. This is where, he thought, we live or die. Would his policemen run?

They did not. Coolly, each took aim and immediately brought down four of the advancing six. Simon himself took aim and missed his man. He worked the bolt of his rifle quickly, fired again and, this time, hit his target squarely in the chest. Amazingly – proving Mzingeli's point about the fighting qualities of these black askaris – the last man continued to charge towards them until a bullet fired from one of the houses brought him down.

Simon turned and saw Jenkins, with Mzingeli

37

behind him, lower his smoking rifle and wave to him from a side street.

'Thank God you're back,' called Fonthill. 'Come with us to the bottom of the street. We're going to need you there.'

The little party, the policemen having reloaded, trotted down warily to where the houses ended. Peering round the last house and scanning the bush, Fonthill could see no sign of the enemy. He called to a policeman who was taking shelter behind a low wall: 'Any more of them come this way?'

'No, baas. Only them six. They came round corner before I could shoot.'

'Well, be quicker next time. There will be more.' He turned to Jenkins and Mzingeli. 'What happened to you? How did you manage to get back so quickly?'

Jenkins sniffed. 'We were able to fire real rapid, like, an' we brought down about ten of the bastards. That stopped 'em comin' down that side of the town, so I thought we'd better bolt for the 'ouses, before we was cut off. An', by the look of it, it was just as well that we did, eh?'

'Absolutely. Thanks for that shot. Now, can you support this chap behind the wall, because I think they might try and break through at this end before long.'

He sniffed the air and looked up. The sky was a bowl of unbroken blue and the sun blazed down so brazenly that patches of the bush seemed to be cracking open in the heat. He wiped the sweat that was trickling down onto his eyebrows and arched his back so that his sodden shirt parted from it. Wasn't he just a bit too old for all this now? Probably, but there was nothing to be done about it for the moment. Suddenly he stiffened. Something had changed. Then he realised that the firing had ceased and a strange stillness had settled on the little town.

'I'll leave these chaps to help you,' he called to Jenkins. 'I'm going to find McCarthy and see what's happening.'

He turned, ordered his three men to remain and set off back up the street until he reached the jailhouse. He shouted, 'Mac, I'm coming in,' darted to the door and wrenched it open. Inside, the heat was intolerable and the stench of gun smoke and cordite filled the air, immediately settling on his lips and making them taste sour. Huddled behind the Maxim, McCarthy turned and shouted.

'Your plan worked. We've beaten them off – at least for the moment. They've retreated, by the look of it. Here, come and take a look.'

Fonthill climbed up and peered along the machine gun barrel out into the bush. The field gun sat where it had been abandoned by its crew, several bodies lying around it – a tribute to the firepower of the jailhouse. Further out, however, there was activity.

'Damn!' Simon frowned. 'They're digging in. It looks as though they are making trenches just out of range of our Metfords – but just in range of their Mausers, or whatever they've got.'

He turned his sweating face to the lieutenant. 'They are going to besiege the town, by the looks of it. They won't be able to reach that gun while it's daylight but, after dark, they might be able to pull it back, set it up out of range of our rifles and the machine gun and start shelling us. How long before help comes from Kasama?'

'God knows.' The strain was beginning to show on McCarthy's cordite-streaked face. 'It's about a hundred miles from here. We telegraphed, of course, as well as sending a rider. But I can't see any reinforcements arriving within the next twenty-four hours. So we will have to fight it out. Have they got into the town from the sides and back?'

'Not so far. And we have already given them a bloody nose.' He clapped the young man on his back. 'You've done a damned good job. That's why they are treating us with respect. And it won't be much fun for them, stuck out on the plain in this heat. Will they risk a night attack? I doubt it. It's full moon and there's not much cover out there. They are more likely to stay back and trust to their field gun.'

McCarthy frowned. 'How can we stop them pulling the gun back?'

'Well, we could try and cut it out, I suppose ... run at it at twilight under covering fire and plant charges. Do we have any explosives?'

'No ... well, wait a moment.' The young man creased his brow as he pondered. 'Yes. I think I could find a couple of sticks of dynamite; they're all that are left from our attempts last year to blast foundations for the new boathouse by the lake.'

Fonthill's face lightened. 'Dynamite would be ideal. Can you get them?'

'Yes. They should be in the station. But who is

going to crawl out there in the semi-darkness and try and plant them?'

'Don't worry about that. We just need two men – and plenty of covering fire. Jenkins and I can do it.'

McCarthy blew out his cheeks. 'With great respect, sir, you are not as young as you were when you crept through the Mahdi's lines at Khartoum. No. I insist. My sergeant and I will do it. Now, let me go and get the sticks.'

Simon grinned ruefully. 'Good man. I must confess I'm not much of a crawler these days. Get the sticks and we'll wait until the sun dips and the shadows lengthen. It's quite a short twilight in these parts now and we must be ready.'

McCarthy was away some time and Fonthill kept watch, swivelling the nose of his Maxim to follow his gaze. The enemy was still there, seemingly just out of range and merrily digging a ring of trenches. He didn't envy them their task under this sun.

The afternoon had worn on, marked only by desultory sniping, when the lieutenant returned. 'Sorry,' he said. 'Couldn't find the bloody things.' He held up the two sticks, looking like candles, but with long fuses instead of wicks. 'Should do the job, I would think. They're all we've got, anyway.'

Fonthill inspected the dynamite. 'Don't know much about these things,' he muttered, 'but they look all right. Trick is to make absolutely sure that the fuses are burning all right before you run away. Fuses can go out and then you have to go back to relight the damned things. Best place for them, I would think, would be the barrel of the gun. It's facing this way, so the gun shield itself should give you a little protection. Pop 'em straight down the muzzle, make sure they're burning and then hop it.' He grinned. 'Easy, really.'

McCarthy returned the grin, but only half-heartedly. 'Have you ... er ... done this sort of thing yourself, sir?'

'Oh yes. During the Boxer Rebellion. Nearly blew my legs off and got knocked unconscious, but I had two bundles of the damned things and you should be all right with just two sticks.' He looked at his watch. 'I reckon we've got just about an hour before the sun slips away. I will use that time to make sure my men dotted around the town are all right. Then I will be back.'

He nodded and then was gone. He found all his men in place, with the exception of the policeman who had fallen from the roof. He had been shot neatly through the forehead. Some of the women from the houses had brought food and drink to the men in the trenches, who all reported that the only activity in the bush was coming from isolated snipers.

'Be particularly watchful at dusk,' warned Fonthill. 'There just might be an attack when the light fades. And take it in turns to stand watch during the night. They might just come then.'

Standing by Jenkins at the southern end of the town, he looked at his watch. 'In twenty minutes time,' he said, 'I want you and Mzingeli to make a diversion by blazing away at whatever you can see out there that might house a sniper. Try and keep it up for about five minutes if you can. Do you have enough ammunition?'

'Still got pockets full, bach sir.'

He felt happier at leaving Jenkins in charge of the defences at the rear of the town and, just when the shadows were lengthening, he hurried back to the jailhouse. McCarthy and his sergeant were waiting for him.

'I suggest you take one stick each,' he instructed, 'just in case one of you gets hit. Do you have tapers and matches?' They nodded.

'Good.' Simon looked at his watch. 'We will give it another quarter of an hour. I have arranged for a diversion to be created at the other end of town, so when you hear that firing you can start crawling. We will not begin firing here, because it could attract attention to you. But, if we see you have been spotted, then we will blaze away. I suggest you slip in the sticks, crawl a few yards away – far enough to be out of range of falling bits of iron and steel from the explosion – then when the gun goes up, stand and run for it. We will cover you.'

The young lieutenant gulped and nodded, but the sergeant gave a flashing white-toothed grin. Fonthill then briefed the men whose firing positions faced to the north. 'Don't fire until I give you the order,' he said, 'then direct your fire at the trenches you can see now. Mark their positions now, because the light will have faded by the time you come to shoot. The lives of the lieutenant and the sergeant could be in your hands.'

The following fifteen minutes seemed endless for the men crouched together in that airless room. Then Simon nodded. 'Go to the door. As soon as you hear firing from the southern end of the street, start crawling. I hope the attention of the Germans will be diverted to that end of town and they'll not see you. Good luck, lads. Move slowly and don't draw attention to yourselves.'

Dusk was falling when the rapid firing from Jenkins's and Mzingeli's magazine rifles suddenly broke the semi-silence. Watching from the Maxim's post, Fonthill caught a glimpse of two dim forms crawling from the edge of the town, from bush to bush, edging towards the gun, which could now just be seen in the gloomy light.

Simon had a sudden apprehension. What if the Germans had left a guard crouching behind the gun's metal plate? He shrugged. Too late to worry about that now. McCarthy and his sergeant would have to deal with him when and if the danger occurred.

The two figures had disappeared into the twilight when suddenly a shout rose from the German lines and two rifles began firing. 'Fire at those flashes,' shouted Fonthill and he pressed the triggers of the Maxim so that its sound was deafening in the stifling room. He swung the barrel round in an arc, hoping to clip the top of the enemy trenches, or, if they were out of range, at least to spurt dirt and dust into the defenders manning the firing line, so making them keep their heads down.

Most of the riflemen in the jailhouse were now joining in and the noise within the room was deafening. It was now impossible to see if McCarthy and his sergeant had reached the gun but, with an explosion that lit up the landscape, the dynamite thrust down the barrel of the gun detonated and, for a brief moment, exposed in that terrible light, Simon saw the barrel split open, like the petals of a flower opening up at a speed multiplied by a factor of at least a thousand.

He heard himself shout 'Run for it!' and opened up his Maxim again, swinging it round in an arc. The noise continued deafeningly until a voice from below shouted, 'They're back, baas,' and two black faces, blacker even, it seemed, than those of the policemen surrounding them, beamed up at him.

'Thank God for that, boys,' he shouted. And letting his Maxim swing round on its own impetus he leapt down and pumped the hands of the two men. 'Well done. I think you have removed the main threat to Abercorn, but we shall have to wait and see.

'Now,' he addressed McCarthy, 'you go and see if you can snatch a little sleep. You have been under great stress.'

The young man wiped a grimy finger across his face. 'Not necessary, sir,' he smiled, a trifle wanly. 'Now that little job is out of the way I can carry on happily, thank you.'

They were interrupted by a cry from above. 'I think they attack now, baas.' And once again the fortress-prison resounded to the sound of the defenders all firing at once, until: 'I think they go back now, baas,' shouted the lookout. 'Had enough, p'raps for time being...'

And so it proved. Fonthill quickly doubled back down the main street and inspected his trenches. No movement was recorded from any of them. The attack was, Simon realised, a kind of knee-

45

jerk reaction from the Germans at having their prized gun, their main weapon, destroyed right under their noses. Would they now retreat back to the border?

It seemed not, however, for throughout that night and the following blisteringly hot day, sniper fire rained down upon the defenders of Abercorn. Dogged tired now, Fonthill suspected that there would be at least one other frontal attack until, at approximately three o'clock in the morning, some thirty hours since the town had been invested, he heard a thin cheer from its southern end. Minutes later, exhausted and hardly able to put one foot now in front of the other, a British major arrived with one hundred troops.

They had marched ninety-nine miles from Kasama in just sixty-six hours and they were quite exhausted. But the Germans were not to know this and, as dawn broke, they could be seen marching back to the north, towards the border with German East Africa.

'Get after the devils,' shouted Fonthill to McCarthy. 'Get the prisoners to carry the Maxim. Harass them all the way back to the border. Dammit man. You have won your first battle. Show 'em that you're a proper soldier, now, because, by George, you are, Lieutenant.'

McCarthy gave him a weary smile and began organising his men for the pursuit. As they marched out, Fonthill, Jenkins and Mzingeli sat down and drank black coffee.

'I think it only fair to sit this one out, see, bach sir,' said Jenkins, putting up his feet. 'After all, we're nearly bloody pensioners, all three of us.'

Simon raised his mug in silent salute to his two comrades.

Jenkins took a reflective sip and mused: 'I wonder what Miss Alice would think of all these bleedin' antics.' He thought for a moment. 'I know what she'd say, o' course. She'd say we were too old for these capers. And you know what? She'd be right an' all, look you.'

CHAPTER TWO

Alice Fonthill, known, however, to her employers at the *Morning Post,* all her competitors in Fleet Street and to a wide range of senior officers in the British army by her maiden (and professional) name of Alice Griffith, was furious.

The fleet which had lumbered across the ocean from India to invade German East Africa had arrived off Mombasa, its jumping-off point, on 31st October. Alice had joined the convoy there with a handful of journalistic colleagues, all of them Afrikaners who had journeyed up from South Africa to cover the invasion, which was confidently expected to meet with little resistance.

Now, however, as she stood on the deck of *Homayun,* the largest of the transports that had brought the troops from India, in the late afternoon of 3rd November, she was alone. To the west, she could clearly see the peaks of the Usambara Mountains rising up from the coastal plain to where the lighters carrying the invading troops had disappeared towards that horizon the previous day.

Alice stamped her foot and swore loudly. Those lighters were also carrying her journalistic colleagues – *her competitors* – who were being taken ashore to observe the triumphant landing at the German East African port of Tanga and the expected frenzied departure inland of the port's inhabitants. She had been told she must remain on board, because it was possible that the landing could be opposed and that it could be 'no place for a woman'.

She scowled at the memory. The order had been conveyed to her from Major General Arthur Aitken, the commander of the 8,000 troops making up the invading army, by a young subaltern on his staff.

'What do you mean, *a woman,*' she had screamed at the young man. 'I am a fully accredited war correspondent for the *Morning Post.* If the other correspondents are being allowed ashore, I must be with them. It is my job, dammit.'

The lieutenant had looked sheepish. 'Sorry, miss … er … madam, but those are the general's orders. You may go ashore once the landing has been effected.'

'Now you listen to me, my boy.' She had taken a step closer to the officer and spoke in tones of suppressed fury. 'Go back to your bloody general and tell him that, while he was sitting on his arse in India playing bloody polo, I was reporting *from the battlefields* of the Zulu War, the second Afghan war, General Wolseley's attack on the bPedi tribe, his invasion of Egypt, his expedition to relieve

Gordon at Khartoum, Rhodes' invasion of Mata-beleland, the Pathan uprising of 1897...' she paused to draw breath.

The lieutenant cleared his throat to interrupt, but she had forestalled him. 'I haven't finished yet,' she hissed. 'I was in Peking during the Boxer Rebellion, then I covered the Boer War and went with Younghusband on his pathetic invasion of Tibet. And where was bloody General Aitken while I was in "terrible danger as a poor weak woman" on those campaigns? I'll tell you, he was in bloody India, that's where. He never left the place.

'Now you go back and tell him exactly what I have said, otherwise there will be trouble. Go on. Tell him what I have said. Go, go, shoo off.'

The memory of the young man's embarrass-ment gave her momentary satisfaction now but that was fleeting as she remembered how she had attempted to board the lighters that were setting off on the seven-mile journey to the port and had been prevented from doing so by a burly sergeant major. She had been forced to stand on deck and see the smiles on the faces of the Afrikaner re-porters as they looked up at her.

Some of them, she knew, were still fighting the Anglo–Boer war in their hearts. They were atavistically anti-British and had made her aware of this during the wait for the fleet to come into Mombasa.

Alice sniffed. The smell on board the *Homayun* remained foul. Like the rest of the transports, she was grossly overcrowded and the convoy's cruis-ing speed of seven knots had done nothing to

49

alleviate the conditions of the 1,000 men of the Indian 'coolie corps' who had been crammed into a ship designed to carry only 800, as the ships had crawled across the hot and humid Indian Ocean, taking a full month to make the passage.

Alice had reported this from Mombasa on first boarding the ship. She had also not flinched from cabling that the invading army seemed singularly ill-equipped for fighting a major battle, in that it was issued with only fourteen machine guns and virtually no artillery – just six guns of the 28th Mountain Battery. Furthermore, its commander-in-chief had never set foot in Africa before and had not even met his two brigade generals until just before departure.

All this implied criticism, of course, had not endeared her to Aitken and was probably behind his decision to keep her on board. The facts that had fuelled her story had been gleaned from the middle-aged major who was in charge of the ordnance and supplies and with whom she had flirted outrageously during the brief stopover in Mombasa (despite the presence of dysentery among his troops and carriers, Aitken had insisted on sailing on to Tanga without delay).

Alice Fonthill, married woman or not, was not above using her undoubted feminine charms to wheedle out the background facts that she needed to write her stories. And she was able to do so, for, although now 59, she remained a handsome woman. Many grey hairs were now mixed with the fair ones, but riding with Simon in Rhodesia and Norfolk had retained her trim figure and her eyes remained a bewitching, cool grey. She could have, perhaps, been called beautiful, with her high cheekbones, long eyelashes and curving, full eyebrows, had it not been for a certain squareness of the jaw, betraying the determination that had earned her her reputation as one of the best war correspondents in Fleet St.

That determination had surfaced when confronted with Aitken's order and, last night, with the general asleep (after seeing off the invading troops, he had spent the rest of the day on board his warship reading a novel), she had lied to the Morse code operator on the *Homayun* and bribed him into sending a personal cable from her to Lord Kitchener, the Secretary of State for War in London, begging him to overrule Aitken's order. She and the great field marshal had forged a mutual admiration for each other when she was reporting on his campaign against the Boers from South Africa. And, of course, the *Morning Post* was a pillar of the establishment, of which K was a prominent member. Would both these factors be strong enough to gain his intervention now?

She bit her lip. Alice had heard no news from the shadowy mainland on the edge of the horizon. Had the invasion been the walkover that had been predicted? Or had it met resistance from the Germans?

She was still frowning and studying that horizon when the same young subaltern approached her now, a wry grin on his face.

'The pinnace awaits you now, Miss Griffith,' he announced, with exaggerated courtesy.

'What?' Alice whirled round. 'Pinnace? What pinnace?'

'The one, madam, that is going to take you ashore.' His face now had lapsed into a broad grin and Alice could not help noticing how white his teeth were underneath his full moustache. 'I must say, you really do have influence. I think the general was impressed.'

'So he bloody well should be,' but she returned his smile. 'Give me two minutes to get my things. Oh,' she turned back to him. 'How has the landing gone, do you know?'

The smile disappeared. 'Not good, I am afraid, madam. I think it has been quite hot. I am anxious to get ashore to do my bit.'

'Very well. I won't be a minute.'

Within ten minutes, Alice was back on deck and scrambling down the companionway towards where the little steam pinnace lay gently rolling at its foot. Nodding to the young midshipman in command and to the boatswain, she settled down and took out her pencil and notebook, anxious to capture her first impressions as they neared the enemy coast.

For the first time since her vicarious confrontation with Aitken, her thoughts turned to Simon. She had heard, of course, of his involvement with the battle at Abercorn and, although his letter to her, penned shortly after the engagement, was typically modest, she had seen the news reports of how he had organised the defence of the little town. Her heart sang a little as she reflected now upon how glad she was that he was not involved in this present invasion. At least he was safe, back on their farm in the north of Rhodesia!

Then she smiled ruefully. This little matter of landing on an assumed hostile shore would be nothing to her husband, a man lauded throughout the Empire for his daring achievements on its furthest borders. And with the great 352 Jenkins, master shot and horseman, and the elegant and equally fearless Mzingeli, the best tracker in the whole of Africa, to make up the trio, there was nothing that that little band of warriors couldn't do! The smile turned to a grin as she crossed her arms across her breast, swayed slightly with the motion of the boat and clutched the thought of Simon to her.

They had been married now for thirty years. Their only child had been stillborn shortly after their marriage and their attempts to raise a family since had failed. However, during their perilous expedition with Younghusband over the Himalayas deep into Tibet four years ago, they had picked up a young Tibetan, who had joined them and proved to be brave, intelligent – and homeless. They had, therefore, adopted him on their return and taken him back with them to Norfolk, sent him to a crammer and, reluctantly, accepted his strong desire to join the British army.

Alice frowned now as she recalled Sunil's smiling face. Despite (or perhaps because of?) his foreign appearance, they had resisted the pressure to enlist him in the Indian Army and the boy had sailed through Sandhurst and pleased them both by being commissioned into the old regiment of Simon's and both of their parents: the South Wales Borderers, previously known as the 24th Regiment of Foot. Now, as a 26-year-

53

old first lieutenant, he had recently been posted with his battalion to France. His last letter had sung of his excitement at the chance of proving himself in battle. Alice bit her lip at the thought. She could not stand the thought of losing both her children, for Sunil had proved to be a warm, caring son.

She was aroused from her reverie by the sound of gunfire coming from the shore, which now appeared as a grey-black smudge, lit spasmodically by flashes as they neared it.

The helmsman called back to the midshipman, 'Are we goin' straight in, sir? Could be dangerous.'

'No. Not to the jetty. Steer away from the town, towards where you see that headland. Where we landed the troops yesterday. Aim for the signal tower, it will come up in a minute. We should beach on this side of the headland.'

'Aye aye, sir.'

Alice took the opportunity to spread out the rough map of Tanga she had bought in Mombasa. It was little more than a street map but the signal tower was marked as was the nearby beach, called Ras Kasone. She realised that the troops landed yesterday would have had to make their way some 2,000 to 3,000 yards, through what looked like a rubber plantation, to reach the town. Had they been able to do it? Not by the sound of firing that came now from the headland.

'We're going in now, madam,' called the midshipman. 'I'm afraid we can't beach her so you will have to get out in the surf and then run for it. It looks as though the beach may be under fire. I'll have a man to help you.'

'Not needed, thank you. I can swim if necessary and wade, if not. But thank you for your thought. As soon as I jump off, go astern and get out of here. I don't want anyone endangered by me. Thank you all. Tell me when to go.'

She slung her notebook around her neck with a cord, hitched up her skirt waist high, tucked it into her belt and unsteadily made her way to the bow of the little vessel, now pitching heavily as it caught the surf. In fact, Alice was so preoccupied with the high waves and the crashing of the surf that she had no idea if the beach was under fire, although she could hear gunfire from up ahead.

'Now, madam!' The burly boatswain, standing waist-deep in the water as the waves surged by him, lifted up his arms, caught her above the waist and swung her high and over into the water. The surf surged forward but he lifted her clear and, head down so that his beard tickled her chin, carried her to the edge of the beach. Depositing her onto the sand he pointed to where a coral cliff face, some twenty feet high, marked the end of the beach. 'You'll have to climb that, luv, but there's a path up there and it doesn't seem to be under fire. Go now – and good luck to yer. You've got guts. Run now!'

Alice could hardly find breath to thank him but she gathered up her sodden skirt and ran as best she could through the slipping, sliding sand until she could huddle under the protection of the bank. Then she turned and waved her thanks to the pinnace, which was now bucking its way astern through the surf.

She put her fist to her mouth. Oh, how awful if the little craft was sunk and lives lost as a result of her intransigence! But the boat turned in calmer waters and, with a puff of black smoke, headed out to sea safely enough.

Now: where to go and what to do? The beach was only about a hundred yards wide and Alice could not help but wonder why it had been chosen to put the first men ashore. It would have been impossible, surely, if the Germans were manning the top of the little escarpment. It would have been like firing at fish in a barrel. The firing now seemed to come from above her and to the left but she could see no sign of troops.

She did, however, see the little path arching up-wards and now well trodden and she began to scramble up it. At the top she glimpsed to her right a brightly painted red house near the signal tower that stood behind it. Turbaned troops seemed to be assembling there – Indians! Thank God for that! – and she became aware that other Indian troops were half-running, half-walking back along the top of the ridge, away from the firing.

'Good God, madam, who are you and what on earth are you doing here?'

The speaker was a young captain, wearing the uniform of the 13th Rajputs, who had suddenly appeared from a patch of scrub.

'Alice Griffith. War correspondent for the *Morning Post*, London. I've just been put ashore. Who is in command here?'

'Brigadier General Michael Tighe, madam.' She realised that the young man's face was smirched with cordite streaks and that he was clearly tired, extremely tired. 'But I must warn you that the general won't exactly warm to your presence here. He's in the middle of fighting and, by the look of it, losing a very bloody battle. I don't think, madam, that you should be here.'

'Of course I should. I am a *war* correspondent, Captain. And I have probably covered more wars than you have had hot dinners.' She relented as she saw the tiredness in the eyes of the officer. 'But I am sorry it's been so bloody. Have you sustained many casualties?'

'You'd better ask the general that. He's over there. His headquarters is the red-painted house there. But I can tell you,' he ran the back of his hand over his brow, 'that I have lost many good men. Very good men.'

'Ah, I am so sorry, Captain. Let me get out of your way and try and find the general.'

He nodded and Alice joined the ragged segments of troops, mainly Rajputs and Indian Pioneers, as far as she could see, who were wearily plodding back towards the red house. She suddenly realised that dark clouds, so close above her that she felt she could almost reach up and touch them, were debouching rain that now came down in torrents, so adding to the discomforts caused by her already wet skirt.

She became aware that the firing was now coming from behind her and seemed static. Had General Tighe been able to establish a line and stop the general retreat? If he had not, by the look of it, he and his recently landed troops would be thrown back into the sea. She must find Tighe.

57

She thrust her way through the retreating troops, earning open-mouthed looks of astonishment from them all, until she had gained the house. 'General Tighe?' she asked of a young subaltern.

'There, ma'am.' The lieutenant pointed to where a group of staff officers were bent over a table. Through the open doorway to another room, she glimpsed medics, wearing bloodstained aprons, bustling to and fro. It was obviously no time to be interrupting the general and, suddenly, she felt cold. She had taken a drenching but the air was warm and humid so it could not be an unseasonable cold – unless she had sweated under her garments and this had chilled. But she began to shudder, so she pulled up a chair and sat down within a discreet distance of the huddled group.

She realised that she must have dozed off because she was suddenly aware that she was being addressed by an officer bending over her and staring at her with the fiercest blue eyes she had ever seen. 'I said, who the hell are you, madam, and what are you doing here in my headquarters? Eh?' The words were spoken in a lilting Irish accent that exactly matched the blue eyes.

'Ah, General.' Alice gulped and struggled to stand.

'No, no, lady. Sit there. You are shivering, dammit. You'll catch yer death.' Tighe turned and shouted. 'Smithers. Bring me my whiskey flask, there's a good chap.'

Alice realised that her teeth were chattering and she grasped the little screw-on cup with both hands and lifted it to her lips. The liquid coursed through her veins almost immediately and she gulped and coughed.

'Ah, thank you, General,' she said. 'I am so sorry to take you from your duties.'

'So you should be, madam. I am in the middle of fighting a battle and I certainly didn't invite you here. So, to repeat, what the hell– No, no...' His voice took on a kindly note. 'No, you're shaking fit to break. Now, take another sip, won't yer. It's the best Irish and will do yer the world of good.'

Alice nodded her thanks and took a gulp of the fiery liquid. 'Thank you again,' she wiped her lips. 'I'm Alice Griffith of the *Morning Post* and General Aitken allowed me to land here,' she gestured with her head, 'on the beach just below the headland. I presume there must be other correspondents here with you?'

Tighe raised his eyebrows. 'Good God, madam. Certainly not. As far as I know, they're all huddled on one of the lighters in the bay waiting to land when the harbour has been swept of mines. I have to say, the general must have been mad to have let you land here. Not to put too fine a point on it, dear lady, we're fightin' for our lives, so we are. Mind you,' he sniffed and the blue eyes seemed to twinkle, 'when I get this lot together again and we get some reinforcements we'll sweep forward and take the town. But we need to ... er ... get our breath back first, so to speak.'

He shouted again to one of his aides. 'Can someone find a blanket for this lady? Quickly, now.' He turned back to Alice. 'Excuse me, now. If yer want to know what's goin' on, we'll talk later. But I've got to fight me battle now, d'yer see.' He nodded and joined his staff at the table.

He had left his hip flask on the floor beside her, so Alice furtively bent down and took another sip. Immediately she felt better, and fumbling for the notebook, still hung around her neck, and pulling the blanket around her, she walked towards the door and peered outside.

Some sort of order now seemed to have been imposed on the Indian troops who had fled back from the general direction of the town of Tanga, with officers shouting and getting the men to fall into lines. She caught a glimpse of the captain to whom she had spoken earlier and, edging out under the overhanging guttering to avoid another drenching, she beckoned to him.

Reluctantly, he came over.

'Captain, I've found the general and he is going to brief me in a moment, but I wanted to get an impression of what has happened from someone who has been there. Just tell me what happened and I promise not to quote you.'

'Well, I'm not sure I should...'

Alice became brusque. 'Oh, of course you can. I am a correspondent accredited by the War Office. Now, in your own words, what happened?'

'Very well, madam. We set off at about 8 a.m. this morning, having waited for our full strength to build with the landings, but,' his voice took on a bitter tone, 'I can tell you that we were ordered to advance towards the town well before our three battalions had landed.'

Alice nodded sympathetically. She was not taking notes. Experience had told her that, under the circumstances, this was a way of alarming her

60

informants. Better to just try and remember it all.

'We were ordered to take the town and had to advance,' he jerked his head to where the firing still could be heard, 'through thick scrub, a sort of mangrove swamp and a rubber plantation. It was hard going, particularly for men who had not yet got their shore legs. We had been told that there would be little, if any, resistance and we made good time at first. Then,' he frowned at the memory, 'machine guns opened up on us from a railway cutting that seemed to surround this end of town. My commanding officer, Colonel Codrington, and two other officers were mown down.

'The same happened to the 61st Pioneers on our left – they are not really supposed to be fighting troops, you know, and they had never faced machine guns before. They lost their CO, too, and when the Germans counter-attacked – obviously having received reinforcements – the Pioneers buckled and ran and our left flank was completely exposed. We couldn't hold on and we were forced to retreat too. Luckily, the Loyal North Lancs have landed now and have entrenched a line covering both landing beaches. It seems they are holding fast, thank goodness.'

Alice nodded her thanks. 'Only one more question. Have you any idea how many men you have lost?'

'Not really. At a guess about fifteen per cent. Far too many.'

'Thank you, I am most grateful.' Alice suddenly realised that she was beginning to shake again and so she made her way back into the comparative warmth of the general's headquarters. He and his staff were now gone, presumably to oversee the holding of the line, but she was delighted to see the little whiskey flask still nestling by the foot of her chair and, feeling slightly guilty, she stole another sip before beginning to scribble in her notebook.

As her pencil raced, it became clear that two elementary mistakes had been made with the landings. Firstly, there had obviously been no reconnaissance on the ground made of the approaches to the town and the troops had been sanguinely told to expect no resistance, with no evidence to support that; and, secondly, to attack what was a well-guarded town with unseasoned Pioneer troops *before* the attacking force was at full strength was foolhardy, to say the least. Her dislike of General Aitken deepened.

Pocketing the flask – she must, of course, return it to Brigadier Tighe – she ventured outside again. The rain, thank goodness, had slackened somewhat and Alice decided to find higher ground that would enable her to gain a view of the harbour, away to the west from Tighe's position on the headland. Surely, given the setbacks sustained by Tighe's command, the attack would now have been switched to effect landings on the jetty in the harbour, so enabling Tighe to gather his force for another advance? She must see.

She scrambled up a hill rising behind the house and at last found the viewpoint she sought. She took out the small binoculars she carried in a case and focussed on the harbour down below. The warship HMS *Fox* was out in the harbour but her guns were silent and there were no attempts to land troops on the main jetty under cover of her fire. Instead, Alice could see that men were being put ashore on the two small beaches in Tanga's inner harbour. Their combined frontage was no more than 400 yards and the congestion was obvious, even to her distant eye, but it seemed that the enemy was not contesting the landings.

Frowning, Alice put down the glasses. It was obvious that the Germans had decided to defend the town – the evidence of Tighe's losses made that clear. But why no firing on the men being put ashore in the harbour? Then slowly, she nodded. The Germans were doing everything they could not to risk the town itself being bombarded by British naval guns. They were obviously waiting until the main attack started from the landed troops and then, when shelling the town would mean inflicting damage on the warships' own men, the enemy would open up, probably from well-defended positions.

Hmmh. Whoever was in command of the German troops defending Tanga knew what he was doing. She had heard that a Prussian colonel was leading the defence of the colony; now, what was his name? She produced her pad and looked at earlier notes. Ah yes, here it was: Colonel von Lettow-Vorbeck. No one that Alice had spoken to had heard of the man. But here he was defending a town that Aitken was convinced would be virtually empty when the 8,000 British soldiers hove over the horizon. Where, oh where, was British intelligence? To land on an unknown enemy coast without reconnaissance was an unforgivable error. She bit her lip. Her heart was full of foreboding.

She scrambled back down to the HQ and saw Brigadier Tighe striding back towards it. 'Do you have a moment now, General?' she called.

'Just two minutes,' he called back. 'Come inside and sit down.'

'Thank you for the whiskey,' she said, offering the flask. 'I think it saved my life.'

'And I'm not too proud to take it back,' he said with a smile. 'It's saved me own on more than one occasion, I can tell you. Now,' he perched on a corner of the table, as she sat on one of the camp stools, 'what d'yer want to know?'

'Will you attack again now? It seems as though troops are being landed without resistance on the beaches in the inner harbour. Now that the Loyals are here, will you move again?'

'Hmmm. You've got a grasp of the situation pretty quickly, I must say. Will I attack now? Well, I'd love to – in fact, I'm itching to attack. But no, I won't – at least not at the moment. I daren't risk ruinin' the whole thing, yer know, until we've got enough men ashore down there.' He nodded towards the town. 'One false move and I could upset the whole applecart.'

'Was not the town reconnoitred properly before you and the others were put ashore?'

The blue eyes stared at her from under bushy eyebrows and he paused before answering. 'Ah now, m'lady,' he said carefully. 'You must ask the commander-in-chief those sorts of questions. I believe there was some sort of nonsense from the navy about sweeping the harbour for mines before goin' in and that caused much of the delay. But once we've got sufficient men ashore, then I will certainly have another go at the Hun at this end. Now, you must leave me alone while I make me plans. Will yer have another tiny pull at this lovely Irish?'

Alice shook her head as he offered her the flask. 'You are very kind and solicitous but I must keep my head.'

'And so must I. Now you must excuse me.'

Throughout the evening, as the rain recommenced, there was no movement on either side, although the sniping continued spasmodically where the Loyals were dug in. Alice heard a rumour that General Aitken himself had at last landed down at the harbour in the late afternoon but if he had done so it did not precipitate any aggressive activity there and darkness fell on what seemed to be stalemate. She retained her by now dry blanket, gathered two cushions in a dark corner of the room where she hoped she would be virtually unnoticed and spent the night fitfully sleeping and dreaming that Simon had come ashore to take command of the landings.

Alice arose at dawn and crept up the hill to her vantage point of the day before. Through her glasses she could see no sign of fighting in the town, even though it was clear that many more troops had been landed between Tighe's position and the town itself, which was still not under bombardment from the navy ships in the harbour. Nor, indeed, did it seem that there were any preparations for attack by Tighe and his men from behind the line of trenches. In fact, it was not until just before noon that the advance began.

Presuming that it would be another day of inactivity, Alice had left her viewing point and was munching a stale sandwich when she sensed from the bustle all around her that the attack was about to begin. Back up the hill, she had a perfect view of Tighe's command begin to leave its trenches and move forward cautiously through the thick scrub. It immediately became apparent that the advance was proceeding at an exceedingly cautious pace, seemingly meeting no resistance from the Germans this time. Had they retreated during the night? wondered Alice, her eyes glued to her field glasses.

If it had taken the 13th Jajputs just half an hour to march to the German machine guns at the railway cutting the previous morning, this present advance was being conducted at a snail's pace. She knew that Brigadier General Tighe had a reputation as a fighting Irishman, but it was clear that he was being incredibly cautious this time – a tribute to the enemy, perhaps, or fear of another collapse by the comparatively untrained Indians in his command? Then it became clear that Tighe's men in the north had made contact with men who had landed after them and that all General Aitken's seven battalions were now advancing on Tanga in one long straight line, moving at what seemed like the pace of a terrified centipede. The line was now disappearing out of range of Alice's small binoculars, but she could not help thinking that to advance in this fashion was to turn back the military clock to the days of Marlborough.

Then she heard the firing begin – particularly the rat-tat-tat of machine guns. Had the British been lured into a German trap? It seemed so, for, as she desperately tried to focus her inadequate glasses, into her view came tiny khaki figures running back from the left of the British line, where she had seen the Indian Palamcottahs advance. This had obviously left a gap in the line but smoke was now obscuring Alice's view and she lowered her glasses and began quickly making notes.

Eventually, she heard guns booming from the harbour and saw that HMS *Fox* had at last opened fire on the town. Did this mean that British troops had been repulsed from it? By late afternoon, she could see that the whole British line had been broken, with some sections still fighting but others in retreat, with troops streaming back the way they had come. The dreaded rattle of machine guns could now clearly be heard in what seemed like a malicious song of victory. She gnawed on her knuckle. Had the much vaunted invasion of German East Africa been defeated so comprehensively and so quickly? She hurried down the hill, anxious to seek confirmation.

The first to arrive back at their starting point were the Palamcottahs, their white eyes staring from dark faces. 'What happened, what happened?' she shouted as she ran towards them. But they streamed by her without response. One British officer had been trying to stem the retreat, revolver in hand, and tears were streaming down his face as she caught his arm.

'Damn it all, they broke and ran,' he hissed,

seemingly not at all distracted by being accosted by a woman on the battlefield. 'It was the bloody machine guns, you see. Not used to 'em. Couldn't hold them. Must get back.' And he turned and, waving his arms, tried to stop the men running towards him.

Soon, Alice realised that English troops were among those streaming back and she scrambled back up her hill to attempt to gain some sort of overall impression of what was happening. Now she could see German troops advancing from where they had obviously delivered a telling right hook on the British left. But she could see that not all was lost. The British line had certainly been broken but she could see from rifle flashes that isolated pockets of resistance were being sustained in the bush and the enemy was certainly not in hot pursuit.

Why did they not follow up what had obviously been a great victory? In fact, she could catch glimpses now of the darker green uniforms of the German askaris moving back towards the town, before they disappeared from sight in the general dust and smoke. Even if the German counter-attack was not being pressed, one thing was certain. This was the end of the attempt to take Tanga.

Wearily, Alice went back down her hill again and waited until she could catch a moment with General Tighe. He eventually came back in the gathering darkness, a bullet hole in his trousers and his face smeared with black powder marks.

'General, for God's sake, what happened?' Alice cried as she ran towards him.

'Can't stop to talk now,' the Irishman grunted. 'But we are goin' to get out of here, I can tell you that. We're goin' back to our bloody ships. It's been a disaster. You'd better talk to Aitken if you want more. Now, I've got to get down to the beaches. Follow me down and I'll see you get into a boat.'

But Alice did not. Pencil in hand, she stayed by the red house, watching the troops wearily file back, some of the officers, she could see, white-faced with anger. She approached one.

'Why the collapse?' she asked.

'God knows. Who the hell are you, anyway?'

'Alice Griffith, *Morning Post*.'

'Ah. Well, tell the folks back home that it wasn't our fault. We had reached the town and even got into the Kaiserhof hotel and pulled down the two German flags on the roof, but the Germans were well positioned in buildings all around us and opened up a withering fire. There were plenty of them, too, I can tell you.'

He wiped a weary hand across his face. 'We lost a lot of men. The Hun must have been reinforced down the railway from the interior and were well positioned – just waiting for us. And they were well commanded. A damn sight better than us...' He tailed away.

Alice jumped in quickly; she sensed caution now creeping into his words. 'If the Germans were in position in the town, why on earth do you think the navy didn't bombard it? That could have flushed the Germans out.'

'Absolutely. I think the bloody fool of a general commanding us,' he frowned, 'you must not quote me now, otherwise I will be in hot water. Aitken, I understand, didn't want the railway damaged because he was relying on it to take us all into our great invasion of the interior. As it was, it was used by the Hun to bring in their men from the east. Now I must get my chaps down to the beaches to re-embark. Thank God the Hun haven't pursued us, for some reason. What a mess!' He summoned up an apologetic smile and walked past her.

Alice scribbled what she could remember of his words and then wrote in capital letters DISASTER! And underlined it. How much of all this, she wondered, would the censors let her relay back to London? One thought, however, brought a slow smile to her face. As far as she could see, not one of her competitors had had as close-up a view of the battle as she. If they had been allowed to land, then they probably would have been kept back from the front line and the street fighting. Good. An exclusive! Thanks to that misogynistic, incompetent old Major General Arthur Aitken!

A wind was beginning to come off the sea and she decided it was time to leave this ill-fated headland, for troops were now being marshalled and were shuffling past her down the paths to the beaches. Tucking her notepad under her now torn blanket and swinging her binocular case over her shoulder, she joined the sad stream of men evacuating German East Africa.

CHAPTER THREE

The general held no press conference to explain what had happened at Tanga and each journalist was left to report back to his newspaper in his own way – except that each cable was strictly censored to avoid giving the impression that the attempted invasion had resulted in a major reversal. Hints, however, were allowed to leak to the correspondents that the navy had been over-cautious in terms of minesweeping the harbour, so giving the Germans time to bring in reinforcements and establish their positions.

These, of course, Alice ignored and, experienced as she was at avoiding censorship and accustomed as were her editors at home at reading between her lines, she was able to cloak the damning evidence against Aitken under such phrases as 'the Germans seemed to spring from nowhere' and 'pre-landing reconnaissance was not clearly evident'.

What could not be disguised, however, were the losses sustained by the British. It ensued that 817 men had been killed, wounded or had gone missing, totalling fifteen per cent of the invading force. The losses had been particularly heavy among the pith-helmeted British and Indian officers: thirty-one dead and thirty wounded. These figures loomed even larger when compared to the German statistics that British intelligence secured: just 150 men.

71

Alice's fury at the incompetence and arrogance of the British commander-in-chief lasted well after their return to Mombasa.

It was compounded when the news trickled down from Aitken's staff that, despite the fact that the Germans were not attacking the evacuating troops (it emerged that a bugle call had been misinterpreted and most of the defending troops had mistakenly retreated to the railway terminus), the general had ordered that re-embarkation could be undertaken more quickly if less portable equipment was left behind. As a result, eight serviceable machine guns, 455 rifles, half a million rounds of ammunition, telephone gear, coats, blankets and even uniforms were discarded, giving the supply-starved Germans an early and most welcome Christmas present.

On arrival in Mombasa, Alice immediately sought a commercial cabling station, one free, of course, from army censorship, and sent a message to her editor, giving the facts and imploring him to reveal what he could in a critical leader, rather than under the byline of 'Our Own Correspondent with the British Forces,' which would, she knew, have resulted in formal complaints being laid against her by Aitken.

Waiting for her in Mombasa was a long letter from Simon, begging her to see if she could earn a little leave and journey up to the farm to spend a few days with him there, during what seemed likely to be a hiatus in preparing the next move of the British army.

The suggestion had immediately appealed to her, not least because of the mounting animosity revealed towards her – and, indeed, towards the British – by one of the leading Boer journalists with the army, Herman de Villiers of the Afrikaner newspaper *Die Burger.*

A tall, thin man with a full, black beard, he greeted her when they met at the quayside: 'Well, Mrs Fonthill,' (he resolutely refused to give her the courtesy of referring to her by her maiden name by which she was known professionally). 'Another Spion Kop for the British, didn't you think? Didn't your people learn anything from we poor farmers fourteen years ago, eh?'

She gave him a mock curtsy. 'Ah, Mr de Villiers. I looked for you in Tanga but couldn't find you. Where were you? Painting word pictures of the invasion from way out at sea?' And she finished with that very Dutch-sounding word 'eh?'

De Villiers scowled. 'None of us caught sight of you, madam. We all wondered where you were. Perhaps comforting your general, eh?'

Alice smiled sweetly. 'I was certainly with a general, sir. A *fighting* general, Brigadier Tighe. And I witnessed a lot of the action – from close up. I agree that there was no delight that anyone who was not a German could take from this so-called invasion, but there were too many good men killed on both sides to take pleasure from it anyway. But now you must forgive me, for I have a follow-up story to file. Good day to you, sir.'

She swept away, grinning inwardly, for she knew that her last words would immediately set the Boer journalistic camp agog with apprehension, for she had a reputation – recently confirmed – for getting the story that eluded most of them. What, she knew they would be thinking, is she up to now?

To get away from that uncollegiate group would be a relief – not least because it was clear that there would be a long lull in the fighting on the coast – but awaiting her at her hotel was a cable from Simon: 'THINK I MIGHT HAVE A JOB AT LAST STOP STAY MOMBASA STOP AM ON MY WAY STOP WILL ARRIVE THURSDAY STOP LOVE YOU STOP'.

Immediately, Alice's heart sang at the thought of seeing him and just as immediately it sank. A job. What sort of job? Her husband was too old to go fighting again. For God's sake, hadn't he done enough at Abercorn to earn him respite from taking up arms in this war at the age of 59? She frowned. She sensed the hand of Kitchener in this. She knew that the great man at the War Office rated her husband highly, first from the early days on Wolseley's failed mission to rescue Gordon in Khartoum when Kitchener was merely a humble intelligence major, to the Boer War, where, as commander-in-chief, he had employed Simon as a colonel – later brigadier – of cavalry. She had always felt that if the need arose in Africa, the Secretary of State for War would find him a job. Now, it seemed, he had.

But what kind of job? K would never contemplate offering him some sort of desk work, he knew that Simon would be wasted wielding a pen. It had to be the sword. She drew in her breath. Ah well, all would be revealed on Thursday.

Alice knew that the journey from Northern Rhodesia to British East Africa's Mombasa would be tortuous because, of course, the great territory of German East Africa lay between the two colonies. It was not surprising, therefore, that Simon arrived a day later than intended.

As she waited at the dockside for his ship to put in, she looked around her in the hot sun, taking in once again the distinctive smells of this part of Africa, the shattering brightness of the bandanas worn by the stevedores, and the flash of their teeth as they joked and languidly went about their work. Alice had grown to love Africa and once more she cursed that that arrogant Prussian Emperor, Kaiser Wilhelm, had broken the tranquillity of this part of the vast continent by his venal invasion of Belgium, so throwing together in conflict people in East Africa who had, hitherto, been warm friends and even working colleagues.

She could not help smiling, however, as she recalled the anecdote that had found its way throughout British-speaking Africa from Lake Nyasa. On the outbreak of the war, a red-haired British skipper called Captain Rhoades enterprisingly steered his ship the *Gwendolen* into the port of Sphinxhafen at the German end of the lake and, with one shot, disabled the *Hermann von Wissmann*, so giving the British navy its first victory of the war. Immediately, the German ship's captain rowed out to the *Gwendolen* and bellowed up to his old drinking partner, 'Gott for damn, Rhoades, vos you drunk?' He and his crew were, somewhat apologetically, taken on board as prisoners of war.

At last, Alice saw the familiar figures of Simon and Jenkins waving to her from the tender that bounced its way towards the jerry and the greetings exchanged at the dockside were warm and tender – as much for the Welshman as for Fonthill.

'Thank God you are all right,' whispered Simon as he embraced her. 'I knew that you would be in the thick of it at Tanga and was terrified that you would take it upon yourself to lead the damned invasion.'

Jenkins's great eyebrows shot up. 'From what I've 'eard of that bleedin' mess up, look you, it would 'ave been better if she 'ad been in command, like.'

'It was, indeed, a disaster,' mumbled Alice from just underneath Simon's left ear. 'But let's talk about it all back in the hotel. I want to know what this new job of yours is going to be.'

They settled into the bar of the hotel, bustling with British officers and bronzed farmers, and, over whiskies and sodas, exchanged their experiences of the last month, as the electric fan whirled slowly above their heads. Aware that Mombasa, the leading port of East Africa and the railhead for the British Uganda Railway, was alleged to house many German spies, they spoke in low voices and when Alice had finished recounting her sad litany of Aitken's mistakes, Simon leant forward and spoke even more quietly.

'Well,' he said, 'I've heard on the grapevine, coming here in the ship, that it is highly unlikely that the man is going to get away with it. While British newspapers have been very restrained...'

76

'Oh damn,' exploded Alice.

Simon frowned. '...one particular Afrikaner paper in South Africa has openly referred to us having sustained a severe beating. And from what I've heard, it seems that the general, while nobly accepting responsibility for the mess, has at the same time been thrashing about blaming almost everybody but the King for it all.'

Alice sniffed. 'That sounds typical. What sort of accusations has he made?'

'That the navy was at fault for taking so much time in double-sweeping the bay for mines that Tighe was left exposed and forced to advance on 3rd November with only one and a half battalions; that almost half the force given was in a deplorable state and that he was sorely let down by the 63rd Palamcottahs and 98th Infantry, both of whom he wants to be sent back to India; and that the Germans had far more manpower available to them than he had been led to believe.'

'Probably all true,' said Alice drawing deeply on her glass. 'But it doesn't excuse the fact that he didn't let his troops disembark at Mombasa for rest and rehabilitation after their long and frightful passage from India and, most of all, for attacking Tanga without reconnoitring the town and its defences before landing his troops. Simon, surely that's all fairly basic, isn't it, and just bad generalship?'

Simon nodded. 'Certainly is.'

'So...' Alice drew out the word. 'Are they going to make you commander-in-chief now? Is this the new job you are going to be offered?'

'Well, Miss Alice.' Jenkins tugged at his moustache. 'They could do a lot worse, I'll tell you.'

'That's all very kind of you,' Simon grinned, 'but I think it a bit unlikely, don't you, what with my arthritis and all?'

'Oh, for God's sake, Simon, tell me what they're offering you.'

'As a matter of fact, my love, I don't actually know. I understand that I am to see Major General Wapshare tomorrow – he was the chap under Aitken in charge of the landings in the harbour at Tanga and has been newly promoted by the sound of it.'

'Ah.' Alice's face brightened. 'So Aitken has been, or is about to be, sacked. Is that true?'

'Don't know yet, but I think it likely. Anyway, I will probably know tomorrow.' He leant forward. 'Everyone has been saying that the two wars – here and in Europe – will be over within a couple of months. Well, I don't believe that for a moment. From what I have heard, the Germans here are well equipped with many machine guns and it will take us months to ship in enough decent troops and guns to equal them. The Germans have well trained their black askaris, who are formidable fighters and it seems that they are well led...'

'I can confirm that,' nodded Alice.

'They can't possibly win this African war in the long run,' continued Simon, 'because they are too far from Germany and I can't see how the homeland can continue to supply their troops here. But their territory is huge. It's about twice the size of Germany itself – and from what Mzingeli tells me, there are few roads and only two railways and it's full of mountains, swamps and waterless deserts. It is ideal country in which and from which to conduct an aggressive guerrilla campaign and I understand that the Germans are already launching raids on our Ugandan railway. This could be the Anglo-Boer War all over again, with us expending lives and millions of pounds chasing the askaris all over the place.'

Simon drained his whisky and beckoned to the blue-sashed waiter for replacements. 'You see,' he said, 'the Germans don't really *need* to win the war in East Africa, anyway, and I suspect this colonel who leads 'em, von Lettow something, realises this and is determined to play the game to the end, so engaging thousands of our troops that could be usefully deployed in France and Flanders. In other words, sort of fighting the War of the Western Front in Africa.'

Jenkins gratefully raised the new glass of whisky placed before him. 'But 'aven't we got plenty of blokes in India,' he asked, 'who could be shipped over 'ere to fight?'

'What? Like the chaps who turned and ran in Tanga?'

'Ah. I see what you mean.'

'And the Germans will be doing their best to raise trouble with the natives in India, as it is. If we denude the place of troops, God knows what could happen.' Simon leant back. 'This is not going to be easy, you know.'

'Now look, Simon.' It was Alice's turn to lean forward in emphasis. 'Whatever this job is, please don't take anything that is going to put you in the front line. Frankly, darling, you are just too old.'

'Heh, Miss Alice.' Jenkins's eyebrows had risen again in indignation. 'I quite understand and emphasist ... emphisose...'

'Empathise?' offered Simon.

'That's just what I was goin' to say. I ... er ... understand your feelin', like, but the colonel is just as good as 'e ever was, as far as I can see. You should 'ave seen 'im in that Aftercorn place. Tearin' about, 'e was, see. Nimble as a twenty-year-old.'

Alice smiled. 'Well, that's nice to hear, 352, but, look, he's all I have – apart from you and Sunil, that is – and I don't want to lose him just yet.'

'Oh, for goodness' sake.' Simon rose. 'Stop squabbling over me as if I was a little boy. Come on. Let's get some lunch.'

The following afternoon Fonthill returned from his interview with Wapshare and was met by an eager Alice and Jenkins. 'Well,' said Alice in some exasperation as Simon slumped into an armchair in their bedroom, 'what happened?'

'Well, I've been offered a job but I have turned it down.'

'Blimey, bach sir.' Jenkins blew out his cheeks. 'I didn't expect that, look you.'

'Thank goodness for that.' Alice's face had lit up. 'You are showing some sense at last.'

'Hmmm. But I have accepted another one.'

'Oh no! What? Oh, for God's sake, tell us all.'

Simon eased himself in the chair and stared at the ceiling. He hated interrogations. 'I was offered command of a battalion that is on its way out here.' He smiled, a touch ruefully. 'They're a

80

strange lot and I suppose that's why Wapshare offered them to me. Kitchener's behind it, of course.'

Alice frowned. 'Yes, I thought as much. Go on.'

'They're called The Legion of Frontiersmen but they've been made more or less respectable by coming out as a battalion of the Royal Fusiliers.'

'Ah.' Jenkins nodded. 'I've 'eard of them. Funny lot, as you say.'

'Yes. They were formed about ten years ago by a strange feller called Pocock, who, it seems, has knocked about the fringes of the Empire and wanted to harness together people who had lived hard in the outback, on prairies, the veldt and so on but who felt themselves patriots. Pocock felt that not enough was being done to oppose the German threat...'

'An' 'e was probably right there,' Jenkins interposed.

'...so he formed them into a sort of territorial outfit, but scattered around the world.' Fonthill frowned. 'The War Office didn't fancy 'em much, so they were never formally recognised. I met the type during the Boer War. Good fighters but undisciplined. Anyway, they've formed a battalion now and they are on their way out here, the thinking obviously being that this is the sort of war that would suit them.'

Alice looked puzzled. 'And you were offered the command?'

'Yes.'

'Well, I am glad you turned it down. But I would have thought the job would have been just the sort you wanted.'

'Well, yes. In a way it was. But I didn't have to think for long before saying no.' A silence fell in the room, broken distantly by the rattle of harness as a wagon was driven by and a little burst of Swahili rose from the street below. Simon leant forward. 'There were two reasons, really, I suppose.

'The first is that the battalion is sailing out with a CO already in place. I know him. Met him in South Africa but only briefly. Great character, named Patrick Driscoll. Got a DSO acting as scout against the Boers and is certainly not a man to be crossed. He has raised the regiment and it would be disastrous, in my view, to replace him once he arrives here. It would also be most unfair.'

'Why did Kitchener and Whipshot want to sack him, then?' asked Jenkins. 'Ad 'e blotted 'is copy book already, like?'

'I don't think so. But I think that K wanted to have somebody with experience in command and he remembered me, of course, from the Boer War, as well as, I suppose, the Tibetan business. Also, he had promised not to forget me out here and this would have seemed something right up my street, given my ... er ... irregular past in the army. So he wasn't really trying to depose Driscoll. They would have given him another command.'

'Well,' said Alice, 'I can understand that you wouldn't want to have him on your conscience. But you mentioned a second reason.'

'Yes.' Fonthill ran a hand across his brow. 'I just didn't want to rejoin the army, particularly as a line officer.'

82

'Absolutely bloody right, bach sir,' Jenkins nodded vigorously. 'We left together once and then rejoined and I think that once was enough.'

'That's all very well, Simon,' said Alice. 'But what is this other job, then, that you have volunteered for? Are we joining the navy now, then? Have you become an admiral?'

'No. You know very well I get seasick in a rowing boat. No. What I offered to do, though, is for 352 and I to go back to doing what we are best at.'

'Oh, my God. And what, pray, is that?'

'Acting on our own, more or less. As scouts. Working between the lines or behind the enemy lines. Intelligence workers, if you like, but not spies.'

Thunder descended on Alice's face. 'No, I certainly do not like,' she hissed. 'You must be mad, Simon. That's even more dangerous and, I would have thought, arduous physically and in every other way than commanding a battalion of ruffians. Living out in the bush again and all that.' Her face softened. 'You are 59 now, darling, and 352 is even older. Let younger men do that job.'

Jenkins switched his gaze between the two. 'But, savin' your presence and all that, Miss Alice, younger blokes wouldn't do it as well as us. We can still live rough and, if the colonel can remember to grip with 'is knees, 'e can just about manage now to stay on 'is 'orse, as well.' He sniffed. 'I reckon there's nobody better 'n us at that sort of business, I really do.'

'Rubbish,' said Simon. 'I'm a damned good

horseman now. Not perhaps as good as you, but much better than I used to be.'

'Oh, stop arguing like a pair of schoolboys.' Alice's voice was beginning to quaver. 'Did the bloody general accept your crazy offer?'

'Well ... er ... yes. To be honest, I think he was glad he didn't have to sack Driscoll as soon as he had landed. And' – Simon paused for a moment, as though to gather courage – 'as a matter of fact, there is a job coming up that will suit us down to the ground.'

Alice shook her head in despair. 'So the two of you are going to smuggle into Dar es Salaam and blow up the German headquarters, are you?'

'No, my love. Now listen, both of you. The army here is very down, of course, after the Tanga disaster. And the news from the Western Front hasn't been good, either, after Mons and the Marne. So Wapshare is anxious to strike a blow to restore morale and, indeed, to placate the War Office in London to some extent.'

He put his hand inside his tunic and pulled out a carefully folded map, opened it and placed it on the table between them. Then he stabbed a finger onto it.

'Look here,' he said. 'This is Bukoba, a largish town on the German side of Lake Victoria, some thirty miles into German East Africa and south of its border with Uganda. Wapshare wants to attack it.'

'Why?' asked Alice. 'It doesn't look of great strategic importance.'

'Ah, but it is. Firstly, it possesses a high-power radio transmitter, which is a precious link to

Germany itself; destroying it would completely isolate this north-west corner of the German colony. Secondly, the surrounding country is of some economic importance to the Germans. It is a huge producer of coffee, which the settlers demand, as well as running a trading business with Ruanda and Urundi in hides and skins, both of which are needed by the German askaris.'

'Is it well defended?' asked Alice.

'Well, that's for us to find out. We are asked to reconnoitre the best way to attack the place, without alerting the Germans, of course, and to assess the strength of the defenders.'

Jenkins's grin seemed to light up the room. 'Just our sort of job,' he said. 'But we shall need old Jelly to 'elp us find the place.'

Simon smiled. One of the Welshman's few de-merits as a soldier and scout was his complete inability to find his way from A to B, even if the road between was brightly illuminated and ran dead straight. 'Oh, yes. I shall ask Mzingeli to track for us. The farm can run itself for a while.'

'Well,' Alice sat back with a sigh. 'It sounds all neatly bound with ribbons. You are going and that's that. I suppose it is no use me arguing any further.'

'Sorry, darling. But no.'

'When do you set off?'

'As soon as we can get ready, say within the week, although, of course, we must wait until Mzingeli gets here. Ah, there is one other interesting point.'

'Yes?'

'What with the mauling we received at Tanga

85

and other activities in the north, we are short of good troops on the ground and so this League of Frontiersmen will be given their first baptism of fire in this attack. They will be in the van. It should be interesting to see how they perform.'

'Well,' it was Alice's turn to sniff. 'I don't particularly care if the whole Brigade of Guards is in the van, as long as you don't have to lead the troops in personally. Oh Simon,' she turned imploring eyes towards her husband. 'This place is deep inside enemy country. How do you propose to get in?'

'It depends. We could creep across the lake from the British side but I would favour slipping over the border from Uganda – I doubt if it is all that well policed. And that is the way, I suspect, that most of the troops will have to go in. But we must wait until we can see the lie of the land. We've been given non-substantive ranks so that we can hold up our heads with the professionals. I am back to colonel and Jenkins here will be paid as a warrant officer Grade I, a regimental sergeant major, no less.

'Look, Alice.' He took her hand. 'I promise we will be extremely cautious and, when the attack starts, do our best to stay out of the way.' He grinned. 'We don't want three elderly gentlemen – including Mzingeli, that is – being shot out of their wheelchairs when the troops go in.'

Alice shook her hand free. 'This is no joke, Simon. None of you can do what you used to do in the old days. You must – you really must – be aware of your limitations now. Promise me you will.'

'Of course, love. Now, if you will excuse me, I must send a telegram to Mzingeli. It will take him some time to get here. Ah–' he stopped and turned at the door. 'No news from Sunil, I suppose?'

'No. But no news is good news now, isn't it?'

He nodded and was gone.

Mzingeli arrived four days later, stepping ashore, a loose bag slung across his shoulder, and, if it were not for the rifle he carried so non-chalantly, looking like an elegant elder statesman of some African nation. Three days afterwards the three of them set off, dressed as hunters in rough, sun-bleached khaki, and boarded the train at the Mombasa railhead of the Uganda Railway.

It was this line that the Germans had been att-empting to disrupt and Fonthill was warned that other raids were expected, particularly as the railway neared the northern border of German East Africa on its long journey to Kisumu on the eastern, British side of Lake Victoria. A small detachment of the King's African Rifles was posted on the train to provide some protection. The train itself consisted of four open-topped cargo trucks and three coaches for passengers, of whom there were very few. The coaches were without corridors, with only running-boards pro-viding means of passing from coach to coach while the train was in motion. As a result, two soldiers of the Rifles were designated to sit in each coach, with other, less fortunate men con-signed to squat on top of the loads in the cargo trucks.

The two Riflemen who joined Fonthill, Jenkins

and Mzingeli in their compartment sat incongruously, their rifles between their gleaming black knees, and wearing their distinctive red fez caps with tassles, broad sashes under black leather belts and the sunniest of smiles. They rarely spoke except to express surprised thanks when Simon shared sandwiches with them, but their expressions remained peacefully beatific as the train rattled along through the barren countryside.

As they had all boarded the train at Mombasa, the transport officer there had noted the rifles carried by Simon and his two companions and had suggested that they be ready to use them if called upon. It was therefore no surprise when a blast from the locomotive's steam whistle midway through the afternoon indicated trouble ahead – quickly confirmed when the brakes were slammed on and the train came to a hissing halt.

Simon hung his head out of the window and noted that the train had stopped just as it approached a defile between two rocky ridges, which rose from the plain on either side. He was just able to catch a glimpse of two boulders that had been rolled down onto the track when his view was blocked by the young lieutenant of the KARs from the first carriage, who jumped down onto the running-board and then onto the track to run ahead.

'For God's sake, don't go down there,' shouted Simon. 'It's obviously an ambush.' But it was too late. Several shots rang out from the rocks above the track and the officer was hit twice, once in the shoulder and secondly, fatally through the forehead. He fell to the ground and lay inert.

Fonthill flung open the door and jumped down. Turning his head, he shouted loudly, 'No one must leave the train,' and, head down, he skipped over the body of the dead man and ran towards the locomotive. As he did so, a rattle of musketry rang out from the rocks above and to either side of the coaches, the bullets pinging away as they ricochetted from the steel tracks and the great wheels of the engine.

Somehow, he managed to reach the footplate unharmed and clambered up into the cabin. The driver and his black stevedore were crouched under the protection of the side plates and regarded him wide-eyed as he squatted beside them. Fonthill suddenly became aware that there were now four in the cab, for Jenkins, sweat trickling down his forehead, had joined them on the footplate.

The Welshman poked the barrel of his rifle over the side plate, aimed quickly and pulled the trigger. 'I don't know what you're doin, bach sir,' he gasped, 'but I'll try and keep the bastards' heads down while you're doin' it.'

'No, don't. It'll just draw their fire.' He turned to the driver. 'Can you reverse this bloody great thing?'

The man looked at him with a crooked smile. 'Aye, laddie,' he said in tones redolent of the Highlands, 'where would yer like me to take her?'

'Get us back out of here as quickly as you can. If I'm not mistaken they will roll down bloody great boulders onto the track right behind us and we will be stuck here. Reverse it now before they do that.'

'Och aye. But it'll take me a minute or two to get the pressure up. Just keep yer hair on, sonny, while we do this. Coal in quickly now, Ahmed. Jump to it!'

Fonthill sucked in his breath and realised that he had not brought his rifle with him. 'Keep your head down, 352,' he hissed. 'Charging back out of here is our only hope.'

'What about the poor chap who took the bullet?'

'He's beyond help. Shot through the head.'

Shots were now raining down onto the steel superstructure of the engine housing and the cab, sounding as though the four men inside were trapped under a tin roof in a heavy hailstorm, and it seemed ages before, with a series of hisses and heavy spinning of the wheels, the train slowly began to move backwards.

'Can you see if the track is clear behind us?' called Simon to the driver.

'Aye, it's clear all right, but I can see some of the varmints tryin' to roll a few wee rocks down onto us.' He turned to Jenkins. 'Can you try an' pick 'em off, d'yer think, Taffy?'

Jenkins swung round and glared at the Scotsman and then immediately levelled his rifle up and to the rear of them and took careful aim. He fired three shots quickly and nodded. 'Got two of the buggers, look you, *Jock*,' he hissed the name with heavy emphasis. 'But it looks as though some of the rocks have been set rollin. 'Ang onto your 'ats and 'old tight.'

The locomotive, fuelled frantically by the shovelling footplateman, had now gathered speed and was clumping its way backwards at a fair pace when the three rocks came bouncing down the cliff face in a flurry of scree. The first caught the locomotive a glancing blow on the buffers and the others crashed down on the line, settling there in a cloud of dust.

'Well done, driver, I think we've made it,' cried Fonthill.

Jenkins turned a face drenched in sweat and Simon suddenly realised that the temperature inside the cab must have passed the 100 degrees level. 'Where are we goin?' called the Welshman. 'All the way back to the bleedin' Indian Ocean, is it?'

'No.' Fonthill turned to the driver. 'Back as fast as you can for about a mile and then stop, but keep steam up, if you can.'

'Very well, sonny. But what are yer goin' to do?'

'Yes, bach sir.' Jenkins's features were a rosy-hued picture of consternation. 'Are we goin' to try and ram the bloody rocks, then?'

'No. But I'll be damned if I'm going to let those Germans get away with this. We will unload the KARs and run back and take the bastards in the rear. With all their rock pushing I doubt if they will be prepared for us to do that. Fast as you can, driver, until I tell you to stop.' He grinned. 'I've always loved steam engines. Pile it on, there's a good chap.'

Within four minutes, Fonthill had given the signal to stop and like a great leviathan the engine hissed to a halt. Immediately, Simon jumped down.

'All troops leave the train and assemble on this

side of the line,' he yelled. 'I am a British army officer. Quickly now. Bring your rifles with you.'

The two riflemen who had shared their compartment were the first to jump down and they called for their comrades to obey Simon's order. Slowly, the rest of the KAR men assembled along the side of the track. They were led by a black sergeant, who said, 'Where is Lieutenant Daniels?'

'I am sorry to have to tell you, Sergeant, that he is dead. He was hit by the first bullets the Germans fired. Now,' he looked along the row of faces, 'we are going to get the lieutenant's body, but first we are going to climb this rise on either side of the track and we're going to run back to where the ambush took place. Then we are going to take the Germans in the rear and give them the surprise of their lives.

'Sergeant.'

'Sah.'

'I want you to divide the men into two parties. You will take one half to the other side of the track and trot back steadily to the defile. It's about a mile, I should say. I will take the others on this side and do the same. Keep me in sight all the time, as we go. When we near the Germans, I shall signal and we will all then take cover and crawl up on those men who killed Lieutenant Daniels. Do not – I repeat, do not – fire until I do. Is that all clear?'

'Very good, sah.' The sergeant gave Fonthill a smile that revealed a perfect set of glittering teeth – a smile that was reflected along the line of his men. It was clear that this detachment of the King's African Rifles was itching for a fight.

Jenkins and Mzingeli were at Simon's side. 'Did you say, *trot* back there, bach sir?' asked the Welshman, wiping the perspiration from his forehead and squinting up at the sun, which hung in the sky like a blazing cauldron.

'Yes. But not too fast, I don't want to get there before the sergeant's men.'

'Oh, goodness gracious me, I quite agree. Slow me down when we get near the bleedin' Germans, then, won't you, in case I run on and overwhelm 'em singl'andedly, like.'

'Mzingeli.'

'*Nkosi.*'

'I would be grateful if you would go on ahead and see what the Germans are doing, taking care not to be seen, of course, and come back to me. It might be that they are guessing what we are up to and are coming back here themselves.'

With a nod of the head, the tracker slipped his rifle over his head by its sling and effortlessly climbed the gradient and disappeared from sight.

The sergeant's party had crept under the couplings to the other side of the train. 'Are you ready, Sergeant?' called Fonthill.

'Ready, sah.'

'Right. Make sure the men's magazines are full and that each has put a cartridge up the spout. Then we will go. Keep me in sight, now.'

'Very good, sah.'

Cautiously, Fonthill led his men up the cutting, his feet slipping back in the loose shale. At the top, he was just able to see the tall figure of Mzingeli disappear between a wizened clump of mimosa thorn trees. The way back to the ambush site seemed clear, from what he could see. Across the track, the sergeant waved to him and he waved back and gestured ahead. The two parties set off at the trot.

Simon soon realised that he had been unwise to suggest that the way back should be taken at the double, or at least a fast trot. It was clear that the pace in no way disconcerted the KAR soldiers, but it was way too fast for two Europeans in late middle age, trying to keep up with the black troopers in this heat. He held up his hand to halt the men.

'Thank God for that,' gasped Jenkins. 'I was about to disappear into a little Welsh puddle.'

Fonthill ignored him and turned to the men bunched behind him. 'We must be near now,' he said. 'Spread out and advance at the walk.' He looked across the line and could see that the sergeant had stopped his men too. He waved and spread his arms to indicate that they should disperse and saw the sergeant repeat the gesture.

The two parties had advanced at this slower pace for less than a hundred yards when Simon saw the tall figure of Mzingeli loping towards him. The tracker came up, waving his arms to take cover and stood before Fonthill in no sort of discomfort at the pace at which he had been running.

'Germans comin' this way, *Nkosi.*'

'How far?'

'About three hundred paces. Comin' quite quick now. They carryin' machine gun.'

'Damn! Did they see you?'

Mzingeli wrinkled his nose, as though offended by the question. 'Of course not, *Nkosi.*'

Fonthill forced a grin. 'Of course not. Sorry to have asked.'

He turned and waved to the sergeant across the track. He pointed ahead and then back again. Then he spread his arms in a spreading, downward motion. The sergeant immediately seemed to understand, nodded and repeated the gesture to his men. Simon thanked his lucky stars that he had some of the best-trained native troops in all Africa under his temporary command. As he watched, the men on the other side of the track seemed to disappear from sight. Good.

He looked around. To his right, there was a low outbreak of rocks, broken by some stunted, leafless bushes and one or two cactus plants. 'Quickly, take cover behind those rocks,' he called softly. 'Move now. Enemy is approaching. Nobody to fire until I do.'

With Jenkins and Mzingeli in close company, he ran to the rocks and spread-eagled himself behind the nearest clump, taking care that his rifle did not protrude at this early stage in the engagement. He looked around. Some of the troops had knelt down and, surely, their red fezes would be seen by the enemy. 'Lie flat,' he hissed. 'And take off those damned hats.'

He turned his head to where Mzingeli was lying beside him. 'Are they advancing on both sides of the track?' he asked.

'Yes, *Nkosi*. But biggest party – with machine gun – this side.'

It seemed to Fonthill that an eternity had passed, lying here under the African sun, the rays of which seemed to bounce off the ochre-coloured rocks in an attempt to fry the little party. In fact, of course, it was perhaps only three minutes before, stepping out cautiously from between a group of mimosa thorns, he saw the first of the enemy.

They were black askaris, led by a white man in long shorts and a pith helmet, a revolver in his hand.

Fonthill turned his head to his left, where Jenkins lay. 'I want you to hold your fire, 352,' he whispered, 'until the machine gun crew come into sight, then take them.' He turned back to his right. 'And you Mzingeli. Can you pick off the officer leading them? You are both better shots than me. Make sure you don't miss. Neither of you fire until I give the signal.'

The two men nodded.

Slowly, Simon eased his rifle up alongside him. How long should he wait? He turned his head to look across the line. No sign of the Germans advancing there. Better to ensure that most of the enemy on this side were clear of cover so that they could be brought down in the open. He ran his tongue over lips that were now so dry that they seemed made of sandpaper.

Then, as he watched, a second party of askaris came into sight, leaving the mimosas behind. This party was carrying a machine gun, broken down for transport into two parts: the barrel with its long belt of ammunition swung over the shoulders of the two men carrying it, and the tripod in the hands of just one man.

Simon turned his head fractionally towards Jenkins.

'I've got the bastards,' whispered the Welshman, almost absent-mindedly as he sighted along the barrel of his Lee Enfield.

Perhaps someone had caught sight of Jenkins's rifle, or it could have been the reflection of the sun off the shining buckles of one of the KAR troopers, but someone in the lead party pointed ahead and shouted.

'Damn and blast,' whispered Simon, 'I wanted more of 'em.' But he pushed the barrel of his own rifle forward, sighted quickly at the man who was still pointing, and fired. To his rather surprised satisfaction, the man flung up his hands and collapsed. It was the signal for the clump of rocks housing the troopers suddenly to come ablaze with firing as the men followed Fonthill's lead.

Through the haze of blue smoke that floated across the rocks, Simon caught a glimpse of the two men carrying the machine gun both fall to the ground. More of the askaris were now breaking cover from the thicket and rushing forward, two of them bending down to retrieve the Maxim.

'Get the machine gunners,' screamed Fonthill and heard Jenkins's gun fire twice, bringing down the men attempting to lift the big gun.

Looking over the track, Simon could see and hear firing as the second party of Germans broke their cover and charged forward. But, as he watched, the leading troops all collapsed and fell under the rapid firing of the KARs – volley firing, for Fonthill could hear, even above the rattle of musketry, the stentorian voice of the sergeant calling, 'Even numbers fire; reload; odd numbers fire; reload.' What splendid training!

97

Suddenly, he became aware that the firing on both sides of the railway track had ceased.

'They've 'ad enough. They're buggerin' off.' Jenkins's voice was a mixture of triumph and relief.

Sure enough, the askaris seemed to have melted away – all, that is, except for the bodies that lay inert among the stones and sand and for the pitiful attempts of the wounded to seek help, raising hands and heads. The scene was repeated on the other side of the track.

Fonthill hauled himself upright. 'Sergeant,' he yelled. 'Do you have any wounded?'

'No, sah.'

'Good. Take your men and pursue the enemy. Take care, though. They may have laid another ambush.'

'Yes, sah.'

He called to his own men. 'Soldiers, on your feet now. Well done. Anybody hurt?'

No hands were raised. 'You three men.' He called to a lance corporal and the two men nearest. 'Do you have first-aid kits?' They all nodded.

'Good. I want you to go with Mzingeli here and see what you can do – on both sides of the track – for the German wounded. Those that can walk, get them to help you with the others and take them all back to the train and put them on board and stand guard over them.' He raised his gaze. 'The rest of you come with me.'

'Not at a bloody run again, bach sir, I do 'ope.' Jenkins had now predictably lost his hat; his black hair was plastered over his forehead and the rest of his face was streaming in perspiration.

'Oh, don't make such a fuss. I want to get back in time to capture a few of those German blacks before these KARs kill 'em all. Someone has got to move those bloody stones off the track. Unless, that is, you are volunteering for the job. No? Come on, then.'

There was a full corporal in the few men left in Fonthill's section. 'Corporal,' he called. 'Get three men to pick up that Maxim. It could prove useful. Then take the men on at a trot. Be on your guard because the Germans may still resist. Those that you find at the place where they rolled down the rocks, put them under guard until I come up. Off you go now.'

He began walking, picking his way carefully between the wounded and the dead, Jenkins puffing along behind him followed by the three men carrying the machine gun. The marksmanship of the colonial troops had been exemplary and, at short range, it had cut down most of the German askaris, with, here and there, a few white faces dotted amongst the dead. Simon wondered about returning to bury the dead, then thought better of it. The ground was hard and vultures were already circling. Better to leave them to clear up.

After a few minutes he heard desultory firing from up ahead and then silence. Ten more minutes of walking and they passed the bodies of three askaris, obviously left as some form of rearguard and witness, once again, to the KARs' skills with their Lee Enfields. Then the railside track began to climb and they found themselves looking down onto the defile through which the line had been cut.

Down below, clustered around the rocks, were a handful of the askaris, plus one European officer, all standing their hands in the air and surrounded by the colonial troopers.

'Well done, Sergeant,' called Fonthill and began to scramble down to join the little group. 'No one wounded?'

'No, sah. We had to kill three more, though.'

'So I noticed. I will make sure that you and your men are commended. Now,' he turned to the white officer, a thin man with a wispy beard.

'Colonel Fonthill,' he said, extending his hand. 'I hope you speak English?

'Lieutenant Wolfgang Schmidt,' said the German, taking Simon's hand. 'Building contractor in Dar es Salaam until three months ago.' He gave a wry smile.

Fonthill returned the smile. 'Now turned demolition expert, I see. Well, Lieutenant, I'm afraid I must ask you to now undo the work you did a few minutes ago. Please instruct your men to take these rocks off the line so that we can resume our journey and we can take you into custody, I'm afraid.'

The German pulled a long face but gave instructions in Swahili and his men, obviously relieved that they were not going to be shot out of hand, began the work.

Simon called to his corporal. 'Jog back to the train,' he said, 'and ask the driver to bring the locomotive and the carriages here. Make sure that the prisoners and the wounded there are under guard.'

'Very good, sah.'

Within the hour, the train had chugged its way forward, using the cattle catcher on the front of the locomotive to ease the largest of the rocks aside off the track, and the prisoners had been safely housed under guard in the open trucks. The body of Lieutenant Daniels had been recovered, wrapped in a blanket provided by Lieutenant Schmidt and laid carefully in the lead compartment. Then with a triumphant toot on the steam whistle the train continued its journey to Kisumu.

CHAPTER FOUR

There were no further attempted attacks on the line but it was long after dark when the little lakeside town was reached. The stationmaster was summoned from his cottage nearby, a magistrate found and the prisoners marched away to the town jail. A small escort was formed to take the body of Lieutenant Daniels to the mortuary and lodgings were found in a hotel for Fonthill, Jenkins and Mzingeli, the latter not without argument, as usual, because of his colour.

The next morning, Simon reported to the senior British officer in the town, who happened to be a naval lieutenant commander, named Evans. The man was puzzled by Fonthill's arrival, for the strictest security had been imposed on his journey and Simon warned the commander of the importance of keeping the news of the impending attack under the tightest of wraps.

'Which way do you intend to go in?' asked Evans, sucking on his pipe.

'I thought it would be safer to go up around the north of the lake and slip south across the border on the other side. I know the frontier is not strictly patrolled and felt that it would probably be the best way for the raiding force to go in, too.'

'Good God, no!' exclaimed Evans. 'There is no way you – and certainly not several thousand men – can tramp right round the lake and enter GEA without the Germans knowing. The alarm would be raised as soon as you sniffed at the frontier. No, no. Go straight across the lake. We can take you over.'

'What, and the invading force too?'

Evans extracted his pipe and used the stem to point at a large map of Lake Victoria pinned to his wall. 'Yes. Straight across as the dear old crow flies, old chap.'

Fonthill frowned. 'But I understood that the Germans have ships on the lake and regularly patrol it.'

'Used to, old boy.' There was a definite note of pride in Evans's voice. 'We've just sunk their eighty-ton steamer *Muensa* and even if they did manage to refloat her, her two seven-pounder guns would be no match now for the little fleet we've managed to put together. We've now got six steamers, including two of one thousand tons each, plus three tugs.'

He leant back and puffed his pipe proprietarily. 'As I am sure you know, Lake Victoria is the largest lake in Africa, with a surface area of about 27,000 square miles. But now we control it completely. We could take Sir John French's BEF across to the German side without the slightest hindrance. And what's more,' he leant forward, 'I reckon we can take your little army across during the night without the enemy having the faintest idea of what's going on.'

Fonthill nodded slowly. 'That certainly does change things. So you could take me and my two men across to the other side of the lake, say, tomorrow night during darkness?'

'Certainly. Where do you want to be landed?'

'As near as possible to Bukoba so that we can reconnoitre the town and be picked up again the following night.'

'Fine.' Evans allowed the pipe to leave his mouth long enough to grin. 'Know the place reasonably well, as it happens. Used to go across and have a drink once or twice with my German opposite number.' He used his pipe stem again as a marker. 'Just north of the town, about here, there is quite a wide beach, shallow enough for us to land you and the chaps to follow, but far enough, I would think, from the town and its defences to escape detection. We will drop you ashore and you can see for yourself. Would you be happy with that?'

Fonthill leant across and extended his hand. 'Very happy. Thank you.'

'Good. But you have probably underestimated the length of the voyage. It's about 180 miles from here to Bukoba, so we shall need to set out tomorrow morning to make the crossing and allow you to land under cover of darkness. So we

would need to set sail at about 10 a.m. Agreed?'
'Agreed.'

Evans insisted on coming with them and the following morning they assembled on the jetty at Kisumu and then boarded a steam pinnace. A course was set to the south-west, and five men – Fonthill, Jenkins, Mzingeli, Evans and the young sub lieutenant commanding the pinnace – clustered together in the vessel's little cabin to drink rum and study an old map Evans had managed to acquire of Bukuba and its environs.

'I doubt if this will be of much use to you,' said the sailor. 'It's quite a bit marshy, as I remember the place. So you will have to be careful in planning the attack. Now, let's have another spot of rum and I suggest you close your eyes for as long as you can. I will wake you when we are near to the opposite shore. We won't run you in. But we will put you in a dinghy and row you onto the beach. Much quieter.'

The moon was high and disconcertingly shedding a bright light across the water when the pinnace hove to, the shoreline a distant but distinctly darker smudge to the west, and the dinghy was lowered into the water. The three men shook hands with Evans, then they clustered together in the little craft as a brawny seaman dug in the oars and they headed for German territory.

The sky was just beginning to redden in the east as the prow of the dinghy crunched onto the shingle shore. Fonthill looked around anxiously, but there were no dwellings on the shoreline, only low shrubbery lining the edge of the beach. They slipped calf-length into the water and waded to the shingle before running to the protection of the greenery, as the seaman backed the oars and the dinghy slipped away into the vastness of the lake.

'Where to now, bach sir?' asked Jenkins.

'Well, according to Evans and this old map, the town is about a couple of miles down there,' he nodded, 'to the left. It straddles the Kanoni River and it's on a small marshy plain, surrounded by hills and a few limestone kopjes. But,' he squinted around, 'the first thing to do is to make sure that this beach is big enough to land about 1,500 troops. You two go that way,' he pointed to the right, 'and I will take a look the other way. Back here in ten minutes.'

The little party broke up and reassembled well within the ten minutes. The three squatted under a low mimosa tree.

Jenkins smoothed his moustache. 'Looks good enough where we've been,' he said. 'There's an 'ouse we could see through the trees right at the far end. P'raps some kind of custom place, by the look of it. But nobody seemed to be there. The good thing was that all the beach is shingle. Firmer, look you, than sand. So we could bring guns ashore.'

Fonthill nodded. 'I quite agree. But the beach is a bit on the small side and it will be some time before everyone gets ashore, so surprise will be everything. Let's take a walk and see what's between here and the town. Remember, if we see anyone, just nod, don't talk. And,' he recovered a revolver from under his shirt 'we mustn't use these unless we are in obvious danger. Right, let's go.'

Through the fringe of trees and scrub that lined the beach, they found a dirt track road lying parallel to the shoreline. The sun was beginning to rise but no one was about. They pushed on up and over a ridge, and made their way through what Mzingeli confirmed was a *matoke* plantation, before being confronted by a larger hill. Simon made a note. This could be a good defensive position for the Germans and would have to be taken quickly by the invaders.

The nearer they came to the town, the more marshy the ground became and it was necessary sometimes to wade through water chest-deep. Fonthill noted that Bukoba itself did seem to be surrounded by a series of ridges that looked down onto the town, all of which would have to be taken by the attacking force.

The trio continued their walk, carrying now a rake, a fork and a spade that they had taken from a farm backing onto the marsh. Splashed by mud, they now looked in the early light like farm workers, but they met only a few black labourers who gave them a surly wave. The town itself did not seem to be large and, in this early morning, was largely unpopulated. When Simon had noted the exact position of the wireless mast and transmitting station, he decided that they had seen enough and that it would be unwise to linger longer and risk their discovery and so reveal the purpose of their mission.

Accordingly, they sauntered back to the beach and crept under the shade of bushes to avoid the heat of the afternoon sun. Taking it in turns to stand guard, they found it not unpleasant, dozing, eating their sandwiches and drinking a little rum and water from their flasks, which they had left hidden before setting off on their reconnaissance.

A few hours later, a pinprick of light flashed on and off out on the lake, and Simon responded with his own torch. Within minutes, the low profile of the dinghy emerged from the darkness and they scrambled aboard, insisting this time at relieving the seaman and taking it in turns to row.

The pinnace, which, with an anxious Evans aboard, had stood out in the middle of the lake while they were ashore, was waiting for them and they immediately steamed back towards Kusumu. Simon disclosed little of what they had seen to Evans, who seemed to respect his reticence, and they slept for most of the return crossing. Fonthill was glad to find the Mombasa train waiting with steam up. He was anxious to report back to General Wapshare but equally anxious that no news of the planned raid should leak from any quarter before he did so. The fewer people who knew about it in Kisumu the better.

They quickly regained their bags and rifles from their hotel and boarded the train, this time guarded by a different section of the KAR, led only by a sergeant, who saluted them and put them in the leading carriage. Although they sat, their rifles at the ready, throughout the dusty, hot journey, keenly looking ahead and to the sides for possible ambush, the trip was uneventful and they regained Mombasa towards the end of the following day.

Having telegraphed ahead, they were met at the station by a grinning Alice. 'News, news,' she cried, as they stepped down onto the milling platform.

'Don't tell me the war is over,' cried Fonthill in mock distress. 'I'm banking on winning the VC in this show.'

'No, no. Of course not. But Wapshare has been replaced.'

'Good lord. Why? He did well enough at Tanga. It wasn't his fault that the thing was a mess.'

'I don't really know, but he has already gone off to command the 33rd Division in Mesopotamia. The word is that he is disappointed because he regards it as a demotion and a censuring for what happened at Tanga.'

'Hmm. Well a divisional command on an active front certainly shouldn't be seen as that. But who is taking his place?'

'My favourite general. Mickey Tighe. He has already taken over and wants to see you immediately on your return.'

Simon pulled a face. 'I hope he doesn't want to cancel the attack on Bukoba. I reckon we can pull it off.'

'I doubt it. He's a fighting general, if ever there was one, and I am glad he has been promoted.' Alice smiled and ran her hand over Simon's stubble. 'Look, you've got time to come to the hotel and have a bath and shave. He can wait. He's only a major general, after all.'

They all grinned and piled into a rickshaw and headed for the hotel.

Bathed and shaved within the hour, Fonthill reported to the C-in-C's Headquarters and, although he was in mufti, of course, received a smart salute from the huge Sikh at the guard post. Without delay he was ushered in to meet the Major General.

The two men shook hands, Tighe's blue eyes twinkling as he did so.

'I've already met your wife, Fonthill,' he said. 'A remarkable woman, as I had always heard. I do congratulate you, my dear fellow. My God, she's as feisty under fire as any young subaltern I have ever met.'

Simon nodded and pulled a face. 'Well thank you, General. You are quite right. She worries the life out of me, even though I have grown used to her, crouching there with pencil and notebook at the firing line in so many campaigns now. But tell me...' He paused and frowned. 'I do hope you are not going to pull out of the Bukoba show, are you?'

Tighe puffed out his cheeks. 'Good God, no. Well I hope not. It all depends on what you tell me. You know, we never met in India, I believe, not even on the frontier during the Pathan Uprising. But I know all about you. So I am anxious to have your report now. Fire away. Is it possible?'

'Certainly. Evans – he's the commander of the Lake Fleet in Kisumu, at the railhead at the lake.'

'Yes, I know.'

'He certainly believes he can take – what is it, about 1,500 men across the lake?'

'About that, yes.' Tighe yelled a command and the door was flung open by a beaming black orderly. 'Tea, yer grinning monkey,' the General cried. 'For two.' He turned back to Fonthill. 'Milk or lemon?'

'Lemon in this climate, thanks.'

'Quite right. With lemon, then, yer rascal. So move your arse and be quick about it.' But he grinned as he shouted and the grin was returned. 'Now where were we? Ah yes. About 1,500 men. Can we get across without detection, presumably under darkness, attack the town, put the radio station out of action and knock the place about a bit with that number, d'yer think, Fonthill? I doubt if I can spare more.'

'Yes, I believe so.' Simon thought for a moment. 'I don't know how many men the Germans have to defend the town. Certainly, I saw absolutely no sign of any military, apart from one or two black askaris guarding the radio station. Evans believes that the standing garrison is only about 300, but he also feels that there are about five times that number within marching distance of the town.'

Tighe frowned. 'Hmmm. That means that we have to get in swiftly and strike quickly before the reinforcements get up. Show me the lie of the land.'

Fonthill produced the rough map he had drawn on the train journey. 'It seems to me, General,' he said, 'that the secret lies in getting swiftly inland and sweeping round the outskirts of the town and taking these ridges that surround the place and look down on it. Once there, you have the town at your mercy. There are hills here and here by the beach,' he pointed, 'where the Germans, if they are sensible, will rush to oppose you shortly after landing. So you will have to take them quickly.'

'What about going along the shoreline this way and attacking from the north?'

'It's very marshy there, sometimes waist-deep. But, if you have the men, it would be worth sending a battalion that way to create a diversion, at least. And there is a plantation here, which could provide defensive positions for the Germans. If I may make a suggestion...?'

The blue eyes smiled. 'Suggest away, old chap. I am listening to every word. I understand that you advised General Wolseley on how to attack the bPedi nation on the Mozambique border. If your advice was good enough for Wolseley, then, for sure, it's good enough for me.'

Fonthill returned the smile, half-embarrassed. 'That's kind of you, General. Obviously, you have to get in quickly and one of the problems is that the beach, while suitable for landing in most ways, is a bit small to take such a large contingent of men. So you will need to buy time, so to speak, to get 'em all ashore.'

'Quite so. So...?'

'You will need a diversion, to create confusion among the defenders and distract from the main landing place. The river here,' he pointed, 'curls round and there is a ferry there. If Evans could send a couple of ships, say just south of the town here, it could lure the Germans into thinking that you intended a landing there and so persuade them to divert troops to defend the ferry crossing. And, also, if the naval guns could direct fire on the custom house, to the north of where the main landing will be, just about here,' he pointed again, 'it would add to the merry dance you

111

would be leading the Huns.'

'Good idea. Let me discuss this with my staff, but it seems a pretty good plan to me.'

There was a brief pause while the tea was brought in. Simon raised his cup and then asked: 'May I ask, what troops do you have for all this? You will need some good men to get in, strike quickly and get out again.'

'Indeed. The 25th Royal Fusiliers – what d'yer call 'em?'

'The Frontiersmen.'

'Those are the boys. They've only just landed but their CO is bursting to get into action and says they need absolutely no acclimitisation, so I shall send 'em straight in. Strange bunch. Lots of elderly fellers amongst them but they look a hardy lot … ah, weren't you involved with them?'

Fonthill smiled wanly. 'Not really. I was offered the command but I felt that Driscoll, whom I knew vaguely in South Africa, didn't deserve to lose his regiment in my favour, so I refused it. I am much happier doing what I am now.'

'Very well. Now finish yer tea and get back to that remarkable wife of yours. You will come in with us, presumably?'

Simon drained his cup. 'Good Lord, yes. If you will have me, that is.'

'Wouldn't dream of leaving you behind – and, of course, bring in old 657, or whatever he is called, and your black tracker.'

'352. Yes, thank you. When do you move?'

'It will take a few days to get the troops together. Ah, there's one more thing.'

'Yes?'

112

Tighe frowned. 'The bloody War Office won't let me take command of the operation. They say that as C-in-C I must stay here and play at soldiers on my desk top. So, I have given command to General Stewart. Know him?'

'No. I don't think so.'

'First-class chap. You will meet him soon.' He held out his hand. 'Give my regards to your wife and thank you for your good work on this – oh, and by the way, for what you did when that train was attacked.' Tighe tightened his grip and shook Simon's hand warmly. 'God knows why the army let you go, Fonthill. You would have been on the general staff, covered in gold braid, if you had stayed on after the Second Afghan War. And I would have been calling you sir by now.'

Back in the hotel, Alice, Jenkins and Mzingeli joined Fonthill in a corner of the bar where they could not be overheard, to take whiskies and soda – a lemonade in the case of Mzingeli. After hearing Simon's story, Alice leant forward eagerly.

'Good,' she said. 'When do we start?'

Jenkins looked at the ceiling wearily as Simon slowly replaced his glass. 'We?' he said. '"*We*"? There is no *we* about this, my love. You are not going on this expedition, Alice, and that is the beginning and end of it. This is an army operation that will involve a great deal of danger and there cannot possibly be a place for a woman in it.'

Jenkins stood up. 'I 'ave a feelin' that I've heard this argument before,' he said. 'If you will excuse us, I will take old Jelly and buy him a glass of milk to sober 'im up, see. Come on, boyo.'

They had hardly left before Alice exploded.

'Army? *Army?* I am in the bloody army as much as you are, Simon. At least, I am formally accredited to it, which is more than you can say. Of course I am coming. This is my job, dammit. I must report on something that sounds as though it might produce the first bit of good news since this bloody war started.'

Simon sighed. 'Ah well, Alice, you might find that you have a problem with Stewart. I can well imagine that he won't want a *woman* in his invasion force.'

'Well that is just jolly hard luck for General Stewart. Kitchener intervened to get me ashore at Tanga and, if necessary, I will get King Bloody George to step in, or even the Kaiser, for that matter.' She leant forward and gripped his hand. 'Simon, my love, I must do my job, just as you must, too. You must understand that.'

Simon lifted her hand to his lips. 'Very well, darling. We've been through this so many times before. I certainly will do nothing to stop you coming with us, of course.' He gave her a wry smile. 'At least I might get a better cup of tea, if you do come. I think 352 is losing his touch. His tea these days tastes like stewed prunes.'

They both smiled and, leaning forward, exchanged a chaste kiss.

The next morning Alice rose well before Simon and crept quietly out into the already sultry morning and summoned a rickshaw. 'To the Army GHQ,' she said firmly. What was the point, she argued to herself as the black boy jogged along between the shafts before her, in having established a good relationship with the commander-in-chief of the British army in British East Africa if she didn't fully exploit that relationship?

Alice returned at mid-morning to find that Simon and his two companions had left the hotel, but those who knew her would have recognised the very self-satisfied smile on her face as she sat in the bar and ordered herself coffee, cold milk and a small chaser of single malt whisky.

It took Tighe about three weeks to assemble his force. He knew that the success of the mission was vital, after the Tanga debacle, and he plundered some of the best troops from throughout his command. They congregated on the eastern shore of Lake Victoria: the newly-arrived 25th Royal Fusiliers; a detachment from the Loyal North Lancs; the 3rd battalion of the King's African Rifles, with two guns of the 28th Mountain Battery; a full machine gun section from the East African Regiment; and the four machine guns of the Volunteer Maxim Company – roughly one and a half thousand men, as originally planned.

The day before the main force set out, Stewart ordered two ships to cross the lake and make a feint away from Bukoba towards the Kagera River. Simon was glad to see that his advice was being taken by the general, whom he had only met briefly before disembarkation.

On the voyage across the lake in the leading ship, Fonthill sought out Lieutenant Colonel Driscoll, the CO of the 25th Fusiliers, 'the Frontiersmen', as much out of curiosity to see what kind of men he had narrowly 'escaped' from commanding, as from desire to meet Driscoll himself.

He found the colonel, sprawled with his men on the deck of the steamer, ready to be the first ashore. Driscoll was a large, good-looking man with a bristling moustache and a very loud voice. In fact, as Fonthill introduced himself, the colonel struggled to his feet and boomed, 'Delighted, Fonthill, absolutely delighted,' so loudly that Simon worried that the German defences would hear and be alerted.

Fonthill squatted down beside him and immediately the two began reminiscing about the Boer War. Driscoll and he had shared similar experiences during that conflict, with each acting as scouts and, in the end, commanding a column. But they had never met.

Simon steered the conversation towards the 400 men who constituted Driscoll's command. 'I gather you've got a rather strange bunch under you,' he said.

Driscoll frowned for a moment and Fonthill feared that he had given offence. 'Well,' responded the colonel, 'I suppose you could call them strange.' He grinned. 'To start with, as you can see,' he gestured towards his men, 'our average age must be well above that of any other battalion in the British army. But they are all fit as fiddles. We include Outram and Selous, the big-game hunters. Splendid shots, of course. And I believe that Selous, who is 63, must be the oldest serving man in the whole damned army. We've got cowboys from Canada and the States, prizefighters, acrobats – including one feller who can climb stairs on his head, or something like that. There's a couple of MPs, some music hall comedians, and even some university professors. Dammit, Fonthill, they know the Empire, they know how to rough it and they're as keen as mustard to have a go at the Kaiser and his Prussians. I am proud to command 'em, I can tell you.'

Fonthill nodded and returned the grins that were being directed at him from the faces looking toward him and the colonel. For a moment, he regretted giving up the chance of leading these men into action. It would have been an unusual challenge. Then Driscoll was speaking again.

'I hear that you have already been on the other side of this pond and sorted out the plan of attack,' he said, one eyebrow raised.

'Well,' Simon shifted awkwardly, 'I gave Tighe a few suggestions, that's all. He's got a good record, as I'm sure you know, and you don't give a fighting major general his plan of attack. Are you going in first?'

'More or less.' The colonel's teeth shone in the moonlight. 'We're going onto the beach first, I gather, which is quite an honour, but my orders are not to go inland but to advance to the town more or less along the shoreline. Then we are to capture the first ridge we meet – you must know it – consolidate there and cover the main force as they land. Do you have specific orders yourself? Do you have to stay alongside Stewart?'

'Er ... no. He probably didn't want me hanging about him. He will have his own ideas of how to attack the town.'

'Well, that's splendid. Why don't you come

along with us? Show us the way, so to speak.'

Fonthill bit his lip. He looked along the serried row of faces of the Frontiersmen turned towards them both. There was a lot of silver hair to be seen under their caps and quite a few gnarled moustaches. It would be good to see how they reacted to being in the van of the attack. But advancing along the shoreline? That would mean struggling through that blasted marsh again and then, in all probability, attacking through the plantation, with its many trees offering cover for the defenders. But, of course, he could not refuse the invitation.

'Delighted,' he said.

Before dawn but under a full moon the ships carrying the troops put their human cargoes ashore at the little inlet where Simon, Jenkins and Mzingeli had landed several weeks before, now identified as Kiaya Bay. The disembarkation, however, was not carried out without some initial vicissitudes. The Germans had posted a lookout station on nearby Busira Island – had they been alerted? – and the flotilla was seen approaching in the full moonlight. The alarm was given but two of the ships executed a feint towards the customs house identified originally by Jenkins and Mzingeli and drew the fire of a German field gun sited there. The landings themselves were carried out far enough away from the town to prevent defenders being rushed to the little bay to prevent the invaders going ashore. It was, in effect, a complete reversal of the Tanga disaster.

Alice and the small group of correspondents allowed to accompany the mission watched the first landings from the deck of a steamer waiting its turn to disembark its troops. She quickly focussed her field glasses onto the little figures – she knew they were the Fusiliers – who were the first ashore and drew in her breath as she made out the unmistakable outlines of Simon, Jenkins and Mzingeli in the first wave, splashing through the water, holding their rifles aloft.

'Ah, your man is there, then.' She turned quickly and found the unwelcome figure of Herman de Villiers standing at her side, also focussing his glasses on the shore.

'What? Oh. I don't know where he is, as a matter of fact.' Alice felt an instinctive desire to tell the Boer nothing – and certainly no fragment of information that would implicate Simon in any way.

'Ach.' De Villiers lowered his glasses and tugged at his black beard. 'I understood that he was going ashore with the first battalion to land, the Fusiliers.'

'Really?' Alice summoned up a smile. 'Ah, you are so well informed Mr de Villiers. Better than I, in fact.'

'Oh, I don't think so, Mrs Fonthill. I don't think so. But we will see.' He adjusted his spectacles, nodded to her and shuffled away, picking his way along the crowded deck.

Frowning, Alice picked up her binoculars again and tried to pick out Simon and his two companions among the khaki figures tumbling ashore and making their way up the beach. He had gone. Where, she wondered, where? Was he being expected to lead the troops in the van? She lowered

119

the glasses. Thank God the first wave of troops had gone ashore without meeting any opposition. How long would that last...?

Simon, Jenkins and Mzingeli had, in fact, landed right in the van of the raiding force, even before General Stewart had gone ashore. Driscoll was the first to tread ashore and he looked enquiringly over his shoulder. Fonthill pointed ahead into the thin line of trees and then indicated a left turn. The colonel nodded and broke into a leaden-footed trot, disappearing into the trees.

'Oh, bloody hell,' shouted Simon. 'Why didn't he wait?' He turned to the others. 'We'd better catch him up before he leads everybody into an ambush.'

'I'm not too sure about the catchin' up bit,' puffed Jenkins. 'Me right boot is full of water and I'm sloshing about. And I'm not the fastest mover at the best of times these days, look you. Send old Jelly to slow the bugger down.'

Fonthill nodded to Mzingeli, and the black man strode effortlessly ahead in the wake of the colonel. 'Tell him,' Simon called after him, 'that there's a ridge immediately ahead on the left, which could be the Germans' first defensive position. He must be careful.'

The tracker raised a hand in acknowledgement and was gone.

They found him a couple of minutes later, crouched by the side of Driscoll and his senior officers, examining the black outline of the ridge that stretched above them.

Simon nodded towards it. 'Any sign of occupation?' he asked.

'Don't know. But my instincts are to march straight in and take it now.'

'It's your show, Driscoll. But may I suggest we send in Mzingeli here to go up it first and find out? He moves like a panther and can scout it and be back within ten minutes. Not too long to wait, I would suggest, eh?'

The tracker's teeth flashed in the early dawn. 'I go if you want.'

Driscoll nodded. 'Good idea. All of my chaps aren't here from the beach yet, anyway. But make it quick, boy. Make it quick.'

Fonthill noticed a slight frown cross the usually impassive face of Mzingeli at being called 'boy', but then he nodded and disappeared into the gathering light.

The Fusiliers had hardly gathered behind their colonel before the tracker was back.

He avoided Driscoll and reported to Fonthill. 'Nobody up there, *Nkosi*,' he said. 'But troops could be coming from direction of town, I think. I did not stay to find out.'

'Good. Quite right.' Driscoll turned his head and spoke to his second in command. 'Advance to the front in open order. No one to fire unless I give the order. On the top, if there is no opposition, take up defensive positions facing the south all along the ridge. Spread the word to the officers.'

'Very good, sir.' Orders were barked and the Frontiersmen quickly and quietly began to spread out on either side of their colonel, moving away under cover of a morning mist that was beginning to rise. Fonthill was impressed at the discipline of the troops. Not the adventurous, individualistic rabble that he had half-expected. They could have been Guardsmen the way they dispersed in an orderly fashion, following their officers.

He nodded to Jenkins and Mzingeli and the three picked up their rifles and followed the large figure of Driscoll, who had already begun the climb up the ridge, the edge of which was now becoming more sharply defined in the early morning light. Simon sniffed the air. Jenkins nodded.

'Yes, it's goin' to bloody rain,' grunted the Welshman. 'Just as me bleedin' wet sock was beginnin' to dry out, we're goin' to get soaked, look you.'

'Good thing, though. If the Germans are coming from the town to face us, they could get literally bogged down in that damned marsh. Come on, keep up. We must get to the top of the ridge before the Hun does.'

They did so, for it was an easy climb. The ridge stretched from just above the shoreline inland towards the north and Fonthill realised that it was a perfect position from which to cover the troops still landing on the beach behind them. Ahead of them, however, stretched an even higher ridge with the *matoke* plantation and swampland to cross before it would have to be scaled. He looked behind him. Troops were pouring ashore from lighters and forming up on the beach.

He called up to Driscoll. 'It looks as though most of the men have been landed on the beach, Colonel.'

'Good. Can't see any sign of us being attacked yet. I'll give it another ten minutes and then advance on that next ridge.'

'Very well. It's difficult ground between the two. Marshland and a plantation.'

'So I understand. But we'd better get on with it before the Hun comes up. They will surely know we have landed by now.'

A runner came up and reported to the colonel, who turned his head and shouted back to Fonthill. 'Everyone's ashore quite safely, thank God. Now I am ordered to push on. Do stay with me.'

'Of course.'

The whole battalion now moved slowly down the hillside and immediately descended into swampland. As they did so, desultory fire began to open up on them from the hill ahead. It was thin and poorly directed and Simon guessed that the main defending force had not yet been able to reach the hill in sufficient numbers to pose a definitive threat to the Fusiliers. Nevertheless, it was unpleasant to have to wade through the swamp, thigh and sometimes chest high, holding rifles at shoulder level to keep them dry, while the odd bullet hissed into the mud around them.

Driscoll shouted an order and several weather-beaten Frontiersmen stopped wading, carefully sighted their rifles and began to reply to the snipers up on the hill.

Predictably, it now began to rain, and at this point, Jenkins missed his footing and slipped neck high into the murky, brown water, before he could regain his balance. 'Oh shit!' he called. 'Now I'm bloody well soaked all over, look you. I 'ave to tell you, bach sir, that I'm gettin' really fed up with this postin', so I am.' His misery suddenly turned to fear as a thought struck him. 'Eh,' he shouted. 'They don't 'ave crocodiles in this wet muck, do they?'

Simon recalled that his old comrade, although a fighter as courageous as a lion and as skilled in battle as a gladiator, held three terrors: fear of heights, water (he had never learnt to swim) and, most of all, of crocodiles and alligators.

'Only little ones,' shouted Fonthill. 'Mzingeli, see what you can do to help the big baby.'

A grinning Mzingeli turned and waded back to the Welshman, offering the end of his rifle to pull him clear. 'Look,' he said, 'follow me. I find better ground, I think. Step where I step, both of you.'

'Thanks, Mzingeli,' called Fonthill, marvelling yet again at the tribesman's instinctive ability to become familiar with new country, though far from home, and to sense its perils and discomforts and avoid them. 'Lead on, we'll follow.'

Soon they came to firmer ground and, stamping their feet to remove the mud, they began to enter the *matoke* plantation, which on their reconnaissance Fonthill had noted as a possibly strong defensive position for the Germans. The banana-like plant grew from trees, thick as palms, which could provide cover for good marksmen – which the German askaris were noted to be.

Simon looked to either side and realised that the Fusiliers had inevitably bunched together as they had waded through the swamp and they continued to do so as they picked their way between the trees. Fonthill opened his mouth to issue orders to spread out but bit his lip and refrained from doing so. He was not in command here.

Suddenly, there was a burst of firing from up ahead and Fonthill caught a glimpse of conical caps, as worn by the German askari, appearing around the side of trees some three hundred yards into the plantation. Puffs of smoke came from their long rifles. At the same time, two Fusiliers to his right staggered and fell.

He heard Driscoll's stentorian voice shout, 'Stretcher-bearers!' and then, 'Advance at the double. Fire as you go, from tree to tree. Push the bastards back.'

The plantation had now become a chaotic battlefield, with the rain settling on the mud underfoot, causing it to cling and suck at everyone's boots, as they slipped and slid from tree to tree. It was difficult now to define the enemy up ahead, but it was clear that the German askaris were living up to their reputation for bravery and musketry, for bullets thudded into the trees behind which Fonthill and his three comrades were trying to find flimsy shelter.

The crackle of rifle fire now seemed to merge with the thunder of the tropical rain as it bounced from the palm leaves high above. Shouted orders, both in German and English, could be heard from up ahead but it was hard to distinguish between friend and foe in the semi-darkness of the plantation.

'Can't see the buggers,' muttered Jenkins as he wiped the rain from his forehead – he had, of course, lost his pith helmet somewhere in the swamp. But he pushed his rifle around the side of

125

the tree, took careful aim and fired. A cry from the depths of the plantation showed that his bullet had struck home.

Fonthill had now lost sight of the colonel but, with lowered head, he ran as best he could from tree to tree, occasionally stopping to fire ahead when he caught a glimpse of a black face peering from the foliage. Jenkins and Mzingeli remained at his side, firing whenever they had the opportunity.

'Keep going,' gasped Simon. 'We can't afford to stop. We must push them out of this plantation, because it's their best cover for miles. Once we get them out into the open we shall have a better chance because, by the look of it, we are outnumbering them.'

'Blimey,' muttered Jenkins. 'Can't see much evidence of that.'

Eventually, however, they found the density of the plantation was thinning and at last they plunged from its edge into more open country, the beginning of the climb up to the next ridge. Nevertheless, the vista ahead was hardly clearer than it had been among the *matoke* trees, for the hillside ahead of them was covered in scrub and long grass, from which the flashes of rifle fire could be seen, as the askaris disputed every inch of territory.

The sky above them had turned a dull yellow but it still bulged with rain clouds and the atmosphere seemed even more humid in the open than it did in the plantation. What was clear was that the Germans' famed colonial troops were fighting a splendid rearguard action, stoically firing

126

from their limited cover, reloading, retreating a few yards and then firing again.

Suddenly, the boom of a distant, heavy artillery piece cut through the cacophony of the rifle fire. It sounded far away, but a great flash of flame erupted from the ground ahead of Simon and his three comrades, sending sand, grit and scrubs rising in a great v-shape.

'Damn,' hissed Fonthill. 'I didn't know the Germans had heavy artillery. Where the hell could it have come from?'

Jenkins puffed out his cheeks. 'I don't know and I don't much care, see, as long as the bloody thing fires at somebody else.'

Only two more shells exploded on the hillside, however, because a distant booming from the lake showed that the British warships were now engaging in an artillery battle with the solitary German big gun. It quickly fell silent – either because of a direct hit or, more likely, because the enemy had moved the gun out of range.

Its removal, however, did nothing to accelerate the dogged retreat of the askaris and their white officers, a glimpse of whose pith helmets and cloth neck protectors could occasionally be caught through the brush. The enemy's fire remained accurate and consistent and the climb to the top of the hill continued to be contested by them, inch by inch, bush by bush.

Eventually, Driscoll and his men reached the top of the ridge and Fonthill crawled forward and slumped by his side. 'Have you lost many men, Colonel?' he asked.

The big man took a draught from his water

bottle, wiped the dribble from his chin in a great swipe and wedged the cork back into the canteen with a savage thump. It seemed that everything he did was larger than life.

'Surprisingly few, old chap,' he grinned. 'Rather amazing, really, because they've kept up a pretty fierce firing and I thought they had us on toast coming through that blasted plantation. But we've cleared this damned ridge. Trouble is,' he nodded ahead, 'there's another one to get up and down before we get anywhere near the town itself. And at the bottom of this hill there's more bloody bogland. Lordy, what a country! And it looks as though the Germans are going to contest every bit of the way.'

Simon nodded to his right. 'Any news about our advance further inland?'

'Not yet. But the askaris haven't tried to out-flank us from that direction so I hope that means our line is holding.' He turned and shouted to his adjutant. 'George, get the men moving again. Can't hang about.'

All through that wet and humid day, the Fusiliers advanced doggedly, wading through more swamp despite strong resistance and, even-tually, taking the third ridge – soon to be known as 'Fusiliers' Knoll'. Fonthill and his two com-panions fought with them, acting as riflemen in the front of the line and, occasionally, whenever Driscoll queried the terrain ahead, giving direc-tions as to the best route to follow.

By late afternoon, contact was established with Stewart's force to the north, where the Loyal North Lancs and the 29th Punjabis had climbed and occupied Arab Ridge. Now the whole line advanced so that, by dusk, the British had taken all the heights commanding the town.

As Fonthill, Jenkins and Mzingeli bivouacked under a bush in a desperate attempt to keep dry, Simon's thoughts turned, for the first time in that fraught and busy day, to Alice. He knew that she would be with the journalistic contingent close to General Stewart, the commanding officer – a comforting thought, for he doubted if Stewart could allow himself to advance too far into danger without compromising his grasp of the strategic situation. Yet would his wife stay so confined? In battle she hated to be anywhere called 'safe'.

In fact, he was completely right to be concerned, for Alice had been prevented from leaving the little group of correspondents who were gathered around the general and his staff. Twice, she had attempted to slip away to move towards the gunfire ahead and twice she had been brought back by the young subaltern who was shepherding the newspapermen.

'Please, madam,' he scolded her the second time. 'I am already feeling extremely frustrated myself at not being allowed to go towards the firing, so don't make it worse for me by having to keep both eyes on you throughout the day. The general will kill me if you make a nuisance of yourself in the front line.'

Alice forced herself to grin pleasantly. 'Young man,' she said, 'I haven't been placed on earth to make your job easy, nor, for that matter, to make myself a nuisance when an action is being fought.

No,' she found herself fluttering her eyelashes and despised herself for doing so, 'I am here to do a job and to report on the action being fought here so that the great British public can understand what is going on. And, dear boy, I can't do that if you prevent me from seeing what the bloody hell is actually going on. Now, be a splendid fellow and just turn your back for a second and let me get to the front. I shall not be a nuisance, I promise. I just want to make a note or two from nearer the action.'

The subaltern sighed. 'It is more than my commission is worth, madam. Please return to where the others are sitting. We will brief you all as the day goes on.'

'Oh, well. Bugger it. On your head be it if the readers of the *Morning Post* are misinformed. Very well, I promise not to stray. But can you tell me one thing?'

A frown puckered the young man's forehead. 'Probably not, madam. But ask me anyway.'

'Very well. Now tell me – and I promise I won't quote you, so you can speak off the record – why do you think that German field gun fired at our ships before we landed? Is there a possibility that they were warned we were coming?'

'Oh, I really don't know that. You must ask the general.'

'Very well, I shall. But I don't want to do it with all my competitors listening.' She laid a hand on his arm. 'Do you think you could be an angel and, perhaps, get your colleagues' views on this point? Just their opinions, you understand. I cannot understand why the gun was mounted there if no one was expecting some sort of invasion.'

'Well, I'll try, Miss Griffith. But I can't make any promises. Now do come back to the journalists' enclosure, there's a good lady.'

'Very well. But try *really* hard, Lieutenant, won't you?'

He did indeed try, for later in the day he sought out Alice.

'The general view amongst the staff, Miss Griffith,' he confided, 'is that someone must have alerted the Germans.' The lieutenant looked uncomfortable, even as he spoke. 'Now, please don't take that as gospel because it's ... it's ... only gossip, really, madam. The gun, it seemed, was very recently moved to its position and the word is ... ah ... that a spy in the British camp somehow gave a last-minute warning that we were crossing the lake in force and, as a result, the gun was ready and loaded.'

Alice nodded slowly. She had refrained from making a note in case it daunted the officer. 'How very interesting,' she murmured. 'But if that were true, surely the Germans would have had troops ready and waiting by the beach to dispute the landing, don't you think?'

The young man shook his head. 'We have captured a German officer and he tells us that the general's feint by two of our warships towards the river crossing worked and that the Germans sent a large part of their defensive force to the south to protect the crossing. Realising their mistake, they have rushed their troops back and this explains why their resistance has been so strong later in the day.'

He looked uneasily over his shoulder. 'Now please, Miss Griffith, do not quote me on this or I will get into trouble. May I have your word on that?'

Alice smiled. 'You certainly do, Lieutenant, you certainly do. I shall treat all you have told me with the utmost discretion and I am most grateful.'

She planted a quick kiss on the young man's cheek, turned and walked away frowning. A spy? In the British camp. Who on earth could that be?

Troops on both sides endured a miserable night in the rain and it was a relief for the British to be able to move forward down the slopes the next day – still in pouring rain – to advance on Bukoba. If they thought that their commanding position on the heights would deter the enemy, they were wrong, for the German askaris and their officers fought with the same obduracy they had shown since the return of their troops from their false errand to the south.

Inevitably, however, the defenders were forced back to the outskirts of the town and then, abruptly, they melted away over the hills to the west, leaving Bukoba at the mercy of the British. The troops surged into the seemingly deserted town and it was an Australian Frontiersman from the Fusiliers, Lieutenant Dartnell, who was given the honour of lowering the German flag in the centre of the town.

In what remained of the daylight that evening, Bukoba's radio mast was dismantled and destroyed by British sappers and a German field gun was removed, only to fall into the lake from the lighter taking it to the waiting British fleet.

Alice was reunited with her husband and she immediately sat down and interrogated him, begging him for details about the Fusiliers' advance and the heavy fighting they had encountered in the swamps and plantation, on their way to capture the ridges.

The four were sitting companionably on a rise above town, by a spluttering campfire after the rain had ceased with the rising of the moon, emptying Simon's whisky bottle (milk, of course, for Mzingeli), when there were explosions from the centre of Bokuba and the sky was lit by a succession of bonfires.

'What the hell's going on?' demanded Fonthill, rising to his feet.

'Looks to me, as though our League of Whatd'yercall'em is 'avin' a bit of fun down there,' grunted Jenkins. 'They was already startin' to do a bit of lootin' when I left the town to come up 'ere.'

Alice climbed up onto a knoll the better to see. 'Yes,' she gasped. 'Those bloody Fusiliers – the ones you nearly commanded, Simon – are sacking the town. I'm going down to see what's happening.'

'No, Alice,' shouted Fonthill, 'don't do that.' But she had already gone.

The three hurried after her and caught her up as she stood, notebook in hand, scribbling away. She noted a Fusilier officer, glass of champagne in hand, laughing as he watched a trooper emerge from the German governor's house with a ladies' toilet set in ivory. Another carried the governor's ceremonial helmet. Everwhere, houses were being looted and then torched, until the very sky seemed to be alight.

'Where the hell is Driscoll?' demanded Fonthill. 'This is disgusting.'

'Colonel is over there,' said Mzingeli pointing. A faint smile played on his lips. He had not forgotten being called 'boy'.

'Simon,' shouted Alice above the crack of the burning timbers. 'For God's sake go and tell him to restrain his men. This is not how British troops should behave.'

'I quite agree.' Fonthill strode to where Driscoll and his second in command were standing watching the looting, seemingly quite unconcerned.

'Colonel,' shouted Simon as he approached. 'Can't you stop this? Putting a defeated town to the torch is something that went out in Wellington's time. Your chaps shouldn't behave like this.'

Driscoll waved a dismissive hand. 'Oh, don't be stuffy, Fonthill. We're not exactly the Household Cavalry, yer know. This is all part and parcel of colonial warfare. And my men are nearly all colonials. They've fought like hell today and I'm certainly not going to stop them having a bit of fun. Nobody's getting injured. The town is virtually deserted. Relax, man.'

Simon suddenly realised that Alice was at his side, notebook in hand. 'Thank you, Colonel,' she said. 'I intend to quote you.' And she turned on her heel and strode away, her head in the air.

Driscoll sniffed. 'Your famous wife, I suppose, Fonthill. Well, let her quote away. People back home should know what happens in times of war.

134

Look at what the Germans have done in invading Belgium.'

Fonthill opened his mouth to respond but thought better of it and turned and followed Alice. Immediately, he felt ashamed. Why hadn't he stayed and argued with Driscoll? Why did he always walk away from arguments these days? Why was it always Alice who showed the moral courage in confrontations like this? Perhaps it was just the advancing years. He must be more... More what? He didn't know. Anyway, it was a bit late to change his personality. He trudged on.

The Fusiliers – who were almost completely responsible for the looting and fire-raising – were quickly dubbed 'The Boozeliers' by the rest of the British troops. But no news of their after-battle behaviour reached the news-stands back home. The army's censorship saw to that, much to Alice's disgust.

Once the British had completed their demolition work, the invaders counted the cost of the expedition. Only ten of Stewart's command had been killed and some twenty wounded, from the total of 1,500. According to prisoners, the completely outnumbered defenders, on the other hand, had sustained casualties amounting to more than fifty from their force of 350.

On hearing these facts, Fonthill shook his head. 'These German colonials can fight,' he muttered. 'They are brave, well led and well disciplined. If they can do as well as that, given how greatly they were outnumbered, then it doesn't auger well for this campaign. We are facing a long, hard slog, from what I can see.'

Jenkins wrinkled his nose. 'Better 'ave a drink, then, while we can. Can you pass what's left of your bottle, thank you, bach sir?'

CHAPTER FIVE

The news of the triumph of the Bukoba raid was greeted with jubilation from a British public starved of success on the Western Front in Europe and from the hard-pressed staff in the War Office in Whitehall. Kitchener immediately cabled his congratulations to Tighe and Stewart and it seemed as though the sacking of the town had been forgotten. But not quite, for Driscoll's Fusiliers were immediately sent on border duty in British East Africa, interpreted by most observers in the colony as retribution for their misdeeds.

On his return to Mombasa, Fonthill received a note of thanks and congratulations from both Tighe and Stewart. Alice had, indeed, raised with Stewart the possibility of a spy in the British camp having alerted the enemy but the general had refuted any such suggestion and Alice had been forced to leave out any reference to possible sabotage in her report on the action. Nevertheless, she made a mental note to pursue the matter when circumstances allowed.

The Germans continued their attacks on the Uganda Railway and they made a second excursion across the border of Rhodesia with an attack on a British outpost at Saisi. It was beaten off, although only after the stiffest of engagements. A second fillip to British morale in the colony, however, was received when news came from Cape Town that enemy forces in German South-West Africa had surrendered to South African troops under the command of General Botha.

'Nice to 'ave that bloke on our side, eh?' commented Jenkins. 'I wouldn't want to be fightin' 'im again, after the runaround 'e gave us fifteen years ago.'

Fonthill nodded. 'Splendid soldier and good politician. He's been having trouble as Prime Minister of South Africa with some of his Boer right-wingers who still hate the British, but he's handled them well. We could do with him up here.'

The three comrades had been given no further roles to play and Simon had begun to wonder if, despite the lauding of his work at Abercorn and Bukoba, he was now regarded as too old to be useful elsewhere in this vast and demanding theatre of war. He was on the point of suggesting that they all return to the farm in Rhodesia when suddenly attention was focussed once again on the eastern seaboard of the colony.

When the war had broken out the Germans had only a handful of warships anywhere south of the Equator and only one, a nine-year-old light cruiser, the *Königsberg,* in Dar es Salaam, the capital of German East Africa. Forewarned that hostilities could break out, the captain of the vessel, Max Looff, had no intention of being trapped within the port by the warships of the British navy who dominated the Indian Ocean. On the eve of the declaration of war, therefore, he slipped out of the port and took to the high seas.

There was no way he could return home to Germany and he had no base from which to operate. But he determined to stay free as long as possible and so pose a threat to the British and to their merchant navy, whose many tramp steamers ploughed the waters off the German colony's coast. Almost immediately he had his first success when he captured the British merchantman *The City of Winchester,* newly built at a cost of £400,000, in the Gulf of Aden. It was the British merchant navy's first loss of the war and the cry 'sink the *Königsberg'* resounded loudly from the Admiralty.

The hunt for the lone German cruiser therefore was launched immediately. In fact, Captain Looff's early success was not repeated and he found it increasingly difficult to stay at sea with his supplies of coal running out and British warships combing the ocean for him. No ports were open to him. Where to go? He needed a hiding place.

He found one in the maze of channels that formed the Rufiji Delta on the southern coast of the German colony at a place called Salale. It was ideal in that the *Königsberg* could penetrate far enough inland for its superstructure not to be seen by British ships patrolling the coast. And – at least in theory – it could slip its moorings at a moment's notice to strike at passing merchant shipping and return to its hiding place without being detected. It was also supported by the German colonists, who sent food and other supplies to the fugitive vessel, tucked away in its jungle refuge. After a few days, coal began arriving in a succession of small craft sent from Dar es Salaam and, eventually, the cruiser was revictualled, refuelled and ready to put to sea. She lay for several days, moored in her deep-water lair, like some giant crocodile waiting for prey to pass the delta's mouth.

Then Captain Looff heard that a British cruiser had put in at Zanzibar, less than 200 miles to the north. Was she waiting there for reinforcements before combing the shoreline for his ship? He could not help but feel vulnerable. The British had so many ships! He decided to deliver a pre-emptive strike before the British Navy could concentrate its forces.

He sailed at night and by dawn the harbour of Zanzibar was visible. Within it was the British cruiser, *Pegasus,* lying at the quayside. In fact, she was undergoing repairs to her boilers and was completely vulnerable. Looff did not know this but his 4.1-inch guns immediately opened fire at a range of some six miles. Unable to manoeuvre, the *Pegasus* was a sitting target and, although she did her best to respond with her venerable, fifteen-year-old guns, they were no match for the German armament and within minutes the British ship was ablaze. Looff continued to fire – fifty shells in all – until the stricken vessel began to sink.

Looff had won the first naval battle of the Great War and he was jubilant. But one of his engines had broken down and he could not afford to linger, so, after firing at several onshore targets, he retreated to the open sea, sinking a recently captured German ship on the way. Within hours, the *Königsberg* was snugly back in her lair in the

Rufiji Delta, leaving havoc and a storm of cables from the Admiralty to Zanzibar in its wake.

To the impetuous Winston Churchill, the First Lord of the Admiralty, the presence of the German warship was an irritant – a constant rebuke to the most powerful navy in the world. She had to be found. Accordingly, he despatched the cruisers *Chatham, Dartmouth* and *Weymouth* to East Africa. As the months ticked by, intelligence began to mount, all pointing to the Rufiji Delta as the most likely hiding place of the *Königsberg.* And then a lookout on the Chatham's masthead at the delta's mouth reported seeing two masts inland. The elusive German cruiser had been found.

Destroying it, however, was another matter. The *Chatham* used a spring tide to inch her way up the delta channels until she was virtually aground. She was near enough, however, to unleash a succession of broadsides on the enemy vessel at a range of 14,800 yards. This time it was Captain Looff's turn to be outgunned and outranged and he was forced to sit and accept the punishment. Somehow, however, not one English shell landed on the German cruiser. For five days, the *Chatham* repeated the bombardment from long range, hampered by the shallow nature of the channel, but still the *Königsberg* escaped serious damage. Looff had erected a series of sophisticated shore defences in the jungle on the shoreline of the main channel, and although Chatham turned her guns on these, they too survived without being harmed.

The change of target, however, allowed Looff

to slip away even further upchannel so that, once again, the exact position of the fugitive ship was no longer known to the ships blockading it. And blockade it was, for although the mouth of the delta was forty miles across, there were sufficient ships available to prevent any attempt by the German cruiser to slip through the cordon.

It was, in effect, a stalemate, and perhaps the sensible thing for the British to do was simply to let the *Königsberg* stew in her jungle juice for the remainder of the war, besieged by malevolent insects, baked by a tropical sun and sweating in the river's intolerable humidity. But inactivity had never appealed to Winston Churchill and he turned to the latest weapon in the modern war-time armoury: the aeroplane.

A 90hp Curtiss seaplane, armed with home-made bombs containing rock-blasting gelatine, was shipped out, complete with intrepid pilot, to find the enemy vessel and bomb her. Ninety horse power seemed to constitute a considerable amount of engineering muscle but, in the atmosphere of the delta, it was insufficient to lift even the very light aircraft to a safe height and it crashed near Okazi Island to the south.

Aeroplane and pilot were saved and took off again two days later. This time, skimming the treetops, the fragile machine spotted the *Königsberg*. She was about twelve miles upriver, moored close to a little island and cleverly hidden by high trees. Her topgallant mast had been removed and verdant branches had been woven around her topmast. It was not possible to make a bombing attack using primitive bombs, and it was clearly

141

impossible for large vessels to venture upstream near enough to bombard her. The strength and clever placing of Looff's coastal defences also made it impossible to attack the ship by sending flotillas of small vessels through the channels to get close enough to launch torpedoes at her.

Alas, the third flight of the Curtiss was its last and it came down about a mile upriver; the plane was lost and its pilot fell into the hands of the Germans and spent the rest of the war as a POW. It seemed that the cleverly hidden cruiser was virtually impervious to attack.

The renewal of the campaigns on land – plus the demands exerted on the Royal Navy by the activities and eventual destruction of Admiral von Spee's South Atlantic squadron off the Falkland Islands – diverted attention from the *Königsberg* for some months, but Churchill, chomping on his cigar in the Admiralty in London, was not the man to let sleeping cruisers lie. It seemed clear that an air attack offered the best means of destroying the cornered ship, or at least putting it out of action.

Accordingly, the bustling, monocled Admiral Herbert King-Hall was despatched from the Cape to take personal command of the East Coast operations and with him came No. 4 Squadron of the newly formed Royal Air Service: twenty men led by Flight Lieutenants Cull and Watkins and two Sopwith 807 100hp seaplanes, specially shipped from Bombay.

Unfortunately, the Sopwiths proved themselves to be little better in tropical conditions than the ill-fated Curtiss. They found it impossible to get airborne in the thin tropical air and one of the two was wrecked beyond repair almost straight away. The aviators found that, carrying bombs, it was only possible to take off in days of high humidity – and then carrying only one hour's fuel and rising to a height of no more than 1,500 feet. Based on Niororo Island, some 100 miles south of Zanzibar, the aircraft were virtually useless.

But Churchill's and King-Hall's faith in attacking the *Königsberg* by air was undiminished and, responding to the message that only 'exceptionally powerful machines' could overcome the tropical conditions, three Short seaplanes were sent out from Britain on board the Cunarder *Laconia*. On arrival, however, they were found to be old machines in a lamentable condition and certainly no improvement on either the Curtiss or the Sopwiths.

King-Hall and Churchill continued their long-range arguments on the best way to crack the German nut. The admiral proposed sending a small boat armed with torpedoes upriver; the First Lord replied, 'I do not think that the chances of a rowing boat with spar torpedo going 12 miles up a creek past a fortified fort with numerous trenches and trying to attack a ship with searchlights and modern guns is likely to be rosy.' Churchill suggested sending in two battalions of Royal Marines with six 12-pounder guns; the Admiralty said that there were no Marines to spare.

But the problem of by-passing the shore defences rankled with King-Hall. And it was here that a despondent, virtually redundant Simon Fonthill and his two companions crept into the picture.

Consulting with his army colleague, General Wapshare, the admiral was told of the scouting role carried out at Bokuba by Fonthill, Jenkins and Mzingeli. He had heard of Fonthill and knew of his reputation for getting and operating behind enemy lines, but his ears pricked up when he was told that a black tracker, who had served with Fonthill and Jenkins for some years, was part of the trio.

So it was that Simon received a message in Mombasa, asking him to meet with the admiral the following day. No reason was given.

'Bloody 'ell,' muttered Jenkins. 'We're not joinin' the navy now, are we? You know I can't swim.'

Simon waved the note. 'This tells me nothing of the reason why he wants to see me, but I am more than happy to go. I'll take any job they offer me, even if it means commanding a rowing boat. I am fed up with moping around Mombasa while people are losing their lives upcountry and, of course, in Europe.'

He told nothing of the appointment to Alice who, in the absence of further military action, was busy writing colour pieces about the terrain over which the war was being fought. Better to delay the inevitable argument about whether she could accompany him until he knew more about what lay ahead.

On arrival, he was ushered into the Naval C-in-C's office with no delay. He knew a little about the admiral: that he had joined the navy, Nelson

144

fashion, as a boy of twelve in 1874, weighing, it was said, five stone and standing just under four feet four inches in height. As King-Hall stood to receive him, hand outstretched, Simon realised that the man seemed to have grown very little, although he had the width of chest and bushy eyebrows, plus the ever-present monocle, of a man of character.

'Delighted, Fonthill,' he barked. 'Glad you could come in at short notice. Do take a seat. Tea?'

'No thank you, sir.'

'Oh, don't sir me, my good fellow. We are almost the same age I would guess? How old are you, by the way?'

Simon smiled inwardly. Ah, the key question early on! This was a man who didn't beat about the bush. Best not to dissemble.

'I am a smidgeon under sixty, Admiral, so older than you, I fear. But I am as fit as a fiddle, as I think I have proven in Abercorn and, recently, at Bokuba. And, may I say, I am absolutely fed up with hanging about Mombasa, waiting for a job. I want to fight.'

'Does you credit, Fonthill.' The admiral extracted his monocle from under one shaggy eyebrow, breathed on it and began to polish it. He had a remarkably formidable face: jowled and heavily lined. Simon recalled that he liked to describe himself as 'the ugliest man in the British Navy.' He wondered idly if he was married and if his wife cared about appearances.

'Not worried too much about your advancing years, Fonthill, but what I have in mind will demand that you really are fit. What do you weigh?'

'Oh, about eleven and a half stone. I've lost a bit in this climate.'

'Haven't we all. Good. A paunch will be rather out of place where I would like to send you.'

'And where would that be, Admiral?'

The little man stood. 'Come over here,' and he walked to where a large wall map of the British East Africa coastline dominated the room. He jabbed his finger onto the Rufiji Delta. 'Ever been here?'

'Ah,' Simon nodded. 'So it is to be the *Königsberg*, is it?'

'It certainly is. Been in these channels, have you? I understand you've travelled widely in Africa?'

Fonthill felt his heart sink. 'Not been exactly there, Admiral.' He paused and then his heart lifted a little. 'But my man, Mzingeli – he's a black man, of course, originally a tracker from the Malakala tribe in what is now called Rhodesia. He has been with me from my days with Rhodes, through the Boer War and would have come with us to Tibet if I had not needed him to run my farm here in Africa – but the point is that *he* does know the delta. He told me so when we were discussing the *Königsberg* the other day. He used to fish there, I gather. He's a first-class chap. I would trust him with my life.'

'Ah, that sounds more like it. Now, let me tell you the background concerning this bloody ship and what I want you to do.'

For the next ten minutes the little admiral, his eyes blazing, described the events of the last year concerning the German cruiser, the search for her, the failed attempts to bomb her from the air, the abortive attacks with light craft up the channels, and the fact that she had now disappeared once again into the tracery of waterways in the delta.

'We've sunk a blockship at one of the delta mouths,' he continued, 'but there are plenty of other ways she can get out. We've also laid some dummy mines in the other channels but I don't think for a minute that these would fool anyone – not least a crafty operator like Captain Looff.'

Fonthill nodded. 'So what exactly do you want of me?'

'Three main things.' He banged his hand, palm extended, onto the map. 'Firstly, find this damned ship. She has retreated further inland, we know that, but we can't pin her down. Wherever she is, she will be protected by the shore defences in the jungle, which this man Looff – first-class feller, by the sound of him – has erected. So the second task is to find out where these are, their armament and so on. Thirdly, I would like you to put forward whatever suggestions you have about destroying this bit of naval Germany in Africa. Simple, eh? Quite straightforward, in fact.'

Simon grinned. 'Oh, absolutely. A bit of a summer cruise up seventeen rivers by the sound ot it.'

'Quite so. Now,' the admiral led him back to his chair, 'I can't tell you how to go about this. But it seems to me that a bit of light sculling or canoeing up the channels is required. The jungle round-about the channels is quite impenetrable by land, I am told. Oh!' He held up his hand. 'One other thing. We will need to have details of the depths of the various channels. Can't have our vessels stuck in shallow waters, allowing old Looff to fire on them from the jungle.'

He stood, held his head to one side, thrust his right hand into the pocket of his uniform jacket in admiral style and looked at Fonthill quizzically. 'Quite a job, actually, Fonthill. Think you can do it?'

Simon paused for a moment before replying. 'To be honest, I don't know until we try it. You said you had tried sending small craft up the various channels?'

'Oh, yes. Most of 'em had to turn back under fire. The Germans are well entrenched and keep a careful look out, of course.'

'Hmm.' Pause again. 'It sounds to me as though this is a task that does not demand sending in, say, a platoon, or a couple of boatfuls of Jacks. Stealth is what will be required – and not from a large party. I think the three of us – Jenkins, Mzingeli and myself, are probably the ideal number. When will you want us to start?'

'Soon as possible. I am fed up with keeping half of the British Navy in the southern ocean steaming up and down doing guard duty at the mouth of the delta. I want to get in after this bloody ship as soon as you can come up with the information we require. Can you – soon?'

'Do you have good maps of the delta?'

'Wouldn't say they are exactly comprehensive or up to date. But you can have what we have. You might even find better snooping around the backstreets of Mombasa.'

'Very well, Admiral. I will need, say, three days

to find the right light craft – no naval longboats, thank you – and to provision, and then we will be off. I presume we can have a ship to drop us off at the mouth of the delta?'

The admiral sniffed. 'Me dear feller, you can have a whole bloody fleet. They are all steaming about, looking for something to do. Take yer pick.'

'Very well, sir. Thank you. We will do our best.'

The two men shook hands and Fonthill swung on his heel and walked out into the hot sun, his head swimming but his heart singing. Just the sort of task he revelled in: out with his two tried-and-trusted comrades, on their own, behind or crossing enemy lines. Then he frowned. He hoped to God that Mzingeli could guide them through the channels. Without that sort of knowledge they would be lost – metaphorically and literally!

Back at the hotel he summoned his two colleagues to meet in his room – Alice was out on some mission of her own. He described the task and gave them a brief rundown on the recent attempts to winkle out the German ship from her jungle shell. Then he paused. Jenkins and Mzingeli remained silent.

'A tough assignment, lads, I know – and much will depend upon you, Mzingeli. You said the other day that you had fished in those waters...?'

The tracker slowly nodded; he rarely did anything quickly. 'Oh yes, *Nkosi*,' he said eventually. 'But it was a long time ago. Perhaps thirty years.'

'Yes, but will you remember the channels?'

Another pause. 'Probably not. But I think I

149

know a man who help us.'

'Ah, splendid. Who is he?'

'He is fisherman who live there. I fish with him years ago. Local native. His son lives in Mombasa. I meet him the other day. He says his father still alive and fishing. If there is big ship hiding upriver, he will know where.'

Jenkins lifted his eyebrows. 'Blimey, Jelly. That's the most I've 'eard you say in years. You must be gettin' verbal diaroh ... deareah ... the shits.'

Fonthill stifled a smile. 'Will you be able to find this fellow?'

'Oh, I think so. Long time ago I see him, but his son say he is in same village, near mouth of little rivers. Yes, I think I find him.'

'That's good. Now–'

He was interrupted by Jenkins. 'One thing, bach sir.'

'Yes?'

'Exactly 'ow do we go up these rivers, then?'

'That's what I was coming to. Mzingeli, we will need native craft – canoes or whatever they use in the delta. Probably two. One for us and one for our supplies. Where would be the best place to buy them, d'you think? I would be worried about trying to get them in the delta. Word could get out to the Germans. They are bound to have made contact and even have working arrangements with the local natives to supply food etc. to the ship.'

'Yes, *Nkosi*. But I see plenty of small boats here in Mombasa like those used in the delta. We buy them here, I think.'

'Good, now–'

Again he was interrupted by Jenkins. 'Would ... er ... these be very small boats, then, Jelly?'

'Oh yes, 352, bach.' A faint smile began to creep across the usually impassive face of the black man. 'Quite small. Trouble is, they easily overturn. So we must be careful.'

'And ... er' – Jenkins own features now assumed a nonchalant air – 'would there be any ... crocodiles in these rivers, then?'

Mzingeli's face had reassumed its normal impassivity, but there was a sparkle to his black eyes. 'Oh, teeming with them, yes.'

'And ... er ... 'ow big would these crocs be, then?'

'Oh, very big, 352, bach. Maneaters.'

A silence fell on the little room and Fonthill bit his lip to hold back a smile.

Jenkins shrugged his shoulders. 'Not that I'm worried about crocs, look you. Seen plenty of 'em in my time. Stood on one once in Egypt.'

Mzingeli shook his head slowly. 'They alligators in Nile. These crocodiles. Much more fierce.'

Tiny beads of perspiration were now standing out on Jenkins's forehead. 'Well, bach, it's no concern of mine. I don't worry about 'em now. Once you've seen one, you've seen 'em all. Just don't fall in the bleedin' water, that's my motto.'

'Quite right, too.' Simon now allowed his grin to lighten his features. 'Firstly, Mzingeli, see if you can buy two reasonably unsinkable,' he turned the grin onto Jenkins, 'craft in the harbour – the sort that would be used by the natives in the delta. Say you want them for fishing.'

He turned to Jenkins. '352, sniff around the

marketplace – you are the best scavenger I have ever met – and see if you can buy three reasonably serviceable German Mauser rifles...'

'Oh no.' Jenkins's face fell. 'Why do we want them old things when we've got our much better Lee Enfields?'

Simon sighed. 'Because, if we are questioned by the Germans, the British guns would be a dead giveaway. There should be plenty of Mausers coming across the border from German East Africa and, if we are stopped, we can say we bought them there.'

Mzingeli's forehead now carried a faint frown. 'If we stopped, who do we say we are? We not local natives of the delta, that would be clear.'

'Quite so. I think we'd better be Portuguese – the border of their colony is not far away. We would have to say that we were looking to set up a franchise in the delta for fishing when the war is over and we are prospecting to judge the fishing stocks. What do you think? Does that sound plausible?'

'Not very.' The black man gave a rare smile, revealing his array of white teeth of tombstone proportions. 'Might work with stupid Germans. We must make sure we only captured by stupid men.'

'Oh, I can arrange that. Now, I must withdraw money from the bank. Stay here, I won't be a moment. It's only next door. Ah, just one more thing.'

Simon put a hand to his brow and looked a little embarrassed.

'What's that?' asked Jenkins. 'Shall we go in on

a battleship, then? Much better idea.'

'No. Now, listen. I don't want Alice to know anything about this. If she hears what we are up to, she will want to come with us and that is impossible.' He blew out his cheeks. 'I don't want another row with her. They are more debilitating than the actual work itself.'

'What do we do, then? Just say we're paddlin' up the bloody ocean, fishin' for sardines?'

Simon frowned. 'I'll have to think about it. But say nothing now. Stay here until I come back with the money.'

He returned shortly with a bundle of notes, which he shared with the others. 'Off you go and see what you can get. But whatever you do, don't spread suspicion. Alice tells me that this town is buzzing with German spies. Oh, and Mzingeli, see if you can pick up an up-to-date map of the delta, showing the channels. If you are questioned, say it is for your master, who collects this sort of thing.'

The thought of what to tell Alice now consumed Simon. In the end, he decided that they would just slip away, after she had left to do her researching. He would leave a non-commital note and then write to her more fully from the British warship.

The admiral made arrangements for one of his ships to pick them up and Simon despatched Mzingeli once again into the markets to buy some old clothes – cotton shirts, trousers, bandanas for their heads – that Portuguese fishermen might wear, and he also shopped at the local pharmacist himself for a stock of anti-malaria tablets. In the delta channels, overhung with jungle vegetation, he felt that mosquitoes would be as big a threat as the Germans.

Within two days, the trio were ready. Importantly, the resourceful Mzingeli – who was turning into as good a provisioner as the arch-scavenger Jenkins – had been able to find an old Arab map that looked remarkably detailed. It showed four main channels opening out into the delta, among the mass of streams and rivulets that made a patchwork quilt of the area. Each of them looked wide enough to offer passage to the *Königsberg*. But how deep were they and which would take them far enough into the interior?

Simon scribbled a brief note for Alice:

Been called away without notice to carry out a scouting job inland. It's just routine and not dangerous. Will write more fully later.
 Not to worry.
 Love you.
 Simon

Then they boarded a small steam launch and headed out to where their long, low, grey warship waited for them, fully coaled and with steam up. Looking back at the bustling, steamy port they were leaving, Fonthill wondered how long it would be before he would see it – and his wife – again.

CHAPTER SIX

The three of them huddled together in the cling-ing, early morning mist in the lead canoe while Mizango, Mzingeli's old friend from fishing days, paddled behind in the craft carrying their supplies. They had picked him up the preceding day from one of the villages on the banks of the Kikunja Channel, on the seaward edge of the delta. He was a very old, thin, wiry man, with white, tightly curled hair and an engaging, toothless grin. He had willingly agreed to serve Fonthill because, he confessed through Mzingeli, he disliked the Germans 'who ordered him about and had flog-ged his nephew for refusing to sell them fish'.

'Sounds a promising bloke,' commented Jenkins at the time. 'Give 'im one tooth and a vest and 'e could be a British general.'

Today, however, 352 was in a less amenable mood. Two crocodiles had swum past their fragile canoes that morning and hauled their scaly lengths up into the mangrove roots, causing their vessels to rock in the swell they had created. He had gripped the sides of the canoe until his knuckles gleamed white in the half-light and pers-piration stood out on his brow.

'Ah, bach,' called out Mzingeli cheerily, 'if you not interfere with them they not interfere with you.'

'I 'ave no bleedin' intention of interferin' with

them. But do they know that?'

Mizango had quickly acknowledged that he knew of a big three-funnelled ship moored at the Salale island deep in the Simba-Uranga Channel but he also knew that she had slipped her moorings and steamed deeper into the delta. Where she was now he had no idea, but he cheerily insisted that he could find her. They had therefore paddled across the mouth of the delta and camped at the mouth of this channel, near where the old British steamer *Newbridge* had been sunk to block the exit. Now, since before dawn, they had been paddling up the channel, thinking it best to establish where the cruiser had originally moored and trace her passage from there.

They had been dropped by their warship at the mouth of the delta and now entered the channel between two narrow headlands, on both of which they had caught a glimpse of cleverly camouflaged German heavy machine gun posts, their snub snouts pointing across the channel. Fonthill had been apprehensive that they might be challenged but, so near the open sea, there were many similar fishing boats paddling or sailing to and fro even at this early hour, some laying nets near the shore, others casting single lines, and they excited no curiosity from the watchers at their hidden posts.

Now, however, the channel, though seemingly quite deep, was beginning to narrow and Mizango indicated that, on their starboard side, they were approaching the big inland island of Salale where the *Königsberg* had been lying up until comparatively recently.

156

'Let's land on that bit of beach on the island there,' Simon pointed to starboard. 'I wouldn't be surprised if the Germans had left a fortified position where the ship had been moored. I would rather steal up on it and take a look before we try and paddle past. But take one of the nets, just in case they spot us and question us.'

Quietly, they slipped their craft ashore, paddling carefully between two hippopotamuses on the way. Drawing up their canoes and hiding them under bushes, they began to make their way through the thick undergrowth along the shoreline. By now, they looked nothing like a British naval party on a spying mission. Mzingeli and Mizango now wore only loin cloths and loose turbans wound around their heads. Fonthill and Jenkins were now both deeply tanned so that their ethnic origins were hard to place. They wore sandals, torn khaki shorts, grimy cotton shirts and had forsaken their white man's pith helmets in favour of scraps of fabric wound around their heads to protect them from the sun. Mzingeli and Mizango now led the way, carrying the big prawn net between them, and the two white men followed, holding their rifles by their slings.

It was not easy going, for they were forced to pick their way over and through the great, arching mangrove roots that marked the shoreline. Overhead, a thousand chattering monkeys seemed to scream at their intrusion and warn of their progress. Snakes, large and small, slithered over the roots and into the water to give them passage. The river mist had now risen to be replaced by a steamy, shirt-clinging heat.

'Blimey,' muttered Jenkins, 'I think it would be better to swim. Not that I can, mind you.'

Fonthill hissed and held up his hand. The others clustered around him.

'If we are stopped and questioned,' he whispered, 'remember that we are two Portuguese fishermen who are investigating the prospects for prawn fishing here, if we gain permission from the German authorities.' He slapped his hip pocket. 'Jenkins and I have rough-and-ready forged passports that I had made in Mombasa, so I hope the Germans will believe us.

'Now, Mzingeli, ask Mizango if he thinks the Germans will speak Swahili. If so, you do the talking for us. If one of them speaks Portuguese we are going to be in trouble, but we have to take that risk. If necessary, I will ask – in my best Portuguese accent – if they speak English. But, I don't want to get taken, so tread with great care through this damned jungle. I just want to observe their armament and placement and then get back to the canoe. If there is no German post here, then let's see what we can pick up from where the cruiser was moored.'

Simon realised that he had no indication of where the *Königsberg* had originally moored. For all he knew, the three of them could be picking their way between these damned mangrove roots and slapping away mosquitoes for the rest of the day. Perhaps they should have paddled on a little further...

Then, Mzingeli, who was leading, froze and held up his hand. He gestured for the others to slip into the jungle and inched his way forward alone, brushing aside the overhanging creepers with great care.

He had disappeared for at least three minutes before he reappeared and joined Fonthill in the undergrowth. He crouched down close to Simon so that his body odour was distinctive.

'There is German post a few yards ahead,' he whispered. 'They have big gun and one machine gun set onto wooden planks put onto edge of jungle and hidden by vines and so on, all pointing across water.'

'How many men?'

'Not sure. I counted five. All white men. Could not see any askaris.'

'Good. They must be sailors from the cruiser. We can't be all that far away.'

'What we do now, *Nkosi?*'

'Take me where I can see for myself.'

Together, the two men carefully picked their way forward until Mzingeli indicated that they should fall onto hands and knees and crawl forward. Fonthill parted the creepers that hung all around them until he could see ahead. He saw the breech of a small-to-medium-size artillery piece – perhaps a 12-pounder – its muzzle pointed away from them, snugly mounted on a wooden base and with a camouflaged net hung overhead, strewn with foliage. Flanking it on either side were two Maxim-type heavy machine guns. The twelve-man crew, dressed in white, tropical uniforms and wearing the distinctive, tasselled sailor caps of the German Imperial Navy, were sitting at their weapons, smoking and all looking out onto the channel. Then three more men sauntered into sight, sat and produced playing cards.

'Back now,' hissed Simon. 'I've seen enough.'

They retreated as carefully as they had come and rejoined the other two.

''Ave they got a battleship tucked away there, then, bach sir?' enquired Jenkins.

'No, but if all their posts are as well equipped and manned as this one, then I can quite understand why our small craft couldn't get through.'

'So ... what do we do now, then?'

'Back to the boats. I don't want to risk being blown out of the water by some trigger-happy German rating. We will hide away, as best we can, in case they patrol this bit of shoreline. Then after darkness but before the moon comes up, we will paddle gently past them – on the other side of the channel. And if anyone makes a sound, he will feed the crocodiles.'

'Ah,' Jenkins nodded sombrely. 'I shall be very, very, very, exceedingly quiet, then.'

Back at the little beach, they covered the boats more satisfactorily and then found what little comfort they could in the jungle, slapping at the mosquitoes and drinking from their quinine-spliced water bottles. The discomfort was extreme, but the dusk fell quickly and when it came they were ready. Their prawn nets prominently displayed in case they were challenged, they paddled to the far side of the channel and crept upstream, hugging the shoreline.

Only one small raw flame spluttering – an attempt, no doubt, to defeat the mosquitoes afflicting the lookout – showed where the gun point was situated. Intuitively, Fonthill ducked his head and

160

averted his gaze from the far shore as, silently, each man in the two canoes dipped his paddle into the water, reaching forward to gain maximum impetus from each stroke. Agonisingly slow, it seemed, the little craft crept past the gun emplacements until they passed a bend in the channel and had reached safe water.

'Well done,' whispered Simon. 'We'll keep on for another hour, then stop and bed down for the night. I want to explore further upstream. The cruiser obviously came this way. 352.'

'Bach, sir?'

'Keep taking soundings with that pole of yours, every two hundred yards or so. I want to chart the water depths as we go.'

'Aye aye, Captain.'

They were up again well before dawn – sleeping in what were virtually African water meadows presented little opportunity for sound slumber – and they continued their passage down the south-eastern side of Salale Island and had put perhaps two miles of the muddy water of the channel behind them when, suddenly, they were challenged from the shore.

'Wer sind Sie und wohin gehen Sie?'

'Damn,' swore Simon. 'Caught napping. Now, remember, we two are Portuguese. Explain that in Swahili, Mzingeli.'

The tracker did so and a man appeared from between the mangrove trees. He was wearing a grubby German naval uniform and was pointing a rifle at them. He shouted at them again in German. 'Kommen Sie ans Ufer. Sonst schiesse ich!'

They could not understand him, but he gestured to the shore with his rifle and his meaning was clear. 'Very well,' muttered Simon. 'If he doesn't speak Swahili then I will have to try my Portuguese English. Paddle in, boys. Are there bullets up the spouts of the Mausers, 352?'

'Oh yes, bach sir.'

'Well, we'll try and keep them in reach but I don't want to fight unless we absolutely have to. The bloody cruiser may be just round the corner and we might be just a bit outnumbered if we start a fight. Mzingeli.'

'*Nkosi?*'

'As we paddle in, keep shouting to him in Swahili that you are acting as guides for two Portuguese fishermen.'

'Yes, *Nkosi.*'

As they neared the shore, two more sailors appeared, carrying rifles, and as the canoe grounded onto the gritty shingle they surrounded the craft and gestured with their rifles for them to get out.

Simon held up his hands and said, '*Nein spraken ze Duetch.*' Mzingeli was still speaking in Swahili to the first German, who scowled and shook his head. Then, a fourth man, in officer's uniform, materialised from among the trees and nodded to the seamen to lower their weapons. Fonthill took a deep breath. If the officer spoke Portuguese they were done for. 'I speaka some English,' he said.

The officer nodded. 'Then tell me who you are and what you are doing in German territory.' His English was perfect.

Simon fumbled in his pocket and produced his bogus passport and gestured to Jenkins to do the same. 'Manuel da Silva,' he said, bowing slightly. He nodded to Jenkins and added, 'Mina colleaga. Frederico Ramirez. We Portuguese fishermen.'

The German inspected both passports with a cursory air and handed them back. 'What are you doing here?'

'We worka for big Portuguese fishing company in Portuguese East Africa. We ... er ... esploring this water to find if enough prawns 'ere to fish 'ere after war. See.' And he bent down into the canoe and held up the large net.

The officer remained looking at them, slowly taking in the baggy torn shorts, the dirty shirts and the scraps of fabric tied around their heads. Then he shook his head. 'I don't believe you. Come.' He drew a revolver from its holster at his belt and indicated that they should follow him.

The little party, with the three sailors at the rear, threaded its way over the mangrove roots until they reached the rear end of a rough wooden shelter that was draped with a camouflage net, through which had been thrust stalks of palm and other leaves. Simon realised that the post had been situated just around the point of a small promontory, which they would have reached with a few more strokes of their paddles. A large machine gun was mounted on a tripod inside the shack and, quite hidden from the outside, commanded this part of the river.

The officer was young, with a fair golden moustache and embryonic beard, but the most distinguishing features were his eyes. They were startlingly light blue, giving his face a cold and even cruel appearance. He seemed to be in command of the post. He gestured for Fonthill and Jenkins to sit on two stools and the others to squat on the floor of bamboo canes that projected over the water. He lowered himself into an old armchair.

'Now,' he said. 'I think you are British spies trying to find the *Königsberg*. You might as well tell the truth now. We will beat it out of you if you don't.' He shouted a command in German and one of the sailors immediately reached up to the roof of the shack and produced a bull-hide whip.

From the corner of his eye, Simon saw Jenkins's fingers creep towards the large knife that always hung from his belt. He hoped the Welshman would do nothing impulsive, for they were well outnumbered.

He rolled his eyes in simulated terror. 'We no lie,' he said. 'Portuguese men want to fish 'ere.'

'These are German territorial waters and Portugal is now at war with Germany. You could not have been given permission to enter these waters. Show me your accreditation to do so.'

Fonthill allowed his jaw to drop. 'Accreditation, sir? What that?'

The German sighed. Simon began for the first time to think that their story might be believed. He knew that many of the fishermen out at the entrance to the delta were Portuguese. Some of them were fishing for prawns at the mouth of the Kikunja Channel, impervious to – and perhaps even unaware of – the fact that war had been declared between Germany and Portugal, England's oldest ally.

'It means the papers giving you permission to

enter these waters.'

'Ah, papers. Si. I 'ave some. In ze boat.'

'Go and get them.' He issued an order in German and the sailor with the bullwhip stepped forward and gestured back the way they had come.

Fonthill took a deep breath. His escort, supremely arrogant, had left his rifle behind, relying only on the bullwhip as a weapon. In referring to his 'papers', Simon was merely playing for time. But now there was a chance he could overpower his guardian. Or could he? As he shuffled through the door he assessed him: medium height, a paunch that hung over his belt (a good sign!), much younger of course, but not looking very fit. Like Jenkins, Simon wore a knife at his belt. It was useful for cutting back undergrowth. It would have to play a more sinister role now.

Deliberately slouching, he made his way towards the boat, stumbling here and there over the mangrove roots. His thoughts raced. Even if he could unearth one of the Mausers hidden in the canoe swiftly enough to fire before the sailor did, the report would alert the others and fetch them running. No. He gulped. It would have to be silent, cold steel. Ah, Jenkins would have been much better at this dreadful business!

They reached the boat and Simon wracked his brains to remember where there might be official-looking papers in the craft. They carried nothing to betray their identity, of course, so there was little that would serve the purpose. There were only the maps. Yet maps always looked like maps. But at least these were carefully folded. Perhaps they would serve, if he could distract the German's attention...

He retrieved them from the boat, held them up for the sailor's inspection as he stepped over onto the shingle, then deliberately slipped, sending them scattering at the German's feet. The man instinctively looked down. In one quick movement, Fonthill withdrew his knife, flung himself upon the sailor and plunged the knife into his stomach, putting his hand over the man's mouth as he did so.

The two went sprawling and, as he fell, the German banged his head onto a mangro root projecting from the shingle, half-stunning him. The impact threw Simon to one side so that his hand fell from the sailor's mouth, but the man emitted only a low groan. Quickly, Fonthill withdrew the knife and, gritting his teeth in disgust, thrust the blade into the man's throat, sending blood over his own face and breast. Within seconds, the German was dead.

Slowly, Simon stood, breathing heavily. He stood listening for a moment but only the chattering of monkeys overhead met his ear. He turned to the canoe and extracted the three Mauser rifles. They were not exactly state-of-the-art weapons but they were modern enough to be fitted with six-cartridge magazines each. He checked to ensure that each rifle had a round inserted into its breech and, stepping gingerly over the body of the dead sailor – he wrinkled his nose as he noted that flies were already gorging themselves on the man's gaping wounds – he began making his way back to the hut.

At the doorway, he took a deep breath, put the butt of the rifle to his shoulder and sprang through the opening. 'Drop your guns!' he shouted.

The officer still had his revolver in his hand and, involuntarily, he fired at Fonthill from his lap. It was his last act. As his bullet crashed into the door frame, Simon's shot took him in the chest and he crashed to the floor. Working the bolt on his Mauser to slip another round into the breech, Fonthill swung round to face the others. He was not as quick, however, as Jenkins.

The Welshman, knife in hand, hurled himself at the nearest sailor who cannoned into the man next to him, sending them both to the ground. One of the rifles cracked, sending a round into the roof of the shack. Then Jenkins's knife rose and fell twice and all became silent.

'Well done, 352,' gasped Fonthill, subsiding into a chair. 'I think that's enough killing for one day.'

Mzingeli moved lithely to the three Germans, put three fingers to each man's jugular artery and nodded. 'All dead, *Nkosi*,' he said.

Jenkins slowly got to his feet, breathing heavily. 'Blimey,' he said, nodding to where the elderly Mizango, his mouth hanging open, was staring wide-eyed at the bodies, 'old Jango 'ere probably thinks we do this every Thursday.' He raised his eyebrows at Simon's bloodstained shirt. 'Good 'eavens, bach sir. You look as though you've been in a bit of a fight. But well done. I was just won-derin' 'ow I could finish off this lot on me own and then come and give you an 'and, see. I might 'ave known you could look after yourself. Are you all right?'

Fonthill nodded dismally. 'A knife, I'm afraid. And I hated doing it. Mind you,' he looked up at Jenkins, 'I think the bastard would have used that whip on us. Now,' he looked round. 'It takes three men to man a heavy Maxim like this so, including the officer, we must have accounted for the full crew of this post. If there were any more they would have come running by now.'

He looked round at the others. 'I am sorry, gentlemen, but I think we must dispose of the bodies. When there is no report back from this post to the German ship, I reckon the captain will send a boat to check. I don't want to alert them by letting them find the human debris.' He thought for a moment. 'Can't bury them among these mangrove roots. I'm afraid it will have to be the river – and the crocodiles.'

'Oh, bloody 'ell, bach sir.' Jenkins's face was a picture of misery. 'We can't do that to the poor bastards. It'll encourage them awful crocs, too, look you. Can't we find a bit of sand or somethin' and put 'em in there?'

'No, sorry. No time. Come on. First the bodies, then the machine gun. We'll put them all midstream and weigh them down. 352, you are excused this duty. Stay here and keep watch.'

'Ah, now that's very kind, bach sir. I couldn't feed them to the crocs. I really couldn't.'

'No.' Simon nodded. 'But first you can help Mzingeli and I carry this damned machine gun. Let's put a couple of rounds into the thing to make sure it's put out of action completely, in case the Germans try and recover it. They are probably treasuring every weapon they have,

168

being so far from their home base. Come on. Let's get moving.' Well within the hour, the two canoes were on their way. Gingerly dipping a rag into the river – when the bodies had been deposited there was an ominious swelling of the surface of the water near the boat – Fonthill had managed to clean most, at least, of the blood from his shirt and face. He was worried, however, that they had blundered so blindly into the machine gun post. If the German captain was as efficient as he seemed to be, there would be many other posts to circumnavigate before they found the *Königsberg*. He lifted his hand.

'I don't think we should continue paddling during daylight hours,' he said. 'I don't want to run into another German post. We will pull over at the next clearing in the jungle we can see and lay up for the rest of the day. I want to talk to Mizango, anyway.'

Once they had hidden the canoes, a fire was lit, a kettle was hung over it and the four gathered around it and sipped tea.

'I don't want to go on more or less blindly paddling up these channels, offering ourselves as bait to the German defences in the jungle. And there are so many of these damned rivers that it will take us months to investigate them all. Mzingeli, would you please ask Mizango if there are any native villages tucked away on the channels?'

For a few moments, the two black men huddled over their tin mugs, talking to each other in Swahili. Then Mzingeli turned back to Simon.

'He say that, yes, there are native fishing villages on some of the islands of the delta. But they will probably be selling fish to the big ship, so may not tell us where she is.'

'Hmm. Good point. Never mind. Can he take us to the nearest of these villages? The people there will surely know where the blasted ship is and I am prepared to pay for the information.'

Again the two men became locked in discussion. Ever since the bloodstained Simon had appeared in the doorway of the machine gun post like some avenging angel from hell and had shot the German officer, and Jenkins had so quickly despatched the two other men, the old man had hardly taken his eyes off both of them, his jaw hanging down in – what? Awe? Fear? Admiration?

Now Mzingeli reported that the nearest village known to Mizango was a good day's paddling away. But the chief there knew most things that happened in the maze of inlets and channels that made up the delta and he might know where the big ship lay.

'Humph,' Jenkins tugged at his moustache in exasperation. 'Now, why didn't 'e say that in the first place?'

Fonthill shook his head. 'My fault,' he said. 'The admiral had advised that we should investigate this, the biggest channel, first. I should have thought it through. Of course the natives would know if a damned great three-funnelled man-o'-war was parked in their backyard. We should have visited this chief first. Thank Mizango and ask him to take us there as soon as it gets dark. Will he know the way to go in the darkness?'

Mzingeli nodded. 'He think so.'

'Good. Let's have something to eat and leave as soon as we can. It would be good to get as near as we can to the village before dawn. Let's paddle on the far side.' He allowed himself a smile. 'Where the giant crocs are.'

Jenkins snorted. 'Everyone knows I am not in the least afraid of the bloody things, bach sir. It's just that I can't swim, see. If I could, I could just swim underneath their bellies, stick in me knife and Bob's your uncle.'

'Of course, old chap. Of course.'

Once they were afloat again the heat at last subsided and, this time led by Mizango, they cleared the bottom of the long Salale Island and turned to the north-west to meet yet another channel (they found later that it was a subsidiary of the Simba-Uranga), where they turned to the north. The night was dark and Fonthill attempted to follow, with his compass, the twists and turns they took, before he gave up in disgust. They had travelled at least four miles before a glow to the east prompted him to call a halt once more. Again they spent an agonising day, slapping at the mosquitoes and trying to find some sort of sleeping space between the mangrove roots. They took to the water again in the dusk and, after two hours of paddling, Mizango held up his paddle and pointed ahead. The embers of flickering fires could be seen through the trees.

'It's the village,' whispered Mzingeli.

'Good.' Simon wiped his forehead. 'We can't enter it at night. Tell Mizango to find us a spot to camp nearby. Then we will find the chief as soon as people are about.'

Sleeping at night in the jungle was almost as bad as by day, for the fear of snakes – Mizango warned that many were dangerous – kept them awake and forced them to light a small fire. As soon as dawn broke, they paddled their way into a small inlet, where dug-out canoes were drawn up.

There they waited while Mizango and Mzingeli disappeared along a beaten path. They returned twenty minutes later, bringing with them a wizened beanstick of a man who, with his tightly curled white hair and toothless grin, seemed a replica of Mizango.

Everyone sat in a semicircle on the grey shingle while the three black men spoke animatedly. Eventually Mzingeli turned to Fonthill.

'Yes. Chief says that big ship with three funnels and plenty guns is moored not far from here, but deeper into channel.'

'Splendid.' Fonthill pulled out from under his shirt a small leather bag and dipped into it, producing five German coins. He handed them to the chief, who grabbed them eagerly. 'Now, ask him if he can draw in the shingle a rough map, showing where we are now and where the big ship is moored. If he can, I will double the coins.'

The chief gave his toothless grin and nodded. Then, with a long black finger he traced a rough outline of a big entrance to the delta, which Simon identified, from the old map he had bought in Mombasa, as the mouth of the Kikunja Channel. Then he traced a line down the channel to the south-west, to an outline of an island. His finger moved to the left and then sharply to the south, past another island. At the southern end of the island he made a cross.

'German ship,' said Mzingeli.

The old man grinned again and began talking again, this time frowning and jabbing his finger into the shingle in emphasis.

'He say,' said Mzingeli, 'that big ship is protected by small boats carrying guns. It is well hidden in trees and there are many posts on mainland and islands where Germans are hidden with guns. He don't think it possible to get there by canoe without Germans shooting at us.'

Fonthill nodded and thought for a moment. He leant forward and indicated the big island at the southern tip of which the *Königsberg* was moored. 'What is this island called?'

'Kikunja.'

'Ah yes, after the channel. Is it possible for us to go ashore there on the island to the north of where the ship is and walk through the jungle to see the ship for ourselves?'

Another palaver followed. Then Mzingeli: 'He say that it is possible but very difficult to get through jungle. We would need to follow island shoreline down but very ... er ... tangled and so on. Will take time.'

Fonthill nodded. He handed over five more coins and sat thinking. Then: 'Sounds too difficult to me. Tell him we will go back to the mouth of the delta and find our ships and go home. Thank him for his help.'

The chief folded the coins in his large fist, nodded and grinned to everyone and then stood and ambled away.

'Blimey,' grunted Jenkins. 'We're not giving up now, are we?'

Simon shook his head. 'Of course not. But, just in case the old boy was going to run to the Germans – valued customers for his fish, I should think – I wanted to set him off our track. We will paddle by night down to the end of this island and then go ashore on the next island where the *Königsberg* is moored. Then we will take a stroll through the jungle and take a look at the ship. From now on, 352, it is particularly important that you keep on taking regular soundings with your pole. We must report on how far upchannel the big ships can go.'

'Very good, bach sir. And I shall look forward to the refreshin' walk through this miserable bleedin' jungle, so I will.'

They spent the rest of the day trying to rest among the mangrove roots on the edge of the village. Fonthill found it impossible to sleep. The sight of the blood gushing from the German sailor's throat and the ease with which his knife had slipped into the soft flesh kept returning to him and making his stomach turn. He and Jenkins had been involved in so many battles and hand-to-hand encounters over the years that he was a little surprised at his revulsion still at killing. The distaste for it was muted when he killed at long range with the bullet. But, ever since the battles of Isandlwana and Rorke's Drift, the necessity of using cold steel always reminded him of those frantic two days when he saw soldiers' bowels ripped open by the assegais of the Zulu and the distinctive *iklwa* sound made by the

174

twisting and withdrawing of the blades after the killings.

Inevitably, his thoughts turned to Alice. He had scribbled a further, fuller letter to her from the ship and asked that it be delivered to her when the vessel returned to Mombasa, which was imminent. She would surely have received the letter by now. He had explained that their mission had been extended and that it would be some little time before he and his two companions returned to the port. He assured her that the task ahead of them was not unduly dangerous, just rather arduous and wearying. She should not, under any circumstance, attempt to discover the nature of the mission as it was cloaked in secrecy and any talk of it could threaten its successful conclusion.

He turned and pushed the end of his headscarf over his face to keep the flies away. Surely the letter would prevent Alice from sniffing at their coat-tails. His mind idled its way to thinking of their adopted son, Sunil. The boy who had been such a comfort to them over the last decade was, now, of course, a subaltern fighting on the Western Front. Even in East Africa the news of the awful carnage of the fighting in Europe had reached them. It was said that the average lifetime of a second lieutenant in the trenches there was less than a month. God, he hoped he was safe! They had lost their first son in childbirth and this boy had become precious to them both. He had also turned out to be a first-class soldier. So that was one comfort. Please God, he prayed, keep him safe. Keep him safe...

The sun went down and it was with relief that

they launched the two canoes and headed, at first, to the north. Then, when well out of sight of the village, they turned and paddled their way to the south, keeping close inshore to reduce the risk of them being spotted out in mid channel, now brightly lit by the moon.

Eventually, they rounded the edge of the island that housed the village and paddled quickly across to Kikunja. They must be nearing the *Königsberg* now, which meant, pondered Simon, that they would soon be coming abreast of the shore gun emplacements set up in the jungle to protect her. Better not risk going too far by canoe down the channel. He peered to the shoreline on his left. It seemed impenetrable. How on earth were they going to cut their way through it without being discovered?

Eventually, another little inlet with its own beach appeared, the shingle glinting in the moonlight. He signalled for the two canoes to pull into it.

They followed the usual drill: Mzingeli, the master tracker with a tread as light as a panther's, disappearing into the jungle to ensure that there were no Germans entrenched nearby and also to find a path of some sort near the shoreline; and the others pulling up the canoes and hiding them, as far as possible, among the mangrove roots. The smell from the latter – or perhaps from the stagnant water between them – added to the general feeling of dismay at the task ahead of them.

This was reinforced when Mzingeli returned to say that he could find no path through the undergrowth and the roots. 'Ah well,' said Simon, 'it's a bad thing in that it is going to make the going very difficult, but good in that it shows there is not much traffic hereabouts.' He took out his compass. 'Come on. At least there is plenty of light from the moon. But tread carefully.'

The next two hours were amongst the worst of Fonthill's life. He did his best to follow the shoreline, catching the occasional glimpse of bright water between the tree trunks, but sometimes his compass bearing took them deeper into the jungle, so that they had to use their one machete to cut a way through to make any progress at all. They all slipped and stumbled over the cursed roots, sometimes splashing into the water between them. Perspiration coated their bodies, attracting myriads of insects, and thorns tore at what was left of the clothing, causing blood to trickle down their skins, attracting yet more parasites. The chattering of the monkeys preceded them and the squawking of parakeets and other birds, fluttering up as they came near, prompted Fonthill to feel that the jungle itself was conspiring to warn the Germans of their approach.

Eventually, the jungle began to thin out slightly and a beaten path of sorts materialised by the side of the channel. Here, Fonthill sent Mzingeli on ahead to scout while the others took a much-needed rest perched on the mangrove roots protruding from the black, fetid water.

'Big gun post up ahead,' reported the tracker, his teeth flashing in the early dawn light. 'It blocks path. We must go into jungle to get round it.'

'Oh bugger,' muttered Jenkins. 'Why don't you

three leave me 'ere, keeping these mangrieves warm? You can pick me up on your way back.'

'No talking from now on,' whispered Simon. 'You'd better lead, Mzingeli. I'll be close behind with the compass.'

It took them at least forty-five minutes to circle around the gun emplacement and then return to the shoreline. As they did so, Mzingeli held up his hand and beckoned Fonthill forward. Simon knelt at his side and, parting the fronds ahead of him, revealed in the early light of dawn the long, menacing outline of a grey-painted warship, moored close up to the shore so that she looked vast, her three funnels and menacing gun barrels draped in camouflage netting, a black and red eagle hanging listlessly from its flagstaff on her stern.

He grinned, turned and gestured for Jenkins to join them. 'Look,' he said. 'It's the *Königsberg*, as I live and breathe. We've found the bastard at last.'

CHAPTER SEVEN

Alice read Simon's second letter, delivered that morning from HMS *Weymouth* on her return to Mombasa, with a growing sense of fury. Why on earth couldn't he tell her where he was going? A 'routine job' indeed! Was she a blabbermouth who could not keep a secret? Was she just another correspondent who couldn't be trusted? Dammit

– was she not his wife who would be concerned about his safety? Why the hell, then, couldn't he tell her, at least to what part of the country it was that his 'mission' was taking him?

Country...? She mused. Country? Presumably, the *Weymouth* had taken him there – the note-paper of his letter was headed from the ward-room of that ship. It should not be difficult to find out what had been her destination before returning home to port. She sat for a moment, thinking. Then she put on her wide-brimmed sunhat, wrapped around its base a blue-grey scarf that she knew complemented her eyes, left the hotel and headed for the harbour.

Using her binoculars she scanned the ships in the harbour. Yes, there was *Weymouth*, anchored quite far out. And yes, what luck! There was her pinnace, clearly marked, heading into the harbour from the ship, quite close into the quay now. She strode forward.

A young midshipman sprang ashore.

'Excuse me, Lieutenant,' said Alice, doing her best to summon up a winning smile. 'I am sorry to bother you but I wonder if you could help me?'

The young man beamed and saluted. 'I am only a midshipman, madam, but I will do my best. How can I help?'

Alice fluttered her eyelashes. 'Oh, my goodness. You look much older than that. But thank you. I am searching for a Lieutenant Commander Hawkins and, I have stupidly left the name of his ship at the hotel. Would he be serving on the *Weymouth*, by any chance?'

'No, ma'am. I don't know an officer of that name.'

'Ah that's strange. I am sure it was the *Weymouth*. His ship had come in from Cape Town. Was that your last destination, pray?'

'No, ma'am. We have just come back from the Rufiji Delta, which is certainly south of here, but not that far south.'

'Oh, I am so sorry to have detained you. I must return to my hotel and ascertain the name of his ship. Thank you so much.'

The young man saluted. 'Not at all, madam. Good day.'

Alice walked away, thinking quickly. The Rufiji Delta. Of course. The *Königsberg!* They had sent Simon, Jenkins and Mzingeli to find the big German cruiser that was tucked away somewhere in that network of channels and islands. What better team to seek her out and pin her down than that wonderful trio!

Her brow darkened. What was it Simon had written? Something to the effect that their task would be arduous but not dangerous. What rubbish! Of course it would be dangerous! She knew that the German ship had defied all efforts to sink her, from bombing attacks from the air to light-craft assaults along the channels, and that she was defended by gun emplacements in the jungle armed with artillery pieces and heavy machine guns. Even the Magnificent Trio could not lightly undertake the task of finding her new hiding place and then planning how to sink her.

Alice sat for a moment in shade offered by palm fronds and closed her eyes, the better to think. At least Mzingeli would be invaluable on this mission; his knowledge of the jungle would be an ideal complement to the guts and courage of Jenkins and the leadership skills of Simon. Jungle? From the little she had read of the delta, she knew that the islands and the mainland fringing it were dominated by thick undergrowth, mangrove swamps and forest. They would not try to wade through that sort of terrain in quest of the *Königsberg*. It would take them a month of Sundays to make any progress.

Alice brushed away a fly. No. They would explore the channels by boat, just as dangerous, but quicker and more likely to bring success. Then a slow smile crept across her sunburnt features. What a story! The search for the German cruiser had captured the imagination of all the readers of newspapers back home. If Simon could find her – *and* if she could find him first and be with him when the discovery was made – it would be the scoop of a lifetime. On a par – no, better than – Stanley's discovery of Livingstone forty years or so ago.

She stood, her mind made up. She would go in search of her husband and his two comrades. There was little time, because they had, what – a week's start on her? But if she could find a really fast sailing Arab dhow in the harbour – and there seemed plenty of them about – to catch a following wind and take her into the delta, she could cut down that lead.

The frown returned, however, as she lengthened her stride to get back to the hotel. The delta was a maze of channels – which one to follow? Well, she would just have to tackle that problem when they reached there. Time was of the essence now.

She strode to the reception desk at the hotel. 'I am going away for some time,' she said, 'but I would be grateful if you could keep my room for me. My company in London will keep up the payments while I am away, of course, and I would like to leave most of my possessions in it.'

The receptionist inclined his head. 'Of course, madam. That will be no problem. When will you be leaving and can you let us have a forwarding address for you, for mail, of course?'

'Well, I hope to leave tomorrow, or the next day at the latest. I have to make some arrangements first, you understand. I'm afraid I can't give you a forwarding address, so please keep my mail for me.'

She slipped a pound note across the counter and the clerk accepted and pocketed it in one smooth movement. 'Of course, madam.'

His eyes followed her as she began to climb up the stairs. Then he picked up the desk telephone and dialled a number. Cupping his hand over the mouthpiece, he said, 'Mr de Villiers? Ah yes, sir. I have some news that I think will interest you...'

Alice changed very quickly into a simple, khaki-coloured, cotton dress, sandals and a pith helmet and retraced her steps to the harbour, this time making for the smelly jetties where the fishing boats, large and small, were moored. She walked along slowly, inspecting each one with care. Then she found one that she felt might fit the bill.

It was an Arab dhow, carrying a huge lanteen sail that was now furled to its spar. Unusually, it had a small cabin amidships, with open holds for the catch and what appeared to be sailors' quarters in the fo'c's'le. Three crew members were washing down the holds, under the direction of what appeared to be the captain, a handsome, middle-aged man, wearing a clipped beard and a turban, his shirt undone to the waist, showing a muscular, dark-brown chest. He looked up quickly at Alice and gave her a quick smile, revealing white, even teeth. It was not intrusive or disrespectful; merely cheerful.

Alice did not respond but walked past and then, from behind a tree trunk, inspected the boat again. She was rakish in appearance, with the gunnels sweeping down from a high prow and then up again to an equally high sternpost. She certainly looked as though she would make the most of the capricious winds that characterised this part of the African coastline. To Alice's not altogether untutored eye, she looked a sleek, speedy craft – and one which, importantly, fitted easily into the environment.

Turning back, Alice hailed the captain. 'Good morning,' she said. 'Do you speak English?'

The smile returned. 'Oh yes, madam. I have sailed to London docks and back. I know your language.'

'Splendid. May I come on board and have a conversation with you?'

The man's eyebrows rose. 'By all means, madam.' He issued a series of commands in Arabic and a gangplank was thrown, bridging the gap between the boat and the jetty. He boarded it and walked halfway along and held out his hand.

'Be careful, madam. This is very slippy, I think.'

Alice nodded and accepted his hand and strode purposefully across the plank, jumping down onto the narrow decking that bordered the open hold. She wrinkled her nose. If her plan came to fruition, she would have to live with this smell, probably for weeks. She coughed to hide her displeasure.

'Is there anywhere we could talk in private, Captain?' she asked.

'Oh yes. I have a cabin.'

He led the way and they both bent to gain entry through the narrow companionway. The captain gestured to a narrow bunk, which occupied one side of the cabin. She noted with approval that its blankets and sheets were carefully tucked and folded. 'Sit there, please. More comfortable. I sit on this silly little thing.' He tucked a small stool made of bamboo under his ample bottom and perched on it. Then, immediately, he stood again and leant forward, holding out his hand. 'I am Mustapha Abdullah. How do you do, lady.'

Alice clasped his hand and found that he had a firm grasp. 'How do you do, Mr Abdullah.' She sat back and regarded him quickly. His features were good, with wide-set brown eyes and high cheekbones.

'Mr Abdullah – ah, would you mind if I called you Mustapha? It was the name of a young Sudanese boy I knew many years ago and learnt to love very much.'

'Of course not, madam. I am honoured.' He put his hand on his heart in an old-fashioned gesture and bent his head.

'Good. Now, Mustapha. May I ask if you own this boat as well as being its captain?'

The Arab inclined his head again. 'Yes, I am the owner. She is beautiful boat.'

'So I noticed. That's why I decided I should talk to you. Now, Mustapha. My name is Alice Griffith. I am married to a very senior officer in the British army and, er, I am working for the British Government.'

Mustapha allowed his jaw to drop for a moment. 'You are working for British government? They let ladies do that in England?'

Alice directed at him her most bewitching smile. 'Oh yes. It is called intelligence work. In fact,' she wrinkled her nose, 'women are much better at this kind of work than men, you know?'

Mustapha shook his head slowly. 'The ways of Allah are strange, lady, but the ways of the British are even more strange.' His great smile returned. 'So, then, lady, what can I do for you?'

She leant forward. 'Can I rely on your complete confidence?'

The Arab frowned. 'I am not sure what that means, madam.'

'It means that I do not want any details of what I say to you given to anybody else. Not even members of your crew.'

He nodded his head. 'Certainly. No one will know.' He grinned. 'Not even my three wives.'

Alice returned the grin. 'Mustapha, have you any reason to love the Germans?'

'No.' He replied immediately and emphatically. 'They too quick to whip people, I think. We have our honour and dignity as well as white people.'

'Oh, that I know. Now, listen. I would like to hire your boat to sail to the Rufiji Delta in the south, in German East Africa. And then take me up the main channels in that delta. I don't know how long we will be away – perhaps a month, perhaps more – but I do not want the Germans to know that you are carrying a member of the British Secret Service if we are stopped. So I must disguise myself. I am prepared to pay you handsomely for this. But I am in a hurry and would like to sail tomorrow.'

He puffed out his cheeks. 'Ah, so soon! First I must sell my fish.'

'Of course. How long will that take you?'

'They already in market. Sell today, I think. Good catch this time. And...' He paused. 'I must ask crew if they prepared to be away that long.'

Alice frowned. 'It is important that you do not tell them where we are going until we are out at sea. You must need to tell them some story.'

'Hmm.' The captain wrinkled his brow now. 'This voyage is dangerous, you think?'

'Oh, I hope not. That is one of the reasons why I chose your boat. It is clearly a simple fishing boat – although,' she smiled, 'to me it has beautiful lines and looks as though it will sail well.'

Mustapha's eyebrows shot up and his chest expanded visibly. 'Oh yes, lady. The *Calipha* is the best boat in Mombasa. Now.' A serious look fell over his face. 'You say you pay well. So you must, because I lose all that time fishing.'

'Quite so.' Alice took a deep breath, mentally calculating the amount of funds she had available to her in the Mombasa bank, both from the

Morning Post and from her own, ample means. 'I will pay you six hundred British pounds for a month's sailing,' she said. 'I will bring three hundred with me to give to you tomorrow when we sail and the rest when we return. If we are forced to stay at sea longer than a month, we must negotiate again.'

Mustapha smiled, making his eyes dance. He was comfortable, she reflected, conducting a bargain, like most Arabs.

'Ah, madam. I think a little more. I could get very close to that with a good catch. Shall we say, seven hundred British pounds?'

'No we shall not. Six hundred and fifty will be my last word. Three hundred and twenty-five tomorrow, the rest on return. Now, Mustapha, if you don't take me I must find another boat, so please, no further bargaining.'

Slowly, he nodded, his eyes still dancing. 'Very well, madam.' He stood and leant forward, extending his hand. 'We shake hands, like English people. Yes?'

'Yes.' Alice smiled and made sure that the firmness of her grip now matched his. 'We have a deal. Good. Now what time can we sail tomorrow?'

'Ah, with this boat, we do not need a tide. We can row, using big oars – I think you call them sweeps?'

Alice nodded.

'Yes, we can row out far enough to catch the wind beyond the harbour. So, shall we say we sail soon after sun comes up: six-thirty by your watch?'

'Good. What about your crew? Do you need to

find out if they will sail?'

Mustapha's great grin returned. 'Ah, they will sail all right. Do not worry. They will agree when I tell them what I will pay them.'

Damn, thought Alice! I offered too much. Well, never mind. Better to have a contented crew than a disaffected one. Her face became serious. 'Remember, Captain. You must not tell them where we are sailing. If they reveal our destination, it will get back to the Germans very quickly, because Mombasa is full of spies. And then we could all be shot, once we reach the delta.'

'No, madam. Not a word. I will not mention the German ship.'

Alice shot him a sharp glance. 'I never mentioned a German ship.'

'No. But we look for the *Königsberg,* of course. Why else would we go to the delta? She is there, I know.'

'Do you know where she is moored?'

'No. But we find her, lady. We find her. You can rely on Mustapha Abdullah.'

'Well, I do hope so. I will see you in the morning at first light, Mustapha. At first light.'

'At first light, madam.'

Alice left the quay, her step light and her heart rejoicing. An adventure at last, with the possibility of an exclusive at the end of it and – most important of all – the chance to join Simon! She smiled and turned towards the street market, which was a cacophony of sound and a kaleidoscope of colour, where the whole of Africa and his wife, it seemed, had congregated to trade and haggle. She headed straight towards a stall, which she had noted before, and which sold fabrics and garments aimed at the native market. She quickly selected a brightly coloured dress, another two-piece of blouse and harem-style billowing trousers, native sandals, a selection of scarves and a bad-weather mackintosh-type cape. Wrapping her purchases, she called at a stall that sold dyes and then hurried back to the hotel.

There, she confirmed to the clerk at the desk that she would need no breakfast in the morning and would be leaving before dawn. She wished to cause no trouble to the nightwatchman so would it be convenient, perhaps, to slip out via the kitchen door, which she understood opened before dawn to receive early produce?

Of course, agreed the clerk. She smiled and hurried to her room. There, she laid out her garments, tried them on – to her satisfaction – and selected the trousers and blouse for wear in the morning under the bad-weather cape. She then packed a soft holdall with the remainder of the garments, underwear, toiletries, a water bottle, her malaria tablets and anti-mosquito cream. Then, she slipped in a heavy Webley service revolver and, as an afterthought, the small Belgian Francotte automatic pistol, a snub-nosed weapon that could be easily strapped to her ankle under the billowing trousers without detection. She unpacked the dyes, selected one and retreated to her tiny washroom to apply it all over her body. Finished, she regarded herself with approval in the mirror. Only the grey eyes seemed to regard her somewhat incongruously from the glass. She must remember to avert her gaze if questioned – and she must remember to spread paper over the pillow before retiring for the night.

It was still dark, a humid, muskily scented night, when a dusky, rather tall native woman slipped out through the service door of the hotel and, head down under her headscarf, made for the harbour. All was a-bustle aboard the *Calipha* when she boarded her. Alice noted with relief that sleeping mattresses had been set out on deck above the fo'c's'le – obviously the captain had given her his cabin and thrown out the crew from their quarters to accommodate him. The sweeps were being produced and put into large rowlocks amidships and Mustapha was coiling fishing nets and putting them into the holds. Good! They must look the part and obviously fish once they reached the delta.

The captain raised his hand in greeting. 'Good morning, madam. I see you have converted to Islam. You look well! We are ready to sail. You have my quarters. I suggest you go there until we leave the harbour. The wives of fishing vessels here do not usually go with their husbands to sea.'

'Very well, Captain.'

Alice stepped inside the little cabin and laid out her things. She felt the boat lurch, gather way and then move forward smoothly as the sweeps were manned, but she resisted the temptation to go on deck and see Mombasa retreat into the half-darkness. She therefore was not aware of the dark figure of Herman de Villiers, who stood on the jetty, partly shielded by a palm tree, carefully making a note of the *Calipha's* name as she swept out to the open sea.

CHAPTER EIGHT

A finger to his lips, Fonthill waved his three companions back and then moved with them into the darkness of the jungle, away from the *Königsberg*.

'Now what?' whispered Jenkins.

'Back to the boats and then we must take careful soundings of the channels leading from the mouth of the delta to the ship. Finding the damned thing is one thing. Getting near enough to destroy her with big guns, within the range of her own guns, is quite another.'

Fonthill pursed his lips. 'And we must be particularly careful. They surely must have sent a boat by now to the gun position we destroyed and will have guessed that the place was attacked. So they will be looking for us. Everyone be on the alert.'

The quartet began retracing their steps, Mzingeli leading, following skilfully the marks of their passage through the undergrowth. If he can do that, thought Simon, then surely the Germans could also – if, that is, they had natives who could track as well as Mzingeli. Once again they skirted the gun emplacement, set about a quarter of a mile hidden in the shoreline north of the *Königsberg*. And once again they suffered from the insects, the humidity and the muscle-aching task of stepping on and over the curving mangrove roots. The animal residents of the jungle continued to mark their passage with a chorus of screeches and chatterings. Once, Fonthill almost put his foot on what he thought was a log, just under the surface of the water between two roots. The log quickly glided away into deeper water. He decided not to tell Jenkins.

It was with huge relief, then, that they eventually arrived back at the little inlet where they had left their canoes.

Except that they had gone.

They paused at the edge of the undergrowth and then drew back. Mzingeli pointed to the marks in the sandy shingle where the boats had been drawn back into the water. Surrounding them were the imprints of many boots. But these did not lead into the jungle, only back towards where the brown water lapped the shore.

'They did not go into jungle to follow us,' said Mzingeli.

'Very sensible of them, I am sure,' muttered Jenkins, scratching at a mosquito bite.

Fonthill stood, frowning. 'Why should they take what appeared to be just two dug-out canoes, fishermen's boats?'

'What did we leave in them, bach sir?' asked Jenkins.

'Perhaps enough to incriminate us. Let me think: nets, of course, including our mosquito nets – would fishermen have them? Unlikely. Blankets, your sounding pole. Then there were our provisions. Not much to give us away there, just rice, dried meat, biscuits, tea and coffee. Luckily we have our rifles, binoculars, maps and canteens with us.'

He sighed. 'Well, this shows that they are looking for the people who attacked their gun post. And we can't make much progress – or take any soundings – without our boats. What's more, we have nothing to eat.'

Mzingeli put a long finger to the side of his nose. 'We don't get off this island without our boats. We don't swim to the next one with all these hippos and crocodiles about, I think.'

'Ah.' Jenkins nodded in fervent agreement. 'You think right, there, Jelly. Very right, bach.'

Mzingeli turned to Mizango and spoke to him in Swahili. The other responded, slowly.

'I ask,' said the tracker, 'if any of his people would fish these waters. He say, probably not this far south because water too dirty. But perhaps from the northern end of this island. If we can cut through jungle up to there we might attract one of boats from his village, if it go by.'

'Aw, not another march through this bleedin' jungle an' sleepin' rough, is it?' Jenkins's perspiring face was a picture of woe.

Simon nodded. 'Our only hope, I would say.' He fumbled in his knapsack and produced the map he had bought from the market in Mombasa, opening it on his knee. He showed Mzingeli where he had roughly marked the position of the *Königsberg.* 'How far do you think we have come from there?'

'I think, maybe one and half miles, *Nkosi*. We march slow in jungle.'

'Hmm. From this map, this island of Kikunja looks to be about four miles from north to south.' He looked up grinning. 'That means we have a happy little walk ahead of us to reach the north

193

coast. We had better get moving.'

He consulted his compass. 'We follow the shore-line as best we can. It should be easier, anyway, than plodding through the heart of this blasted jungle. And we should be able to sleep more comfortably on the odd beaches we come across. Right, let's start. I will lead this time, Mzingeli, with the compass, so give me the machete. But keep those keen eyes of yours looking out into the channel. The Germans will almost certainly be patrolling.'

So they began the incredibly wearying trudge again through the mangroves, carefully putting their feet on the roots and sometimes jumping over the dark water in between, with Fonthill hacking away with the machete when the under-growth became too tangled ahead. Once again the birds and animals of the swamp sounded their disapproval, and monkeys sometimes hurled branches and sticks down at them. The forest seemed to teem with life. Fonthill noticed large ants seeming to walk stiffly on the surface of the water. He put his finger in and sucked it. Too salty to drink, alas – but surely a source of food.

He turned back to Mzingeli. 'We can't go hungry. Mizango is a fisherman. Even without fishing tackle, can he catch anything that might feed us?'

'Oh yes, *Nkosi*. I already ask him. He say that cannot get shrimps without nets but further along there should be place where he maybe get crabs and perhaps lobster.'

'How the hell are we going to cook 'em?'

'We have matches and mangrove leaves will

194

burn – when we find dry beach.'

'Good.'

Eventually, they did so and each man slumped down in gratitude onto the still damp sand, studded with young, soft, mangrove shoots standing up like small sentinels. Mzingeli and Mizango immediately rose, however, and began searching under the green undergrowth that edged the beach and arched over the water. Soon, there was a cry of triumph and Mizango held up a wriggling red-shelled crab, as big as his fist, which he threw onto the beach, where Jenkins killed it with a blow from his rifle butt. Then another followed and another until a small pile of the crustaceans had been deposited onto the sand.

Then the two black men began scavenging for dry wood.

'They'll never find any,' mumbled Jenkins. 'Every bloody thing around 'ere is drenched.'

But they did and soon a small fire was lit close to the undergrowth, which quickly absorbed the smoke that rose and died among the greenery. The men used rifle butts to crack the hot shells and soon they were hungrily devouring the soft meat inside.

'I've 'ad better in Rhyl,' observed Jenkins, sucking his fingers, 'but not all *that* much better, I'd say. Well done, lads.'

Fonthill held up a hand. 'Shush,' he cried – and then, 'Throw sand on the fire, quickly now. Back into the jungle.'

Then the others heard it: the throb of a marine engine. They had hardly time to douse the fire, scatter the crab shells, spread the ashes and crawl

195

into the protection of the overhanging foliage when, nosing round the edge of the inlet, a motor launch appeared, the German eagle ensign draped over its stern. It was manned by four men, three of them armed with rifles, scanning the jungle, and a fourth at the tiller.

Suddenly, an order was given and the launch swept round in a great arc and headed for the shore.

'Damn!' swore Fonthill. 'They've seen something. If they land, we will have to kill them. We cannot afford to take captives. Mzingeli, 352, put a cartridge up the spout of your rifles. Don't fire until I do. Stay very quiet now.'

The launch crunched into the soft sand, an order was shouted in German and the three men jumped into the shallows, their rifles at the ready, the fourth man – obviously an officer or petty officer – remaining at the tiller, staring into the jungle.

'Wait,' breathed Fonthill.

The men cautiously walked up the beach and then one of them pointed to where some ashes from the fire still smouldered. He turned and shouted back to the officer.

'Now,' cried Simon. The three Mausers sounded as one. It was impossible to miss at that range and the three Germans crumpled and fell onto the sand. The officer immediately gunned the engine of the launch, swung the tiller around and the craft swung back out into the channel. Jenkins's rifle sounded once more, however, and the helmsman slumped over, pushing the tiller back so that the craft swung round again and surged up onto the sand, where the engine coughed, spluttered and died.

'Pull it up before it slips back into the water,' shouted Fonthill, and Mzingeli, closely followed by Mizango, hauled up the craft so that it nestled snugly halfway up the beach.

Fonthill ran to the four inert Germans. He put his fingers to each throat in turn. 'They're all dead,' he said. 'Good shooting. Sad, but we had to do it. Mzingeli, wade out a little past the spur there – watch out for crocs – and make sure this boat was not one of a fleet. I doubt it, but you never know. Now, we must get rid of the bodies again. Into the jungle, this time, 352. Be careful of snakes but we must tuck the bodies out of sight, where they won't float out again.'

The grisly work was soon done, with Mizango helping them.

Jenkins nodded to where the black man was hauling one of the dead Germans by the heels, almost nonchalantly into the undergrowth. 'Poor old bugger must think we're fightin' this war all on our own, like. Must be used to dead bodies by now.'

Mzingeli reported that the channel seemed deserted and they all climbed into the launch, Simon returning for a moment to pick up the discarded German naval caps that had been left on the edge of the undergrowth and throwing them into the launch.

'We have saved ourselves more tramping through that blasted jungle, anyway,' he said. Then his brow furrowed. 'I've just got to learn how to drive this damned thing. Now let's see.' He looked

197

up at Mzingeli. 'Can you and Mizango see if you can push the boat into deeper water, while I start the engine?'

The controls were set aft, by the tiller, and seemed simple but they were marked, of course, in German. He dredged his mind for the remnants of the language he remembered. 'Hmm. "Start", of course, must be start and this stick seems to be a simple gear lever, with "Rückwärts" meaning reverse.' He looked up. 'Did we get the Germans' rifles?'

Jenkins held one of them up. 'All aboard, Captain. Let's get the hell out of here. I don't much like this island. But don't hit any crocs. I've grown quite fond of 'em.'

Mzingeli and Mizango pushed the craft back into the water, so that the propeller was well and truly submerged, Simon turned the start switch and the engine coughed into life. He thrust the gear lever back and the boat backed out into the channel.

'Right,' he called. 'I intend to go slowly, up to the northern tip of this island. 352, use the boathook as a sounding pole...'

'I mean lower it into the water, as you did with your pole in the canoe. Do it every fifty yards or so, so that we can measure the depth of the water. It means that we shall have to sail in mid channel, in plain view of both shores, but it can't be helped. Right,' he thrust the gear lever forward and opened up the throttle, 'here we go.'

Jenkins sniffed. 'We've still got the German flag up at the back.'

'Leave it. It will give us precious time if we pass

a gun emplacement on the shore.'

'What if we meet another German boat?'

'Hope that this one goes faster than that one does. But put one of those sailors' caps on and throw me the other. Mzingeli look in that little locker by the bow and see if there is something to eat and drink in there. Oh – and keep the rifles ready.'

Fonthill set the German officer's cap at a jaunty angle and steered the boat towards mid channel. He knew that he – and the others – would look incongruous, dressed in what were left of their fishermen's garments, now torn and hanging in shreds from the ravages of the thorns and sharp branches of the forest. He tore his off and gestured to Jenkins to do the same, hoping that any German observers would think that they were sunbathing. It was a forlorn hope but the best he could do. There was no way they could disguise the black skins of Mzingeli and Mizango.

Then Mzingeli threw back to him two dirty white naval tunics he found stored in the forward compartment. Holding the tiller with his knee he donned one and threw the other to Jenkins. Now, at a distance, they looked like a German boat, manned by a German crew, plus two natives. They had a fighting chance, at least, of reaching the mouth of the delta.

So the launch continued its serene voyage up the Kikunja Channel, Fonthill keeping the engine revs low so that the bow wave that curled back to lap the forest on either side of them was modest and the exhaust note muffled. Jenkins poled regularly, finding the channel deepening, and it was not unpleasant cruising in this way, for the passage made by their progress through the humid air gave them some relief from the heat of the sun at midday. Mzingeli had found a small package of German frankfurter sausages in the bow locker and these they shared.

For some time now, Mizango had been keenly looking ahead.

Now, as the channel began to narrow he called out to Mzingeli.

'He say,' said the tracker, 'that small island splits the channel ahead and makes it much narrower. German guns likely to be on either side.'

'Damn!' Fonthill frowned. 'Thank him, Mzingeli. Put down your pole, 352. You and Mzingeli pick up your rifles but I will want Mzingeli and Mizango to duck down below the gunnels out of sight of the shore when I tell you. It is likely that we shall have to run the gauntlet under fire before we get to the open sea and it could get rather hot and noisy. If so, I shall just jam the throttle open and go like hell. If that happens, 352 and Mzingeli blast away at the shore positions with your rifles. Mizango stays low at all times. Translate please.'

An air of expectation now descended onto the launch and gone was the air of a gentle day out on the Thames near Bray. Fonthill settled the German cap more firmly on his head and opened the throttle slightly. He narrowed his eyes the better to see ahead.

Ah, yes. The island had now appeared – no, dammit – there were two, so decreasing strongly the distance between the channels. And which one to take? Both seemed incredibly narrow.

Then Mizango, still looking ahead, called back. At the same time he gestured to the starboard with his hand.

'He say,' shouted Mzingeli, 'that right channel is narrower and less deep, so no ships expected to come that way. So he think no German guns on shore either side there. But he don't know for sure.'

'Thank him. Now get down. I am going through.'

Fonthill opened the throttle slightly so that the speed increased but only by a little. He wondered how quickly this old stately launch could go if she were really put to it. Well – they would soon find out!

He gently leant on the tiller, pushing it to port and the snub nose of the boat inched towards starboard, aiming for the centre of the channel, which was, by the look of it, only about one hundred yards across – perhaps one hundred and fifty. The foliage on the narrow southern tip of this island seemed undisturbed and, for a moment, he felt relieved. But only for a moment.

A voice in guttural German suddenly challenged him from the right. Then the snouts of two heavy German machine guns came into sight. Thank God, they seemed unmanned, except for one sailor, outstanding in his white garb against the green of the jungle, who stood between them. The man called again, waving this time, gesturing, it seemed, for them to pull into a little inlet by the guns.

Simon waved back, shook his head and pointed ahead. He shouted something in what he hoped sounded like German and gently opened the throttle.

Suddenly, the foliage opened and six sailors rushed through it to their guns, three to each. They settled down behind the triggers and wheeled them round to follow the passage of the launch.

'Right,' shouted Fonthill. 'Shoot at the buggers.' At the same time, he knelt low and pushed forward the throttle. For a heart-stopping moment the launch did not respond, then, like an elderly racehorse spurred once more into life, she bounded forward, sending Simon falling back against the stern. At that moment Jenkins and Mzingeli opened fire.

There was no response. Scrambling to his knees, he saw that the German crews were feeding their long belt of cartridges into their guns. How disgraceful that they were not prepared already! Where was that German efficiency he had heard so much about? But Jenkins, his naval hat characteristically hanging from one ear, was shouting at him.

'Can you stop this bloody thing from swinging all over the place? We're shootin' into the trees, look you.'

Suddenly, the German guns stuttered into life and Simon felt the breath of bullets winging over his head. Too high, thank God! The bow of the boat now rose as she pounded into the waters, once placid, now rippling with the effect of the tide coming in from the delta mouth. At the same time, the two rifles from the boat began replying, until they rounded a bend in the river and were safe and away.

'Well done,' shouted Simon. 'Anyone hurt?'

Mizango's eyes shone white in his black face but he was grinning. Jenkins shook his head. 'But I shall be sick if this thing keeps bouncin' about like this.'

Fonthill eased back the throttle. They were now out of the narrow channel and he could see ahead the sun glinting on the open sea. In the distance, out near the horizon, he could make out the indistinct shapes of two of the patrolling British warships. They were out!

'Better pull down that German flag,' he called out to Jenkins. 'And see if you can find a bit of white rag or something like that we can hoist in its place. I don't want to be sunk by British guns. Throw the German hats and tunics overboard. They've served their purpose.'

Within the half-hour, he was sitting in the stateroom of Admiral King-Hall's flagship, HMS *Hyacinth,* reporting to the little man.

'My God, you've done well, Fonthill,' cried the admiral. 'So how far into the delta do you think she is moored?'

'About six or seven miles down the Kikunja Channel. But you won't be able to get down there, going directly. There are two islands blocking the way.'

'So what do we do?'

Simon took out his well-creased map. 'The obvious passage is to sail down south here, down the Simba-Uranga Channel. Trouble is that the water level falls down to as little as five feet at low tide, so you would never be able to get near enough with cruisers carrying six-inch guns – which you will need to sink the *Königsberg*. There is one solution, though.'

A slow smile spread across King-Hall's face. 'I think I know what you are going to say, Fonthill.'

Simon's eyebrows rose. 'Yes?'

'Monitors. Am I right?'

'Absolutely, sir. I am no sailor and certainly no gunnery expert, but as I understand it, these strange vessels are virtually gun platforms, drawing only about five feet but able to mount six-inch guns. No good, of course, in anything like a seaway but the waters of the channels are placid. You should be able to get near enough to fire at the *Königsberg*, even over an island. But...' he paused. 'I suppose it would take months to get them shipped out here from home.'

The admiral's grin widened. 'My dear Fonthill,' he said, 'you have something in common with our worthy First Lord of the Admiralty, Mr Winston Churchill.'

'Oh really. What's that?'

'An inventive mind. Churchill has had the same thought. Two monitors – the *Mersey* and the *Severn* – were found at Malta. Churchill ordered them to be towed through the Suez Canal and down the African coast. They have just arrived and are being fitted out at Mafia.'

'Ah, that's splendid. But can they do the job, do you think?'

King-Hall's monocle gleamed in the late sunlight. 'Well we are painting 'em green to help them fit into the background. We're stuffing 'em with empty kerosene tins below decks to maintain buoyancy if they get hit, and piling sandbags around their conning towers etc. They're not small, of course. They measure 265 feet in length and they displace 1,260 tons, yet they only draw just five or six feet. Ideal for the job, really.'

'So it seems. And their guns?'

'Each of 'em carries two six-inch guns, two 4.7 inch guns, four 3-pounders and six machine guns. They bristle with armaments. Enough anyway, I would think, to sink this bloody cruiser.'

Fonthill thought for a moment. 'They are, of course, self-propelled?'

'Oh quite. They may seem to be just bloody gun platforms, but they *are* ships.'

The frown on Simon's brow deepened. 'By the sound of it, it is not going to be easy to manoeuvre them in these tight channels. I think you will have to anchor them as near as you can get to the target and then fire blind, so to speak.'

'Not quite. Now you have told us where the ship is moored, we can pinpoint its position by aeroplane. We have more efficient machines now and I hope they can spot for the guns, radioing back where the shells are falling and so on.'

'Ah, that sounds excellent, sir. So...' Fonthill returned to his map. 'When you intend to attack, perhaps you could create a diversion somewhere else along the coast and then send the monitors in down this channel, the Simba-Uranga. But they will almost certainly be too ponderous to navigate round this island, behind which the *Königsberg* is hiding. I think it should be possible to anchor the gunships on the blind side of the island, so to speak, and to shell the cruiser over the top, with the air machines spotting for the guns.'

'Exactly. But we need to know two things.'

'Sir?'

'We need to know the depth of the channel all the way down to the *Königsberg,* to make sure that the monitors can get down it. If they run aground halfway down, they will be at the mercy of the small torpedo-carrying boats that I understand the Germans have set up as part of their defences – like the craft that you came in on. As I understand it, you were not able to take soundings down this particular channel?'

'I'm afraid not, sir. What's the second thing?'

'We need an exact measurement of the rise and fall of the tides at the entrance to the delta. They could play a crucial role in deciding whether we can penetrate far enough down the channel.'

A silence fell on the little cabin. Fonthill's features registered his dismay. 'And you will want us to go back to do all this measuring...?'

'Afraid so, old chap. The German shore defences – as you have experienced – are fairly extensive and sending in our small boats to do the job would be tantamount to offering them up as sacrificial lambs. A native fishing boat on the other hand...' He left the sentence unfinished but shrugged his shoulders and offered both hands out beseechingly.

The silence returned. Then Fonthill nodded. 'Well, my chaps won't be exactly delighted to hear that we must run the gauntlet of crocodiles, hippos and trigger-happy Germans again, and neither am I, for that matter.' Then he grinned.

'But if it has to be done, I reckon we're the very best Portuguese fishermen to do the job for miles around. How much time do we have?'

King-Hall removed his monocle and polished it vigorously with a snowy-white handkerchief while he thought for a moment. 'Well,' he said, 'we won't have the monitors ready for at least a couple of weeks and we ought to give them a few days to practise gun-to-aircraft co-ordination. So ... let's say three weeks.'

'Phew. That's not long and there's much to do.'

'Sorry, but my ships that are poncing about off the mouth of the delta in case the *Königsberg* comes out to fight are urgently needed to chase U-boats in northern waters. We need to sink this damned German cruiser quickly so that we can free them. Do your best, Fonthill. I am sure you will.'

'Very good, sir. We're all filthy, though. Time for a bath first.'

The admiral stood. 'Of course. You will need to hire some new dug-outs from wherever this native feller of yours has his village – my purser can provide funds in German currency. I suggest you do that first thing in the morning. My launch can take you there. Then get fishing again the next morning. Right?'

'Right, sir.'

So it was that Fonthill and his three companions slipped down the side of the *Hyacinth* before dawn two days later and resumed their precarious positions in the two canoes, now in danger of shipping water as they rolled in the choppy seas off the delta. Dipping in their paddles they made for the opening of the large Simba-Uranga Channel, turning to port as they neared the headland to skirt what Mizango said was a German heavy-gun emplacement on the mainland to starboard.

The work upon which they were now embarked was repetitive, arduous and dangerous, demanding as it did that they took their soundings and measurements almost under the noses of clearly visible enemy gun positions onshore, while also pretending to fish – in shallow waters inshore where the shrimps were to be found.

Thinking through their brushes with the Germans, Fonthill realised with relief that none of the enemy had survived, of course, to warn of the presence of English spies posing as Portuguese fishermen. To that extent, then, they were reasonably safe, particularly as the waters at the opening to the delta were studded with native boats fishing there.

The problem lay, however, in plotting the depths of the channel further into the delta, where the locals rarely fished. Nevertheless, their luck held for two and a half weeks until, when their work was nearly done, they were taking soundings deep into the delta off the large island of Kikunja, on the opposite side to where the *Königsberg* was moored.

Jenkins had just put his sounding pole inboard and was making a note of the depth – a dangerously shallow 5.6 feet – when the distinctive noise of a German marine diesel came from behind a promontory that jutted out to their right.

'Quick,' shouted Fonthill, 'throw out the nets.'

Mizango and Mzingeli had just time to hurl the shrimping net in a great arc when the boat appeared with, this time, a rating at the tiller, what appeared to be an officer in the bow and two sailors amidships bearing rifles.

'If they hail us,' whispered Simon, 'answer in Swahili and repeat that we two are Portuguese.'

Inevitably, the hail came, from the officer in the bow, who gestured towards them with a pistol that he withdrew from a holster at his belt. As he did so, Jenkins slid his hand under the tarpaulin where the rifles were.

'Be careful,' hissed Fonthill, 'they have us covered with their guns.'

The launch cut its motor and eased alongside the canoes. Once again the question came from the officer. Simon knew enough German to realise that they were being challenged and asked what they were doing fishing so deeply into the delta in German waters. He could not understand Mzingeli's reply in Swahili, of course, and it was clear that neither could the German, for he indicated to them to pull up their net and paddle closer, alongside the launch.

'If they search us and discover the Mausers we're done for,' whispered Simon. 'So take plenty of time getting the nets up. I will help and deliberately tangle them. We need to play for time.'

While Jenkins, paddling deliberately badly, turned the lead canoe in a circle, the others pulled hard onto the great net, entangling it round the high bow post of the dug-out and causing the German officer to scream at them in frustration. Simon realised that he had to intervene.

'I no speaka German, but speak some English,' he called, with what he hoped might sound like a Portuguese accent. 'You speaka English?'

'Nein,' shouted the officer and he waved his revolver urgently, indicating that Fonthill should climb into the launch.

'What you wanta me to do?' asked Simon plaintively, hunching his shoulders and spreading out his hands beseechingly. The frantic and clumsy net hauling of Mzingeli and Mizango was now beginning to rock both of the canoes and it was clear that Jenkins was certainly becoming alarmed, far more concerned about joining the crocodiles in the black water than being imprisoned by the German navy.

'Oi, steady on lads,' he shouted.

Fonthill did his best to cover up Jenkins's involuntary lapse and immediately called out, 'We fishermen. Portugesa fishermen. No fighters, please. Don't shoota.'

But Jenkins's cry had been enough to alert the officer and he lifted his revolver into the air and let off a round. Instantly, all net hauling ceased and an apprehensive silence descended onto the launch and two canoes. Simon's mind raced. If he created some sort of diversion, would it enable Jenkins to withdraw one of the Mausers from under the tarpaulin and shoot ... what? All three of the Germans, who now had all of their guns pointing ominously at the canoes? Ridiculous! The Germans would bring him down before he could work the bolt of his rifle to reload the magazine. Simon did, however, have his Webley revolver, containing six cartridges, tucked under a cloth by the stern of the canoe.

He waved acknowledgment to the officer. Turning his back on him and picking up the cloth, he ostentatiously wiped his hands with it and then his brow, while slipping the revolver into the waistband of his trousers underneath his shirt. 'I come on boarda,' he shouted and waving to Jenkins to follow him, he left the rocking canoe and clambered into the launch.

Jenkins, not at all averse to leaving the fragile dug-out, followed him and quietly moved towards the nearest sailor, standing there with his hand just above the knife at his belt. From the corner of his eye, Simon noticed that Mzingeli had managed to throw the end of the fishing net around the propeller beneath the launch's stern.

The German officer waved to Mzingeli and Mizango to climb aboard also and shouted an order to the rating standing at the tiller behind the engine housing. The man put down his rifle and bent down and pushed a switch to start the motor. It coughed into action, then immediately whirred to a stop as the wings of the propeller wound themselves around the net.

The officer cursed and joined the helmsman leaning over the stern to examine what had caused the motor to cut. Simon half-turned, pulled out the Webley, dropped on one knee and fired at the officer, wounding him in the shoulder and causing him to drop his revolver. At the same time, Jenkins struck up the rifle of the sailor standing next to him and pushed him into his mate, sending them both reeling.

'Drop your guns,' shouted Fonthill. One did so

211

but the other fired a bullet, which flew over the officer's head as the latter knelt, gasping and holding his wounded shoulder. The rating received Jenkins's knife in his ribs for his courage and he too collapsed onto the deck of the launch.

'Mzingeli,' ordered Simon. 'Get the rifles, quickly.'

The tracker sprang around the deck, barefooted and as lithely as any seaman before the mast, gathering the weapons.

'Good.' Still holding the revolver, Fonthill tore off his shirt and threw it to Jenkins. He nodded to the wounded seaman. 'Pull out your knife and tear up my shirt to make a dressing and bandage. We mustn't let him bleed to death. I will do what I can to help the officer.'

He waved his revolver at the helmsman and gestured to him to remove his shirt. Wide-eyed, the man did so. Simon mimed to him to tear the shirt similarly into strips and then knelt down to remove the bloodstained jacket from the officer, who lay moaning on the deck.

Inspecting the wound, Fonthill nodded. 'You have been very lucky, Fritz,' he said. 'My bullet has gone clean through under the bones and out the other side. Throw me your knife, 352.'

The knife clattered along the deck and Simon used it to cut away the shirt, double a part of it into two pads and apply them to the wound at the front and back. He gestured to the helmsman to use one of his shirt's strips to bind the dressing to the chest. Then he stood, blowing out his cheeks at the effort and speed of it all.

'Mzingeli,' he said. 'Stack the rifles. You did well

to disable the motor but we're going to need it pretty damn quick to get out of here. The sound of shots may attract more boats or crewmen from the *Königsberg*. Please ask Mizango to drop into the water to untangle the net from the prop and you keep watch over him with a rifle to make sure the crocs don't fancy his legs. We've got to move quickly.'

Simon moved to where a little companionway led into a small cabin. 'Now,' he waved his revolver to the seaman who had dropped his rifle, 'you take your mate down below and give him water.' He pointed to the wounded man, whom Jenkins was now helping to his feet, and mimed giving him a drink.

The unwounded man nodded and, putting his hand around the waist of the wounded man, helped to go below.

Jenkins nodded. 'It was only a flesh wound, see,' he said. 'I must be losin' me nerve 'cos I didn't want to stick 'im proper, like. Must be gettin' soft in me old age.'

'Good. Take over from Mzingeli watching for crocs and get him to get into the canoes and salvage our maps and what supplies we've got left. I want to get out of here as soon as we can. We can leave the dug-outs behind.'

'Very good, bach sir.'

A cry from the water from a triumphant Mizango indicated that the propeller had been freed and he was hauled aboard. Fonthill indicated to the helmsman to help the wounded officer to his feet and to take him into the little cabin. Once they were below and had joined the other two, Simon locked the cabin door and turned back to the motor. To his relief the engine kicked into life immediately. Slipping the gear into reverse, Simon swung round in a welter of white wake out into the channel and headed due north, revving the motor as high as he dared to elude whatever pursuit might be mounted from the cruiser or the shore.

'352,' shouted Fonthill above the roar, 'you and Mzingeli man starboard and port with the rifles, ready to fire back if we are fired upon from the shore.'

'Er ... starboard and what?'

'Oh, for God's sake, each take a side and watch out for movement in the jungle. Ask Mzingeli to tell Mizango to watch ahead from the bow – the front of the boat – to warn of any trouble coming up. I can't see too clearly here from the stern.'

'Aye aye, Captain.'

The launch was considerably faster and seemed better equipped than the first they had captured; Fonthill estimated that it was probably the captain's own boat and chuckled at the thought of robbing him of it. But his delight was short-lived, for a cry from the bow alerted him to possible danger.

Handing the tiller to Jenkins and cutting the motor to just allow the boat to make headway, he walked ahead to see where Mizango was pointing. Shading his eyes from the sun, he saw that a small motor craft, carrying the German flag at its stern, had pulled alongside an Arab dhow in mid channel. The dhow had dropped its anchor and its skipper appeared to be in earnest conversation with a man in German uniform on its deck.

'Damn!' Fonthill's mind raced. The smaller of the two craft was a speedboat and could easily overtake the launch. Should they sail by with an airy wave or stop and deprive the Germans of their catch, whatever it was? Yes, better the latter. They outnumbered the crew of the little boat, anyway, which seemed to be manned by only two men. A high-speed patrol boat, obviously.

Simon moved back to Jenkins at the tiller. 'You and Mzingeli get your rifles,' he said, 'and be prepared to jump aboard that little boat and the Arab vessel at its side. Disarm the two Germans and bring 'em back here and put them down below with the others. Move quickly, now. I'm going alongside.'

He increased speed again and then dropped the revs so that the engine noise fell away and let the momentum of the boat approach the two boats from the rear and gently pull alongside the patrol boat. Both of the Germans remained looking ahead but the officer had been joined on board the deck of the dhow by a slim Arab who was now addressing the Germans.

With a gentle bump the launch slipped along-side the speedboat and Mzingeli leapt aboard, pushed the helmsman to one side and climbed on board the dhow, thrusting his rifle into the side of the German officer, indicating that he should drop his revolver. The man did so, his face a picture of surprise and consternation.

'Well done, lads,' shouted Fonthill. '352, you get on board the Arab ship and take over watching the Germans. Mzingeli, come back here and tie us up to the speedboat. I don't want to drift away.'

Within minutes, the three boats were lashed side by side and Simon had joined a grinning Jenkins on board the dhow. 'What the hell are you laughing at?' he demanded of the Welshman.

Jenkins nodded mutely towards the slim Arab.

'Hello, Simon,' said Alice. She turned towards the captain of the dhow, standing at her side, his face matching the astonishment on that of the German officer. 'Mustapha,' she said, 'I would like to introduce you to Simon Fonthill, my husband.' She smiled and sighed at Fonthill. 'He's always rescuing me. It's getting very embarrassing and rather boring.'

CHAPTER NINE

Simon Fonthill's jaw dropped as he regarded the figure before him. Her so-familiar grey eyes and white teeth shone from a face that was almost as dark as that of the sailor standing next to her. She was dressed in a tangerine-coloured blouse that was open at the neck, revealing a cheap, Arabian necklace, above pantaloons that flared, houri-like, at the ankles, and she wore open-toed native slippers on her brown feet. Her fair hair, turning grey, was tucked away under a brightly coloured scarf. His heart missed a beat as he regarded her, looking as though she had just stepped from a native bazaar – half her age and ridiculously attractive.

216

He regained his composure, his face a mixture of surprise and indignation. 'Alice!' he cried. 'What the hell are you doing here? And dressed up like something from the *Arabian Nights?*'

'Doing here? Well, looking for you, actually. And it looks as though we've found you.' She looked him up and down, her eyes twinkling in her dusky face. 'As for the Arabian Nights, my darling, you look as though you have stepped from the stage of *Aladdin* – and, my goodness, I think you could do with a bath.'

And then she stepped forward, put her arms around his neck and kissed him soundly.

Simon untangled himself, coughed, and looked at the two Germans in some embarrassment. Then he turned to Jenkins. 'Get these two into the cabin on the launch, where we've got the rest of the bloody German navy. And make sure the door is bolted behind you.'

Jenkins waved his rifle towards the two prisoners who stepped reluctantly – their faces still a picture of bewilderment – into the launch.

Fonthill turned to Mzingeli. 'Put a couple of rifle shots into the hull of the speedboat and set it adrift. It should soon sink.'

Then he spoke to Mustapha. 'I presume, sir,' he said, 'that you are the captain of this craft?'

'Yes, indeed, effendi. I bring your wife from Mombasa, here to look for you.'

'Well, I am obliged to you for looking after her. But you must get your vessel under way now and beat back up the channel towards the open sea, for we might both be pursued from the German cruiser.'

Alice's eyes lit up. 'Oh, Simon. You've found her! I knew you would.'

Three rifle shots from the speedboat showed that Mzingeli had opened up the hull of the little boat and he pushed the craft away and then climbed back aboard the dhow. Jenkins, his task as jailer completed, followed him less adroitly. Mustapha shouted orders and the crew of the *Calipha* began to haul up its anchor.

'Where are we going?' asked Alice. 'I wanted to catch a glimpse, at least, of the *Königsberg*. Is it far from here?'

'No. But all this shooting will have alerted the crew and they must have at least one boat left that could pursue us. So we must get out of here. We will take you aboard the launch to one of our warships off the delta.'

Alice drew herself to her full height. 'Certainly not. I can't leave Mustapha and his crew to the mercy of the Germans. They have been magnificent in getting me here. I shall stay with them, thank you very much.' Then her tone altered and she put her hand on his arm. 'But, Simon, you must tell me what you have been up to. It will make a wonderful story.'

'I will do no such thing. But what the hell are we going to do with this bloody boat? Is it a good sailor?'

'Oh, first class. She ghosts along in light airs and really puts her lee rail down with a bit of wind.'

'What? Good lord, Alice. You've certainly picked up the jargon. Very well, we will accompany the dhow until we reach the open water. There are

German gun emplacements to pass before we do. What's the chap's name again?'

'Mustapha.'

'Very well. Now, sit over there until I've had a word with him. I want you to tell me how you found us.'

Mustapha was supervising the hauling up of the mast of the great lanteen sail as Simon approached him.

'Captain,' he said, 'it looks as though the tide is with us. Can we make good time with this wind and the tide back to the open sea, do you think?'

Mustapha's nostrils flared as he sniffed the wind. 'Oh yes. Offshore wind has sprung up. We should sail well.' He smiled and looked down at the launch. 'Faster than that boat of yours, perhaps.'

Fonthill returned the smile. 'Well, we won't have to tack, of course. But we will keep you company until we are past the German guns on the shore. Did you pass many coming down this channel?'

The Arab shook his head. 'I saw nothing, effendi. Busy sailing boat, of course.'

'Of course. Well, they are there. So we must sail quickly past them. Put on as much sail as you can.'

'Very well, effendi.'

Mustapha barked more orders and Simon walked back to Alice. 'Now, my love, I apologise for laying down the law, but we are still in some danger here and I must insist that you join me in the launch. I think it would be better for this crew if you were not on board if the Germans do

219

catch up with the dhow.'

'Oh, very well, Simon. But you must allow me to go back on board when we are out at sea for I must pay these good fellows off. They are all my friends now.'

'Of course. Explain to Mustapha and tell him to deny all knowledge of you if they are caught. Then join us in the launch. We must go on ahead, for I have to report to the admiral and we have prisoners to unload.'

The lashings coupling the launch to the *Calipha* were untied and Fonthill steered the launch away from the dhow. Immediately, however, as the newly-risen offshore wind filled her giant sail, the native boat gathered way, heeled over and began almost to skip across the water.

'My word,' Simon shouted to Alice, 'she is a good sailor. Now, come and sit next to me while I steer and tell me how you got here and why. No nonsense, now.'

Meekly, Alice did as she was told. Mustapha had proved to be not only an excellent sailor, skippering a fast and seaworthy boat, but a man who knew the delta extremely well, having fished its channels in the past. He also knew many of the fishermen's villages and they had systematically called on them, until they found one who acknowledged that they had recently sold two dug-out canoes to two Englishmen who had paddled away down the Simba-Uranga Channel.

'So we followed you, in the hope that we would catch you up,' said Alice. 'And we did.'

'No you didn't. You were stopped and captured by a German patrol boat.'

Alice frowned. 'Yes.' She leant forward. 'And this is the funny thing, Simon. That boat came straight for us, as though it was expecting us. I hid in the cabin, of course, pretending to be Mustapha's wife...'

'Not completely, I trust?'

'No. Don't be silly. But, as you know, my German isn't too bad, and I heard him demanding Mustapha to produce the English lady whom he had on board who was, in fact, a spy. That's when I stepped out and began arguing with him because I didn't want Mustapha to get into trouble – and that's when you arrived, thank goodness.'

'Hmm.' Simon thought in silence for a while. Then, 'Who knew in Mombasa what you were up to?'

'Absolutely nobody. I was very careful.'

'Well, my love, somebody knew. We need to look into this when we get back. But for now, let's get out of here.' He looked behind him. 'My word, the *Calipha* is a lovely sailor. She's almost keeping up with us. But, as far as I can see, neither of us is being pursued. Now all we have to do is race past the German gun emplacements. Hold on to your hat, darling.'

He opened the throttle and a white wake spread out behind them. Best now, he thought, to move away from the dhow in case the Germans somehow linked the two craft together. Mustapha would have a better chance on his own – and without Alice on board, of course.

In the event, they sped past the only shore gun emplacement they could see without being challenged and then, once clear in the mouth of the delta, waited for the *Calipha* to appear. She did so in fine style, the sail billowing out and the lee rail kissing the top of the white foam she was creating. Alice went back on board, retrieved her few belongings, paid Mustapha the balance owed to him – plus a little extra – and rejoined Simon on board the launch.

Alice's main concern now was whether Admiral King-Hall had already revealed the discovery of the German cruiser to the correspondents all desperately waiting for news in Mombasa, while she herself was plodding round the delta villages. To her relief, he had not and, what's more, the admiral – in gratitude for Fonthill's work – allowed Alice to use the ship's radio to send a brief cable back to her office in Fleet Street, announcing that the *Königsberg* had been found (although she was forbidden to say where) and that an attack was now being planned, although, again, she was not allowed to say how and when.

It was just the exclusive that she had dreamt of and she was allowed to remain on board the *Hyacinth* to await the imminent arrival of the monitors.

The strange vessels, looking more like floating gun platforms than ships, came ponderously into view two days later, behind their tugs, and Fonthill and Jenkins were immediately ensconced with their skippers to explain tidal times and channel depths. Almost as important as these maritime matters was the efficiency of the communications linking the spotter aircraft to the monitors, and exercises were conducted out at sea to test this.

'Surely the Germans must know we're comin',

said Jenkins to Simon.

'Of course they do. The local natives will have told them of the arrival of the monitors and they will be improving their defences as best they can. The poor devils, however, can't turn and run or twist and turn. That ship is stuck where she is now, like a fly caught in aspic. It's just a question of how near the monitors can get before they can open fire.'

He frowned. 'And, of course, whether the monitors can survive the fire that the *Königsberg* will rain down on them. She has already proven that she has splendid six-inch guns. It's going to be a terrific artillery duel and some battle, that's for sure.'

Fonthill reported that, depending upon the tides, the main channels were navigable by the monitors for a depth of some seven miles into the delta and it was decided that the two great gunships, the *Mersey* and the *Severn,* would, in fact, sail as far as possible down the northern of the two channels, the Kikunja, the one in which the *Königsberg* was moored, deep in the delta. Accordingly, they anchored some ten miles off the mouth on the night of 5–6th July and steamed off at 4 a.m. reaching the entrance of the channel just before light at 5.45 a.m.

At roughly the same time, three ships of the fleet staged a diversion at Dar es Salaam and a plane dropped four bombs near the *Königsberg.* Under cover of this activity, the two monitors edged their way down the channel and, despite being severely attacked by field guns and machine guns from the shore, had reached their firing positions between five and six miles into the delta by 6.30 a.m.

By now, Mizango had been paid off and thanked for his hard work. The German marks he received would, he grinningly announced, pay for at least four fishing boats. Simon thought it unfair to subject Mzingeli to the rigours and danger of a naval artillery battle and, overcoming the tracker's objections, insisted that he should stay in Mizango's village until the fighting was over.

Alice's fury at being ordered by the admiral to remain on his flagship was abated somewhat by the fact that she was the only newspaper correspondent to be present at the battle, albeit at a distance. Simon, however, insisted that he and Jenkins should be in at the kill and the captain of the *Severn* happily agreed to their presence on board his ship, not least because of the help they could offer with navigation as the gunship eased its way down the channel.

It was, in fact, the *Severn* who was first into station and it was she who opened up the fire on the *Königsberg*, out of sight, of course, at a range of 10,600 yards. No hits were reported but the cruiser immediately responded, getting the range of the two monitors quickly, showing that the firing was being directed by observation platforms erected amidst the jungle onshore.

In fact, it was the *Mersey* who suffered. Fonthill and Jenkins watched with horror as the monitor was straddled by a salvo from all five of the German ship's starboard guns. One shell landed just short of the monitor's quarterdeck, another destroyed one of her motor boats and a third put one of her six-inch guns out of action, killing most of its crew. A shell that was being loaded at the time exploded, and then another, and it was a miracle that the consequent fire did not flash down to the magazine below, so completely destroying the ship. As it was, the kapok life jackets worn by the crew to protect them from shrapnel splinters, caught fire, severely burning two men who were to die later in the day.

It was enough, and the *Mersey's* captain slipped her anchors and steamed 700 hundred yards downriver to escape the barrage, leaving *Severn* to bear the full brunt of the German firing.

'I thought this bloody aeroplane was supposed to be directin' our guns,' wailed Jenkins as huge water spouts leapt up on either side of the monitor. 'They're 'ittin' us, but are we don't seem to be 'ittin' back.'

In fact, it emerged that the method of communication between the spotting plane and the guns down below had broken down, despite all the practice. One of the problems was that the pilot could not distinguish between the shells landed by each of the two monitors and so was unable to correct their fire.

At 8 a.m., however, he was able to signal that *Severn* had hit the *Königsberg*, and *Mersey* then steamed upstream to rejoin the fray and anchored on the opposite bank, firing with her aft gun and registering a hit on the enemy ship. The *Königsberg's* firing had now become a little less fierce, for she was forced to harbour her precious ammunition (it was revealed later that her highly competent gunnery officer had also been badly wounded). But she continued to fire and, at 3.30 p.m. the two monitors were forced ignominiously to retire to the mouth of the delta, blasting the still active German shore defences in a gesture of defiance as they did so.

'Well, that's wasn't a great bleedin' success, look you, now was it?' Jenkins, his face a misery, was clinging to a stanchion as the ocean swell began to cause the *Severn* to pitch.

Fonthill nodded. 'Bloody awful, in fact. But at least the monitors got within range. You have to hand it to those German gunners. They stuck to their task and were damned accurate. We need to try and take out those gun-spotting platforms on the shore and find some better way of communicating with the aircraft. And I shall tell the admiral so. This is becoming a damned expensive way of destroying one stationary ship, I must say.'

Simon requested an interview with King-Hall and was ferried to the flagship, where, of course, he was closely cross-questioned by Alice before he could see the admiral. He was suitably discreet with her, but not with King-Hall.

'If you don't mind me saying, sir—' he began.

'I *will* probably mind you saying, Fonthill,' the little man barked. 'I am bloody furious with those monitors. Didn't do their damned job. One of the aeroplanes has just flown over the German ship and reported that only one of the *Königsberg's* big guns has been put out of action.'

'With respect, sir, I doubt if it was the fault of the monitors. From what I could see we were "out-spotted", so to speak. The observation platforms onshore could see our monitors and report how the German shells were landing and our aeroplanes couldn't do the same job for our guns. So we were firing blind.'

'So...?'

'If the monitors can take it in turns to fire, then the spotting planes can report the results more precisely. And can your cruisers get close in, do you think, and put the German spotting platforms – the main one is on Pemba Hill – under fire?'

'Humph. Already ordered that and we'll bombard all the shore defences, too. But it's a good idea to alternate the firing. I intend to have another go as soon as we've patched up the monitors. That's going to take four or five days. But we will sink that bloody ship yet, I promise you, Fonthill.'

On 11th July the breaking dawn saw the British offshore fleet steaming into position, much closer this time to the German shore. At 10.40 a.m. the two monitors hove into sight after their twenty-mile voyage from Mafia and, as they approached the entrance to the channel, the British fleet began their bombardment of the shore defences and the German observation platforms.

This time, Fonthill and Jenkins were invited to board the *Mersey* as she led the two gunships over the bar and into the channel. Immediately, she was put under fire from a German shore-based field gun and three men manning her aft six-inch gun were wounded. Simon and Jenkins took shelter behind steel shields mounted on the deck and bent their heads as machine gun bullets pinged off their shelter.

As the shells from the British cruisers began to find their targets, the fire from the shore began to lessen and the two monitors continued their laborious progress down the channel unhindered. Eventually, the *Mersey* swung into position broadside onto the *Königsberg* on the other side of the island. Immediately she came under fire from the German ship but, this time, thanks to the fleet's targeting of the spotter platforms, it was noticeable that the enemy firing was far less accurate, and she opened up her big guns in retaliation.

As she did so, the *Severn* moved around her sister ship 100 yards upriver, so drawing the German fire. As soon as the *Severn* was in position, *Mersey* ceased firing and the *Severn* began. But the German guns had got their range now and the *Severn* came under heavy fire.

'Blimey,' said Jenkins, poking his head above the steel shield, 'we seem to have chosen the right ship. They're gettin' plastered, look you.'

Water spouts were rising vertically all round the monitor and the clatter of shell splinters could be heard from her sister ship as they struck the deck and superstructure of the vessel. Somehow, however, she did not receive a direct hit. She continued firing and it was clear that the more precise reporting of the origin of the British shells from the aeroplanes up above was working, for, at 12.35 p.m. the *Mersey's* guns gained their first direct hit on the enemy ship. Immediately a column of black, oily smoke rose from the other side of the island and a great cheer went up from the crews of both monitors.

It was soon noticed that the accuracy of *Königs-berg's* firing began to falter. *Severn* now took over the bombardment and the spotter plane signalled two more direct hits and reported that only three of the German ship's guns were still firing.

At that point, however, one of the last of the cruiser's shrapnel shells exploded in front of the aircraft's nose, just before it climbed into clouds at 2,400 ft. Immediately its engine cut out and it began to glide down towards the river, its observer still coolly recording *Severn's* hits as it descended. It hit the water near *Mersey*, sending one of its crew catapulting into the river. The other, still wearing his safety harness, was trapped under the wreckage.

'Oh my God,' wailed Jenkins. 'The crocs will 'ave 'em.' But the reptiles had long since been sent packing by the noise of the shelling and both men were eventually pulled on board the *Mersey*, where they coughed up a considerable amount of the Rufiji's brown waters before being given hot tea.

Now *Severn* was scoring hit after hit on the *Königsberg* and a huge explosion was heard from the German ship, followed by another and then another. It was *Mersey's* turn now to take up the execution and her skipper carefully conned her past her sister ship until she was within 7,000 yards of the enemy. The cruiser was still out of sight but the columns of smoke now rising made her a much easier target and the monitor ruth-lessly continued firing until 2.45, when the ceasefire order was given.

'Thank God for that,' murmured Fonthill. 'It's not just the noise – I think I have already gone deaf – but I couldn't help thinking of the poor devils on the receiving end of all those shells. I just hope the German captain got his crew ashore some time ago.'

It later transpired that one of the many great explosions heard from the stricken vessel was caused by Captain Looff ordering the ship to be blown up by a torpedo warhead. But the tide was falling rapidly and both of the monitors had to retire downstream before any sort of examination could be carried out on the cruiser. It was clear enough, however, that nothing more would be heard from the *Königsberg*. It was the first time that aircraft had been used to spot targets for ships below them and, indeed, it was one of the longer continuous engagements in the history of the British navy. The smoke-covered monitors were cheered through the fleet as they emerged from the mouth of the delta and began their voyage back to their base at Mafia.

In fact, the task of making absolutely sure that all was over with the cruiser fell to Fonthill and Jenkins. Continual rain had prevented air reconnaissance, but after six days, King-Hall ordered them to lead a landing party sent off down the channel in one of the captured German launches.

As they cautiously rounded the southern tip of Kikunja Island, an astonishing sight met their gaze. What was left of the *Königsberg* lay, submerged up to her upper deck, lying on her starboard side like some mortally wounded dragon, trails of smoke rising from her superstructure. The pennant of the Imperial German Navy still flew from her mainmast but the once proud warship was now a mass of twisted, black and grey metal. The channel banks on either side were scorched black where her protecting shore gun emplacements had been blown to bits and the jungle set ablaze.

'We've seen enough,' said Fonthill. 'I don't want to stand and gloat. Turn her round, helmsman, and let's return to the mother ship. It looks as though the British Navy has won this battle at last.' Then, quietly to Jenkins: 'I wonder at what cost?'

It was Alice, in fact, back on board the *Hyacinth*, who, by ceaseless questioning, managed to worm out from the admiral's staff the cost, at least in ordnance, of the two days of the battle.

In those two days, she told Simon, the monitors between them had fired 943 six-inch shells, 389 4.7-inch shells, 1,860 three-pounder shells, and 16,000 rounds from their machine guns.

'Yes, but,' Simon frowned, 'you're not going to report that the whole engagement was a disaster, are you? King-Hall has removed a prodigious threat to our shipping in the Indian Ocean and maybe even further afield.'

'Yes, yes, I know that. But there have been twenty warships of different types hovering about off the delta for weeks. Those ships and those shells could have been used in the North Sea or the Atlantic, where the German U-boats are beginning to prove a real menace. And our dear little admiral has earned the enmity of his captains by his brusque manner and blaming them for his own temerity. I don't think he will get away from this lightly.

'So,' she continued, 'I am itching to get back to Mombasa to file my report, because I am not allowed to do that now from on board. Don't worry, I shall tread carefully between the daisies and my story will be censored anyway, so the true story can't be told to the great British public. It will come out as a triumph for the British Navy once again.' She smiled. 'It wasn't really, in my book, but at least that bloody ship is sunk.'

They were talking in the wardroom of the *Hyacinth*, which, with the rest of the fleet, was steaming back to Mombasa. The admiral, a stickler for rank, had banished Jenkins to the Petty Officers' mess and Mzingeli to the Stokers'. Now Alice and Simon sipped coffee, sitting on the plush banquettes of the large cabin, in makeshift clothing provided by the navy, their tans still evident, and felt vaguely guilty at the distinction shown to them.

Alice looked round and smiled. 'Now, darling, what's next for you, I wonder? A posting to be commander-in-chief of the British army in East Africa, at the very least? You jolly well deserve it.'

'Good lord, no. I don't want to be a soldier again, thank you very much. Particularly in this campaign.' He frowned. 'I fear it is going to be just as bad as the Western Front, from what I can see. The German leading their army here is proving to be one of the most able on any side in this bloody war. I don't know how I can be involved now, at my age, but I certainly don't want to sit on my arse for the rest of it. We shall see.'

They anchored in the bay, off the harbour, and King-Hall summoned Fonthill. The little man rose from behind his desk, extended his hand and gripped Simon's fiercely.

'You've done a first-class job, Fonthill,' he said. 'In fact, I doubt if we could have got anywhere near the *Königsberg* if it hadn't been for you.'

'Delighted to have been of use, Admiral.'

King-Hall coughed. 'I have submitted a request that special payments of £50 and £100 should be made to your black feller and that remarkable ... er ... 423, or whatever his number is.'

'352, sir.'

'Ah yes. Now look here, I've looked at what we could award to you.' The simian features screwed up into a scowl of embarrassment. 'Trouble is – you're a civilian, y'see, and it's proving difficult. You've already got two DSOs and a CB. Short of making you Admiral of the Fleet and Viceroy of India I'm buggered if I know what we can do. But it doesn't mean that your country – and me – are not profoundly grateful.'

It became Fonthill's turn to look embarrassed. 'Well, my two chaps will be appreciative of the payments but I need nothing. As you know, I have ample private means and, as you say,' he smiled, 'enough gongs to sound dinner in a thousand private hotels throughout the south of England. I want nothing more. Except, perhaps, another interesting job. I don't want to sit this war out down here, Admiral. I know I can still be useful.'

'I am sure you can. Thank you again, my dear fellow, and my best wishes to your wife.'

Fonthill, Alice, Jenkins and Mzingeli were given the honour of being conveyed to the shore in the admiral's barge and they all repaired to the hotel for stiff whiskies and, in Mzingeli's case, a large glass of milk. What was more, there was a letter awaiting Simon and Alice from their adopted son, Sunil, sent from France and assuring them that he was well and fit.

CHAPTER TEN

Simon immediately sought an interview with General Tighe to plead for more work but also to report on Alice's suspicion that there was a German spy somewhere in the British ranks in Mombasa. It was clear that the land war was going badly – put into vivid relief by the success in German South West Africa of the South African prime minister, Louis Botha, one of the Afrikaner heroes of the Anglo–Boer war, who had personally led South African troops in invading and defeating the Germans in that colony. He had also put down a rebellion by diehard Boers in South Africa.

In contrast, Tighe's men in the north had received several setbacks. An attempt by the British to eject German troops from Mbuyuni, twenty miles east of Taveta, had failed miserably with the loss of 100 British troops. Soon afterwards, an attempt to retake Longido with a force 450 strong was beaten off with heavy casualties.

It was not surprising, then, that Simon found Tighe to be in an untypically depressed mood and comparatively uninterested in the task of flushing out spies in Mombasa.

'Ah, Fonthill,' he said, 'we know that the bloody place is steaming with them,' he said. 'But our intelligence is doing its best and I am not convinced that anything of value gets out to the Germans.' He gestured to Simon to take a chair and resumed his own seat behind his desk, drawing heavily on his cigarette.

'I've got bigger fish to fry than a touch of espionage back here,' he went on, leaning back in his chair. 'My intelligence wallahs tell me that von Lettow-Vorbeck has been conducting a pretty successful recruiting campaign in his colony and that an extra 2,000 Europeans – *Europeans*, mind you, Fonthill, reservists he's called up – have joined his ranks and that he can now put 20,000 troops into the field.'

Tighe frowned as he watched the blue smoke from his cigarette rise to the ceiling. 'What's more, do yer know, he's got sixty-six machine guns and sixty field guns at his disposal which means that he has superior fire power to me. It's true that the ration strength of my force rose to 15,000 in the summer, but of that lot only 4,000 British and Indian troops and 3,600 of the King's African Rifles were fit for duty. In other words, I have a fighting force now no bigger than the army we started with a year ago, mainly thanks to malaria and dysentery. At this very moment, the greatest force I could put into the field in British East Africa is 2,500 infantry with eighteen field guns and thirty-five machine guns. I hope to God von Lettow-Vorbeck doesn't come at me in force.'

A silence fell on the room, broken only by a

shouted command and stamp of feet in the distance as a troop was drilled.

Fonthill shook his head. 'Sounds pretty bad, General. But presumably you will get reinforcements?'

'Indeed. The best news I've had so far is that the South Africans, bless 'em, have offered to send troops from the south. Botha and his deputy Smuts – you'll remember them from eleven years ago, no doubt?'

Simon nodded. 'Only too well. Chased 'em both. Superb soldiers.'

'Quite so. Well, they're proving to be superb politicians now, as well. It's only a few years ago the Kaiser was supporting old man Kruger in his fight against the British and half of the Afrikaners in South Africa still blame us and hate us for that war. Yet Botha has assured the government back home that, now that he has cleaned up German South West Africa, he can send a considerable force to fight von Lettow-Vorbeck up here.'

Tighe tapped the ash from his cigarette. 'It means that I shall probably be superseded in command here by a South African – the Boer population would never stand for their troops being commanded by an Englishman – but I don't mind that at all, as long as they leave me here to carry on fighting the Germans. I have the greatest respect for those Boer chaps.

'In any case,' he continued, 'I have requested that the War Office ask Cape Town for 10,000 men as soon as possible, so that I can clear all enemy troops from the border between German and British East Africa and give us a clean start for a possible offensive. I hope we'll get them soon.'

'Glad to hear it, General. In the meantime, is there any sort of job I can do, do you think? I am anxious to be of service.'

'Well, you have been of great service already, Fonthill. Your role in knocking out the *Königsberg* has been splashed all over the papers back home and you are even more famous than you were before.' Tighe smiled. 'No doubt thanks, to a large extent, to that remarkable wife of yours, Fonthill. Please do give her my regards.'

'Of course I will.' Despite his age, Fonthill felt himself flushing. He always hated the inference that his so-called fame was due to Alice. 'I don't know about being famous – I doubt if I am – but I am seeking another job. Is there anything you might have for me, General?'

Tighe stubbed out his cigarette. 'I am afraid not at the moment, Fonthill, but leave it with me. As I have explained, things are about to change here at the top, so I am not really in a position to be of use to you. But let's see who comes in and I will certainly try to put you forward. Now, my dear fellow, if you will excuse me, I have much to do.'

The next few months were a difficult time for Simon Fonthill and his wife and comrades. Alice was denied permission to go out into the field – as were the other correspondents – and once again was trying to write strategic appreciations of the war from Mombasa, without much real idea of what was going on out in that vast bush.

237

Accordingly, she was short-tempered and began to conduct her own, abortive, search for whoever might be spying on her from within the British camp. Jenkins, with little to do, was drinking too much and on one occasion came back to the hotel with the blackest of eyes and bleeding knuckles. He had, he said, walked into a door. Mzingeli made a formal submission to Simon for permission to return to the farm in Northern Rhodesia, as a response to which Fonthill stalled awkwardly, asking for time to think about it.

For himself, Simon took to going for long, rather slow runs out into the countryside surrounding Mombasa, to get himself, he told Alice, into condition for whatever might be asked of him next. Both he and his wife took to watching out for the afternoon post in the hope of a letter from Sunil in France.

None came – he had explained that he was being trained for a big new push that was in the offing and that he would be too busy to write for a while – and so the weeks dragged by for the strangely ill-sorted quartet staying in the Empire Hotel; a quartet because Simon and Alice had insisted that they would immediately end their stay if Mzingeli was not accepted as a guest there. In the end the management conceded, but with ill grace.

Rumours abounded that a South African contingent was due to arrive soon and indeed they did in December: 2,500 men forming the 1st South African Mounted Brigade, led by Colonel Jakobus van Deventer, a giant of a man, who had been Jan Smuts's second in command during the latter's famous drive into the Union of South Africa.

Alice soon buzzed around her contacts in Tighe's staff and found that by no means all of Deventer's men were Boers. For instance, a squadron of the 1st South African Horse were British, as were the majority of the troopers in the 4th South African Horse.

'Do you know Deventer, Simon?' she asked.

Fonthill shook his head. 'Don't think I ever met him or crossed swords with him at all. Knew of him, of course. He and Smuts scared the life out of Sir John French in South Africa. French thought it was a full-blown invasion. It wasn't, but Smuts and Deventer caused a hell of a lot of trouble down in the south before the armistice.'

The arrival of the first of the South Africans lifted Fonthill's spirits and raised his hopes of gainful employment to the point where he begged Mzingeli to stay with him and Jenkins, for, if he was given some kind of 'freelance' scouting job, he knew that the tracker would be invaluable. In fact, Mzingeli – a man of very few words – confessed that he enjoyed what he called 'the soldiering' more than farming and was quite happy to stay, with the promise of action soon. As for Jenkins, after a wigging from Simon, he undertook to stop his drinking for a full month to prove that he could do it. The promise held for a full week, but Fonthill was glad that some effort, at least, had been made by his old comrade.

Their patience, however, was tried when reports came in that the South African Brigade, backing up a large British force, had been well and truly blooded when Tighe's attempt to retake Salaita had completely failed. It seemed that the British General Malleson, whom Tighe had entrusted with command, had ignored all advice and blundered in every way.

There was general relief all round, then, when Jan Smuts arrived in Mombasa in February 1916 to become commander-in-chief of all South African and British forces in British East Africa.

'But he's more of a politician than a general, surely?' Alice asked of Simon. 'He was mainly Attorney General to Kruger during the Boer War and, since then, he's been deputy prime minister. Botha did all the fighting in the South West, didn't he?'

Fonthill nodded. 'Yes. But don't underestimate Smuts. He was the best lawyer I've ever known on horseback commanding troops. He invaded South Africa with a handful of horsemen and was never captured, knocking back our chaps all the time. He's a first-class fighter. I hope to God he will have something for me.'

It was a delighted Simon, then, who received a hand-scribbled note from Smuts himself, asking him to attend his office in Mombasa the following day.

Although Fonthill had attended the armistice meetings that ended the Boer War in 1902, meeting and talking with Generals Botha and de Wet, he had somehow missed encountering the little man with the Van Dyke beard, who had so loyally supported Botha's premiership during the last decade in South Africa. Nevertheless, his welcome from the lawyer-general was warm in the extreme when they met now.

Smuts had somehow acquired a small, airless office with only a solitary fan leisurely stirring the leaden air that hung over the place. The heat and humidity were high but they did not deter the slim, erect figure that bounced up from behind his desk and bounded towards Fonthill, his hand outstretched.

'My dear Fonthill,' said Smuts. 'I have long wished to meet you.' He spoke in a high-pitched voice with only a trace of an Afrikaans accent and Fonthill remembered that he had been called to the bar in London before the war. 'In fact,' Smuts went on, 'when we could have met but didn't, I remember you were a Brigadier General. Why didn't you stay in the British army? You could have been commander-in-chief here now, instead of me, just a humble pen-pusher.'

'I think you flatter me, sir. I was a regular soldier, in fact, years ago and fought against the Zulus back in '78, but I am afraid I got disillusioned with the British army and resigned my commission. I managed, however, to carry on serving here and there in the Empire afterwards in ... what shall I say ... a more irregular role. It was Kitchener who talked me into coming back into the regular ranks for our scrap with you fellows fourteen years ago.'

'Yes, de Wet and Botha have both told me that you gave them a particularly hard time of it.'

'Well that's kind of them, but I never caught either of them, you know. Wonderful horsemen and tremendous guerrilla fighters.'

'In fact, it's what they told me about you – plus Paddy Tighe's strong recommendation – that

241

made me ask you to call in.'

Fonthill's heart leapt. A job at last! Perhaps...

'Really, sir? I am really very anxious to try and do something useful again. I have been kicking my heels here, waiting for some sort of call since the *Königsberg* some months ago now.'

'Yes, well you certainly did wonders there.' A wry smile crept over the thin lips under the grey moustache. 'It seems you managed to kick poor old King-Hall into some sort of life. Oh, by the way. Have you heard that he is to be recalled and put in command of the Scapa Flow base, up there on the cold North Sea?'

'No, I hadn't. That seems a trifle harsh, if I may say so.'

'I rather tend to agree with you. But he's lost his protector in Winston Churchill, who has been forced to resign over the Dardanelles disaster. And someone had to be blamed for all the time it took to knock over one German cruiser, given that it was hugely outnumbered.'

'Hmm. So heads are falling all over the place.'

The cold blue eyes staring into Fonthill's seemed to harden for a moment. And Simon remembered that Smuts had a reputation for possessing a brilliant, legally honed mind, which could be completely ruthless if it had to be.

'Yes, when war breaks out there is often no time to be, what shall I say? – completely fair, perhaps, in attributing blame.' The little man, looking cool and crisp in his light-grey general's uniform, despite the heat in the room, leant forward.

'It was your reputation for being, now what was your word, ah yes: "irregular" that interested me about you. You made your mark during the Boxer Rebellion in China and you impressed my colleagues who fought against you in the South African war for the way you operated like the Boers. Unlike the other soldiers of your rank and experience in the British army, you did not fight by the book. You behaved, in fact, like a Boer guerrilla, living with your men out on the veldt, travelling light with little, if any, baggage train, and attacking at dawn, out of the darkness.'

The enthusiasm in Smuts's voice was unmistakable. It sounded, felt Fonthill, as though he was being made an honorary Boer. But the general was continuing.

'You did something similar, I understand, in Tibet during that,' the faint smile came back, 'rather strange and regrettable adventure of Lord Curzon's. I am told that you formed a force of cavalry that did immense service while the main British force plodded behind you over the passes.'

Fonthill shifted uncomfortably in his chair. 'Not quite, sir. The nucleus of our cavalry arm was formed before I took command. I merely knocked it into shape.'

Smuts's smile broadened, now lightening his whole, rather austere countenance. 'That may be so, Fonthill, but now we find you popping up here in East Africa, organising the defence of a border town, taking a raiding party across Lake Victoria and now, with your equally amazing little team, turning native and showing the fleet how to sink the *Königsberg*. I have to say, my dear fellow, that you seem to be a man of many parts – and just the man I am looking for.'

Ah, thought Simon. At last he was getting to the point, after all the compliments.

'And what sort of man would that be, General?' he asked.

'Intelligence. Good intelligence. As far as I can see, that – and more reactive, quick-thinking generalship – is what has been missing in this campaign so far. Von Lettow-Vorbek has both. It's my job to improve the second, but I want you and your small team to get out into the bush, behind enemy lines if necessary, to provide the first. I will give you a roving commission' – he held up his hand – 'No, don't protest, I know you don't want to rejoin the army, I use the term loosely, I don't propose to give you a formal rank. I want you to be as irregular as you can.'

Fonthill frowned, belying the joy he felt in his heart. 'This war in East Africa,' he said, 'is being fought over a huge area, on several fronts. I will need direction on where you wish me to operate.'

For the first time, Smuts gave a sign of impatience. 'Bah,' he snorted. 'Of course I don't expect you to wander over half of Africa, trying to pin down these,' the smile returned, 'Boer-like Germans who seem to be proving so elusive. No. I am now making plans to launch a substantial attack. I can't tell you where at the moment, but I want you to be ready with your two chaps to leave at a moment's notice and get out into the bush, where I direct, and sniff out German positions.'

'That sounds fine, sir.'

'Good. Now you will answer to me on all matters of – how shall I put this? – a disciplinary nature.

But, of necessity you must provide your information to whoever I appoint to lead the attack. The general commanding in the field. Understood?'

'Of course.'

'I understand, Fonthill, that you are lucky enough to have private means and that you have not been paid so far for any of the work you and your people have done.'

'That is correct, sir.'

'Well, that seems to me to be quite unfair. So I propose that you will be paid at the level of a substantive full colonel and your man Jenkins similarly at the rank of warrant officer grade one. Your tracker will be paid according to our wages for black fellers working for us.'

'Ah.' Fonthill thought for a moment. 'That is very kind of you, sir, and although I would have been prepared to have funded the party myself, perhaps this time I must accede, since we will need some rather more expensive equipment, like modern rifles, horses etc. But my man Mzingeli is not just a black servant, you see. He is, in fact, my farm manager in Rhodesia and I value him highly. I would prefer to keep him in my employ at his present salary, if this causes you no problems.'

Smuts waved a hand. 'As you wish.' The blue eyes hardened again. 'However, you must realise, Fonthill, that what you will undertake will be dangerous in the extreme. I will expect you and your chaps to live out in the bush, travel light and be concealed at all times. If the Germans catch you, it is quite likely that they will flog your black feller to death and shoot you and Jenkins out of hand.'

'Hmm.' Fonthill frowned. 'Well,' he said, 'I don't fancy that much and I certainly wouldn't intend to be captured, anyway. I don't want us to wear uniform, which would protect us to some extent, but I would appreciate a simple letter from you appointing the three of us as army scouts. That might help if we are caught.'

'Very well. I will see to it.' The little man stood and offered his hand across the desk. 'You will have a day or two to sort yourselves out and buy some provisions. I have already prepared this chit,' he selected an army form from the mass of papers on his desk and offered it, 'giving you free choice of whatever you want – weapons, transport etc. – from the quartermaster here.'

The two men shook hands. 'I don't have to tell you, of course, that you must tell no one about this mission. Not even Mrs Fonthill,' he gave his wintry smile, 'who I understand is one of the most resourceful and intrepid of all the correspondents out here.'

'I understand, General.'

'When I have completed my plans, I shall send a highly confidential letter to you at your hotel – and I shall want you to acknowledge its safe receipt – giving you their outline and telling you where and when to report. Good luck, Fonthill, my thoughts will be with you and I know I can rely on you and your fellows.'

'Thank you. You can be sure of that, sir.'

As Simon stepped out into what seemed like the pleasant cool air of Mombasa, after the stifling humidity of Smuts's office, his heart sang. Just the sort of job he was after: a free-ranging commission with his two trusted friends and comrades, out in the bush, on their own, with no senior officer breathing down their necks. Like the *Königsberg* stunt. But without the wet feet. Jenkins would be pleased. Ideal!

Then he paused. What the hell was he going to tell Alice? She would insist on knowing about his mission and if he wasn't careful she was quite capable of coming after him again. He raised his eyes to the heavens. What a damned awkward, infuriating and wonderful wife!

Alice was waiting for him on his return, sitting in the bar by the doorway, watching for him to arrive. Jenkins was out, obviously drinking, and Mzingeli had gone for one of his 'long walks'.

She rose and clutched his arm. 'Come on,' she said. 'I can see from your eyes that you've got some sort of job. Let's have a whisky to celebrate.' She pushed him into a chair and summoned the waiter. 'Two large scotch and sodas,' she ordered. 'Now, tell me, darling. How did you get on?'

Simon sighed. It would be no good dissembling. She was as good a cross-examiner as any High Court barrister. He would have to tell her the truth – or, at least, as much as he was allowed to.

'Well,' he began, hesitatingly. 'Smuts was very flattering...'

She interrupted. 'So he jolly well should be.'

'Yes, well... He has offered me work – and 352 and Mzingeli too.'

'Ah,' she interrupted again. 'He wants Mzingeli as well, does he? That means tracking work out in the bush. I suppose,' she sighed heavily, 'that means behind enemy lines. Just the sort of stuff you three are good at, eh?'

It was Simon's turn to sigh. 'Look here, Alice. What we have been asked to do – and, to be honest, I don't know the details yet – is highly confidential. I have been sworn to secrecy by Smuts, and he particularly ordered me not to tell you anything. Neither he nor I want you trailing after us disguised as a leopard or elephant or something.'

'Hmm. Well, if I have the choice I would prefer leopard, thank you. Not some great galythumping bloody great elephant, if you please.'

'Well, he didn't exactly say that, darling. But he did say you had earned a reputation as one of the most resourceful and intrepid journalists out here. And so you are.' He sought desperately to change the subject. 'Have you had any luck in sniffing out who might be the spy who knew you had sailed on the *Calipha?*'

'No. But I have my suspicions. I might see if I can set a trap to catch him. But more of that later. Where you're going is going to be dangerous, isn't it?'

'Could be, my love. I don't know yet.'

'Of course you know,' she spluttered. The drinks arrived at just that moment, much to Simon's relief. He buried his nose in the glass. But Alice was undeterred. 'Come on, darling. You know I wouldn't say or do anything that would put you in any sort of danger. Just give me a clue about where you might be heading.'

'Sorry. Can't do that. And that, my dear, is the end of the matter.'

Alice took a deep breath but Simon was saved

by the arrival of Jenkins, walking suspiciously slowly and erect and heading, of course, straight for the bar. He hailed them.

'Private converssashion or can anyone join in?'

Simon sighed. 'It sounds as though you've had enough already. What would you like? A beer?'

'That would be very kind, bach sir. Just one small one, thank you. Where's old Jelly? I wash goin' to buy 'im a huge glass of milk.'

'He's gone walking,' said Alice. 'Sensible man – but not from bar to bar, unlike some people.'

'As smarrer o' fact, Miss Alice, very little 'as passed my lips so far today.' Then he recalled that Simon had had a very important meeting that morning. 'Ah, bach sir. You've been to see–'

Simon fluttered his hand. 'Come on, 352. Keep your voice down. I'll tell you all about it later.'

'Very good indeed, sir.' Jenkins nodded his head lugubriously. 'I shall wait in antishipation.' He raised his glass. ''Ere's to it, whatever it is.' And he drained the glass in one gulp. Then he got to his feet, a trifle unsteadily. 'If you'll both excush me, I think I'll go and 'ave a bit of a lie down, see. Sun's got to me a bit, I think.' Alice and Simon watched him walk away, his gait suspiciously slow and his bearing stiff and artificial.

'The sooner I can get him out of here, the better,' said Simon, shaking his head.

'I know you can't tell me what you will be up to, darling,' said Alice, leaning forward and putting her hand on her husband's knee. 'But can you tell me when you might be going?'

'Sorry, love. I just don't know. Smuts is going to write to me. Within the next couple of days, I should think.'

She nodded slowly. 'Well thank you for that.' She drained her glass and gave him a mischievous grin. 'Shall we go up now, then...?'

The invitation was implicit. 'Very well, my love. But don't come all Mata Hari with me.' He grinned. 'Oh, I don't know. You could try, of course.'

Smuts's letter came two days later, carried by a young subaltern who insisted on having a receipt for it. Luckily, Alice was away on some nefarious expedition of her own, so Simon was able to put it in his pocket and open it in the safety of their room.

The letter was straight to the point. 'I intend to launch a full-scale attack within the next three weeks to clear our border with German East Africa and to remove once and for all any threat of invasion,' he wrote. 'Stewart will advance with the 1st Division across the border, take Longido and then attack Nagasseni Hill, to the west of Kilimanjaro. I shall be attacking on other fronts, too, and Stewart should meet me at Moshi, to the north-west of Taveta. But this need not concern you. I want you to get out in front of Stewart as soon as possible – there are semi-desert conditions there, with limited water and little cover. So take care. I want you to assess the German positions and report back to Stewart as soon as possible, as he advances. Get as much detail as you can: will he need heavy guns to dislodge the enemy from their positions and so on? Move quickly. Good luck.'

Fonthill read the letter again. Good. Kilimanjaro

meant the Taveta Front on the northern edge of German East Africa, near the frontier, only about 200 miles from Mombasa. A comparatively short distance in this vast territory. But if Smuts intended to attack within three weeks then the three of them had to get a move on. Luckily, they were already well equipped, their horses, provisions and rifles held at the barracks so as not to attract attention at the hotel. Now, he rose, where the hell were Jenkins and Mzingeli?

The next day they took a train to the north-west bound for the small town of Kio, still some seventy-five miles from the frontier. Alice had seen them off, tears in her eyes, but making no attempt to plead with him again. There was fuss in getting the horses, plus one pack mule, into the freight carrier at the back but all was completed and the three settled down, Fonthill sharing with his two comrades the old copy of a map of northern German East Africa that Smuts's office had provided for him.

Simon pointed to the large open spaces of the map immediately south and west of Kilimanjaro. 'You're going to be key to this operation, Mzingeli,' he said. 'This looks like the desert territory Smuts told me about. There's not much cover there and we probably will be able to be spotted from miles away if the Germans have patrols out. We are going to need you and your sixth sense to warn us of trouble on the way.'

Mzingeli gave one of his rare smiles. 'I got no sixth sense, *Nkosi* – whatever that means. Perhaps I should go on ahead of you when we get there.

One man less easy to spot in that country than three, particularly if he can merge into background. I good at that.'

'Good idea. As far as I can see, you're good at most things.'

'Trouble is,' Jenkins intervened. ''E's no bloody good at all at drinkin'. You drink too much milk, Jelly. It's bad for the constip, consput...'

'Constitution?' offered Simon.

'That's just what I was goin' to say. It's bad for you. Makes you moo like a cow.'

The tracker showed his great white teeth again but did not reply.

They had to ride the seventy-odd miles to the border from the rail station, where they were told that the frontier was comparatively unmarked – the odd signpost or border stone, but little else. But both sides regularly patrolled their own sides of the border, of course, so Fonthill decided to cross at night.

Before doing so, as the sun descended to their left, the three of them stood at a border signpost, which announced in German that the colony began at that point, while Fonthill scanned the territory beyond with his field glasses. The country looked very unwelcoming: sand and gravel, dotted with low cactus and other miserable-looking stunted bushes and a few trees. To the south rose the intimidating peak of Kilimanjaro, but until then the plain seemed to stretch out with few undulations.

'Nowhere to 'ide, bach sir,' observed Jenkins, frowning. 'What do we say if we are nabbed?'

'I don't intend to get nabbed,' said Fonthill,

slowly twirling the focus wheel on his binoculars. 'If we do get spotted – and on this plain we should be able to see trouble coming from some way ahead, dust on the horizon is a dead giveaway – we either run for it or fight our way out.'

'Perhaps we should travel in the dark?' offered Mzingeli.

'No. Trouble with that is we could stumble into a German patrol so easily. And, anyway, to do our job I shall need to know exactly where we are going.' He put down the glasses. 'We'll eat now and cross over in two hours' time.'

They did so without incident, Fonthill setting a course to the south-west by the light of his illuminated compass. They stopped after two hours, lighting no fire but tethering the horses and allowing them to eat the poor yellow grass that poked its head up above the sand. Fonthill set a three hours' watch, taking the first turn as the other two huddled gratefully into their sleeping bags.

They were up at dawn, watering the horses and setting out. This time, however, Mzingeli rode on ahead with the compass after Fonthill had shown him the bearing until he was a black dot in the distance. 'Must keep him in sight, otherwise we shall lose him,' said Simon to Jenkins.

'Blimey. Let's not lose 'im. I'll get lost in this bloody place in no time.'

The sun beat down on them unrelentingly as they plodded on, keeping the tiny figure of the tracker just in sight ahead of them at all times, but with Fonthill regularly scanning the horizons with his field glasses on either side and behind them as he rode.

Even so, it was Jenkins who gave the alarm first. 'I think old Jelly is riding back to us, bach sir,' he said shielding his eyes to gaze ahead. 'Can you put your glasses on 'im?'

'Yes, you're right.' Fonthill adjusted the focus to look beyond Mzingeli. He could see nothing but – perhaps – a cloud of dust. He put down the glasses and looked around.

'It looks as though Mzingeli is riding fast. That means he has been seen. I don't fancy making a run for it and leaving him behind. At the moment, we must be out of sight of his pursuers. So ... 352, leave your horse here but take your rifle and take cover behind that low tree over there. It won't hide you completely, so you'll have to scrape a depression in the sand. Don't fire unless I give you the signal. I will just put my hand in the air, like this. Go quickly now, before you get spotted.'

'An' what will you do?'

'Stay here and try and argue my way out of it. But be prepared to shoot to kill if you have to. I will do the same. I've got my revolver tucked under my shirt.'

Fonthill walked unhurriedly to his horse – he did not know yet whether he was in binocular sight of the Germans – and casually threw a blanket over the modern British rifle in its saddle holster. Then he sauntered back to a rock protruding from the sand, perched on it and took a drink from his canteen, while raising his field glasses.

Yes, he could see the Germans now, riding fast

behind Mzingeli, raising a dust cloud more visibly now. He tucked the glasses into the sand at the base of the rock and pushed them down out of sight, eased the revolver under his shirt and sat and waited.

Mzingeli thundered to a halt and shouted: 'Germans behind me, *Nkosi*. Can you not see them?'

'Yes, old chap. I can see them. How many, three or four?'

'Four and they see me. I could not ... what? ... "meld" in time. Sorry *Nkosi*. Why did you not ride away? And where is Jenkins bach?'

'I did not want to leave you to fight them alone. And 352 is behind that tree over there. Don't get between him and our visitors. I shall try and talk my way out, but if that fails, Jenkins will fire when I raise my left arm vertically. That means we must attack, too. So be ready.'

'Very good, *Nkosi*. I sit and wait with you.'

Mzingeli dismounted, keeping his rifle with him, but sliding a cartridge into the breech and removing the safety catch. He tethered his steaming horse and sat down, seemingly unconcerned, on the sand beside Fonthill, his rifle at his side, the stock and barrel half-covered with sand.

Within minutes the German patrol had galloped up. There were, indeed, four of them, all black askaris, the most feared troops in East Africa, wearing fezes and pointing their Mausers at the two men on the ground.

The sergeant dismounted warily, not letting the muzzle of his rifle drop for a moment.

He looked at Fonthill angrily, his forehead

dripping sweat, and shouted at him in German. Simon stood easily, shrugged his shoulders, held out his hands in supplication and said: *'Nein spraken ze Duetch. Me Portugesa. Portugesa.'*

The sergeant hurled imprecations in German again, stepped forward and slapped Simon hard across the face. At the same time, the other askaris began to dismount. It was just the opportunity that Fonthill had been waiting for. In administering the slap, the sergeant had dropped the muzzle of his rifle and the others were engaged in dismounting.

Simon raised his left hand and immediately looked to the sky. The sergeant could not resist following his gaze, allowing Fonthill a split second to withdraw his revolver and fire it into the broad chest of the soldier less than a foot away from him. At the same time, Jenkins's rifle fired twice, bringing down two of the askaris and, firing from the hip from where he sat, Mzingeli killed the fourth of the party.

Amazingly it was all over within seconds and, half in awe, Simon gazed at the four bodies sprawled inertly on the sand while their horses, startled by the shooting, galloped away before idly beginning to crop the yellow grass beneath them.

'Good shootin', lads,' called Jenkins, rising arthritically from behind his tree. 'I wasn't sure we could get 'em all before they got you two.'

'Good shooting yourself, 352,' called Fonthill. But he felt nausea rise in his throat as he watched the blood ooze and form rapidly draining pools in the sand. 'Dammit,' he half-whispered. 'I wish we hadn't had to kill all of them. I'm getting a bit fed up with all this killing – and we haven't even started yet.'

Mzingeli laid a hand on his arm. '*Nkosi,*' he said softly, 'I remember how you did not want to kill sleeping lion all those years ago in Matabeleland. You thought, like good hunters do, it was unfair to kill while he sleep. But these askaris are bad men. They would kill us – see how he hit you. Next step would be pointing gun and firing. We did right.'

Jenkins had joined them now. 'Old Jelly's right, bach sir,' he said. 'It's war, look you. Kill or be killed. It's a fair bugger all right and even I am not too 'appy with doin' 'em in cold blood, so to speak, and I've been killin' people all me life. But it 'ad to be done. Now, what do you want to do with the bodies, like?'

Fonthill sighed and looked at the four horizons. He could see no sign of life anywhere on that arid plain. To the south-west the foothills of the great mountain were wooded but nothing stirred on the desert leading to them. 'I'm afraid we're going to have to bury them,' he sighed. 'If their bodies are found then other patrols will know that we are in the territory and come actively looking for us. Trouble is,' he frowned, 'that means killing the horse, too, for the same reason.'

'Ah no, sir!' Jenkins had been brought up on a farm in North Wales and was a horse-lover as well as a superb horseman. 'Can't we just bury the bridle and saddles, slap 'em on the arse and let 'em go?'

Fonthill shot a glance at Mzingeli. The tracker, now a farmer, of course, was looking down but he was nodding in slow agreement. Simon took a deep breath.

'No. We can't risk it. There are no wild horses on this plain and they are bound to have cavalry markings on them. We must leave no trace here.'

Jenkins made one last appeal. 'But, look, bach sir, we ain't got no shovels. It'll take us hours to do all that diggin'.'

'Then we will use our bayonets and hands. Shouldn't be too difficult in this sand and gravel.' He gulped. 'Neither of you need to kill the horses. I will do that. Let's start.'

It was hard work, for the earth was more gravel than sand and the sun beat down on them relentlessly, causing them to perspire prodigiously, their sweat dropping into the depressions they were scooping out. Fonthill kept scanning the horizons, but it seemed they were alone on that vast plain. Eventually, realising that he could no longer put off the unpleasant task of killing the horses, he left the others to carry on digging and walked over to the askaris' mounts, whistling to them softly through parched lips. They were, in fact, poor beasts, their ribs beginning to show through their matted sides – a reflection of the difficulty the Germans must be having at finding suitable horses for their cavalry.

He killed the first two quickly, with his revolver, but, before he could turn, the others took fright and galloped away.

'Damn!' Their own horses had drifted away a little and he thought about galloping after the German mounts but realised they would be difficult to catch now and, head down, he rejoined the others.

Jenkins looked up, his face streaming with perspiration. 'Now what are we goin' to do? Just let 'em go?'

'No.' Fonthill turned to Mzingeli. 'I hate to ask you, but they are still galloping, so it will probably be a tracking job. Will you please track them down and finish them off? They mustn't escape. We will finish here.'

Wearily, the black man nodded and retrieved his horse, mounted and cantered away.

It was an hour before he returned. He dismounted and called to Simon: 'I could not bury them, but I pushed sand on them and found stones to put on top. I think no one find them.' Then he looked up. '*Nkosi*, I think these give us away.'

Fonthill dashed the sweat from his eyes and followed Mzingeli's gaze. High above, vultures were circling in ominous spirals. He then remembered, of course, that they could see or at least sense a kill from miles away and would congregate above the corpses within minutes and wait on high to make sure that they were dead before landing to make their pickings. They were a dead giveaway that a killing had been made.

He shrugged. 'Can't be helped. Do they uncover corpses when they are buried?'

'No. I don't think so.'

'Good. Thank you for doing that miserable job. We are almost finished now. I want to get out of here well before nightfall.'

Jenkins called, 'Do you want to save the Mausers?'

'No. I don't want us to be linked to these chaps in any way, so bury them. And, in any case, our Lee Enfields are just as good, if not better.'

Within the half-hour they were able to smooth the sand, retrieve the horses and ride away. Looking back, Fonthill could see no signs at all that four men and two horses had been slain on the site. He shook his head but the little party rode on, going north and then north-west roughly parallel to the border, until he called a halt and they camped for the night.

They risked a small fire, for darkness prompted a severe drop in temperature and they were not only cold but hungry after all the exertions of the day. By the soft glow of the flames, Simon took out his map and examined it. His orders were to precede General Stewart on his advance to Nagasseni to the west of Kilimanjaro and all day they had been skirting around the mountain that stood ahead of them. The trouble was, Fonthill was not exactly sure of their position now. This damned desert was so featureless. It was some days yet before Stewart could begin his advance, so they had time. But not much of it. They must travel faster the next day to reach the German positions to the west of the mountain in time for them to scout them and report back to Stewart. He crawled into his sleeping bag with a worried frown on his face.

They rose before dawn again and, once more, Mzingeli cantered ahead until he was almost out of sight. They skirted laboriously round the great mass of Kilimanjaro and Fonthill thanked his lucky stars that he had the great mountain towering into the sky as his landmark. Even so, he felt vulnerable on this semi-desert, flat, open plain. He knew that, to prevent being surprised, he and Jenkins should split and spread out but he knew that the Welshman would unintentionally explore every possible way of drifting away from his companion and getting well and truly lost, so that was out of the question.

They rode on during the heat of the day, being careful not to gallop or even canter to prevent raising dust. They were forced to nurse their supplies of water for they passed no wells or oases, but eventually they turned north again towards the hill of Nagasseni and behind it the rise that was the little town of Longido – hardly more than a dot on Fonthill's map – and, well outside its straggling perimeter, they camped that night on the wooded slopes of its hill.

During the course of the day, although they had seen no sign of any living thing apart from a few snakes and desert rats, they had crossed two sets of horse tracks, obviously German patrols, so Fonthill ordered no fire to be lit.

'We are well and truly in German territory now,' he said, 'and those patrols were most likely based in Longido or Nagasseni, where there is bound to be water.'

'Ah good,' beamed Jenkins. 'Can we nip in and get a drop durin' the night, d'yer think?'

'No. Too risky. Take a sip or two of water and a couple of biscuits and turn in. You take first watch, 352, and I'll do the middle stint. We will need all the sleep we can get.'

The night was uneventful and once again they

rose at dawn. Fonthill walked through the trees to look down on Longido, which seemed deserted, so he risked lighting a small fire so that they could make coffee and eat dried biltong.

'I would like to take a look at Longido,' said Fonthill, kicking sand to extinguish the embers of their fire, 'but I daren't risk the three of us riding in. I want to know if there are any German troops based there. I hate to ask you, Mzingeli, but you are the one who will most easily merge into the populace.'

The tracker nodded his tightly curled white-haired head. 'I go, *Nkosi*. Better I walk down than ride on good horse.'

'Absolutely. I will keep my glasses on you as best I can and if I see you get into trouble we will come and get you out. Just amble, don't hurry.'

'I get into no trouble and I happy to amble.' He grinned, slipped off his shirt, discarded his riding boots and, from his saddlebag, pulled out a pair of old slippers that natives wore.

'I can see no trenches dug to protect the town from this side,' said Fonthill, 'but see if there are any on the other side. And look out, of course, for German barracks. We need to try and assess how many are garrisoned there, if any.'

'Very good, *Nkosi*.' And he shuffled away.

Jenkins watched him go with a faint smile stretching his great moustache. 'That bloke is worth 'is weight in gold, look you,' he murmured. 'We'd be a bit lost without 'im, I think, bach sir.'

Simon nodded. 'Absolutely. Salt of the earth.'

'Oh, bugger it!'

'What's the matter?'

262

'We could 'ave asked 'im to bring two or three bottles of beer back with 'im, couldn't we?'

'Mzingeli doesn't drink. He wouldn't know what to ask for.'

Jenkins lifted his eyes to the heavens. 'It's 'is only fault. That's the trouble with bringing with us a tracker who's completely teetotal. With respect, bach sir, you should 'ave thought of that when we started out.'

'Oh, do shut up.'

Mzingeli was away for just under three hours and Fonthill was beginning to worry, when his glasses picked him out as he suddenly appeared from the end of one of the streets that petered out on the edge of the town. He rejoined them within ten minutes.

'Any trouble?' asked Fonthill anxiously.

'No, *Nkosi.*'

Jenkins pulled a face. 'I don't suppose you thought to bring back a bottle or two of beer, did yer?'

Mzingeli's features seemed carved out of stone. 'No, Jenkins bach. I don't drink beer. Terrible stuff.'

The Welshman turned his melancholy countenance to Fonthill. 'There you are, you see. What did I say?'

'Oh, give it a rest. Now, old chap, tell me what you've learnt.'

The black man extended a long finger and drew a circle in the dust. 'Town don't seem to have any proper defences,' he said. 'But some trenches have been dug here, on north side of town, opposite British border. Just recently, by look of it. They

263

not finished. Easy to out ... out ... what is the word?'

'Outflank.'

'Yes outflank. Easy to get round.'

'Good. What about troops?'

'Yes, there is big barracks on other side of town. Cavalry, because there are many stables. Nobody there at moment but one of the Masai who work in stables tell me that–'

Fonthill interrupted. 'You were not suspected, I hope?'

'No, *Nkosi*. I said I was interested in getting work there at stables. Man tell me that there are five German companies there. Even told me name of boss man: Major Fischer, spelt with a "c".'

'Splendid work, Mzingeli.' Simon's smile was all-embracing. 'Where are Major Fischer with a "c" and his companies now?'

'Out on patrol. This time to the north. They think big attack is coming from British across the border. They expecting it. That's why they dig trenches. They patrol all the time.'

Fonthill's frown replaced his grin. 'Damn! Our security is as leaky as a bloody sieve. Alice is right. There must be a spy or spies in the British camp in Mombasa. They know what we're going to do before we do.'

Jenkins pulled at his moustache. ''Ow many men in a German cavalry company, then, bach sir?'

'I don't know because I suspect that they are nothing like our squadrons. Enough to cause Stewart problems, anyway, when he begins his

264

march across the border, which is wooded and broken up on this part, and then the desert.' He held out his hand to Mzingeli. 'You have done splendid work, old chap, and I shall see that the general hears about it.'

'Ah, it was nothing, *Nkosi*. Most difficult part was stealing this from bar in town.' And, with a great smile, he produced a native beer bottle from his tattered knapsack and handed it to Jenkins. 'Sorry, *Nkosi,* I felt it dangerous to take more than one. But Jenkins bach's need is greater than ours, I think.'

Jenkins's grin was like the moon coming up on a dark night. He solemnly accepted the bottle, wrested the stopper off with his teeth and took a deep swig. Then he carefully wiped the top and handed it back to Mzingeli.

'You, old Jelly, are a gentleman, my dear old bach. But share and share alike. I've taken the first drink to see if it's all right for you two, now I insist you take a swig. No. Go on. I insist. We share and share alike on this postin'. Go on. Take it.'

Mzingeli looked at Fonthill in despair but Simon kept a perfectly straight face and nodded. 'Old regimental custom,' he said. 'We share and share alike on this posting.'

With a frown that wrinkled his nose as well as his brow, the black man took the bottle, slowly raised it to his mouth and took a tentative sip. Then he gulped, gurgled, spat out the beer and thrust the bottle back at Jenkins. 'It is terrible, bach mate,' he coughed. 'Awful.'

'Good lord.' Jenkins was clearly shocked to the core. 'That was a terrible waste, that was, spittin'' it out, see. I wish I'd never offered now, look you. In fact, it was a court martial offence. Now, bach sir.' He offered the bottle to Simon. 'Show old Jelly 'ere what it means to be a real soldier.'

Fonthill took the bottle, refrained from wiping its mouth and took a sip. It was, without doubt, foul. But he maintained his equanimity and swallowed it. 'That will do for me, thank you, 352.' He handed the bottle back. 'Now we have shared and shared alike, but I think your need is greater than ours. So you finish it.'

'Thank you, bach sir.' Solemnly he lifted the bottle, tipped it back and emptied its contents in two seconds. Wiping his mouth, he nodded. 'Thank you both, particularly you, Jelly. Very kind to think of us.' He looked across at Simon. 'What now, bach sir? Do we ride down and empty the bar, d'yer think?'

'No. I think not. I want to ride back to the frontier, the way that Stewart will advance, and see if I can get a glimpse of Major Fischer's companies without getting caught by him. I also want to spy out the territory between here and the border so that the general will know what to expect. But we must move quickly. I want to put miles between us and this place before we stop for the night. Come on.'

They rode away, breaking cover out of the woods with care, before taking to the desert again, once again heading virtually due north. Once again they could not travel fast for fear of sending up a dust cloud that could be visible for miles with anyone carrying field glasses. But once, far to their right, they saw just such a cloud, travelling as far as

Fonthill could see, parallel to them. They dismounted and took whatever cover they could find in the stunted scrub until the danger was past, then they continued riding until dusk when they made camp.

It was still open, desert country and Fonthill felt that they dare not light a fire, for a clear flame could be seen for miles in such territory. So, once again, they bedded down, cold and hungry, taking turns to stand watch until dawn.

For another full day they rode, once more seeing dust clouds, this time behind them, until they had to pick their way through wooded, fissured ground and, at last, had crossed the border, where in the distance they could see what could only be the many campfires of General Stewart's column, glimmering in the dusk.

'Thank God,' croaked Jenkins. 'I can smell army beer at last.'

'Do you know, Jenkins bach,' nodded Mzingeli earnestly, 'I think I can as well.'

They were challenged by Stewart's pickets and quickly ushered to the general's tent. Stewart was sitting at a table finishing his dinner with his ADC at his side, both dressed in the smart, all-green of the Gurkha Regiment, a decanter of wine and two glasses by their plates.

The general rose immediately, threw down his napkin and advanced towards Fonthill, meeting him at the tent opening, his hand outstretched.

'My dear Fonthill,' he said, 'my apologies for not organising a meeting between us before you set out. Now come in – yes, all three of you – and have a glass of wine and tell me what you know.

Have you eaten?'

'No, General, your pickets have brought me straight here. We've been riding for two days. These are my chaps, Warrant Officer Jenkins here,' he indicated the Welshman, who immediately sprang to attention and delivered a guards-like salute, 'and Mzingeli, formerly my farm manager and the best tracker in all Africa.' The general shook hands with both men, Mzingeli inclining his head in some confusion. He had never met a general before.

'Delighted to meet both of you,' said Stewart, 'particularly you, 352. You're almost as famous as Fonthill here.'

'Thank you, bach sir,' said Jenkins, grinning broadly.

Stewart turned back to Fonthill. 'By all means dismiss your chaps and Major McCloud here will see that they get something to eat and organise sleeping for all of you. But, if you are not too tired, I would be grateful if you would give me your report here and now. We have wine and I will summon up something for you to eat.' He nodded to Jenkins and Mzingeli. 'Goodnight, gentlemen.'

Fonthill, delighted at meeting such courtesy from a general directed to a black man, nodded to his comrades who smiled back and left in the company of the major. Then he remembered that Stewart was a Gurkha, universally popular and famed for handling his native troops with kindness and understanding.

Reheated stew and bread was quickly brought and his glass was filled with excellent claret. 'When do you advance, General?' he asked.

268

'Shortly after dawn tomorrow, that's why I am so glad you pushed on to meet us before we set off. Now, tell me, have you any idea if there are any German troops nearby who are likely to contest my advance?'

'Yes.' He shovelled a spoonful of stew into his mouth – only lukewarm now but very, very welcome. 'There are at least five enemy companies – cavalry, almost certainly – who are patrolling the country between here and Nagasseni. The cavalry probably number about five hundred but they will know the terrain like the backs of their hands. They are commanded by an officer of major rank, called Fischer.'

Stewart nodded gravely. 'Yes, I've heard of him. Good soldier by all accounts.'

'You have some eighty miles of rotten country to traverse between here and Longido,' Fonthill continued. 'It's steppe country with no water and little cover. It's dusty and dry and you will have to carry your water with you.'

Simon took another mouthful. 'We believe that Fischer knows you are coming and from which direction. We suspect there is an active spy working in Mombasa sending back privileged information to the Germans.'

'Humph!' Stewart wrinkled his nose. 'We've been massing here for quite a few days now. It would have been a miracle if the news of our presence hadn't crossed the border. But pray continue, my dear fellow.'

'Incidentally, sir, most of this information was picked up by Mzingeli, my tracker. He risked his life to enter Longido and sniff around. He deserves your commendation, if I may say so.'

The general made a note. 'He shall get it. Now, take me back to the country we must cross.'

'The desert. It's pretty terrible to cross: blistering heat, gravel and sand to make soft-going, no cover and absolutely no waterholes that we could see. But I doubt if Fischer will attack you here, because you will have ample warning of his coming. You can see for miles across the desert.'

'Hmm. Go on.'

'Longido itself shouldn't be difficult to take. There are some half-finished trenches on the northern, i.e. the border side, but it should be easy to outflank them. There are no walls to hinder your attack, so you should not need your artillery to besiege the place. I believe the cavalry to be based there.

'After Longido, you will be in trouble again with the terrain. It's completely arid, semi-desert, steppe, with no water. Most of the men will be advancing in a thick cloud of dust, marching or riding, and they will be parched. It's about thirty miles-odd of this sort of travelling to reach Nagasseni Hill. This means that your lines of communication will be exposed.'

'Quite so. Pray continue.'

'As I understand it, your orders are to approach the town of Geragua in the foothills of Kilimanjaro and then to march on to Moshi to link up with Smuts. Well, this is rough country of a different sort, wooded and broken with ravines and hills, which will make it difficult to bring up your guns. My guess is that it will be here that Fischer – and maybe others – will attack you.'

'Anything else?'

'That's about it, sir. We weren't given much notice by General Smuts of your advance, so we had to move quickly and not linger.' He put down his spoon and drained his glass. 'I would think that the worst part of your advance will be in the broken country just across the border.'

Stewart leant across and filled his glass from the decanter. 'You've done remarkably well, Fonthill. And I am most grateful. Now, finish your wine and look for McCloud to see where you are to sleep. I would think it will probably have to be a sleeping bag in the officers' mess – that's the big tent on the left, just outside. You will probably find him there.'

The general raised his glass to him and Fonthill reciprocated. 'I benefited from your work at Bukoba and didn't get a chance to thank you there. I have always heard that you were the best scout the British army ever had in its ranks – as a uniformed scout, that is – and you've certainly proved it out here. Now, get you to bed. We march soon after dawn.'

'Very good, sir. Goodnight.'

CHAPTER ELEVEN

It had been some time since Fonthill had experienced the sounds and smells of an army awakening and limbering into life, preparing to face the enemy: the bugles piercing the predawn, the delicious odour of coffee freshly made, the orders screamed by non-commissioned officers and the snorts of horses and mules and the creaking of harnesses.

'Ha,' said Jenkins. 'Ain't it great to be back in the army again? What could be better, eh, bach sir? Actually, when I think of it, I could suggest about a thousand things, mind you.'

'Well, at least we had a good night's sleep at last. Come on, we need to ride out ahead of the advance and get out of the dust.'

Stewart had pushed his cavalry pickets out ahead of the vanguard of his division, of course, and Fonthill chose to ride out ahead of them. If the Germans were out there, waiting, he argued, three men riding quickly would be far better placed to sniff them out than cavalry troops, raising the dust.

It was back to the desert for them, stiflingly hot, and Simon was surprised to see the leading picket troop riding up to them by mid afternoon. 'Are we being recalled?' he asked the subaltern in command.

'Good lord, no,' said the lieutenant. 'We are being pushed on by the general. The old man is setting a blistering pace. I gather he wants to get to this place – what's it called...'

'Longido.'

'That's the spot, a day before he is supposed to. To impress our new boss, Smuts, I suppose. Sorry, old boy, but you'd better ride out faster, or the general's rearguard will overtake both of us.'

'Good lord.' Fonthill wiped his brow. 'He can't have men advancing in field service marching order in this heat – and with little water. He must be mad.'

'To be frank, old man, I think all generals are mad. At least, ours are. Better push on or we'll have to ride through you.'

Simon dug in his spurs and urged the others on, despite their protests. They rode back just before dusk to rejoin the main army for the night – it was the pickets' jobs to stand guard out in the desert. The next two days and nights were a repetition of the first and, true to Fonthill's word, Stewart was able to take Longido without any trouble. He immediately pressed on and reached the little town of Geragua in the wooded western foothills of Mount Kilimanjaro by 8th March. It had been a remarkable march, but it had taken its toll in terms of the effects of heat exhaustion and thirst on his men.

And it was here, when his division could hardly put one foot before the other, that he met Fischer. It was, inevitably, Mzingeli, who was letting his horse find its own way as they entered the trees and declivities of the foothills, who first caught the flash of sunlight reflected from brass harness.

'German cavalry ahead,' he reported to Fonthill. 'They waiting to ambush main column, I think.'

'Right. You go to the left and 352 to the right. Both of you keep me in sight in the middle. I want to get some idea of the size of the enemy. Don't take risks. See how widely they stretch ahead.'

They returned to him within minutes.

'They lined up on edge of woods, right across there,' reported Mzingeli, pointing.

'About the same to the right,' said Jenkins.

'Hmmm. That's a front of, what, about four hundred yards. This must be Fischer's cavalry retreating before us and waiting to pounce. All of five hundred men. Better ride back and report to Stewart.'

The general nodded wearily when they found him at the head of his column. His horse's head was down and perspiration was pouring down his face. Fonthill sighed when he looked at the line of men plodding behind him, none of them looking in a fit condition to fight. Stewart's effort to impress his commander-in-chief with the speed of his march – if that's what it was – had sadly misfired.

Stewart turned to his ADC. 'Jock, ride back quickly and get battalion commanders to deploy their men to receive a cavalry charge. Infantry are to form squares behind whatever cover they can find. Cavalry are to form a screen ahead of the column, between here and those woods half a mile ahead. Artillery are to load with shrapnel. Off you go.'

But he was too late. Before McCloud could dig in his spurs, the leading pickets were riding back across the plain from the edge of the woods. Close behind them thundered two companies of Major Fischer's command, spreading out in an arc to take the long file of the advancing British column at its head and sides.

Yet they did not charge. Instead, maintaining their arc, they dismounted, knelt and, raising their carbines, delivered a crushing volley into the ranks of the British, who hardly had time to raise their own rifles to respond. Tired men fell all around Fonthill, Jenkins and Mzingeli as the three dismounted and did their best to return the fire that came in from both sides.

A hoarse command in German rose from the enemy and they launched a second volley into the torn ranks before them. More men at the head of the column fell, but some sort of retaliatory fire was now beginning to emerge from their tattered ranks. In addition, men from the middle and rear of the column were jogging forward, firing as they came. It was enough for the Germans. Another command was given and, with impeccable discipline, the black askaris mounted their steeds, turned and rode away, back to the woods ahead of them.

A thunder of hooves from the rear of the column showed that Stewart's cavalry had belatedly mounted and had summoned up their own charge, joined by the mounted pickets. But their horses were clearly exhausted and the gap between the two sets of cavalry widened quickly, until the British were forced to halt and lead their gasping mounts back to the column. The Germans disappeared out of sight, still galloping, round the southern edge of the wood.

General Stewart mopped his brow, wearily replaced his revolver in its holster, and gave Fonthill a sad smile. 'What a capital cock-up!' he exclaimed. 'We were caught short, I'm afraid. Caught very short.' He gazed around him at the figures, some twitching and moaning, some lying inert on the sand. He lifted his voice. 'Bugler. Sound for stretcher-bearers. Bring up the doctors.'

Fonthill turned to his comrades. 'Are you two all right?'

Jenkins grunted and examined a tear in his sleeve. 'Just missed me. We was bloody lucky, look you. They were firin' at what I'd say was point-blank range.' He raised a puzzled frown to Simon. 'Why didn't they charge us, bach sir? Ain't that what cavalry are supposed to do to infantry?'

Stewart raised his head from where, with his dirk, he was attempting to cut away the sleeve of a wounded man. 'I would say that they were not proper cavalry,' he said, 'more mounted infantry. Not trained to use sabres – and, from what I could see, not even equipped with them. But they could shoot, all right. Here, man, give me a hand with this bandage, will yer.'

Later, camp was set up on the open plain and the column licked its wounds. Only three of the askaris had been brought down by British fire but six times that number had been either killed or wounded at the head of the line.

'It could have been worse,' murmured Stewart as, later, he sipped tea with his staff and Fonthill in the semi-darkness round a campfire. 'They were very well handled. I had heard that this man Fischer was good. Well, I shall be better prepared the next time we meet.'

He turned to Simon. 'I am mounting extra guards tonight but I intend to let the column rest tomorrow. But first thing in the morning, Fonthill, I want to go out with you and your scouts and a squadron of cavalry to examine the ground ahead.' He gave a rueful smile. 'You warned me that it would be where Fischer would attack, I should have taken more care. But I want to see whether it would be better to continue the advance without the artillery and cavalry. It doesn't sound the sort of territory for them and I don't want to be delayed. So we set off at dawn. Now let's all get some sleep. We deserve it, although I'm not looking forward to the despatch I must send off to Smuts. Goodnight, gentlemen.'

General Stewart's reconnaissance the next morning showed no sign of the enemy. It did, however, show that the way ahead was difficult in the extreme, with thick woods, ravines and rocky outcrops. Yet if he had to reach Moshi in time to link up with Smuts before the rains came, then there was no way he could detour to find more acceptable country. He decided his cavalry – this was no place for horses – and his artillery would have to be left behind under guard while he pressed on with his infantry.

It was at this point that a message was received from Smuts ordering Fonthill and his two comrades to press on to assist General Tighe's assault on Latema and Reata Hills: the nek between them was occupied by the enemy who threatened Smuts's own advance on Moshi.

'It will be dangerous country you will be riding through,' said Stewart, gripping Fonthill's hand. 'It looks to me as though the Germans will be retreating from the Taveta front and you could well run into them. Not to mention our old friend Fischer, who is out there somewhere. So take great care. I will see you in Moshi – I hope.'

'No doubt about it, General. Good luck.'

At first, the broken nature of the territory provided excellent cover for the three and they rode as fast as the ground allowed them, without the constant need to scan the horizons. They rode in all for some sixty miles, taking to the plain and giving Moshi a wide berth and meeting no opposition as they turned north towards Taveta. They were eventually met by British outriders at the foot of the nek that connected the two hills.

'Who is in command?' called Fonthill.

'General Malleson,' came the reply.

'Oh, bloody 'ell,' swore Jenkins. ''E's useless.'

Malleson's task was difficult. The Germans were known to hold the nek in force and dislodging them meant taking the two hills, which rose some 700 feet above the plain. Easier said than done, for the hills rose steeply and were covered in bush and rocks.

On their arrival at noon, Fonthill found that Malleson had ordered forward 1,500 troops in broad daylight to climb the hills under withering fire. The men were completely pinned down and unable to advance an inch. On enquiring where he could find General Malleson, Fonthill was told that the general had left the field shortly after giving the order to attack suffering from dysentery and that General Tighe had taken command.

'Glad to have you, Fonthill,' said the Irishman. 'Now that Malleson has gone – Smuts's choice for command, by the way, not mine – I've been told to take those two bloody hills by frontal attack. You stay out of it for the moment. I will need you later if I fail.'

'I don't want to interfere, General, but getting

278

up there in broad daylight sounds impossible. The men sent up by Malleson have already been wiped out, by the look of it.'

'Nevertheless, I've been ordered to attack. I'm throwing in my reserve of Northern Rhodesians – they're stout fellers – and I've asked Smuts for reinforcements. Now, go and get some rest after your long ride.'

But the three could never rest as they watched as Tighe's men began to climb the heights under heavy fire in daylight. For five hours the attackers scrambled up from the slopes below and then were forced to relinquish the ground they had gained each time.

Tighe recalled his troops and decided on a bayonet attack on the summits after dark. Fonthill obtained permission for he, Jenkins and Mzingeli to press forward in the van.

'That's all very well, bach sir,' said Jenkins, 'but I've always 'eard you say that night attacks are very dangerous. If we lose dear old Jelly 'ere, we'll never find our way anywhere, see.'

'You're right, but I want to sniff what it's like up there, even though it's dark. We're supposed to be scouts, after all. Come on. Fix those bayonets.'

Amazingly, some of the attackers did reach the ridge and hold it for a while but Jenkins's predictions proved correct. Half the men who reached the summit were lost and the rest were forced to slither and slide back in the dark the way they had come up. They clashed with men of another battalion and the scramble back became chaotic.

Even so, Tighe was not deterred and he sent in

another wave at 1.30 a.m., but they too became enmeshed with the retreating troops and Smuts himself sent in orders for Tighe to withdraw his whole force by dawn.

Simon and his three comrades had found themselves pushed to the periphery of the advance in the dark and, breathless, had sought shelter in a ledge shared by other British troops.

'Who are you?' demanded Fonthill.

'We're the remnants of the Rhodesian from the first attack this morning,' shouted back the shadowy figure of a subaltern. 'We've been almost intermingling with the enemy and fighting 'em off all day. I guess we can get back down now, if we can find the way.'

'How many are you?'

'We've got handfuls of the 3rd King's African Rifles hanging on and, round the corner, there are a few more of the Rhodesians and 7th SAI there, too. Lower down, Major Thompson is with 170 of his men.'

'Pass the word that they are to hold on. I'm going down to get reinforcements for you. We might just turn it yet.'

The three scrambled down the hill as best they could and found Tighe.

'There are men still there in good positions just below the nek,' shouted Fonthill. 'I reckon that one last good push to reach them could well turn the tables.'

'Good man. I'll give it a try. To hell with Smuts. Runner, tell Colonel Taylor I want his men to make one last attack. Signaller, send a message to Taveta that I need reinforcements immediately. I am going to take these bloody hills. Are you game to come back up with me, Fonthill?'

'Of course, sir.'

'Permission to 'ave a swig of whisky first, sir?' asked Jenkins.

'Very well, er, 267, but make it quick.'

'I'm not 26 ... ah never mind, sir. Thank you, General bach.'

'Where on earth did you get that bottle, dammit?' demanded Fonthill.

'Jammed in between the rocks up there, bach sir. It seemed a pity to leave it for the Jerries, so I decided to rescue it. Would you like a dram your-self, now?'

'No, thank you. Throw away the damned thing and pick up that rifle. We've a hill to climb.'

There seemed a renewed energy and dash about the men of Colonel Thompson's South Africans and within minutes they had reached the ledges where the survivors of the first attack sheltered, despite the shot that came down around them. Then with a cheer, those survivors rose as one man, leaving the protection of the ledges and climbing upwards.

In the van were Fonthill and his comrades, pre-senting their bayonets to the perspiring black men who faced them on the ridge – and no one more fiercely than Mzingeli.

'Have you ever fired a machine gun?' shouted Simon to Jenkins.

'No. But I've always wanted to.'

'Good. Neither have I, but now is your chance. Come on, both of you. Grab that gun over there and turn it round.'

It was a heavy German Maxim, not unlike the British Vickers – mounted on a tripod and with a continuous belt of cartridges fed into the magazine. Its three-man crew lay dead, their sightless eyes glaring at the blue morning.

'Mzingeli,' shouted Simon above the din, 'feed the belt through from the left, while I take it through on the right. Jenkins, just aim the bloody thing and fire it. I think it's that little round trigger there.'

With a shuddering jolt the machine sprang into life and Jenkins, a demonical grin stretching his moustache, swung it round bringing down askaris who were still manning the ridge. They toppled over, screaming, for they had never faced machine gun fire at such a short range before. In moments, the German troops that were left were running as fast as their unbooted feet could take them down the hillside. Other guns were now seized and turned on them.

'Stop firing, you Welsh madman,' shouted Simon, 'or you'll kill half of our chaps.'

Jenkins blew out his cheeks, wiped his moustache and the cordite from his cheeks and grinned. 'If only we 'ad one of these little beauties against the Zulus at Ishiwannee,' he said. 'I wouldn't 'ave got that bump on me 'ead from that knobkerrie thing.'

Fonthill stood. 'Come on, let's leave this disgusting carnage and go and find the general. Perhaps he'll give us all medals. At least Mzingeli will deserve one. He fought like ... a ... Zulu.'

The Matabele grinned sheepishly. 'I don't like Germans,' was all he said.

They found General Tighe, his blue eyes dancing, drinking tea from a metal cup and balancing on a tiny, folding stool. 'Sit down, all of yer.' There were no more stools so the three crouched, cross-legged on the ground. 'Another pot o' tea and three mugs,' he shouted to his orderly. 'We're goin' to celebrate.'

The tea was brought and, rather self-consciously – particularly Mzingeli – they all saluted the general with their mugs.

'I'll tell you somethin', boys,' said Tighe, his Irishness clearly more marked now, in his enthusiasm – or was it relief? 'If I'd have lost this one, I would have lost me command, and all the hard work I've done over the last eighteen months would have gone down the drain, so it would.'

He returned their salute with his own mug, then turned and confided in a lower voice to Fonthill. 'I'll tell you somethin' else, too. This bloody commander-in-chief of ours is damned ruthless. I'd have been off before you could have said Spion Kop. I hear poor old Stewart is getting hell for advancing so slowly.'

'Ah, but that's unfair, General,' retorted Simon, frowning. 'Stewart had to advance over much more difficult ground than either Smuts or you coming from Taveta.'

'Aye,' Tighe nodded and absent-mindedly reached up to shake the hands of several of his colonels who came to congratulate him. 'I agree with you. It seems Smuts thought it mad for Stewart to separate his infantry from the cavalry and artillery and he's sent him orders to bring 'em up immediately. You know, I don't think these

South African generals – van Deventer is the same, he's closing the trap now by coming from the north – I sometimes think that they don't realise just how difficult this terrain is. When it's not much hotter and more waterless than the veldt of South Africa, then it's raining and we're wading through swamps or grass as high as your shoulder, concealing not only snipers but rhinos and buffalo.'

He took another swig of his tea. 'I've got to thank the three of you for really saving the day by telling me that we had troops left up there at the top. Apart from not sacrificing them to the Hun – they'd all been reported missing by that idiot Malleson and we shall be seeing no more of *him* on this campaign, I'll wager – apart from not losing them, they helped Thompson to turn the tide. I'll see that all three of you are mentioned in my despatches.'

'Thank you, General.'

'Now, you must excuse me. As Wellington, or somebody said, there's far more to do after winning a battle than losing it.'

They all stood and turned away. 'I'll go and make some proper tea,' said Jenkins. 'If this is the bloody stuff they give to generals I don't want to be promoted, thank you very much.'

The three took their tea gratefully, quickly munched the bacon sandwiches which the ever-resourceful Jenkins mustered from somewhere, and then turned into their sleeping bags, for they were all now completely exhausted.

From a member of Tighe's staff, Fonthill learnt later that Smuts had cabled London to say that the first phase of his campaign to clear the Germans from the border had been completely successful.

'Can't be true,' he confided to Jenkins. 'We've got rid of this lot on the Nek, and it looks as though Stewart has frightened off Fischer, but we haven't brought the Hun to battle yet, and they are almost certainly massing somewhere south of here. It's funny, really. This bloody war seems to be a kind of repeat of us fighting the Boers, only the other way around. It's the Germans who are fighting on the retreat and proving to be as slippery as the Boers were, and it's the South Africans now who are desperately trying to corner them and bring them to battle. God, it could go on for months and months yet.'

'Yes.' Jenkins nodded. 'An' I've just been talking to one of the English lads who've been brought down 'ere from the Western Front. 'E says 'e'd rather be in the mud and blood of the trenches back there than fightin' 'ere under the blazin' sun an' in the swamps, an' that.'

If the three thought that they might be rested after the battle, they were wrong. Orders came through, from Smuts, via Tighe, that Fonthill and his men must now get back in their saddles immediately and scout to the south before the town of Kahe, where von Lettow-Vorbeck was alleged to be concentrating his troops. If this was true, it was clear that he would be in a position to harry Smuts's lines of communication when he resumed his attack after the rains had abated.

So the three set out once more, this time huddled in their saddles under inadequate waterproofs, with Mzingeli riding out ahead as their eyes and ears. Twice he galloped back to warn that German patrols were ahead and they had to take cover in gullies, with their horses up to their fetlocks in water that raged down from the hills onto the plain.

Eventually they reached hills surrounding the town and saw plenty of evidence that the German general was, in fact, massing in defensive positions before it, preparing to stand and defy Smuts here.

'Bloody 'ell,' said Jenkins, pointing. 'What's that bloody great thing down there, look you? It's bigger than any of the guns that we've got, surely?'

'Get down, for God's sake!' ordered Fonthill. 'If they've got field glasses focussed on this hill, then they'll see you prancing around like some fat rhino. Let me go forward and take a look at that gun.'

He wriggled forward, poked his binoculars carefully under an overhanging bush and focussed them. Still twirling the focussing knob, he hissed back over his shoulder, 'My God. It's huge! Bloody great barrel. It must be at least a four-inch gun.'

He crawled back. 'Where on earth did the Germans get that from? It must be as huge as these "Big Berthas" they've got on the Western Front. Yet we were told that the Hun had no heavy artillery in East Africa. How did they get it?'

Mzingeli crawled forward to take a look – his keen eyes needed no magnification. 'We see that gun before,' he said on his return.

'No.' Fonthill shook his head. 'I've never seen anything that big in this part of the world before.'

'Oh yes, *Nkosi*. On big German ship in delta.'

'What?' Simon looked puzzled, then enlightenment dawned. 'Ah, yes, of course! It's one of the *Königsberg's* guns. We thought they had all been put out of action. My God, the Germans must have some damned good engineers out here. They've unbolted it, drained it of water, slapped it on a wheeled gun platform and trundled it out all the way here overland.'

Jenkins nodded. 'Not to mention divin' down to salvage the shells from the magazines below water.' Then his jaw dropped in horror. 'Amongst all them crocs, too!'

Fonthill shook his head slowly. 'It shows how desperate they must be getting now for artillery and ammunition. The whole colony must have been put on a hundred per cent war footing. Talk about turning ploughshares into swords... Come on, we'd better hurry back and warn Smuts what he will be up against if he tries a frontal attack here. Keep your eyes peeled for patrols.'

They rode back as fast as the territory would allow to the town of Moshi where, to their delight, they found that Smuts had forged on ahead with his main force to link up there with Tighe, Stewart and the South African General van Deventer, so that his army was now consolidated, ready for the big push against von Lettow-Vorbeck at Kahe, once the rains ceased.

On arrival, Fonthill, dust-stained and weary, was ushered directly into the commander-in-chief's tent. Smuts, smart and elegant in buttoned-up general's tunic, his riding boots polished and his beard precisely trimmed, looked up and, without speaking, indicated a stool facing him on the other side of his camp table. For a while he continued writing, his pen scratching across the paper.

Then, without looking up: 'Why did you let Stewart be caught on that plain in defenceless marching order by Fischer's cavalry, eh? You were supposed to be scouting out ahead to warn him of the enemy's presence. And what about the column's pickets? They must have been right up your bottom.' The high-pitched accent of the Afrikaner seemed to add to the acerbic tone of the questions.

Fonthill cleared his throat and spoke slowly. 'It was rough, broken, wooded country, General. We had to halt at a wood that barred our way and nose into it slowly and carefully to see if it was housing the enemy. We caught the flash of a bridle buckle and stayed long enough to assess the strength of the Huns before riding back as quickly as possible to warn General Stewart.

'The reason that we and the cavalry pickets were not further ahead of the main column was that General Stewart was advancing at such a pace that he kept catching us up when the terrain caused us to walk our horses through it. I understand, sir, that you have been unhappy at the pace of Stewart's advance. With respect, I can only say that I honestly don't see how much quicker he could have marched in that heat and through that sand. His infantry were completely exhausted when they were attacked.'

For the first time, Smuts laid down his pen and looked up. 'I will be the judge of that, Fonthill, thank you. Now, report on the situation at Kahe.'

Inwardly fuming, Simon drew a deep breath

and shifted on the narrow stool. He had heard rumours of Smuts's arrogance but this was the first time he had directly experienced it.

'The Germans are massed in the hills around the town, sir,' he said, 'and they appear to be well dug in. We were able to ascertain that von Lettow-Vorbeck himself is in command and it looked as though he is determined to make a stand there and make you fight to take the town.'

Smuts pursed his lips and nodded. 'Good. It looks as though I have brought him to heel at last. Please continue with your report.'

'The Germans have artillery – the usual light field guns – but also they have salvaged one of the *Königsberg's* big 4.1-inch naval guns. They've put it on wheels, salvaged the shells and it is waiting to greet you at Kahe. It seems to me, sir, that it would be inadvisable, given the rough ground and the nature and sophistication of the German defences, to make a direct assault on the town.'

Smuts looked up sharply. 'When I want your advice on handling my army I will ask for it, Fonthill.'

The tent was silent for a moment, while Simon pondered. Then he made up his mind. He was not going to take this from some jumped-up lawyer-politician, even one who had proved to be a good horseback guerrilla fighter.

'With respect, General,' he said, 'I have always considered it part of my duty, in scouting in various parts of the Empire over the last three decades or so and reporting back to my superiors, to give my view of the situation direct from the front line, so to speak.'

Smuts frowned and opened his mouth to speak, but Fonthill hurried on. 'This I did to General Roberts in Afghanistan, General Wolseley in Mozambique, Egypt and the Sudan, to General Colley in Natal, General Gaselee in Peking and General Kitchener in South Africa. They did not always take my advice, sir, and that was their prerogative. As you well know, being in command is an awesome responsibility and only the soldier in your shoes can make the final judgement. But I still feel it is my duty to give my view – and I do feel you could suffer heavy losses if you make a direct attack at Kahe.'

The general pushed his chair back, wiped the edges of his silver moustache with an elegant finger and a slow smile spread across his face, although it did not reach his eyes. 'Well, thank you for the lecture, Fonthill. I appreciate that you are a man of great experience – even if some of those generals you advised took a bit of a hiding...'

Simon allowed himself a grin and nodded. 'Indeed so. Mainly from the Boers, if I remember rightly.'

'Quite so. But – as you rightly point out – the responsibility is mine and I must make the decision. I can't afford to hang about and let von Lettow-Vorbeck slip away as – and I have to say this – British generals seem to have done for the last eighteen months or so. I shall march on him quickly and attack him in force before he knows what has hit him.'

'Very well, sir. I hope you will allow me to scout ahead of you as soon as you begin your march?'

'Of course. And I have just heard that you saved

Tighe's bacon on the nek, so well done. In fact, I want to appoint you formally as chief scout to my army, Fonthill.' The smile came back. 'I don't dislike the idea of my chief scout having the confidence – and impertinence – to advise his generals and ... er ... how did you diplomatically put it? Ah yes, report directly back from the front. What do you say?'

Simon thought for a moment. Then: 'That is most gratifying, sir, and I do appreciate the offer. But I fear I must decline it.'

Smuts smile disappeared. 'And why would that be, pray?'

'I presume, sir, that being chief scout would mean having line responsibility, much of it at your headquarters, for other scouts on other fronts across the field?'

'Yes, it would.'

'Quite so, sir. You see, both myself and my two comrades would much prefer not to come back into the army, so to speak. I feel we are much better operating as a small unit out in front of – and sometimes between – the two opposing armies, scouting on our own, words I seem to remember you saying to me back in Mombasa. I am sure you have other good men from whom you can choose to do the staff job. We will go anywhere you send us, but let us operate on our own, as ... well, as Boer scouts did so well when you were always one jump ahead of us. I remember it well. I learnt a lesson during that long campaign.'

Smuts threw back his head and laughed out loud. 'Well, I must say, Fonthill, that you are a good debater, as well as a good scout. Not above using a bit of oleaginous flattery if you have to. Well, have it your own way. From now on I can expect to have my work done for me when you report.'

He leant forward again. 'I shall indeed send you out as soon as we get a gap in these damned rains. Oh, and by the way, your reference to good Boer scouts is not only pleasing for me to hear but very apt, in the circumstances.'

'Oh. Why is that, sir?'

'Because you now have operating against you in the field, as the chief scout for von Lettow-Vorbeck, an Afrikaner – a Boer born in the saddle who fought against you twelve years ago and hates all Britishers to this day. I have just heard from home on the grapevine that he is now working for the Germans.'

It was Fonthill's turn to lean forward. 'Hmm. Sounds formidable. What is his name and what does he look like – in case we ... er ... brush against him in the bush, so to speak?'

'His name is – and this won't be easy for an Englishman – Piet Nieuwenhuizen. Tall, thin man, as far as I can remember, with a full beard. A good tracker and knows the ways of the bush backwards. But on one level you and he will be equals.'

'What's that?'

'He's an Afrikaner and he knows the veldt. You are an Englishman who is learning about this damned desert-bush country. But the Boer won't have an advantage here. It's not his country. You have been here probably longer than him now and ... anyway ... I have complete faith in you, Fonthill.'

'Thank you, sir. May I take advantage of your faith in me now, to ask you a question which, I fear, you might find impertinent?'

Smuts sighed. 'If I do feel it's impertinent, Field Marshal Fonthill, then I won't answer it. Ask your question.'

'You are on record, I seem to remember, when writing about the Anglo–Boer war, for saying that English generals always regarded Boer positions that were well prepared defensively as challenges that had to be attacked in a gung-ho, full on, offensive kind of way. The Afrikaners, on the other hand, always believed that the best way to handle such a situation was, to put it simply, to go around it. Leave it isolated, if you will.'

'Did I write that? How interesting. Do go on.'

'Well, sir, now you are saying that the situation at Kahe demands a frontal attack. Have you changed your mind?'

Smuts's icy features once again lapsed into a similarly glacial smile. 'Hmmm. Good question. No, Fonthill, I have not changed my mind. But the situation here is different. I am not fighting a guerrilla campaign, as I and my colleagues did, not so long ago. We are now the British – in more ways than one, of course – in that we must fight a war of aggression. We are the invaders now. On the whole, we outnumber the enemy when we can corner him, and we have the added problem of this damned weather at the moment, which doesn't give us time to hang about. So I must attack Lahe full on. Fiercely and with deter-

293

mination. Good enough answer for you?'

'Good enough, General, thank you.'

'How kind of you to say so. Now clear out of here. I have much work to do. Oh – and take a few days' rest with your chaps while you can. Which reminds me: on Tighe's recommendation, I have put through an order for £50 to be paid to your black feller for his good service. I don't usually appprove of *ex-gratia* payments to blacks but Tighe felt it fair, so I have done so. I shall be giving you new orders as soon as I am able. Good day, Fonthill.'

'Thank you, sir. Good day to you.'

Once outside, Fonthill stretched his back and realised that perspiration was gathering on his brow. And not simply, he reflected, because the day was humid and even hot. He had caught a glimpse of the two sides of General Jan Smuts: the impulsive, arrogant leader; and the thinking, wily lawyer-politician. Impressive, encapsulated in one man, faced across a desk. But were they the qualities needed to command a large army in the field, stretched across alien territory on three or four fronts?

He shrugged his shoulders. Only time would tell. But at least they now had a few days' rest. Would there be a letter from Alice, he wondered? He had not heard from her for nearly three weeks or more, mainly, of course, because they were miles from military post offices. Good! There might be more than one. He walked back to find Mzingeli and 352.

They had pitched their bivouac tents near to the lines of the British cavalry, had seen to the horses and were now, predictably, fast asleep under canvas. Fonthill left them to their slumbers and went to find the mail officer. To his delight, there were three letters waiting for him. He also picked up an envelope addressed to Jenkins, in rounded, immature handwriting, posted from South Africa.

He decided to open his letters in postmarked date order and lay back on the freshly cut wood branches that Jenkins had thoughtfully thrust under his sleeping bag as a makeshift mattress and indulged himself, the odour of the cavalry lines – a mixture of horse manure, urine, and oats – reaching his nostrils in warm, comforting waves.

Alice's first letter was short and to the point: complaining predictably about being held 'as though by damned curfew' in Mombasa, and being forced to pick and choose between formal army press releases to report on the progress of the war and wishing – oh how she wished! – to be with him out in the bush. The next, written quite quickly after the first, was apologetic for being so winsome and assuring him that she had found ways of busying herself usefully (all would be revealed on his return...!). She still yearned, though, to be with him. She was worried, she confessed, because she had not received a letter from Sunil now for some three weeks. She well understood that she could not hear from Simon, but no news from the Western Front disturbed her.

The last letter was quite thick and it became immediately apparent why. It contained a joyful letter from Alice and enclosed one from Sunil, serving in France. Simon turned to it quickly. It informed them both that he had been promoted to captain and made adjutant of his battalion. He confided that this was probably because of the casualties his regiment had received rather than his competence as a soldier, but he had been patted on the back quite effulgently, he added, by his CO. He worried about his 'dear mother and father' – particularly Simon (he had rarely called him 'father' and had taken to using his Christian name in addressing him since he had joined the army) and said that they were both probably in far worse danger than himself. He sent his warmest love to them both and deep affection for 352, with the admonition 'not to drink too much'.

Simon lay back and read it again with a warm smile – a smile that turned to a frown when he read the reference to danger. Of course the boy was in danger! The life of a front line infantry officer in the trenches of France and Flanders, he knew, was likely to be short. How long before dear Sunil, the smiling lad they had recruited to serve with the three of them (Mzingeli had been spared the snows of the Himalayas) in Tibet and then schooled and adopted, joined the casualties that were mounting day by day in Europe? Both he and Alice had grown to regard their adopted son as a gift from God in their middle age. It was unthinkable that he should be taken away from them before they had time to live together as a proper family. He grunted and turned to Alice's joyful covering note.

It was clear that she was vastly relieved to have heard from Sunil and her own news was happier, almost jaunty, as a result. She was, she said, 'very busy now' but wished so much that she could be out covering the skirmishes that were going on now throughout German East Africa. Even the Portuguese and Belgians, she wrote, had joined in on the side of the Allies. Writing at arm's length from Mombasa was not her idea of being a war correspondent and she was about to write directly to General Smuts to alter 'this state of affairs'.

Simon put down her letter with a smile. Poor old Smuts. About to be lambasted on two sides now from the Fonthills! Then he looked at his watch and crawled out into the sunshine. It was time for a cup of tea. And he wanted to share Sunil's good news with his two comrades.

Jenkins nodded sombrely. 'Always said the boy would make a splendid soldier,' he said. 'I taught him to shoot, you may remember, bach sir. In fact, the little blighter saved your life right at the end of the Tibetan business, did he not?'

'He certainly did. Made a change from you and Alice doing the same. I felt quite happy about it, I can assure you.'

'Ah, bach sir. Got a bit of news for you, now. Picked it up from one of the sergeants working on the boss's staff. Old Smuts has sacked Malleson, which we all expected, I suppose. But Tighe's bein' sent to India and Stewart 'as got the old 'eave-oh, too. All a bit unfair on the last two, it seems to me.'

Fonthill frowned. 'I quite agree. This man is certainly ruthless. Have you heard who is taking Tighe's place?'

'A bloke from the East African Rifles called

Hoskins. Never 'eard of 'im.'

'Ah yes, Reginald Hoskins. I know of him, I think. A respected officer, if I remember him properly.'

'Yes, well, I'm also told that old Smutty is bringin' in a lot of South African mates of 'is from the Boer War onto senior positions. P'raps 'e don't trust the British, look you.'

'Well, with the exception of Tighe, he hasn't had much reason to so far, I must say.' They were silent for a moment, then Simon struck his forehead with his hand. 'Oh, 352, forgive me. You have a letter. I have left it in my tent. I'll get it.'

Jenkins's jaw dropped. 'It'll be from the girls,' he said, his face splitting into a great grin. 'I'm so glad they've remembered to write.' He quickly brushed away a reluctant tear. 'I'm not used to receivin' letters, like. Nice change. Thank you, bach sir. Thank you very much.

'Blimey,' Jenkins's favourite exclamation was more a howl of delight. He looked up from his letter – he had been studiously following each word with his forefinger – this time with tears unashamedly streaming down his cheeks. 'I've become a grandfather, TWICE!' He wiped the tears away with the back of a grubby hand. 'Well, I suppose, not an actual grandfather. A sort of step-grandfather. But it'll do me. Two more little girls, one each. Lovely!'

'Grandad,' Fonthill leant across and shook the hand of his old comrade. 'Warmest congratulations.'

Mzingeli did the same in his own style: with a smile but unspokenly.

'As a matter of fact,' said Simon, 'we all have reason to be pleased. You, Mzingeli, have been awarded an *ex-gratia* payment of £50 by General Smuts, on the recommendation of General Tighe for your scouting work, particularly at Longido.'

The Matabele's grin widened. '*Nkosi,* like the rest of us, I am getting old for this work. But it is good to be rewarded.'

Jenkins slapped him on his back so that the tracker was nearly knocked to the earth. 'It certainly is, old Jelly. Well, bach sir, I think this calls for a glass of milk for you an' me, an' a bloody great big pint for Jelly here. What d'yer say?'

'Quite agree, 352. Let's get cleaned up. You light a fire and I'll go and raid the officer's mess, if they let me in without a shave, that is.'

'Good idea, bach sir.'

It turned into a most convivial evening around the campfire, with Jenkins cooking stew, Simon providing wine and, later, a bottle of good Scotch whisky, and Mzingeli doing his best to down a small glass of whisky and water but being forced to spit it out and resort to milk, much to Jenkins's disgust.

Just before they scattered the ashes of the fire and retired to their sleeping bags, Jenkins raised a pensive and rather bloodshot eye and asked, 'What did you shay Miss Alice was up to, bach shir?'

'As a matter of fact, I haven't the faintest idea, old chap. As long as she keeps out of trouble I shall be happy. I must say, though,' he mused, 'I do miss her terribly at the moment.'

'We all do, bach. We all do.'

CHAPTER TWELVE

Alice, in fact, was busily writing her report on Smuts's staff changes when Simon's letter in reply to her previous three arrived. She sighed with relief when she saw the familiar handwriting on the envelope and tore it open quickly. It was posted from the north-eastern front, which did not surprise her, for, as the most active in the vast territory over which the war was now being fought, she had always felt that that was where he and his two companions would be operating.

Simon had deliberately included some juicy details of the attack on the nek, which he knew she would appreciate and would liven up her cables which, perforce, had to be based on the anodyne army HQ briefings. He told of the inferred incompetence of Malleson, in contrast to the feisty aggression and eventual success of Tighe. But what, he asked, had she actually been up to? What was the nature of the 'quite busy' work she was doing in boring old Mombasa?

Alice smiled and quickly put aside her story on the staff appointments and added a rider to her previous cable on the action near Taveta. 'Information has just been received on the story behind General Smuts's success in the north-east...'

Good old Simon! He knew she would appreciate these discreetly dropped crumbs from the battlefront. She finished writing the piece – carefully concealing the source of her information, of course, and wrapping in diplomatic language Malleson's leaving of the field when the battle was at its height – and took the cable to the censor's office. As a very experienced correspondent and an old hand at not incurring the censor's displeasure, she was sure that his blue pencil would not be used on her copy. But she had other, additional, fish to fry that day.

She turned on her most bewitching smile for the benefit of the staff sergeant on duty. 'Staff,' she said. 'Could you leave your desk for a minute, do you think?'

He returned her smile, looked round at the empty office and tugged at his moustache. 'Of course, Miss Griffith. I will see you at the usual place in about five minutes, if that is convenient? But I must be quick.'

'Of course, that will be most convenient, thank you.'

She had less than that to wait in the narrow alleyway round the corner from the censor's office, before the staff sergeant came furtively to her side.

'I could be shot for this, you know, Miss,' he said.

Alice pressed a golden guinea into his hand. 'Now, as I explained before, you are not betraying the army, Staff,' she said. 'I just want to check that this man is not scooping me with his stories, that's all. It's just commercial competition, you see. We correspondents are all in competition with each other. Dog eat dog and all that. You and the staff captain see everything that I write, so you will know that I am not robbing him of his exclusives. I just want to keep an eye on him, that's all.'

'Very well, Miss.' He gave her a copy of a long cable. 'It's in Boer language, as usual. We have to get a South African army bloke to censor them, 'cos neither the captain nor I can understand a word... Hasn't been censored yet, though, so I shall need this back pretty smartly, please.'

He sniffed. 'I have to say that I haven't got much time for the bloke. He's a surly so-and-so, never passes the time of day. He's still fighting the Boer War, if you ask me. I'd better have this back within a couple of hours, Miss, please.' He pocketed the coin, touched the brim of his cap with his forefinger and marched away, ramrod tall.

Alice hurriedly put the cable in her handbag and walked back quickly to her hotel. Back in her room, she drew down the blind, for her bedroom looked across the street directly into a busy office whose window faced hers. Then she locked the door and smoothed out the cable on her dressing table. It was in Afrikaans, of course. Addressed to the office of the Boer newspaper *Die Burger* in Pretoria, it was signed Herman de Villiers and seemed innocuous enough.

Alice had only picked up a smattering of Afrikaans in her many sojourns in South Africa and so she found it extremely difficult to decipher the cable. Brow furrowed, however, she did her best to wade through the story, tracking through the place names and comparing it to her own story, and realised that it was a fairly straightforward account of the battle of the nek. However ... she stiffened. There was something strange about the middle of the story, which seemed to be a distinctly discrete section, even, perhaps, written in a different language and with a signature at the bottom – *Lowe*. Some kind of story within the story. No more than – what? – two hundred and fifty words, perhaps.

She looked up at the ceiling and sucked hard on her pencil. Why a story within the story? She looked down again at the text. Ah, of course. The umlaut over the 'o' of Lowe. The insert was in German! And Lowe was probably a code name.

Alice stood and opened the top drawer of her dressing table and sorted through her underwear. She had studied German in a perfunctory way at finishing school in Switzerland and she had kept her German dictionary and grammar somewhere ... but where? Eventually, with a cry of joy, she found it and began to work, her tongue poking out in concentration.

Within the half-hour, she had finished. She could not accurately translate the message slipped so innocuously into the copy but the meaning was more or less clear. And Lowe was the German word for lion, certainly a code name. The German section stated that Smuts intended forthwith to attack the German defences at Kahe and that when von Lettow-Vorbeck was forced to retreat Smuts would aim south-east for the Central Railway to cut him off.

Alice licked her lips. This meant that, in addition to de Villiers, there were probably two or even three more spies working with the British

Army HQ – certainly the South African interpreter in the censor's office and someone out in the field with the army command. Perhaps there was a whole network of them? No wonder von Lettow-Vorbeck always seemed one jump ahead of the British and South Africans in the field!

She must act quickly. But what to do? Alice frowned. Smuts, of course, was not at his Mombasa HQ so she could not turn to him. But who to approach? Whoever was feeding de Villiers with information was reasonably senior in the army hierarchy, or at least very much involved with communications between the general in the field and his HQ.

She snapped her dictionary tightly shut. Obviously, she must warn the head of Smuts's staff here at Mombasa that the general's plans were being relayed back to a pro-German source in the Boer capital of Pretoria, presumably for onward transmission to von Lettow-Vorbeck out there in the wilds of German East Africa. Alice frowned. She would like to set her own trap for Mr Herman de Villiers, if she could think of a way. She had a personal score to settle with him, and Alice Griffith was not one to let a score settle and fester. It was now perfectly clear that he had spied on her when she employed the *Calipha* to take her into the delta. She had begun to suspect him recently when she saw him slip money into the hands of that obsequious clerk at the hotel desk. Unnoticed, she had observed them whispering in conclave for some time and referring to the hotel register. Yes, before delivering him up to the army, she must first devise a plan to trap him, to ensure that, when he was caught, he would be caught for good!

But first, she must ensure that no more of the general's plans were passed to the enemy. She pinned up her hair, which had become a little bedraggled while she was attempting the translation, placed her smartest straw hat on top of it and left her room, carefully putting the cable in her handbag and locking the door behind her. She left the hotel by the back entrance and made sure she was not being followed before hailing a cab.

Once at Army HQ she asked to see the brigadier who was Smuts's chief of staff in Mombasa. Brigadier Lawrence had served under Alice's father as a young subaltern and, although she had not traded on the acquaintance before, she decided it was time to play this card.

Lawrence sat, jaw in hand, listening to her as she told her story. Then, without speaking, he held out his hand to read the original of the German cable from 'The Lion', then her translation of it.

'You translated well, my dear Miss Griffith,' he said. 'Luckily, I learnt German myself some years ago when I was on secondment to the Kaiser's staff in Berlin...' Then, seeing the alarm materialise in Alice's eyes, he held up his hand. 'No, madam, I am not your spy at headquarters, and I think my record in the army, particularly in the Anglo–Boer war, will prove that. But,' he tapped the German letter with his forefinger, 'I might just have an idea who it might be.'

He sniffed. 'Certainly, a rocket has to be administered to the captain in charge of the censor's office for letting this cleverly inserted stuff slip through. And, of course, we shall arrest the South African interpreter pretty damned quickly now. But first...' he pondered. 'I think we might just alter one or two key phrases about Smuts's intentions so as to misdirect our German friends in the field.'

Lawrence looked up quickly. 'You obviously have to return this cable?'

'Yes, I have only "borrowed it" so to speak.'

'Good. Leave it with me while I get this central bit retyped, so that it can be passed on. Then we can certainly arrest the interpreter. And, presumably, this de Villiers chap. He is undoubtedly a traitor.'

'Indeed, sir. But may I suggest you leave him be for the moment? I would like to make sure that we catch him red-handed, so to speak. I have a personal score to settle with him.'

'Very well. But don't leave it long. The man must hang before he can do any further damage.'

'Of course. I will be back within the hour for the rewritten piece and I hope to have a suggestion for you then.'

'Splendid. Thank you, Miss Griffith. Your father would have been proud of you.'

She smiled. 'How kind of you.'

Back in the hotel, she perched on the bed and thought hard. There was probably enough circumstantial evidence of de Villiers's guilt already to hang him, but the final nail in his coffin would be, somehow, to catch him in the act of betrayal. And she wanted, very much, to be involved in that. How to trap him?

The newly installed electric fan whirled slowly above her head but did little to stir the heat within the room. Somewhere, in the distance, a command was barked and boots slammed onto sandy ground – a reminder that this picturesque, previously peaceful port was now also an army town. Slowly, a plan began to form within Alice's brain. She slowly nodded and smiled. Yes. That would do.

She moved quickly to the writing table and began scribbling on a cable form, addressing it, as usual, to the foreign editor of the *Morning Post,* Fleet Street, London. Then she tucked the cable into an envelope but did not seal it. Looking down from her first-floor landing, she was glad to see that the treacherous clerk was on duty down at the hotel desk.

Picking up the envelope, she walked slowly down the stairs, pulling down a strand of hair to let it fall, languidly across her brow. She smiled at the clerk and put a hand to her brow.

'I wonder if you could do me a favour?' she asked.

'Of course, madam.'

'I think I have caught a touch of the sun and am feeling rather unwell and very tired.' She held up the envelope. 'This is a most important cable I wish to send to my newspaper back in England and it should go to the army censor's office without delay. You know where that is?'

'Oh yes, madam. Quite near.'

'Quite so. Good. Could you arrange for someone to deliver it to the staff sergeant on duty there? I am afraid I am too unwell to take it myself.' She discreetly passed over a ten-shilling note. 'Get someone you can trust to take it, for it is most important. I must go back to my room to lie down.'

'Of course, madam. It shall be done right away. Would you like tea in your room?'

'No, thank you. I wish to sleep and not to be disturbed.'

'Very well, madam. It shall be done.'

Slowly Alice climbed back up the stairs, pausing at the stairhead to look behind her. Yes, the clerk was on the house telephone. Good, the plot was in motion. Then, she hurried past her room, hung a 'do not disturb' sign on the door handle and then slipped down the back stairs, out into the alleyway and walked quickly to the censor's office.

The staff sergeant was still on duty. She quickly explained to him that a communication from her to London would shortly be delivered but that it should not be censored or transmitted. He frowned but Alice gripped his hand. 'Staff,' she said in a low voice. 'I am working for Brigadier Lawrence now. All will be explained to you in due course, but do not, I repeat, do not, mention any of this to your staff captain. He will hear soon enough.

'Oh, and I shall be returning Mr de Villiers's cable to you very shortly. Let it be submitted to your Afrikaner translator for censoring and transmission in the normal way. Staff,' she leant forward. 'Treachery is afoot and these are important moments. Say nothing to anyone, not even your captain. Do you understand?'

His jaw sagging, he nodded. 'Whatever you say, Miss. Whatever you say.'

She hurried on back to Army HQ and was immediately shown into Lawrence's office.

'We have changed the cable, Miss Griffith,' he said, handing it to her. 'We should let it go now. But you mentioned a plan. What is it?'

'Thank you, Brigadier. Yes it's pretty straight-forward. This is what I propose. I have concocted a story – a fake cable from me to my office – which tells of a move by General Smuts to outmanoeuvre von Lettow-Vorbeck south of Kahe by pretending to attack the town full on but diverting most of his troops to the south to take the Germans in a pincer movement as van Deventer moves up. To give the story some validity to de Villiers, I have hinted that my informant is my husband, who is with Smuts and scouting for him. De Villiers will know this and has long suspected that Simon has been feeding me confidential information.'

'Hmm. How will the South African get the story?'

'The clerk at the hotel where the press are all staying is in de Villiers's pay. I pretended that I have a touch of the sun and asked the clerk to send the story to the office to be censored. But he will, of course, show it to de Villiers, who, I am sure, will incorporate it into his next cable.'

'Yes, but how do you propose to catch him red-handed, so to speak?'

'If you can give me two soldiers – military policemen will be ideal – who can be hidden away in the censor's office, in disguise as clerks, say, we can arrest de Villiers as he hands his story over for censorship. The story in his hand will be sufficient evidence to convict him. And I would like to be there when it happens.'

'Very well. That seems straightforward. I will see to it. Now you had better get his original story back to the office. I want my own "amendments" to his story to be sent off to Pretoria to mislead our Teutonic friends.' He grinned impishly. 'You are not the only one to play games, my dear Miss Griffith. Let's catch them both ways.'

'Indeed, sir.'

Alice took the altered cable and hurried with it back to the censor's office. 'This can be censored now, in the normal way, and released, Staff,' she ordered. 'No one is to know I have intercepted it.'

'Very good, madam.'

'Now, has a new cable from me to my office been delivered to you from my hotel yet?'

'No.'

'Good. Now, Brigadier Lawrence will shortly be sending round to you two military policemen, who will pretend to be clerks working here in this office. Let them pretend to be working, but they will actually be here to make an arrest – Mr de Villiers. I want to be here when this happens. Is there a little room, say round the back, where I can wait for a while?'

'Yes, our supper room. But the captain's not here yet.'

'That doesn't matter. The fewer people who are involved in this the better. Let me go and sit in there and wait. This may take some time.'

'Very well.' The staff sergeant tugged at his moustache. 'I wish I knew what the bloody 'ell

310

was goin' on, Miss. But I suppose you know what you are doing?'

'I hope so, too. Show me the way.'

The MPs arrived quickly. Burly men who had changed their tunics, with their chevrons, for plain, clerks' jackets. It was some time, however, before de Villiers put in an appearance, which made Alice edgy. But she realised that he would have had to write a new story, incorporating a new German passage embedded into it, and this would take time.

At last, however, as she peered around the open door of the inner office, she saw the tall, bearded figure of Herman de Villiers walking up the slope towards the entrance to the censor's office. He walked with the indolent grace of a bushman, a slim, tall, fit man striding along, his step light and springy, seemingly without a care in the world. 'Your man is approaching,' Alice hissed to the two 'clerks'. 'Arrest him as soon as I identify him by name. Be alert now.'

Looking about him carefully, de Villiers walked through the door, a cable in his hand. Alice chose that moment to appear from the inner office, lift up the flap on the counter and walk toward the South African.

'Ah,' she said, 'Mr de Villiers. How good to see you. Have you come to file another story you stole from me?'

'What?'

Alice turned towards the MPs. 'This is your man. Take him now!'

Immediately, de Villiers seized Alice, swung her round and threw her towards the gap in the counter so that she collided with the two men as they tried to move forward. The first fell to the ground, Alice on top of him, but the second, with great presence of mind, attempted to vault the counter. Unfortunately, his boot caught on the top of the counter, which sent him sprawling backwards.

De Villiers turned and ran through the doorway and down the hill with all the speed and agility of a veldt springbuck, his long legs pumping.

'Ah blast!' cried Alice. 'He's got away. After him! He mustn't escape. After him!'

The portly nature of the two military policemen, which gave them such an air of command on patrol, alas, did nothing for them now. Scrambling to their feet, their faces red, they made for the door. But de Villiers, with a ground-consuming stride, was out of sight before the soldiers could push through the narrow doorway, disappearing around a bend in the pathway below them.

'Oh, for God's sake, don't let him get away,' screamed Alice. 'He's a German spy. After him. After him!'

She herself ran after the MPs and, in fact, soon caught them up as they paused at the bottom of the hill, gasping and gazing at the empty path before them.

'He must have gone up that side street there,' shouted Alice. 'One of you go that way. The other follow me.'

But there was no sight of the Afrikaner. It was as though he had disappeared into thin air – or, more likely, into the myriad backstreets of down-town Mombasa.

'Follow me back to my hotel,' shouted Alice. 'I doubt if he has returned there but you need to make one more arrest and we need to search his room. Come quickly, now.'

The three stormed into the lobby. The ferret-like clerk was there, his narrow eyes widening as they approached the desk. 'That man there,' said Alice, 'arrest him. But first,' she leant across the counter, 'Give me the key to de Villiers's room.'

'Oh, I can't do that, madam,' he began.

Alice drew back her hand and slapped him hard across the face, so that he staggered back. 'You are already under arrest,' she shouted. 'These men are military policemen and we have a warrant to search his room. Don't you dare delay me any further. Give me his key.'

Jaw sagging and holding his cheek, the clerk gave her the key. 'Good. Now, Constable, take this man into custody.' Then to the other, 'Come with me. We need to search the room and take whatever evidence we can find.'

She leant across and picked up the desk telephone and rattled the cradle. 'Operator, put me through immediately to Army Headquarters in Mombasa. Quickly now.

'Yes, hello. I wish to speak to Brigadier Lawrence urgently. It is Miss Griffith calling.' She tapped her fingers impatiently while she waited. Then: 'Brigadier. The bloody man got away. Slipped away like an eel and disappeared into the backstreets of Mombasa, where, no doubt, he has accomplices who will give him protection. Is there anything you can do to stop him leaving the city, do you think?'

'Give me his description now and I will do my

best. I doubt if we will find him. He might go upcountry or, more likely, find a boat to take him to Dar es Salaam in German country. I will alert the naval authorities. I have already set in train the arrest of their man here in our censor's office and the subeditor on the Pretorian newspaper. As I understand it, we managed to get our fake message back to the paper before startling the fox, so to speak, so perhaps we've been able to cause some confusion amongst von Lettow-Vorbeck's staff. Now, the description, if you please.'

Alice described de Villiers as best she could. As she finished, she said: 'Brigadier, I am so sorry we let him escape. It was undoubtedly my fault for wishing to be there to gloat when he was arrested. Revenge is never sweet, you know. It's a fallacy.'

Lawrence grunted at the end of the line. 'Do not blame yourself, dear lady. You found the scoundrel in our midst, you baited the trap perfectly, we failed to snap it shut, I fear we must give our military policemen more exercise. Now, do search the room thoroughly – I will send you another couple of chaps, skilled in this sort of work, and make sure we pick up everything that might condemn him. We might have a court case on our hands and we will need to convict him properly. Thank you, again, madam.'

'Thank you, Brigadier. You are very kind.'

Alice joined the MP who was scouring the room. When the other two men arrived, she decided to leave. She had much to think about.

Lying back on her bed in her hot little room, she mulled over the events of the day. Well, at least they had dug out the spy and spies in their midst. Presumably, Lawrence would inform Smuts immediately and, perhaps, some credit might accrue to her account. Like all generals, it was known that Smuts, for all his legal training and democratic leanings, was not overly fond of the press, keeping his plans close to his chest and refusing to meet the correspondents fretting around the fringes of his headquarters here in Mombasa. And yet ... and yet... An idea began to form in her mind. General or not, Smuts was very much a politician now, and anxious to impress the Cabinet members fighting the war back home. The *Morning Post* was undoubtedly a true-blue Tory supporter and, perhaps because of Alice's coolly impartial reporting from the front in Africa, it generally cast an approving eye on the African campaign. But, despite Tighe's recent success at the Nek, it must be apparent that things weren't going completely Smuts's way. She had heard that the South African was not without vanity. He could do with some good press back home.

Frowning, Alice drew a piece of *Morning Post*-headed paper towards here, scribbled her Mombasa address at the top and began to write:

My Dear General,
Alas, we have not met, but perhaps you may know that I have been reporting on the German East African campaign for my newspaper, the London Morning Post, *since the war began. I feel we have done our best to give an accurate account of the events of the campaign so far.*
In the last few days, I have been able to carry out

work that has led to the unmasking of a German spy amongst the ranks of the correspondents reporting on the war here from Mombasa and, indeed, others working in the censor's office here and, from back in Pretoria, supplying vital information to von Lettow-Vorbeck in German colonial Africa. Brigadier Lawrence knows about this and will, no doubt, have already informed you of the details.

I need no reward for merely doing my duty and am happy to have been of assistance – although sorry that, at the last moment, the spy, Herman de Villiers, was able to escape. Efforts are in hand to apprehend him as I write this.

I am writing to you, however, on another matter. My newspaper is anxious to give our readers – who, I might add, are among the best-informed in Britain, including many members of government – a balanced view of the man who is leading our, and South African, troops fighting the Germans in this hugely difficult terrain.

To this end, would you please consider granting me permission to visit you at your headquarters in the field and allow me to interview you? Obviously, anything I write will be subject to the usual military censorship, although I flatter myself that, after covering from the front line the fighting in the Anglo–Zulu War of 1879, the campaigns that followed in Egypt, the Sudan, the first Anglo–Boer War and, of course, the second, plus the uprising of the Pathan Rebellion in the nineties and the British mission to Tibet under Colonel Younghusband, I can claim to possess skills that ensure that I impart no secrets or covert forms of encouragement to the enemy.

On a personal note, perhaps I should add that my

husband, Simon Fonthill, is now working for you with his two comrades between the lines as a scout. It would be a wonderful blessing to me, having been apart from him for a month or more now, if, in visiting you, it enabled me to share a few moments with him.

Please forgive the intrusion on your valuable time, but I look forward to hearing from you.

With respect and most sincerely,

Alice Griffith (my professional name)

She read it through carefully and then sealed it and addressed the envelope. Then she settled down to write to Simon and tell him all the happenings of the last few days. On reflection, she decided not to reveal her approach to Smuts. Oh wonderful, to arrive out of the blue and surprise him! If her luck held, that is...

A reply came from Smuts surprisingly quickly. It read:

After the remarkable service you have rendered to us in unmasking what I can only call a spy network in Mombasa and Pretoria, it would be churlish of me, my dear Miss Griffith, to refuse your request. In fact, perhaps now would be the best time for you to venture into the field, for we are forced at the moment to rest and recoup as a result of the heavy rains that afflict us.

I shall give instructions to Brigadier Lawrence as to my precise whereabouts and ask him to arrange for your transport here. Do bring a raincoat!

Alas, I cannot send you the best wishes and love of your husband because he is currently out in the bush, where he and his old comrades continue to render me

317

valuable service. But I can assure you that, as of this time of writing, they are all perfectly safe.

I have been a devoted reader of your writings from the days when your troops pursued me from pillar to post in the last war between our nations and it will be a delight to make your acquaintance at last, dear lady.

With every good wish,
Sincerely,
J. Smuts, General

Alice hugged herself with delight. An exclusive interview with the commander-in-chief and a possibility – just a possibility – to see her dear husband after all these weeks. What joy!

CHAPTER THIRTEEN

The next couple of days became of whirl of activity for Alice. A warrant arrived for her rail journey to the Taveta railhead at the old border with German East Africa – similar to the journey Simon, Jenkins and Mzingeli had taken about a month before. At Taveta, she was met by a young captain of the South African Horse – Smuts's influence was already being exerted in the ranks of the staff, she noticed – and a horse and buggy took her and her few belongings into the bush towards where the British and South African armies were grouped on the outskirts of Kahe, still held by the Germans.

It was, inevitably, raining as she penetrated the fringes of the Allied forces, but she looked around her with great interest. Alice was far from unfamiliar with the smells, sights and sounds of an army in the field, but it had been some time since she had seen such a gathering.

The first thing she noticed was the disparity of uniforms on display, although in the humidity and general wetness of the climate smartness had been allowed to lapse in favour of comfort, with mufflers tucked under chins and oilskins thrown over the uniforms. Nevertheless, she noted the wide-brimmed hats of the South Africans, one side of the brim pinned up to show their colonial origins, contrasted with the pith helmets of the British, the little green pillboxes of the Gurkhas and the turbans of the Punjabis. Mud was underfoot everywhere and the soggy dampness of the clothing seemed to exude steam, matched by that which rose from the horse lines, where the poor beasts stood in rows in silent misery.

The general dampness seemed also to stretch a sodden blanket of near silence over the troop lines, muffling the usual noises of troops under canvas: the clink of kettles hanging over fires, the jingle of harness from the cavalry lines, the badinage issuing from within the tent flaps, and the calling of the sentries from the periphery of the camp.

As she rode in, Alice desperately searched for some sign of Simon. She was not sure what she was looking for: probably a man who must now resemble some kind of bearded, drenched scarecrow if he had been out in the bush for weeks on end, as seemed likely. She herself attracted

319

several interested glances, for despite the rain she held herself erect, smiled and attempted to hold eye contact with everyone she passed.

She was led to a small bell tent at the edge of what appeared to be the officers' quarters. The captain handed her down, saluted and said that the commander-in-chief would expect to entertain her for dinner that evening at seven under his own, rather more luxurious, canvas a hundred yards away.

Her belongings were handed inside to her and she found, propped up on her camp bed, a half-bottle of single malt Scotch whisky. Alongside it was a small card containing the brief message: 'Welcome. This might help to keep out the damned rain! J. Smuts.'

Well! She smiled. Things had started well. At least the army was still here, and the bottle was a thoughtful welcome – the sort of thing a man would leave to greet another man; a masculine gesture, ignoring the recipient's gender and underlining the professional nature of Alice's visit.

Alice poked her nose out into the drizzle and looked around. No sign of Simon, of course. She had hoped, remotely, that maybe Smuts might have called him in from the cold and have him waiting for her. But only darkly shrouded figures trudged through the mud on seemingly un-military errands. She shrugged and lay back onto the bed, took out her notebook and tried to marshal her thoughts. It looked as though the interview would take place virtually immediately. She must prepare her questions.

An hour later, she dressed for the dinner with the

commander-in-chief, sampling the delicious malt whisky as she did so. She had packed one smart dress – not exactly evening wear but an efficacious mixture of formality and femininity that pleased her. She had no intention of attempting to flirt with this cool and reputedly ruthless Afrikaner, but she knew of no man who would not respond to a touch of elegance and grace in these spartan surroundings. She therefore applied a touch of lip rouge and powder to soften the sun's ravages and dressed her hair in her favourite light-green silk scarf.

Promptly at seven, she ignored the drizzle and hurried to the general's tent. She could see that the interior was lit by candles and coughed at the entrance. 'General, may I come in?'

'My dear Miss Griffith, please do come in out of this awful rain. You are most welcome.'

Three men were waiting inside for her. The general himself, unmistakable in his severely cut khaki uniform, his grey beard smartly clipped and his eyes dancing; a huge, darkly bearded man towering over him at his side and wearing the stars and pips of a major general; and a younger, fair-haired man, perhaps in his mid thirties, obviously a member of the general's staff.

The general advanced and took her hand. 'May I introduce to you, Major General Jakobus van Deventer, in command of the second division of our army' – the tall man bowed – 'and this is Deneys Reitz, son of the former President of the Free State, my ADC whom I had the honour to command during our so-called and, I fear, short-lived invasion of the Cape, some thirteen years ago now.'

Alice summoned up a curtsy. 'Gentlemen, I am honoured,' she said.

'Now, madam,' said Smuts, 'we Afrikaners are not great drinkers, I fear, but to have such a distinguished lady with us on campaign demands champagne.' He clapped his hands and two black attendants, wearing white jackets over which red sashes had been draped diagonally, appeared carrying opened bottles of champagne.

The glasses were filled and sipped. 'Gentlemen,' continued Smuts, 'this lady has been responsible for uncovering a quite substantial spy ring in Mombasa and Pretoria, which has been feeding important information to the Germans in the field. I regret to say that it was run by fellow countrymen of ours – I suppose we must call them "Never Say Die Afrikaners" – who are still, it seems, fighting the Anglo–Boer War.'

Alice frowned. 'Is there news, General, about the apprehension of Herman de Villiers?'

'I fear not. He seems to have disappeared off the face of the earth. But we shall find him, have no fear.'

'May I ask what news, then, sir, about my husband, Simon Fonthill, and his two companions? Is he still out there somewhere in the bush in this terrible weather?'

'I fear so, madam. As you must know, we are preparing to launch a strong attack on the German forces holding Kahe – I can't wait for ever for this damned rain to pass – and I have sent back Fonthill and his men to carry out one more reconnoitre of the defences there. This will be a tough nut to crack and I shall need all the intelligence I can get.'

The general nodded to the two attendants. 'We mustn't keep you up too late after your long journey here, Miss Griffith, so may I suggest we begin our meal? Do please feel free to ask me whatever questions you wish during its course. Shall we sit?'

'Thank you, sir. I welcome the opportunity.' Alice took out her notebook and pencil. 'May I begin?'

'Please do. I shall ask my colleagues to help me if I falter.'

The champagne glasses were refilled as soup was served. Alice cleared her throat. 'From what I hear from my colleagues back in London, General,' she said, 'it seems that you are happy with the conduct of your campaign up here in the north-east so far?'

Smuts nodded slowly. 'That is true. We have been able to administer some very hard knocks to von Lettow-Vorbeck since my offensive began.'

'Quite so. But forgive me if I remind you: you have not been able to bring the German general to a full-scale battle yet. He is always slipping away from you. Isn't that so, pray?'

'To some extent yes. But we have been able to clear all German troops from British colonial territory at the border and it looks as though I have them cornered at Kahe now and should be able to deliver a decisive blow to them there.'

Alice scribbled furiously while attempting to drink her soup, quaff her champagne and keep her mind sharp.

'Since taking command, sir, you have carried out some rather drastic reorganisation of your staff here, at the expense of the British senior soldiers who have been fighting here since the war began. General Tighe has been sent back to India to be Inspector of Infantry there and Generals Stewart and Malleson have also left. They have been replaced, as far as one can see, by South Africans who are personally close to you.' Alice put down her spoon and smiled sweetly. 'Such as General van Deventer here, who has been given a division, and Manie Botha, the president's son. Does this not smack, perhaps, of favouritism or, at the least, criticism of the standard of senior British officers? After all, your command is supposed to be a multinational force, is it not?'

For the first time an embarrassed silence fell on the room. Young Reitz cleared his voice to speak, but Smuts held up his hand.

'Dear lady,' he said, 'I am in the middle of an extremely difficult campaign, fought over ground that gives the enemy every advantage. In these circumstances, I must have full confidence in the people I appoint. This comes from knowing the men I can trust.' The ironic smile returned. 'In addition, I have to say that the results obtained by my predecessors – Tighe perhaps excepted – have not inspired confidence.'

'Quite so, but perhaps the government back home might have some difficulty in accepting that. It could seem like a criticism of the British army and its commanders.'

'So far, they have accepted it. Now, Miss

Griffith, try the lamb. We have to live off the land to some extent here but I am told this is excellent.'

It was, and Alice was enjoying both the meal and the encounter, although it seemed that General van Deventer either spoke no English or did not intend to and took no part in the discussion, merely smiling behind his beard and nodding from time to time. Reitz for his part seemed too junior to be allowed to intervene. She was glad, however, that Smuts – and she had never met anyone who appeared so self-confident – seemed happy to answer questions in a straightforward fashion.

Alice put down her knife and fork. 'It seems to me, General,' she said, 'that, given the huge size of the territory in which you are fighting and the fact that the Germans are fighting over ground with which they are very familiar, plus that their askaris have proved to be formidable warriors who are extremely well led – given these facts, isn't it likely that this campaign will last for months yet?'

'No, madam, it is not. I am confident that my next offensive, which is now poised to strike, will pin down von Lettow-Vorbeck and I will destroy him.'

'Do you have enough men to do that?'

'Yes, I do. I have 18,000 combat troops in place to attack here, with another 9,000 Indian troops manning our lines of communication. In fact, our total ration strength amounts now to about 45,000. I discount the Belgians, fighting at the west and the Portuguese – who are, I confess, an embarrassingly doubtful ally – in the south. Yes, I can defeat a force which is continually in retreat and fighting many thousand miles from home and reliant on "make do" supplies and reinforcements. You will see for yourself, because I have every intention of attacking within the next few days now.'

They were interrupted by the arrival of a young lieutenant, who excused himself and whispered into Smuts's ear. The general frowned and nodded.

'I am afraid, madam,' he said, 'that I must ask you to excuse me and my colleagues now. A message has just come from your indefatigable husband to say that the Germans seem to be moving their large gun forward, preparatory, probably, to shelling our positions and forcing me to make a move. Well, they will succeed in that direction, at least.'

He stood, dabbing his mouth with his napkin.

'A large field gun, General? But I thought the Germans were not particularly well equipped.'

'Not so, I am afraid. In fact, they started this war in Africa much better equipped than the British. And I have to give them credit for being remarkably self-reliant. We thought we had sunk the *Königsberg,* and indeed we did. We left her a tangled mass of metal, badly holed and up to her funnels in water. No further threat, of course.'

He gave his wintry smile. 'But the Germans returned, removed the ship's heavy shells, then unbolted the least damaged of their 4.1-inch guns, reassembled it on the shore, put wheels on the damned thing and moved it overland to the front here, where, as the largest piece of ordnance for miles around, it poses a considerable threat to us. These people are a remarkable race, Miss Griffith, and it doesn't do to underestimate them. But, even so, I shall defeat them.

'Now, please do forgive this rudeness in leaving you to finish your meal alone, but we now have much work to do. I intend to attack before that gun can be brought into position. Goodnight, my dear.'

Alice, now in some confusion, inclined her head from her chair to each of the three and watched as they marched away, barking orders to the servants. She sat for a while, thinking hard, then began scribbling furiously. After a while she looked up, a faint smile on her face, and was glad to see the last of the champagne bottles – mercifully still half-full – just about within her reach. She refilled her glass and then continued writing.

It seemed as though the attack would begin in the morning. Splendid! She was not being asked to retreat to the rear or even to return to Mombasa. She would have a ringside seat at what, if Smuts was to be believed, would be a decisive encounter with the wily von Lettow-Vorbeck and, with any luck, she would be overlooked and allowed to watch and report on the encounter. Then the half-smile on her lips froze and she looked up, unseeing, at the canvas ahead of her.

The message had come from Simon. He would be out there somewhere, but undoubtedly caught between the two battle lines, obviously in great danger. Alice bit her lip. How disgraceful of her that only now did she think of her beloved husband and his two companions, undoubtedly in great danger. She laid down her pencil and sighed. Yet there was nothing, absolutely nothing, she could do to help him. Only God could do that. She said a silent prayer.

The subjects of the prayer, in fact, were crouching in a small wood overlooking the defences of Kahe, kneeling in damp undergrowth, hugging their oilskins around them and, in Simon's case, desperately trying to focus through his field glasses on the *Königsberg* gun by the light of a capriciously vanishing moon.

'What are they doin' with the bloody thing?' grunted Jenkins. 'It's a bit 'eavy to keep pushin' about, ain't it? Why are they doin' that?'

Fonthill shook the raindrops off the end of his binoculars. 'It's a deliberate move by a pretty damned good general, I would say, to provoke Smuts to attack ... to draw him within range and to get him to launch a full-scale frontal attack on an enemy who are extremely well entrenched, by the look of it.'

'Didn't you advise the general not to do just that, look you?'

'I did, indeed, and I was told to mind my own business. I doubt if Smuts is going to resist the urge to go in hell for leather. For a wily lawyer, politician and cagy ex-guerrilla fighter, he's become a rather impetuous general, I would say.'

Mzingeli gave a rare grunt. 'So, *Nkosi*, when general attacks, do we join in?'

Fonthill pulled a face. 'I'd rather not. We are all worn out, living rough, eating poorly and have got very very wet over the last few days. I wouldn't want to have to deal with a face-to-face fight with damned great askaris in our present miserable state. This is one I would rather sit out.'

A twisted smile came over his bearded face. 'And we've done our bit. It wouldn't give me much pleasure to sit and watch Smuts get a bloody nose, because it would be our chaps getting knocked about. But at least we warned him. I can't see the three of us making much of a difference. Let's see if we can bunk down here in this wood and let our little general advance around us. They should know by the willows that this bit of wood is housing a swamp, so they should skirt around it – same with the Germans if they leave their lines, which I don't think they will do. Dig in a bit and put our oilskins over us, covered with leaves. We probably won't be noticed.'

'What about the 'orses?'

'Well, if they see them and take 'em, we'll just have to walk back. The best thing we can do now, I think, is to try and get some sleep. You two try and close your eyes. I'll take first watch. You take second, Mzingeli – keep a close eye on that German front line – and 352, you take the dawn watch. Wake me if there is any sign of movement from either of the front lines.'

As the damp dusk crept in around them, they settled down to spend an uncomfortable night, their heads on their saddles and their oilskins spread over them.

'Proper little babes in the woods, that's what we are,' observed Jenkins, his moustache protruding from the edge of his groundsheet. 'Get the fairies to cover me with leaves, there's a good chap, Jelly. Goodnight, children.'

There was no need for Jenkins to alert Simon at dawn, for the blast of the big gun shook them all awake. It sounded as though it came from the edge of the wood but it was now, by the look of it, stationed among the second line of trenches on the hill below. But it was definitely firing over the wood, towards the British lines.

'Smuts will advance now, that's for certain,' said Fonthill. 'Stay hidden. I want to watch the attack.'

Simon was right that the wood would be ignored by the British advance and, from the cover of the trees in the early light, they watched as the 29th Punjabis, 129th Baluchis and the 2nd South African Infantry Brigade split and advanced on either side of their hiding place like the waters of a rippling stream surging by a rock protruding from the river bed, and walk, rifles and bayonets extended, down into the broken ground – and into the German fire.

In fact, the defenders had chosen their ground carefully, for they were embedded on the sides of a series of hills surrounding the town that were immediately given identifying names by the attackers; 'Masai Kraal', 'Store', 'Euphorbien Hill', and so on. The British, Indians and South Africans came under heavy and accurate fire, as Fonthill had predicted. The role of the *Königsberg's* great gun became peripheral as the troops attacked and it fell silent, proving to Fonthill that it had been cleverly used by von Lettow-Vorbeck to tweak Smuts's pride and tempt him forward onto the waiting rifles and machine guns of his entrenched troops.

The day wore on and it became apparent that the attackers were making no definable impressions on the Germans but were indeed suffering heavy losses as they struggled up the hillsides under heavy fire.

By dusk, Fonthill had had enough. 'Get out your first-aid kits,' he called. 'We must go down and help those poor bastards who have been wounded. Leave your rifles behind.'

They laboured through the hours of darkness, giving what help they could to the medics who were crawling between the dead and the wounded.

Fonthill met one of the colonels he had befriended, who was himself giving aid to the stretcher-bearers and medics. 'Smuts is going to continue with this crazy attack, is he?' he demanded.

'Looks like it. He is determined to deliver what he calls a knockout blow, but it looks to me as though it's us who are being knocked about. I don't see how he can keep up this frontal assault in daylight. It seems crazy to me.'

'And to me.'

But the attacks continued throughout the second day, through a third and into a fourth, before Smuts called off the attack, pulling back what were left of his troops to lick his wounds.

'For God's sake, bach sir,' said a weary Jenkins. 'Can we get out of 'ere now? Apart from anythin' else, I've become bloody deafened by all this bangin'. Don't you think we should get back and report to the general, wherever 'e is?'

Fonthill's face was covered in grime and mud. He shook his head. 'That's just what we shouldn't do,' he said. 'It's our job now – exhausted as we are – to scout and see where the hell the Germans go from here. It's clear what von Lettow-Vorbeck has been up to. He never intended to put up a grand-stand fight against Smuts's army here. That's not what he's about. He wanted to draw Smuts on into this well-defended trap, knock him about as long as the man kept coming at him and then...'

Mzingeli nodded slowly. 'And then, *Nkosi?*' he asked.

'And then he is going to slip away while Smuts is tending his wounded and counting his dead and escape back down into the old German colony again. My guess is that he will abandon the whole Ruwu line that he has established here and just melt away down to the south-east into the dense bush that flanks the Northern Railway. That's the sort of hit-and-run fighter he is – just, in fact, as the Boers were in our battles against them. But it's no use going back to Smuts with a supposition. We have to track the Germans and then tell the general where the hell they've gone.'

Jenkins shook his head from side to side; the action of a man dead beat.

'So it's back into the saddle again, is it?' he asked. 'With 'ardly any food or water left. Another little jaunt into this fuckin' desert or swamp, whatever it decides to be? Is that right?'

Fonthill wiped a filthy hand over his mouth and jaw. 'Dead right, old chap. Now go and fetch the

332

horses, there's a good little scout.'

Slowly, they rode through the detritus of the battleground and marked the deep tracks in the mud where the *Königsberg* gun had been dragged back. The trenches were deserted and the town itself an empty ghost town. Its German defenders had, indeed, melted away into the interior of their vast colony, much of their ammunition and ordnance preserved, ready to fight another day.

'Well,' observed Simon, 'it's easy enough to track them.' And so it was for the first two days but, as the terrain became firmer and the bush more extended the retreating army spread out, slipping out on either side of the railway into the semi-desert again, to the point where even Mzingeli could not be sure whether von Lettow-Vorbeck had split his army to confuse pursuers.

Fonthill reined in his horse. 'That's enough,' he said, running his tongue along his cracked lips. 'We can't go on like this. If we do, we shall probably run into a German patrol. It's time to turn back and report.'

'Thank God for that, bach sir,' muttered Jenkins. 'Let's go an' find a beer.'

The country had now become a strange mixture of hard and soft terrain. Uncultivated, arid, dusty and studded with low bush flanking the railway line and offering shelter for lion and rhino – much of it impenetrable – it would sometimes without warning turn into semi-swampland, with head-high reeds flourishing from some underground aquifer and giving home to water buffalo and the occasional crocodile. It became difficult to make any sort of progress through the pools, the mud and the tufty clumps that offered the only firm purchase.

It was in one such strange patch that Mzingeli gently urged his horse alongside that of Simon's. 'We bein' followed, I think, *Nkosi*,' he said in a low voice. 'Horsemen behind us. I think they follow us a little way back, so must be tracking us.'

'Damn!' Fonthill wiped his brow and looked around. 'There's a patch of higher ground up ahead, by the look of it. Let's get up there, hide in the bush and wait for them to catch us up. The horses don't have the strength to pull away, so we will have to wait anyway. Tell Jenkins. Rifles at the ready.'

The trees on the high land were plentiful enough to offer shelter and they drew back into their friendly cover, levelled their rifles and waited.

Eventually, a lone horseman rode into sight. He was a black Askari, wearing a tattered German uniform and riding bootless. He rode, his head down, studying the ground ahead of him, obviously a tracker. Then he reined in, turned his head and called softly behind him. Three more men then came into sight: two of them similarly ethnic and poorly uniformed, the third a white man, with a long black beard and swarthy countenance. They all carried Mauser rifles.

The lead tracker pointed up ahead to where Fonthill and his comrades were hiding among the trees and said something to the white man, who nodded. Slowly, they urged their horses forward and began the climb towards the knoll.

'When I ride forward to confront them,' hissed Fonthill, 'stay behind amongst the trees and cover me. I want to talk to them.'

'Steady, bach sir,' muttered Jenkins, 'they've got guns too and we're outnumbered. What's more, they're bigger than us and I'm tired.'

'Oh, don't be such a ninny. Now, stay quiet.'

As the quartet approached the brow of the little hill Simon urged his mount forward and approached them, holding his rifle steadily aimed at them from the saddle.

'Forgive me if I get your name wrong, Mr Nieuw...' he began and paused. 'There you are, got it wrong already. Do you mind if I call you Piet?'

The swarthy man's jaw dropped for a moment, then his face broke into a grin, revealing great white teeth behind his beard. 'Not at all, English,' he called back. 'Real, African name – *proper* Afrikaans names that is – always were difficult for you. So I shall return the compliment and call you Simon.' The man spoke with easy English and only a trace of an Afrikaans accent.

Fonthill returned the grin. 'Ah yes, you know me. Please do. Much easier. After all, we are plying the same trade, I think.'

'Oh yes. Very much so. But I think you had better put down that English rifle before my black fellows here fire at you. They've been tracking you for hours and getting very tired and very impatient.'

'Ah no, Piet. I think not. My men have you covered from the protection of the trees. Tell your men to throw their guns to the ground. We will not fire if you do.'

The Boer narrowed his eyes and looked into the trees. 'Very well, if you give me your word. I think we are both far from reinforcements, anyway.' He turned and gave an order and the three askaris sullenly slipped from their saddles and put their rifles to the ground. They were then joined by General von Lettow-Vorbeck's chief scout.

'Come on out, boys,' called Simon. 'Come and join the party.'

Slowly and frowning, Jenkins and Mzingeli appeared, rifle butts at their haunches, the muzzles aimed at the four men.

Fonthill gazed down at his opposite number. 'May I put forward a proposition, Piet?' he asked.

'What is that?'

'I suggest that we stop this bloody ridiculous war for, well, maybe an hour, and share a cup of tea. We are tired, you are tired, and frankly I am weary of killing people and watching them being killed. Now, I understand that your ersatz coffee is pretty foul and we don't have much tea left. But if you would care to join us, we would be honoured to share what's left of our tea while we all take a break. What do you say?'

'I say you are right about this bloody awful stuff we are forced to drink and I would welcome a cup of English tea.' He lifted up his hand. 'We have a truce, I think, yah?'

Simon took his hand and shook it. 'We have a truce. Come on, 352. Put the kettle on.'

The three askaris had been watching the dialogue and listening to it without understanding it with troubled frowns on their faces. Now those round, black, glistening countenances broke into grins, as a fire was lit and Jenkins's little black kettle was hung over the flames and a pinch of black tea sprinkled into it. Somehow the Welshman had salvaged a few broken Huntley & Palmer digestive biscuits and these were shared all around as the seven men sprawled on the ground.

'So, Piet,' asked Simon. 'How far ahead is your army, then, and where is it heading?'

The warm smile broke above the Boer's beard. 'Ah now, man, you wouldn't expect me to tell you that, now, would you?'

'No, I wouldn't. But I have to compliment you for the way that you, your German masters and their askaris move so quickly and fluently across this accursed country.'

'Well, it is their land.'

Simon sniffed. 'Well, they haven't done much with it. No real farming that I can see. A complete waste of territory.'

'Probably. Imperial Germany was just beginning to put resources into it when the war broke out.'

'Hmm.' Fonthill gently inserted the last piece of precious biscuit into his mouth. 'So, tell me, Piet. Why are you fighting for that pompous, conceited emperor thousands of miles away in Europe? What did he ever do for you?'

The frown returned. 'He gave us support when we needed it against you Britishers sixteen or seventeen years ago, when you invaded our country.'

'But that war's been over for years and most of your leaders in that conflict happily support the Empire now: Botha, Smuts and so on.'

'But not the best of them – de Wet, for instance.'

Simon sighed. 'Ah well, I have a feeling that this conflict here now, in Germany's old colony, is going to go on for many months yet and many men are going to lose their life fruitlessly. The Germans can't continue to fight for ever without the support of their home country, so far away. It can only end one way.'

The Boer's black eyes gleamed as he leant forward. 'Yes but, English, before it does, von Lettow-Vorbeck will have given you so many hidings that you will wish you were never born. He exists purely as a nuisance value to keep your troops occupied here and prevent them from being sent to the Western Front in Europe. And he is by far the best general fighting in this campaign. There is a long way to go yet.'

A silence fell on the little gathering. Somewhere, down in one of the marshy hollows, something heavy moved and splashed and, much further away, a lion roared. Mosquitoes were gathering and dusk was approaching.

Simon sat up. 'Well,' he said, 'I guess our truce must end. We for our part are riding back north to report to Smuts. May I have your word that you will not follow us?'

The Boer extended his hand. 'Yah. You have that. We go south now to find our own men. We picked up your tracks way back and I asked myself who were these three men riding out alone in this wilderness. Then it occurred to me it might be the famous Simon Fonthill and his trackers and I was curious.'

He smiled. 'But it was good to meet you – if only for the tea. If we do follow you, it will only be to capture your tea.'

'Alas, sorry old chap. None left now.'

Within minutes the two little parties had mounted and, with waves of their hands, began to ride their separate ways.

'Well,' Jenkins urged his mount alongside that of Simon's. 'What a bloody funny little tea party. I wish all wars could be conducted like that. Except that we've got bugger all to drink now. Unless, that is…?'

'Oh yes. I have about half a bottle left. I'm not sharing good Scotch whisky with these strange, never-say-die Boers.'

'I should bloody 'ope not.'

Two days later, the battered little trio met the first outriders of Smuts's army, marching south. Fonthill could see straight away that some of the confidence, the *joie de vivre*, which had characterised its bearing before the Kahe had disappeared. The battle had taken its toll on the various ethnic elements of the British–Indian–South African force. Simon recalled the words of Nieuwenhuizen: 'von Lettow-Vorbeck will give you so many hidings…'

Fonthill was immediately ushered into the presence of Jan Smuts. 'Where the hell have you been, man?' queried the general.

'We couldn't play much part in the battle, because we were caught between the two armies. So we did what we could to help with the wounded, and then,' Simon paused, 'when it became apparent that you had taken a bit of a beating with that direct attack, I felt it my duty to follow the Germans and track the way they were retreating. I sent two messages back with natives we met and bribed upon the way. I hope you received them?'

'Yes,' Smuts nodded – a trifle wearily, Fonthill thought. 'That was the right thing to do. It enabled me to give chase, although not, I fear, very quickly.' He looked up and engaged Simon's eyes. 'But you were wrong, Fonthill, to say that we took a beating. It is true that we lost more men than I would have liked but we forced the Germans back on the retreat once more. I doubt if they will try and impose themselves on the border again. Now, where do you think they are going?'

'Well frankly, sir, I cannot be sure. They are clearly going into the hinterland, probably towards their Central Railway, but where they will move from there I have no idea. It is obviously important, of course, that they are not allowed to settle in the corridor on either side of the Northern Railway and prepare attacks from there. I would guess that he has already moved supply depots and his hospital southwards to anticipate you pursuing him. But we were dead beat, sir, and had to return to report to you, anyway. Give us a few days' rest and we will ride off again to track them down.'

'You shall certainly have that, but I intend to continue to pursue my offensive to the south, so I shall need you.' Then a faint, rather ironic smile came over the general's impeccably shaven features. 'But first, I have a surprise for you, Fonthill. Someone has been waiting for you to arrive for quite a few days now.' He turned his head and barked an order in Afrikaans. The two men sat in silence for a moment or two before the tent flap was disturbed and a flushing Alice came through it.

'Good God, Alice!' Simon rose and stumbled towards her, arms outstretched. They embraced and then a smiling Smuts stood and said, 'Let me leave you together for a few minutes. I must talk to van Deventer.'

Alice pulled back. 'That is a disgraceful beard, darling. Do you really have to go so native on these expeditions?'

'Only to annoy you, my love. But what on earth are you doing out here in the field? I thought the correspondents were safely housed in their hutches back in Mombasa.'

'So they were.' Alice pushed him onto a chair and perched on a stool opposite him and told him of her attempts to arrest de Villiers, her request to interview Smuts and of his acceptance – as, she felt, a part reward for unmasking the spy ring.

'And the big bonus, darling,' she continued, 'is that I was able to stay and report on the Battle for Kahe and then wait here until your return. Now I am to be shipped back to Mombasa to be put back into my kennel. But I saw the battle. Heavy-going, I think – and where were you?'

'In between the armies, lying low. Nothing much we could do, except help the wounded. It was a terrible mistake of Smuts to attack like that. I warned him not to, but he chose to ignore my advice.' He frowned and lowered his voice. 'He has his merits as a commander, Alice, but one could not call him a good general.'

Alice frowned. 'Ah, but he sent the Germans

packing, didn't he? That's what I have reported, anyway.'

'Yes, but that was not his intention. He thought he had cornered von Lettow-Vorbeck but, in fact, he had been drawn into a trap and lost far too many men. The askaris waited until they had inflicted the maximum damage and then slipped away again, as they always do.'

Alice's frown deepened. 'Perhaps I have been seduced by Smuts's briefings but I had gathered the impression that our South African troops are good warriors and probably outfighting the Germans' askaris.'

Fonthill pulled a face. 'Nothing of the kind. The Germans have become masters of concealment and defence and of moving quickly across this difficult country. The terrain here is as unfamiliar to the Boers as it is to our British and Indian troops. The enemy troops are well officered and remarkably brave and resilient – and, it seems, perfectly loyal to the German cause. Strange, given the Germans' reputation for beating them. But, apart from the ill-treatment, we have much to learn from the Hun here, darling. Don't be misled.'

'Oh dear. We have much to talk about. How and where are 352 and Mzingeli?'

'Putting up our tents. They are like me – terribly tired but quite fit. Come and meet them. We have only just arrived back, but I could do with getting away from Smuts for a time.'

That night the four of them sat, ate and drank around the campfire before crawling into their bivouac tents, Alice sharing Simon's, despite the cramped space. They made tender, scratchy love before falling into a deep sleep in each other's arms.

The next morning was illuminated by a letter addressed to Alice and forwarded to her from Mombasa. Sunil always sent his letters to her, as the least mobile of the two. It announced that he had been promoted to Brigade Major and was now stationed somewhere near Ypres, the battered little town on the French–Flemish border, which fringed probably the most fought-over patch of shell holes and mud on the Western Front.

'Oh!' Alice smothered a gasp. 'That means he must be in greater danger.'

Simon shook his head. 'Not so. He's become a staff man at Brigade Headquarters. He will be back from the front line. He's much safer there.'

'Thank God for that.'

Simon, Jenkins and Mzingeli saw Alice off later that morning as she began the long buggy journey back to the railhead. They waved to her until she eventually disappeared over a rise, her green scarf fluttering from her hand.

Fonthill blew his nose. He could not help but wonder if this would be the last time he would see his wife. Smuts wanted them back, following the railway line to the south to catch up with the phantom German army as it prepared for another gruelling march.

Jenkins squinted up at the high sun beating down on them. 'I think this one's goin' to be tough, bach sir, ain't it?'

'Hard slogging, 352. Hard slogging.'

CHAPTER FOURTEEN

And so it proved.

The ensuing months produced the most arduous and bitter fighting of the whole campaign. Fonthill, Jenkins and Mzingeli hung onto von Lettow-Vorbeck's coat-tails and, fed by their information, Smuts's three columns pressed along behind, advancing down the tracks of the Northern Railway and constantly engaging the German rearguard. They advanced through a hundred miles of dense bush and blistering heat, with the Germans disputing every inch of the territory. The British lines of supply and communication were stretched to twanging point and Smuts's men were subsisting on two biscuits a day. Sickness became rife.

It became clear that one of the main reasons for the Germans' remarkable resilience lay in the considerable number of doctors in their ranks at the start of the war: sixty-three, far more than the British. Their network of field hospitals established in the north-east had been moved to the south, matching von Lettow-Vorbeck's retreat. In addition, the improvisation of the German medical staff was ingenious. Home-made quinine was manufactured from the bark of the cinchona tree, bandages were fashioned from soft bark and stocks of all-important typhoid treatment had been taken from towns and cities and distributed round the field hospitals on the line of retreat, ready for immediate use.

The war was now being waged on many fronts, for the German commander had split his force into several columns, scattering throughout the interior and on the periphery of the old German colony. In the south, the British General Northey, attacking from Nyasaland, was having a particularly hard time of it pursuing the Germans across some of the most mountainous and inhospitable territory in all Africa.

As always, it was the native carriers who suffered the most. Some 160,000 were needed to maintain supplies. Bewildered by the conflict – they called it 'the White Man's Palaver' – they were pressed into service, often unwillingly, and suffered great deprivations from the climate. They were also under constant attack from lions in the dry and crocodiles in the wet.

With the vastly outnumbered German columns twisting and turning, fighting and retreating, it had become a will-o'-the-wisp war, with Smuts's strategy of trapping the enemy by executing sweeping flanking movements across the open country proving completely ineffective. But the Germans were not Smuts's only antagonists. Large numbers of wounded and exhausted South African troops were now being returned home and he became the centre of mounting criticism in South Africa. The earlier sweeping success of Botha's invasion of German South West Africa seemed a distant irrelevance compared with the hardship of this gruelling warfare in the north. The political far right in the Cape, Natal and

Pretoria was growing more vociferous in its criticism of Smuts's waging of the war.

Not so in Britain, however. Here the little South African was hailed as one of the few successful Allied generals of the war and Smuts was called to London in 1917 to join the Imperial War Cabinet. On his arrival, he claimed complete victory in German East Africa, pointing out that he had wrested more than a million square miles of German territory from the enemy. But his sudden departure and the return home of almost all of the South African troops caused chaos. The British General Hoskins, who took command, was left with a severely diminished force and in March 1917 he was forced to report to the War Office that although his military establishment exceeded 40,000 on paper, only about 12,000 were fit for combat.

Hoskins pleaded with Botha to send him more South African troops but the South African prime minister refused. He could not trust the Afrikaner nation, he said, to support the sending of more men to the maelstrom of the war in the north. To all intents and purposes the large 'South African Expeditionary Force' had melted away and, in particular, Hoskins bewailed the loss of the South African horsemen who constituted virtually his only cavalry in the field. In the circumstances, Hoskins could not see how he could continue to pursue Smuts's offensive.

In Whitehall, the powerful Smuts maintained that Hoskins was 'dawdling'. Once again he had his way and in May the British general, highly regarded and even loved by his officers and men, was reassigned to Mesopotamia and van Deventer became commander-in-chief.

The big, burly Afrikaner – his hands were said to cover most of the maps when he gave briefings, so that it was difficult to follow him – could not be termed pro-British, having fought hard against Kitchener in the Anglo–Boer war, but he was fiercely loyal to his superiors; if Botha and Smuts believed it was right to defend the Empire against the Germans, then so did he. He was also a strong leader, if he lacked the complete self-conviction of Smuts.

He had quickly set up a good relationship with Fonthill, as his chief scout. Completely abandoning his habit of not speaking in English unless forced to, he put a great arm around Simon's shoulder on his appointment. 'You do good work, man,' he growled. 'Keep out there and tell me what the hell is going on. I shall rely on you.'

With Smuts supporting him in London, van Deventer began a systematic campaign of splitting his command and doggedly hunting down the German columns wherever he could find them. Five months of almost continuous fighting ensued across the most difficult country, with every waterhole being defended by the Germans. In many areas, the bush was so thick that large bodies of troops could pass each other within a mile without one being aware of the other. As the heat increased, bush fires sprang up and the ground became blackened and smoking.

'I know where we are fightin' now, bach sir,' observed Jenkins one day, his face smeared with soot so that his eyes stood out like white marbles.

347

'We're fightin' in 'ell, that's where we are. We're fightin' in bloody 'ell. I always knew what it felt like, because I'd suffered enough terrible 'angovers in me time. But I always wanted to know what it looks like and now I know. It looks like this.'

The three of them had ranged far and wide over the war-torn territory of the old German colony, for van Deventer had given them freedom to pursue the various German columns – some of them now little more than companies – and to report to the local British generals their positions and possible intentions.

Now, the three were just outside Narungombe in the south-east, forty miles from the coast of the Indian Ocean. With the rains – the worst in living memory – just ended, van Deventer was under strict orders to defeat von Lettow-Vorbeck on the firmer ground once and for all. Fonthill sensed that months of fighting in the unhealthiest area of the entire colony lay ahead. As they bivouacked on the plain, on the edge of where a bush fire had roared, he cast a critical eye on his comrades.

They were exhausted, he knew, for their supplies were running low and all of their waking hours were spent in the saddle so that their backs and thighs ached miserably. Now, however, they *looked* exhausted, too. Although they were no longer young – Jenkins at sixty-six was the oldest, with Mzingeli and Fonthill now in their early sixties – they had led outdoor lives, escaped wounds or serious injury and remained fit throughout their long campaigning. Today, it seemed as though all their narrow escapes and risk-taking over the years had caught up with them. Mzingeli bent over his tin of mealies, his nose almost touching the edge; Jenkins lay on his side, slowly ladling native sausage meat between his blackened lips. Underneath the soot, their faces were cracked and lined. They were three elderly men living young men's lives and, clearly, nearing their end of their tether.

Fonthill frowned. Was it fair to ask his two comrades to continue this dangerous, demanding life – particularly Mzingeli, who had no vested interest in the outcome of this white man's war? He cleared his throat.

'What do you think now boys?' he asked. 'Do you think we've done enough? Is it time we struggled back to van Deventer – wherever he might be now – and suggested that it was time we called it a day?' He forced a smile. 'We're not as young as we used to be and there are plenty of young scouts in the field now. Perhaps we should pass on the baton. What do you think?'

From somewhere behind the sausages, Jenkins emitted a deep growl. 'What? Give up, you mean? Pack it all in and go back to growing tea or petunias, while these bloody 'Uns are still maraudin' all over the place? Not for me, bach sir, but if you've 'ad enough, then I'll do what you say, as I always do.'

Simon turned to his tracker. 'Mzingeli. This has never been your war, although you have served magnificently through it so far. Would you like to go back to the farm now?'

The black man looked up and gave his life-affirming grin. 'I do what you want, *Nkosi*,' he said.

349

'The farm is looking after itself under my cousin. I think, though, like 352 bach, that we ought to finish job. Much more to be done. Get rid of these Germans and their cruel askaris, I think. But you lead. We follow.'

Fonthill gave a wry smile and nodded slowly. 'Very well, then,' he said. 'We stay and finish the job and I couldn't wish for better comrades–'

Mzingeli raised a long, thin finger to interrupt him. 'Men coming,' he said. 'We take cover quick.'

Not for the first or last time, Simon thanked his lucky stars for the acute hearing and bush awareness of his tracker. 'Fire out, Mzingeli,' he said. '352, take the horses behind those smouldering bushes and get them to lie down. We'll take cover with you.'

Moving with quiet, practised skill, they removed all traces of their stay and crept back into the blackened undergrowth about a hundred yards from their picnic site, their rifles at the ready. Within minutes a small squad of seven or eight black askaris came into view, thrusting back the charred branches and stamping out smouldering patches of grass with their bare feet, all the time looking around them carefully.

'They're onto us,' whispered Jenkins. 'Must have seen us back there, or followed our tracks.'

'No shooting yet. I don't want to draw in any other patrols that may be nearby. These look as though they've come scouting from Narungombe. Keep low, they might just pass us by.'

At that moment, one of the horses stirred in the ashes of the bush fire and neighed in pain as he burnt his side. Immediately, the German patrol flung themselves to the ground and the pith-helmeted officer let off a round from his revolver, in the general direction from which the sound had come.

'Fire,' bellowed Fonthill. His shot caught the officer as he bent to join his men on the ground, spun him round and felled him. The others, however, had somehow disappeared into the fire-torn bush and couldn't be seen. Well trained, they embraced the undulations in the ground and lay, obviously waiting for a target to present itself.

'Can't see the bastards,' muttered Jenkins.

'No. We will have to draw their fire.'

'No, bach. Don't do anything silly, now. We're outnumbered.'

'Listen. I will run to the right. They will open fire. That will reveal their positions. Rapid fire on them when they do. Tell Mzingeli. I will run in ten seconds from now. Get ready. Begin to count.'

Fonthill lay prone on the earth, his breast heaving. Then, he gradually began to draw up his legs and hunch his back. He took a deep breath, sprang to his feet and ran to his right, dodging between the blackened bush stubble. He was conscious of bullets whipping into the ground beneath his feet and the staccato of Jenkins and Mzingeli's Lee-Enfields rapid firing in reply. Then he flung himself down.

'Think we've got 'em, bach sir. Are you all right?' Jenkins's voice was anxious.

'Yes, I'm all right, just out of breath. But get the horses up quickly. We need to get out of here, fast as we can. I can hear others coming up!'

Fonthill and his comrades had been following a large and well-armed force of Germans – some 2,000 rifles with 48 machine guns and a battery of captured Portuguese artillery – back from the coast as it approached the town of Narungombe, north of the Mbemkuru River. He suspected that its commander, Captain von Lieberman, had decided to stand and fight there, for it offered a last source of water sufficient to sustain his force. Fonthill was on his way back to contact the three pursuing British columns to lead them onto the enemy when the bush fire had overtaken them. Now it looked as though the Germans were out patrolling in some depth. They must dash through their lines if they were to escape.

There was a squeal as the horses were dragged to their feet and their packs, which had been un-loaded to give the beasts some temporary respite, thrust back behind the saddles. There was also shouting in German and then a ragged salvo of shots as a second group of askaris burst from cover, knelt and fired as the three men, heads down, spurred away.

'Thank God they'd got no cavalry,' shouted Jenkins as their horses galloped over the hard ground. 'Where to, now, bach sir?'

'To the east, towards Kilwa. We must find General Beves and bring him up to attack Nar-ungombe before the bloody Germans decide to turn and run again. This could be a really decisive battle.'

''Ow far away is this general, then?'

'I don't know. But I know he's coming in from the coast and if we keep heading east we should meet him. We could be in trouble, though, if the Germans have thrown up a defensive screen this side of the town. Head down and ride hard.'

'Very well. But don't fall off, for God's sake.'

They galloped as far as their panting mounts allowed them, then they slowed to a walk and, as darkness approached, looked for and found some sort of cover where they could spend the night out of sight of German patrols.

They met the first of General Beves's extended pickets halfway through the next morning: a small troop of cavalry of the 40th Pathans out in extended order, all clearly showing the effects of advancing too quickly from the humid coast into a hinterland wracked by bush fires under a burning sun.

Within the half-hour Fonthill was reporting to General Beves, a red-faced man with an abrupt manner.

'Where the hell is the enemy, Fonthill?' he demanded. 'We've lost all touch with him.'

'They're waiting at Narungombe for you, General,' responded Simon. 'I believe they are going to stand and fight there, so you must be prepared for a battle.'

'Humph! I've heard that before. Get there, bayonets fixed, and the buggers have disappeared into thin air once more. What makes you think this chap is determined to fight?'

Fonthill sighed. 'Because von Lieberman has managed to put together a strong force by combining about a dozen companies. He has been fighting hard on the retreat for over a week and desperately needs a few days to regroup. This

353

town has water; it's the last main source able to provide for such a large gathering north of the Mbemkuru River, and he will want to give his troops a break. He also wants glory – at your expense.'

Beves raised his eyebrows. 'Do you know his dispositions?'

'Yes – unless he has moved them. The Germans are deployed across the main track approaching the town. It's a good defensive position he has adopted. His left flank is in thick bush and his right rests in a swamp teeming with crocodiles. His machine guns are placed on high ground on either side of the track and they and his rifles have a good and clear field of fire. I reckon he will be pretty confident in waiting there for you. I would advise caution in making a frontal attack, General.'

'Ah, you would, would you.' Beves's face seemed to have deepened in colour as Fonthill reported and a small tic had appeared under his right eye. 'Well, let me tell you, *scout*' – the word was emphasised as though to emphasise Fonthill's status – 'I have orders to attack these bloody Germans as soon as I come up to them. I am under pressure to put them out quickly and I intend to do just that.'

'Now,' his voice suddenly softened as his gaze took in the blackened nature of Fonthill's face and limbs, the tears in his clothing from the thorn bushes through which they had ridden hard over the last few days and the general weariness of his posture. 'You clearly need a rest. How long before we come to this damned town, d'yer think?'

'This time tomorrow, I would say.'

'Very well. Fall back through the lines and get some rest. I shall continue to bring up my three columns and we will attack as soon as I am in position. Oh – and thank you, Fonthill.'

'Not at all, General. All part of the service.'

Simon raised a leisurely forefinger to his brow and walked away. He had become used to being under-regarded by these commanders in the field and now wasted little time in exchanging courtesies with them. He, Jenkins and Mzingeli certainly needed rest, for Fonthill had decided that they would attack with Beves's men. This was no time for hanging back, with the opportunity at last of defeating a sizeable German force in the offing. He wanted to be there. But first: sleep.

At dawn, a messenger arrived to wake Fonthill and order him to ride ahead to be with Beves as the defended town was approached. He reached him just as his three columns had ground to a halt at midday and extended across the plain, in front of the German positions.

'I see what you mean, Fonthill,' said the general, studying the enemy lines through his field glasses. 'He's dug in pretty well, too. But at least he hasn't done a runner. He *is* here waiting for us and looking as though he wants a fight.'

'Oh, I think he does that, all right.'

'No easy way round those lines, you say?'

'Afraid not.' Fontill pointed. 'As you can see, the bush thickens considerably where he has rested his left flank and I can't see how troops could get through there under fire. And the other end of his trenches stop at that damned great

355

swamp there. No real way through there, either. Particularly as it's home to so many crocs.'

Beves put down his binoculars. The nervous tic was more marked now, Simon noticed. 'Then I shall launch a frontal attack. Only way. Just knock 'em out of the way. Can't hang about. I hear that von Lettow-Vorbeck is on his way with fresh troops. Know anything about that? You didn't tell me.'

The tone was petulant. 'Didn't know, General,' replied Fonthill. 'He could well be, but I've heard nothing about it from the natives we questioned locally. Could well be true, though. He will not want to risk so many of von Lieberman's men against your three columns without supporting them.' He paused for a moment, then: 'This could turn into the biggest battle of the campaign, General. If you don't mind me saying so, you must be careful you don't lose your command, attacking across this open ground against these well-defended positions.'

'Well, I do mind you saying so, Fonthill. I shall go in at dawn tomorrow and that's that.'

'Very well, General. Good luck.'

Rejoining Mzingeli and Jenkins, the Welshman gave Simon an appraising look. 'Attacking at dawn, eh? Will the three of us go in with them?'

'To hell with it now, unless ordered to do so – and that won't happen because we've done our job. Beves's force is going to be terribly mauled as it advances across that open ground. I don't want to be involved in that, thank you very much. I think this is another one we'll sit out.'

The three did rise early, however, just as the

sun was turning the horizon scarlet to the east. On a slight ridge behind the lines, they settled down – Fonthill with a heavy heart – to watch as Beves opened the attack with a barrage from his artillery. The Germans immediately reciprocated and within minutes the view ahead was shrouded in smoke and then flames as the brush caught fire.

'Gawd,' grunted Jenkins, 'I wouldn't want to be in that lot.'

As they watched, they saw the Gold Coast Regiment trudge forward into the maelstrom, then a detachment of the 3rd Punjabis and the great black soldiers of the King's African Rifles, heads down as though their fezes would protect them from the bullets that swept across the track from the German machine guns.

All day the battle raged, with four German counter-attacks on the British flanks being repulsed. The smoke had cleared somewhat now and the extent of the attackers' losses could be seen from the inert bodies strewn across the track leading into Narungombe. Yet Beves continued to hurl fresh troops into the inferno.

For some time, Fonthill had been scrutinising the German right through his field glasses. Then he struggled to his feet. 'This is ridiculous,' he muttered. 'The man must be mad. I'm going to have a word with him. Stay here. I will be back soon.'

'For God's sake don't volunteer to do anything,' shouted Jenkins as he walked away.

He found the general, surrounded by his staff, a little way back from the front line.

'What the hell do you want, Fonthill?' snarled Beves. 'Can't you see I'm busy?'

'With respect, General, you can't keep attacking into those machine guns, otherwise you will lose all your men. I have a suggestion to make, if you will listen for a moment.'

'What?' Beves's face was now quite red. 'I am convinced von Lettow-Vorbeck is near now. I must break through before he reaches us. A suggestion, did you say? What sort of suggestion?'

'Give me a company of men – preferably from the Punjabis, for they are splendid fighters and light on their feet.'

'What will you do with them?'

'I have not properly scouted that swamp on the German right but there's just a chance that I could lead a small body of them through it, despite the crocs, and emerge from its cover just where the German line ends. Too many men will just draw down the artillery on the swamp, but give me a company, say, and if we can get through and survive the crocodiles I reckon we could then spring a surprise and maybe even turn the line.'

Beves's jaw dropped. But he turned to one of his colonels. 'What d'you think?' he demanded.

The colonel nodded slowly. 'Worth a try, sir. Let me find some Punjabis.'

'Oh, very well. But only a company, mind.'

Within minutes some eighty turbaned Punjabis reported for duty, led by a young, English subaltern sporting a ridiculously immature ginger moustache and wearing a white pith helmet that appeared too large for him. To Fonthill, he appeared as though he should still be studying algebra in some pukka English public school.

He saluted Fonthill, although Simon wore no uniform. 'What ho, General,' he said. 'I hear you've deliberately asked for Punjabis. Quite right, too. Best troops in the Indian Army. But,' he grinned, 'if anybody asks for Punjabis it usually means dirty work. Is that right?'

Fonthill returned the grin. 'Oh no, not really. I just want to take you through that swamp on the German right over there, avoiding probably about forty or fifty man-eating crocodiles that live there, and then attack the German line and turn it. Are you up for it?'

'Er ... did you say crocodiles?'

'Yes. Are you any good with crocodiles? By the way, what's your name?'

'John Jones, sir. Distinctive name, eh?'

'Most distinctive.'

'Yes, and I am the best crocodile fighter in India. Yes, we're up for it. Shame, though. I specially cleaned my puttees this morning.'

'Stand the men down and explain what's needed. I have a little persuading of my own to do. I will be back to lead you into and through the swamp in five minutes.'

'Very good, General.'

Jenkins was predictably unenthusiastic at the thought of wading through the swamp.

'What? With them bloody great crocs in there?' His face was contorted and sweat immediately sprang out on his brow. 'It's not that I'm afraid of them, see, but I might tread on one and 'urt it. Couldn't I go round the edge a bit?'

'No. I shall need your marksmanship when we

get through. Don't be such a baby. The crocs will be more afraid of you than you are of them. They will just get out of your way.'

'Oh yes. If you ask them politely. I didn't sign up to get eaten by a crocodile, look you. Beyond the call of duty, I'd say.'

'Come on now. We must try it. I promised the general.'

Fonthill led his two companions back to the Punjabis. He addressed the men. 'It will be difficult wading through that swamp,' he said, 'but at least we will be under cover from the reeds and bushes. Don't be afraid to shoot at the crocs – a few more shots won't alert anyone in this battle. But, whatever you do, watch out for their tails. They can knock you down and are potentially more dangerous than the snouts. I shall lead, with Mzingeli and Jenkins here. Once we are through the worst of the swamp, we will form up under cover on the edge. Is that clear?'

Eighty turbans nodded.

'Right, fix bayonets,' he grinned, 'you'll need them to push the crocs out of the way, then follow me.' He shot a glance behind him at Jenkins. The little Welshman seemed to have lost all colour from his face, despite its grime and underlying tan. He had sucked his great moustache below his lower lip, so that his features were distorted.

'Mzingeli,' hissed Simon. 'Look after 352. Stay close to him.'

Then he called back to Jones. 'Right, Lieutenant. Stay close behind me and keep to the right. Tell your men to be careful where they put their feet.'

The smell hit them before they reached the edge of the marsh: a fetid, sour odour, redolent of mud, excrement and of things long decayed and left to die in the mud and foul water. The first thing Fonthill realised as he crept up to the edge of the swamp was that it was far larger than he had thought. He could not see through to the end of the tangled vegetation for there was little light coming through it. He took a deep breath and took a quick compass bearing before, revolver in hand, he lowered himself into the brown water.

It came only up to his hip but immediately his feet seemed to be sucked into some glutinous substance at the bottom, so that he could only extract them after some considerable effort. He strode forward as best he could, and put out a hand to steady himself against a floating log. Immediately, it kicked into life and slithered away.

'Oh my God!' Jenkins's voice was a croak.

Wherever Simon looked now, it seemed that scaly logs were sinuously moving through the water, some coloured a ubiquitous brown, others a glistening green. He shot a glance behind him. Jenkins, his eyes now firmly closed, had his arm around Mzingeli's shoulder. The tracker, watching the water ahead carefully, was gently urging his comrade forward, his rifle pointing the way down and ahead like a direction finder. Behind them, the Punjabis were wading forward steadily, some with the water up to their chests.

Fonthill felt a nudge to his left leg under the surface and then, with terrifying suddenness, a ghastly head broke the surface ahead of him and giant jaws opened up. Blindly, he fired his revolver into the maw and the crocodile thrashed for a second, its tail sweeping round in great arcs and sending plumes of water high into the air, before it gently subsided into the depths, a pool of blood showing where it had slipped away.

Gulping in air, Simon plodded on, frequently forced to consult his compass in the gloom. It was terribly hard going and there seemed to be more crocodiles about than ever, some seemingly keeping pace with him and regarding him with basilisk eyes. Ahead, he glimpsed what appeared to be a mossy bank to his right. He plunged towards it and found it was a huge plantain root. Strangely coloured snakes were wriggling among the roots but he pulled himself half out of the water, high enough to perch his bottom on the bank and bend down to give Jenkins and Mzingeli a hand and then look behind them to the following Punjabis.

Jones and his men were making slow progress. Another splash of water towards the rear marked another crocodile attack, followed immediately by a rifle shot and huge disturbance in the water as the reptile was despatched. Then a startled cry as a soldier was seized, followed immediately by another rifle shot as he was released from the jaws of the crocodile.

'Seems as though they are deliberately attacking us,' gasped Mzingeli.

'No. The poor devils think we are attacking them. We are disturbing their environment, to say the least. We'll just have to keep going. Maybe there is firmer ground further ahead. Hang onto

352, there's a good chap. Here, I'll help you.'

Jenkins, bravest of warriors, was now almost a wreck. His mouth was open, gasping in air, but his eyes were completely closed. Simon thrust his rifle sling over his shoulder, placed one of the Welshman's arms round Mzingeli's neck and the other around his own, and began wading again, his revolver pointing ahead of them at the surface of the brown water.

It was, in fact, as though the crocodiles were retreating before them. The glistening, scaly creatures were now attempting to get out of the way of the men wading behind them, swinging their tails in the water to get leverage and scrambling with their great, long-clawed feet in the mud to get onto higher ground.

Fonthill turned his head. 'I can see light from the edge of the swamp ahead. But keep your voices down, we must be near the German lines now.'

He gripped Jenkins's hand tightly and whispered into his ear. 'Nearly there, old chap. Nearly over. Open your eyes, 352. I will need you to kill half the German army once we break out of this foul-smelling place. Come on. Open up.'

One eye opened. ''Ave they gone?' he asked. 'One of them touched me, I swear it. Oh, thank God, that's nearly over.' He tried to summon a grin. 'Sorry, bach sir. You probably 'adn't noticed, like, but I am not very fond of crocodiles, y'see.'

'Never noticed. Now we have to fight. You going to be all right?'

'As long as we don't turn around and back the

way we came, I'll be fine, look you. Can you 'and me me rifle?'

The ground beneath Fonthill's feet began to rise and became much firmer. Now crawling on hands and knees, he edged his way through the reeds and, gently parting them, found himself looking right down on the German trench. He was facing the snub muzzle of a heavy Maxim-type machine gun, whose crew were idly lying by its mounting. The two lines of the German trenches stretched away beyond them, with askaris still firing steadily down at Beves's men.

Fonthill turned his head. Behind him, bedraggled Punjabis were emerging from the water and, in response to his waving arms, spreading out on either side of him, lying panting on mossy tussocks.

John Jones, his body covered in mud and his pith helmet hanging down his back by its strap, now crawled up beside him.

'If you don't mind, General,' he whispered, 'next time you have a difficult job to do could you send for the bloody Grenadier Guards instead of my nice clean Punjabis. Look at 'em, what a mess!'

'Well done, John. Any casualties?'

'One rather nasty croc bite, that's all. Amazing, considering.'

'Good. Now, listen. Deploy the men along the edge of the swamp. Tell them to stay hidden and make sure that their rifles are free of mud and have bayonets attached. Just there,' he indicated with his head, 'there is a heavy German machine gun fixed to fire directly at us. So if we break out too soon we shall be cut down. Obviously, the

364

Hun felt the swamp could be a danger point.'

'Can we put the gun out?'

'Yes.' Fonthill nodded to where Jenkins was now imperturbably wiping his rifle clean. 'I have the best marksman and strongest lover of crocodiles in the British army there. He will pick off the crew.'

Jones flicked a piece of mud from the end of his nose. 'Do you want us to attack up the trenches? How many are there?'

'Two. But we enfilade them so I want a couple of crushing volleys first, when I give the order. Then we can charge. But to the right, up the hill, there are other machine guns dug in. They could be the problem. Can you take half your men and put them out? At least they will be firing down the hill away from you, not expecting an attack from here.'

'Very well, sir. Consider it done. I will await your order.' Jones slipped away to supervise the positioning of his men.

Fonthill crawled to join Jenkins and Mzingeli on the edge of the reeds.

'You all right, 352?'

'O' course, bach sir. What do you want me to do?'

Simon gently parted the reeds ahead of them. 'There are three men manning that gun facing us,' he whispered. 'When I give the order I want you to put them all out. Stay positioned, and if others come forward to man the gun, cut them down. Understood?'

Jenkins, now cold-eyed and composed, nodded. 'Understood.'

'Mzingeli.'

'*Nkosi.*'

'Please direct your fire on the other machine guns up the hill. I will support you. Once this end of the two trenches is opened I shall send in the Punjabis with the bayonet and we will work our way up them to clear them.'

Jenkins carefully fixed a bayonet to the muzzle of his Lee Enfield. 'I shall come with you, then, of course,' he said, matter-of-factly.

'Very well. But stay close.'

'I always do.'

Simon looked along the edge of the swamp and saw that the Punjabis had crawled forward into the reeds fronting the edge of the swamp and were now well positioned. Jones was looking towards him expectantly. He put his finger to his lips and gestured to Jenkins.

'Right, 352,' he murmured. 'Shoot.'

Immediately, the Welshman fired once, worked the bolt, fired again and then a third time. 'Got 'em,' he called.

Fonthill rose to his knees and screamed. 'Punjabis, open fire!'

It seemed as if the reeds on the perimeter had suddenly burst into flame, as the Indian troops sent a succession of volleys into the trenches before them. 'Right, go for the guns now, John,' called Simon, and saw the little lieutenant break cover, waving his men forward, as they slipped and slithered out of the reeds and began climbing the gentle slope towards where the other German machine guns were dug in.

Fonthill now rose to his feet and shouted,

'Punjabis, charge!'

He was dimly aware of the men behind him as he, in turn, broke cover and bounded down the hill towards the end of the first trench. The machine gun lay, its muzzle pointed to the sky, its crew dead around it. Other bodies lay further along in the narrow trench, a testimony to the marksmanship of the Indian troops.

Simon now caught the sleeve of an Indian non-commissioned officer. 'Havildar, take a troop and work your way up that trench up above us,' he ordered. 'I want it cleared. I will do the same down here.'

'Very good, sahib.'

Realising that they were being attacked from their flank, the Germans were now rallying and askaris were bounding down the trench, firing as they came, to meet the new assailants.

'We're with you, bach sir.' Jenkins's reassuring voice came from just behind him.

Immediately, the battle became a chaotic affair of hand-to-hand fighting in the restricted space of the trench, with bayonet clashing with bayonet and bullets fired at point-blank range. Both sides were having to cope with finding footholds on the bottom of the trench where bodies were lying – some of them still moving – as a result of the Punjabis' opening volleys.

Fonthill fired at and brought down a giant black Askari who had thrust at him with his bayonet but had no time to rework the bolt before another was upon him, a smaller man this time, more agile, who sprang from body to body beneath his feet, presenting the tip of his bayonet in parade-ground fashion. Simon hooked the end of his own bayonet around that of his opponent and swung it up and round, and then down and into the man's breast.

A shout of 'well done, bach' showed that his old comrade was still behind him and Fonthill realised that the force of his charge had cleared the trench ahead. Had the Germans retreated? Had the line been turned? The chatter of machine guns from up the hill, however, showed that the engagement was far from over.

Indeed, more German reinforcements were now appearing up ahead and from above the earthworks thrown up on either side. The enemy, however, had made the mistake of not building zigzag buttresses into their trenches, so that Simon, at the head of the Punjabis, had a clean line of fire towards the men running towards him.

He knelt and took careful aim, conscious that Jenkins and Mzingeli were at his side. Immediately, three askaris at the head of the attack fell, and then others, as the Punjabis opened fire from behind.

'Up the trench,' shouted Simon. 'Keep running. Clear the damned thing.'

The enemy were making sporadic attempts to counter-attack and groups of askaris kept appearing to offer bayonet-to-bayonet resistance as the Punjabis worked their way up the trench. Fonthill became aware that he had sustained a bayonet wound in the left shoulder but hardly noticed it in the excitement of the attack before slipping on a bloodstained body and falling at the feet of two black askaris who were fighting defiantly with rifles and bayonets.

As he fell he caught a glimpse of a bayonet poised above him and realised that, at last, his time had come. But as the gleaming steel came down, it was diverted by Jenkins's knife blade, who, having lost his rifle, was now fighting with his favourite weapon. The deflected bayonet plunged into the side wall of the trench and, with a twist of his wrist, the Welshman ran his own, more manoeuvrable blade up along the man's arm to sink into his chest.

Simon rose onto his hands and knees and heard Mzingeli's rifle bark into action as the second of the askaris pushed forward.

'On your feet, quick, bach,' called Jenkins. 'There are more of 'em comin'.'

But in fact the askaris, seeing the Punjabis storming down the trench behind Simon and his comrades, thought better of it and melted away. Suddenly, the noise of the battle lifted and Fonthill staggered to his feet.

'I think you've done it, bach,' cried Jenkins. 'The buggers are runnin' away.'

It was true. The trench ahead was deserted. The German line had been turned. Looking up the rise above him, Fonthill became aware that the metallic chattering of the machine guns up above had also ceased. He anxiously scanned the view of the hill to catch a glimpse of John Jones but all he could see were the turbans of his troops.

In fact, the dusk had fallen quickly on the battlefield and allowed the Germans to melt into the dark confusion without being pursued. If von Lettow-Vorbeck was in the offing he never, in

369

fact, materialised and once again the Teutonic will-o'-the-wisp had slipped away into the blackness of the German colony.

It was not a clear-cut British victory, or if it was it was pyrrhic, for Beves's strategy of direct attack on von Lieberman's position and of throwing men into the battle throughout the day had produced heavy casualties. Among the 800 men of the Gold Coast Regiment who had led the attack one in five lay dead or wounded, six of the officers of the King's African Rifles were lost and 200 men killed and the troops who had supported the Gold Coast Regiment had lost one-third of their men.

It seemed clear that Simon's flank attack had swung the day in the end. But it, too, had its cost – not least in the person of the perky, brave Lieutenant John Jones, who fell as he led his men against the German machine guns.

That evening, as Jenkins was dressing the gash in Simon's shoulder, a message came through from General Deventer congratulating Fonthill on his initiative. It also – and more rewardingly – stated that he and his two comrades should immediately take three weeks' leave back in Mombasa.

'Good,' said Simon. 'I can see Alice.' He looked up at the creased face of Jenkins who, tongue protruding from blackened lips, was trying to adjust a sling with a final knot. 'Once again, my dear old 352,' he said, 'I owe you my life. Thank God you were there.'

'Well, actually,' said Jenkins, concentrating hard, 'I wanted to slip back into the swamp to tickle the tummies of the crocs, 'cos I think I've got the 'ang of them now. But I thought I'd just 'old on for a minnit and finish off that black bloke first.'

He looked shyly at Simon. 'I dunno what the score is now, bach sir, but I'd 'ave been dead in that swamp without you and old Jelly 'ere. So I think the count on who's saved who over the years 'as to be about even. Now let's bugger off back to old Mombasa and 'ave a beer with Miss Alice.'

CHAPTER FIFTEEN

At that moment Alice's thoughts, in fact, were not with Simon. Although she pretended to be examining the melon in her hand at a stall in the market near the harbour in Mombasa, she was trembling slightly and thanking God that she had slipped her little automatic pistol into her purse before setting out to shop. The reason for her excitement – no, anxiety – was a tall, thin white man of swarthy appearance who was buying vegetables three stalls away.

The full beard had been replaced by a neatly-trimmed Vandyke and a wide-brimmed hat was pulled well down over his eyes but she was convinced. It was Herman de Villiers all right.

The man had been dominating her thoughts since she had returned from Smuts's camp weeks ago. It was not just a growing irritation of a sense of unfinished business that occupied her mind, nor even the anger that he had been allowed to

371

slip so cleanly away, but more a growing feeling that the traitorous Afrikaner had not, in fact, fled Mombasa for the old German colony but was still somewhere near – even perhaps watching her. She had taken now to carrying the little Belgian Francotte automatic in her purse whenever she went out and always checked her surroundings carefully. He could be anywhere, watching, waiting...

It was with a leap of the heart, then, that she had observed the man walking ahead of her in the market. There was something immediately familiar about that long, loose gait that had stood him so well in his escape from the censor's office. He also had the slightly bow-legged walk of a Boer life spent in the saddle. She had quickened her pace and, moving into a lane between the stalls to his right, had examined his face covertly from that angle. His narrow spectacles, balanced on the long nose, convinced her. He was dressed in typical hand-me-down Boer garments – open-necked flannel shirt, cotton corduroy trousers with the knees worn well – as befitted a man who had lost his employment. Undoubtedly, here was the spy who had tried to deliver her into German hands, who had obviously warned about the attack on Bukoba. The man, in fact, for whom she had been searching, both consciously and unconsciously, for so long.

Alice replaced the melon and looked around her. Not a policeman or soldier in sight, of course. This was the native quarter and the obvious place for de Villiers to have gone to ground. She bit her lip. What to do? Well, follow him, obviously, taking great care not to be recognised, and then mark where he lived so that she could return later with the military. But she must be careful and, this time, he must not escape. She grasped the little handgun in her bag gratefully.

De Villiers bought his vegetables and then sauntered away. Alice pulled down her sun hat well over her eyes and dropped behind a little. As a white woman in the native market she would stand out like a sore thumb if he turned his head. But he did not do so. Obviously, after so long on the run, he had become confident of his anonymity. Nevertheless, Alice grabbed a long, pastel-coloured shawl from a stall, paid for it without haggling – earning the stall-keeper's surprise – then wrapped it around her and hurried on after her quarry.

Eventually he turned away from the market and strolled down a narrow lane fringed by native houses. Alice discarded her sun hat, swung the top of the shawl over her face and head and hurried after him, following as he turned again into the labyrinth of the native quarter.

She was just in time to see de Villiers climb a flight of stone steps and open a door to allow him entry to a second-storey dwelling of some sort. Now ... Alice hesitated. She knew enough about this poor part of town to know that this would not necessarily be the entrance to a separate house or apartment. These native homes were often like terraces, with dwellings opening off corridors. Should she follow or presume that this is where he lived and return later?

She took a deep breath. No. She must be certain.

Alice caught a glimpse of herself in a bead-fringed window. With the shawl covering most of her head and body she appeared native enough. But she was betrayed by the very European court shoes that she wore. Cursing, she kicked them off and mounted the steps in her bare feet, pausing at the top to look behind her. No one. She gulped and softly turned the handle of the door. It opened invitingly and, after waiting a moment to accustom herself to the semi-darkness within, she stepped inside.

'Ah, how delightful to see you again, Mrs Fonthill, after so long.'

The voice, in that well-remembered, clipped Afrikaans accent, came from behind her. De Villiers moved forward and closed the door. In his hand he carried a long-nosed Luger automatic pistol, the end of which seemed disproportionally large.

Alice swallowed hard. Damn! The very thing she had feared had happened. How could she have been so foolish? But better remain cool.

'Fellow journalists don't address me by my married name,' she said. 'I am Alice Griffith to them. But then, you are not a journalist. You are a traitor and a spy, are you not?'

'No. I am not. I am a South African patriot who continues to fight against the people who invaded his country and decimated it.'

'That is finished. An honourable settlement between Britain and the Boer nation was made years ago.'

'Not with my family, madam. Your troopers killed two brothers of mine and put my wife and two children into a concentration camp on the veldt where they nearly starved to death.' His voice was cold and bitter.

Alice paused for a moment. At least, while he was talking he was not shooting. 'There was much cruelty on both sides during that war,' she said. 'That happens in wars. And as for the concentration camps, my articles in the *Morning Post* attacked the concept and, I am told, helped to end the practice.'

'Ah,' the cold voice had become a sneer. 'So you are now a champion of the Boers, are you?'

'No. But I am loyal to my country and to concepts of honour and duty. I don't believe that is true of you.'

'Your view of me is of no concern to me. You will shortly be dead, in fact.'

A chill ran through Alice. 'So in addition to being a traitor, you are also a murderer?'

'No. But in just one moment I shall become an executioner.' He gestured around him. 'This tenement is uninhabited. I don't live here. I chose it some time ago as the place for your death. Yes, I have been watching you.' He held up the Luger. 'This thing on the end is a new accessory called a silencer. When the gun is fired the noise is muffled by this chamber at the end. No one will hear your passing, woman. There is no one to come to your aid.'

Alice's mind raced. After all the years of adventuring with Simon, of sharing front-line dangers with him, what a way to end – in this cheap, dirty little room, facing this fanatic. She had perhaps, though, one last hope.

'It is customary,' she tried to keep her voice level, 'to grant a condemned person one last wish. Will you do so now and perhaps earn some redemption for your act in the eyes of a Christian God?'

His eyes behind the spectacles narrowed. 'What wish is that, then?'

She shrugged her shoulders. 'If I am to be killed, I do not wish to be found looking filthy and unkempt in this foul place. Would you allow me to open my purse and apply just a little face powder and rouge to soften my appearance when, at last, my husband is brought to me?'

He sneered. 'Oh yes. Of course. And in that little purse you will no doubt be carrying a small hand pistol, which you will take out and shoot me with. Do you take me for a fool?'

'No.' She offered the purse to him. 'Open it and look for yourself. It only contains cosmetics. A feminine trait, you must know.'

For one fatal moment, de Villiers lowered his gaze and the muzzle of his Luger dropped slightly. It was all that Alice had hoped for. She tightened her grip on the purse and, through the knitted cotton and silk of its texture, found the contour of the trigger with her index finger. Pointing the purse directly at the Boer, she fired twice.

Both bullets took the man in the chest. Alice's gun had little velocity for it was designed only for close-quarter fighting, but the range here was short indeed. De Villiers's jaw dropped, his eyes widened and, as he attempted to lift the heavy Luger, his legs crumpled beneath him and he collapsed onto the floor.

Immediately, Alice sprang to his side and found the artery under his ear. It was still beating. He turned his head to look at her. 'English bitch...' he began. Then blood seeped from the corner of his mouth and his head fell to one side. Alice took the gun from his fingers and presented it to the door, but no one entered. All was silent.

Slowly she stood, examined the holes in her still smoking purse and realised that she was trembling violently. She gulped. She had killed him. What to do now? Report it to the police or the army? With the South Africans in such control of the military now in Mombasa, was this a risk worth taking? She had killed an Afrikaner. There would be a trial...

No, dammit. There would not! Let the bloody man lie here until he was found, perhaps by his compatriots. There was nothing to say who had killed him. Quickly, she went through his pockets and emptied his wallet. There was nothing to identify him and whoever found him could only now presume that he had been shot and robbed. She stood, checked that she still had four small cartridges in her handgun, wound the scarf around her head and face and stepped through the door. Down below, her shoes lay where she had left them. She put them on and walked quickly away.

As she walked, tears streaming down her cheeks, she promised herself that this was the last time, the very last time, she would kill another human being.

CHAPTER SIXTEEN

The border between Northern Rhodesia and
German East Africa, 25th November, 1918

The four riders sat on their mounts looking
down on the town from the exact place where
three of them had stood, a little over four years
ago. Abercorn itself had hardly changed but the
scene now was very different from that which
Fonthill, Jenkins and Mzingeli had observed
then. The town was hardly awake that morning in
1914. Now, despite a rain-filled sky, Abercorn
was *en fête* and prepared to accept a surrender.

The war in Europe had formally ended two
weeks before. At last, von Lettow-Vorbeck, whose
own campaign had started before the first shots
were fired on the Western Front, had reluctantly
agreed to surrender. Now the quartet – Alice had
now joined the three comrades – watched as the
little general, dapper in smart uniform, with the
brim of his colonial hat turned up on one side,
led what were left of his troops up the main street
to where an obscure British brigadier waited to
receive his sword.

'Appropriate that the bloody war should end virtually where it started four years ago,' murmured
Fonthill.

'Why did the stupid man fight on, so hope-
lessly, for so long?' asked Alice.

Jenkins sniffed. 'Generals are like that. Cocky little buggers. They always think they can win.'

Fonthill, Jenkins and Mzingeli had joined Alice in Mombasa, to her great surprise and delight, the day after de Villiers's death. She was on the point of confessing to the army when Simon's arrival persuaded her to keep silent. His presence had assuaged her guilt and the delivery of a letter from Sunil in Ypres, announcing that he had been awarded the Military Cross, had cheered everyone and prompted a celebration. The cable that arrived the next day, however, had been particularly cruelly timed. 'I regret to inform you...' it began. Sunil's job as brigade major behind the lines had not saved him. A shell had landed at Brigade HQ, killing him instantly.

When news arrived from van Deventer that the Germans were threatening to attack Portuguese East Africa and ordering Simon and his companions to cut short their leave, Alice had insisted on going with him. This time, Fonthill did not have the heart to argue. Nor did he seek permission for her to accompany him. Alice just packed a saddle roll, bought a good horse and rode with them.

They had followed the twists and turns of von Lettow-Vorbeck – this time without clashing with his troops – as the determined little German led his men in and out of the Portuguese territory and, finally, headed towards Rhodesia where he planned one last invasion and where the news of the Kaiser's abdication had reached him. Chastened at last, he had indicated that he would surrender at Abercorn.

A guard of honour provided by men of the King's African Rifles and the Northern Rhodesian Regiment formed up, providing an avenue through which von Lettow-Vorbeck rode to where Brigadier General W. F. S. Edwards – the British local commander – awaited him. Solemnly, the German withdrew his sword and presented it to Edwards. Equally solemnly, Edward handed it back to his adversary, marking his respect for a noble opponent.

'Oh to hell with it,' exclaimed Fonthill suddenly. 'I'm not watching them dance this bloody gavotte any longer. Let's go.' He pulled his horse's head round and headed away from Abercorn. The others followed. They rode in reflective silence for two hours before they camped and ate sandwiches and drank coffee.

No one spoke until Simon said, 'By the way. Did I tell you that van Deventer offered me a knighthood?'

'Blimey!' Jenkins jaw dropped. 'What, making you a sir, a proper sir?'

'Yes. I refused, of course.'

'What? It would 'ave been wonderful! What was it – forty years ago, look you – they was trying to 'ang you as a coward in the Zulu war. Now they're tryin' to knight you. It would show everyone 'ow stupid the army can be.'

'Well, I turned it down.'

'And with it,' Alice pulled a mock face, 'my chance of being a proper lady.'

'Ah, you've always been that, Miss Alice.'

Fonthill reached into his saddlebag. 'Speaking of rewards,' he said. He handed a large envelope to

Mzingeli. 'Inside this are the deeds to the farm,' he said. 'I have formally transferred ownership to you, old friend. I hope you will always allow us to visit and I will have funds to help you should you ever need them. But the farm is now yours.'

Mzingeli did not speak, but he bowed his head and covered his face with his hands.

'Oh, and by the way,' Fonthill continued. 'As you know, your army pay has been paid into accounts under your names in Cape Town. The same bank holds two additional accounts for you. I have continued to pay your wages as my employees into them throughout the war. Gentlemen, you are both now quite well off. I should get married quickly if I were you. You will be good catches.

'And,' he reached out and took Alice's hand, 'I can recommend the state of marriage to you.' Then: 'For God's sake woman, stop crying, or you'll start us all off again.'

He turned to Jenkins. '352, I presume you will go back to South Africa to see your girls and your grandchildren now?'

'Bach, sir,' began Jenkins, his eyes moist, 'I just wanted to say...'

'For God's sake, man, I've just asked you a question.'

The Welshman nodded. 'I suppose so, yes.'

'Good. When you've done that, why don't you bring them all over to Norfolk and stay for a while? Alice and I will be terribly lonely after we get home. That would help us adjust.' He handed a small envelope to Jenkins. 'I know you are a rich man now, but this could be expensive, so this is a cheque to help pay the cost.'

As he spoke, Simon took his watch from his pocket. 'Good lord,' he said, before anyone could interrupt. 'It's late. We shall never make the farm before nightfall if we don't get on. Come on. Up-saddle.'

The four of them mounted slowly – as befitted their ages – and rode away, Simon and Alice hand in hand and Jenkins and Mzingeli, briefly saddle to saddle, arms around each other's shoulders.

Somewhere ahead of them a hyena laughed. Could it be, wondered Fonthill momentarily, sounding the death knell of the British Empire? He shook his head. What a ridiculous idea! They rode on.

AUTHOR'S NOTE

This story is a work of fiction but based on actual happenings and, as always, I owe it to the reader to explain which is which. The war in German East Africa ranged far and wide across this part of Africa and it became quite as hard fought and in conditions different to but quite as arduous as those on the Western Front. The battles I describe are as accurate as a study of respected accounts allow. The exception is the attack through the swamp outside Narungombe. The swamp existed but the British chose not to brave the crocodiles. I felt it right and proper for Jenkins to have one last brush with them.

As for the cast list, von Lettow-Vorbeck very much existed, as did all of the British generals mentioned, as well as Geoffrey Pocock, Lt Commander Evans, Admiral King-Hall, Colonel Driscoll, Captain Max Looff of the *Königsberg,* Captain Lieberman, the scout Piet Nieuwenhuizen, General Van Deventer, the Boer leaders Botha and de Wet, as well as, of course, Smuts and Winston Churchill.

Fictional characters, in addition to Fonthill, Jenkins, Alice and Mzingeli, include Lt Daniels, Mustapha the boat captain, Herman de Villiers (although a Boer spy *was* caught helping the

Germans and hanged), Brigadier Lawrence, Mizango the fisherman and the cocky little Lt John Jones.

I should add that I based some of the exploits of Simon and his comrades in the search for the *Königsberg* on the real life work of the intrepid Boer scout Piet Pretorius, who spent days in the delta measuring tidal flows and channel depths.

The war rambled across such a huge territory and took so long that I have only in my comparatively short narrative been able to include some of the actions or to describe some of the strategies and tactics employed. There is no doubt that von Lettow-Vorbeck was a brilliant leader (only a colonel for much of his time in desert and swamp) and he became a hero in Germany during and after the war. In fact, in 1939, Hitler gave him the honorary rank of *General der Infantrie*. He lived on into his nineties.

There were those, later, who said that it would have been better just to have left von Lettow-Vorbeck to stew in his own juice in his remote colony until he would have been forced to surrender from lack of food and other support from his distant homeland. As it was, the British lost 11,189 soldiers and sustained total casualties of nearly 22,000 chasing him. Nothing like the losses on the Western Front, of course, but if the deaths of the native carriers are included, then the bill rises to far more than 100,000. Nevertheless, that figure represents double the number of Canadian, Australian and Indian troops who perished in Europe.

At the Versailles Peace Conference the new

'scramble for Africa' – the apportioning of Germany's colonial possessions – to the victors began. After months of haggling, German East Africa became British Tanganyika, South Africa inherited German South West Africa, Belgium (until comparatively recently regarded as a pariah for its treatment of the natives of the Congo) picked up Ruanda–Urundi, and Portugal – whose humiliating incompetence in the struggle was regarded by the Allies as a minus factor – received the scraps of the Kionga Triangle.

It was not quite as cynical a carve-up as that sounds, however, for – at America's insistence – the territories were declared to be 'mandates', to be administered by their new colonial masters under the auspices of the League of Nations. The difference between colony and mandated territory, however, never became clear and, in the interwar years, little capital was invested in the lands that once represented the Kaiser's dream of empire.

In these present, post-colonial years that sombre picture has changed little. The 'other 1914–18 war' did little, in the event, to stamp its mark on the formidable terrain of swamp, mountains and desert of this part of Africa, except to drown it in blood.

ACKNOWLEDGEMENTS

Once again I acknowledge my debts of gratitude to my agent, Jane Conway-Gordon and to Susie Dunlop, my publisher at Allison & Busby, for their ever-present support. It was rewarding, too, to know that the staff of the London Library was always there to point me to the appropriate shelves to find books on the period.

Alas, my wife Betty, my much-loved research assistant and critic, became ill during the writing of the book and was unable to help this time. As I write, she remains ill and is constantly in my thoughts as in those of our daughter, Alison, other members of the family and our friends.

I am particularly grateful to my friend, Simon Thompsett, for lending me a precious family heirloom: a bound book of sepia photographs, taken during the campaign, and beautifully captioned in a copperplate hand by his grandfather, Harry Thompsett, who fought throughout it. They were a most useful graphic reference for me.

For what was inevitably termed 'the forgotten war' a remarkably large number of books was written about it. The ones I found most useful were:

Tip and Run, Edward Paice (London, 2007), a

magisterial history of the whole war, and which I gratefully acknowledge as the source of many of the facts and figures I used in my novel.

An Ice-Cream War, William Boyd (London, 1982), the novel, loosely based on fact, which first made me interested in the war.

The Legion of Frontiersmen, Geoffrey Pocock (Chichester, 2004).

African Crossroads, Sir Charles Dundas (London, 1955).

Jan Christian Smuts, Kenneth Ingham (London, 1986).

The publishers hope that this book has given you enjoyable reading. Large Print Books are especially designed to be as easy to see and hold as possible. If you wish a complete list of our books please ask at your local library or write directly to:

Magna Large Print Books
Magna House, Long Preston,
Skipton, North Yorkshire.
BD23 4ND